THE
SHADOW EATER

Other Avon Books by
Adam Lee

THE DARK SHORE: BOOK ONE OF THE DOMINIONS OF IRTH

THE SHADOW EATER

Book Two of *THE DOMINIONS OF IRTH*

ADAM LEE

AVON • EOS

AVON BOOKS
A division of
The Hearst Corporation
1350 Avenue of the Americas
New York, New York 10019

Copyright © 1998 by Adam Lee
Map by John Bergin
Interior design by Kellan Peck
Visit our website at http://www.AvonBooks.com/Eos
Visit Adam Lee's website at http://www.qed.net/rebnj/adamlee.html
ISBN: 0-380-79073-4

Library of Congress Cataloging in Publication Data:

Lee Adam.
   The shadow eater / Adam Lee.
      p.   cm.—(The dominions of Irth; bk. 2)
   I. Title.   II. Series: Lee, Adam. Dominions of Irth; bk. 2.
PS3562.E317S53   1998   97-34990
813'.54—dc21   CIP

First Avon Eos Trade Printing: April 1998

AVON EOS TRADEMARK REG. U.S. PAT. OFF. AND IN OTHER COUNTRIES, MARCA REGISTRADA, HECHO EN U.S.A.

Printed in the U.S.A.

OPM   10   9   8   7   6   5   4   3   2   1

For one, none, no one, *thou*—light of my darkness.

I will make darkness light.
—Isaiah 42:16

Contents

Cast of Characters   xi

PART ONE: SOMEWHERE AT WORLD'S END

The Author of Worlds   3
Meet the Ælves   14
Broydo   22
Into the Dark Labyrinth   30
The Witch   38
The Necklace of Souls   47
The Serpent Sword   55
Pursued by Dwarves   64
A Battle of Dwarves and Ælves   72

PART TWO: DOWN THE WELL OF SPIDERS

Lara   83
Eating Shadows   91
The Magus of Elvre   98
To the Ether Ship   107
Wraith   116
Down in Saxar   126

Ghost Ship   136
Ripcat   146
The Well of Spiders   155

PART THREE: GABAGALUS

Alliance in the Qaf   167
Massacre on Nemora   177
Broydo Blunders   186
Ripcat in Gabagalus   196
Prisoners of Zul   204
Hellsgate   213
The Sibyl   219
Devouring Giants   227
Duppy Hob   236

PART FOUR: EMPIRE OF DARKNESS

Devil's Work   249
Deadwalker   258
Interlude with an Ælf   266
Beastmarked in Manhattan   276
Duppy Hob's Trap   287
Death on the Dark Shore   295
Reclaiming the Dead   304
Dark Song of the Soul   313
Return to the Garden   326

Cast of Characters

The Nameless Ones—supernatural, godlike entities that dwell inside the Abiding Star, the energy source of the universe.

The Lady of the Garden—a noblewoman of the Nameless Ones, who has magically created the worlds of our cosmos to serve as a learning tool for her as-yet-unborn child.

The Lady's Consort—the Nameless One who has fathered the Lady of the Garden's unborn child; he now sleeps within the Abiding Star, his nightmarish dreams of malformity, cruelty, and madness darkly influencing the worlds that his lady's magic has created.

The Four Mystic Worlds—consist of the original reality that is the *Abiding Star* and the three realms created by the Lady of the Garden's magic in the void outside that radiance:

- The **Upper Air**, the turbulent corona of the Abiding Star in which dwell numerous energetic beings, including ether-devils, spawns of the nightmares that trouble the sleeping consort.
- The **Bright Worlds**, numerous planets, including Irth, Nemora, and Hellsgate, that range through the brilliance surrounding the Abiding Star.
- The **Dark Shore**, cold, dim worlds, among them Earth, cast like shadows into the void by the brilliance of the Bright Worlds.

Old Ric—a geriatric gnome from Nemora summoned by the Lady of the Garden to help determine what has gone awry with her magic that the unborn child in her womb has ceased to move; his lifelong knowledge of the Bright Worlds and his awareness of the Dark Shore qualify him as an expert of the lady's magical creation.

Asofel—a luminous sentinel, known as a Radiant One, posted by his superiors to watch over the Lady of the Garden; she has assigned him to accompany Old Ric on his quest through the Four Mystic Worlds to find out why the lady's child has ceased to thrive.

Broydo—a young ælf from World's End, the Bright World closest to the Abiding Star, who befriends Old Ric and escorts him on his quest.

Smiddy Thea—grandmother of Broydo and leader of their ælfen clan on World's End.

Tivel—fellow ælf of Broydo and Smiddy Thea's clan possessed by an ether-devil from the Upper Air.

Duppy Hob—devil worshipper skilled at crafting amulets that trap devils in the ethers of the Upper Air to do his bidding among the Bright Worlds and on the Dark Shore.

Dwarves—fashioned by Duppy Hob's magic from maggots in the flesh of world serpents, behemoth, now-extinct vipers from World's End; they ultimately rebelled against their master and cast him into the Gulf, the dark abyss that falls away from the Bright Worlds to the Dark Shore.

Blue Tipoo—the one dwarf who has remained faithful to Duppy Hob, exiled by his fellows to a volcanic wilderness, where he crafts talismanic weapons in anticipation of his deposed master's return.

Jyoti—margravine of Arwar Odawl, the smallest and most ancient dominion of Irth.

Reece Morgan—a magus from the Dark Shore, endowed on Irth with astonishing magical powers, including the capacity to transform himself into Ripcat, a beastmarked man of great agility and physical strength.

Caval—deceased sorcerer and weapons master of Arwar Odawl, who once worked magic on the Dark Shore and there trained Reece Morgan to serve as his assistant.

Lara—the ghost of a witch who served Caval and Reece on the Dark Shore until she was brutally slain by local settlers fearful of her powers; Caval, out of respect for her service to him, delivered her wounded soul to the Abiding Star to be healed.

Dogbrick—a former thief from Saxar in the dominion of Zul on Irth and friend of Ripcat.

Amara—Old Ric's daughter, who died in childhood and remains his greatest sorrow.

PART ONE

Somewhere at World's End

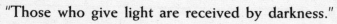

"Those who give light are received by darkness."

—THE GIBBET SCROLLS, SCREED 3:23

The Author of Worlds

Somewhere at World's End, a young woman with long tresses of red hair bathed her swollen belly in a garden's marble pool. Her bright ringlets spread like flames in the ice-green water under temple columns and a sky of mauve dusk.

The cobbled garden spun with golden leaves. Among its mossy bluestone pillars and valved architraves, horned lizards slept and doves fluttered about the flower-laden trellises between the columns. Black-and-green butterflies danced on a breeze that carried scents of distant woodsmoke and leaf drift. An owl sobbed.

The pregnant woman sat up taller in the pool, grave concern troubling her pale features. Her hands trembled as she massaged her taut abdomen, and a tear glinted at the corner of her eye. With dismay, she looked about the garden, searching for the one she had summoned to help her and her unborn child.

Atop a stone jar slued with red ivy sat an eldern gnome in breeks of browncord, a green blouse serrate with silk ruffles, and a slantwise cap of crushed blue velvet. His gaunt and sunken cheeks wore a week's pink beard, and he gazed hard at the naked bather with large eyes of cold gray mist.

"Why is the child within me not moving?" the woman demanded. She turned upon the gnome her long eyes cored black within irises of attic blue. "Is my baby dead?"

"My lady—" With bulb-jointed fingers, the gnome gripped the lip of the jar where he perched, bowed forward, and addressed the pouring leaves. "Darkness encroaches upon the worlds of light."

"How can that be?" the lady frowned, hands of slender, tapered fingers describing small circles upon her gravid belly. "I have poured forth all my soul to drive the dark hard away from us that my child may be born in the light."

"Yours is a soul of magic, lady, and what you have poured forth has broken the dark and authored the wonders of the void that are the bright worlds. And yet—" The gnome sat up and showed the worry upon his nut brown face. "One of darkness has climbed into the light."

"From whence?" she asked, with casual disdain masking her worry. "Out of darkness? Are there worlds then in the outer darkness?"

The gnome nodded vigorously. "Oh yes, lady. But not worlds as we know them. Not the worlds that are the effluvia of your magic, a radiant magic that prefigures for all time in the void the orders and histories of the Bright Worlds. No, the one who has climbed out of darkness and into your light has arisen from the shadow worlds in the cold deeps of the void."

She draped a languorous arm over the edge of the pool, weary with concern for her child. "What are these shadow worlds, gnome?"

"Just that, lady." The gnome wagged his rooty fingers emptily in the air. "Shadows cast into the void by the Bright Worlds that you have created and that move within your dazzling light. Shadows cast into the void. No more than that."

"And you are telling me that a shadow has climbed into my light?" She did not look at him but lifted her attention to the parcels of purple cloud overhead. "A thing without substance thrives within my radiance?"

"There is a magic of shadows by which this is so."

"My child is still," she said to the gathering night, and tears brightened in her eyes. "My child within me does not move."

"Lady, your child yet lives and will move again when the shadow is cast out of the light." The gnome leaned far forward to add emphasis to his words. "The light into which your child is to be born must be pure."

She angrily turned her head toward him, distraught with anxiety. "Then why have you not already cast out the shadow thing from my light?"

The gnome jolted backward and nearly fell into the jar. "Lady, I am no more than a gnome among the worlds you dream into being with your magic. My knowledge is gleaned from a lifetime of gnomish magic, a mere wisp of your power that created me and all the worlds of my experience. I am aware of the shadow thing, but I have no power to dispel it."

She fixed him with an irate stare before returning her worried gaze to the dusk hung above her like a black-and-gold mask. "I will awaken the child's father, then. He will protect what he has created within me."

"No!" The gnome leaped to his feet and stood precariously upon the jar's brim. "Lady—please! Do not awaken him! Your magic will melt into the void for the dream it is. The Bright Worlds will vanish, and your child will not be born into the warmth and brilliance of your light."

"And you as well will vanish, gnome," she said distractedly, contemplating ending her magic to save her child.

"Yes, I, too, will vanish," the gnome admitted morosely. "And the child will be born under the father's dark gaze."

"Perhaps that is best," she said, and circled her hands about her belly. "This is his child. Let it be born in the dark as he wishes. The child will grow stronger for that."

"Stronger, most certainly," the gnome pronounced somberly. "Yet the babe will be born less kind, lady. Less gentle. Less wise of love."

"Better the child be born strong and know less of love than die in my belly." She lifted herself from the green water and sat upon the side of the pool. "I will waken the child's father."

"No!" The gnome trembled from head to foot. The child's father was of the Nameless Ones, who were indifferent to the worlds that this pregnant lady had created with her magic. Even she was cool to her creation except to the degree that it served her unborn child. The purpose of the worlds she had summoned into being with her dream-magic was to educate her child. The aeons that carried all the dynasties of evolution in the universe had amounted to only a few months here in the garden. High above the cosmic mirage that was the gnome's reality, her child grew in her womb, nourished not only by her physical strength but also by her magic, by the illusory worlds whose lifetimes offered their energies to the developing soul. The child's father would have found these energies superfluous and attempting to educate a child before it was born foolish. But the mother, who wanted the best for her infant, believed that her magic would distill the lifetimes of ages and teach her baby compassion for the yearnings of all life-forms.

The gnome scurried down the spun ivy and ran through the golden leaves to stand in the woman's shadow among the ferns. "Let the child's father sleep. Let him sleep a little longer. Give your baby the radiance of a mother's love. Soon enough the father will come. Soon enough."

"Then you must dawdle no longer, gnome." She stepped from the pool and walked to a potted tree whose strata of branches upheld a blue damask veil patterned with figures of stars, comet hair, and quarter moons. "You must cast out the shadow thing from my light."

"This I cannot do, lady." The wizened creature climbed the coils of the serpent to stand upon the stone perimeter of the pool. "After all, I am but a gnome. You created me to witness and report."

"What am I to do then? I don't want observations. I want my baby to live." She draped herself in the damask veil. "Do not vex me, gnome."

"Never, lady! Never!" He hurried across the mossy grouts to stand at the end of the pool nearest her. The gnome knew that this lady was not cold by nature. Her concern for her child evoked anger and frustration in her. The worlds that she had fabricated in her dreaming and that persisted independently now, even when she was awake and paying them no heed, had defied her, their creator. This troubled her. Something from deep within her unconscious had arisen and laid claim to her dream worlds. Was that something the child's father, who himself was asleep and dreaming now, perhaps intruding upon the dream of the lady who carried his child? The gnome, a creature of the lady's dream himself, could not possibly know, but he feared this was so. Instead, he said, "What has happened is a rare thing. A hazard that can be corrected. A turn of chance that will never repeat itself."

From beyond the garden's ranks of yews came dulcimer music that turned the woman's head. "Gnome, how can this hazard be set right?"

"Send one of the Radiant Ones."

She turned a perplexed look upon her gnomish counselor. "Send a Radiant One into my dream?"

"They themselves are dreams," the gnome declared, "dreamt by what has been watching over you."

"Yes," she replied absently, turning once more to face the chimeful strains sifting through the evening air. "They are set upon the garden and this palace to watch over me. I dare not dispatch them into the dark."

"You have several to watch over you, lady." He parted the belled lilies that blocked his full view of her. "Send one, one only. By such radiance the shadow thing will be extirpated." Unless, of course, it was the father himself who intruded. And the gnome prayed this was not so.

The pregnant woman stood under the arbor, beneath an aspiring helix of clematis and hanging roses white and yellow and afreight with golden bees intoxicated by attar. "I send you, Old Ric," she said, forcing her attention away from the alluring music. "I charge you to go ahead of the Radiant One and find this shadow thing."

"It shall be done." The gnome bowed, and the lilies he had parted closed and slapped him as he rose. He impatiently shoved them aside and spoke urgently. "Let the Radiant One you send be Asofel, the sentinel upon the Gate of Outer Darkness, for he already knows of the magic you work for your child. And command this Radiant One to go forth immediately so that when I call, the power I need shall be at hand."

"As you say," she said quietly, then fixed him with a stern gaze. "But be quick about this task, Old Ric. If my child does not stir by tomorrow night, I shall awaken the father. I will have nothing more to do with this foolishness of magic and its hope for warmth, light, and love. I shall trust in the father and his dark strength that my child may live."

At that she departed the garden, and the blooms and fronds dimmed under the slantwise shadows of enclosing night. Evening's purple bleared into violet overhead, fading toward the ultratones of the invisible, and within the utter black of the void no stars glimmered, no moon glided, only shoreless depths of emptiness ranged. Upon those alien reaches, another life dreamed, fugitive of all light, the child's father who even in sleep informed the ill-shapen, deranged, and malevolent forms of darkness that circled closer out of the night.

The eldern gnome leaped from the stone pool and sprinted through the fallen leaves. He was grateful for the rinds of distant music scattered upon the floor of the wind that masked his frantic footfalls. Hurriedly, he exited the garden, passing dead beetles hung like onyx baubles in the jointed webs of sleeping spiders.

The clustered light of fireflies flurried as he thrashed through the deranged shadows of bracken and flowers fallen among cinders. He arrived breathless at the garden's selvage and the well by which he had climbed to World's End. The well was ancient, its massive skewed stones held in place by iron straps twisted into the shapes of magical sigils whose power connected the depths of this fount with the worlds in the abyss below. Through this conduit, she had worked her magic to pour light into the void and generate a cosmos of radiance within the dark.

He climbed up the twisted iron and jarred stones to the mouth of the well and peered in. The apertures of his lungs opened wider with relief to see that the ladder of plaited vines lowered for him by the Lady of the Garden remained where he had left it. The soft luster of its magic wavered far within the nether depths.

Old Ric stood upon the edge of the uncovered well and gazed hard about him in the dark. The throb of frog songs and the brittle trill of crickets offered meager restitution for the absolute silence that reigned in the upper heavens, where not even bats whirred.

By the nightglow of luminous plants and insects he found sufficient illumination to view the terraced lawns, with their fish ponds and tarns, upon whose mirrored surfaces drifted black swans. Beyond them was the bridge-gate with the brimstone light of its one lantern. Upon the far side of that gate stood Asofel, sentinel of the Beginning.

Not even the father of the child could withstand the might of such a Radiant One. The Nameless had set them upon the verges of World's End to guard the young woman and her growing child. Nearest to the well, Asofel had watched from his high, broad terraces as the woman worked her magic to summon the eldern gnome.

Old Ric stared up at the zigzag road that led from the terraces to the bridge-gate, remembering the sentinel, the molten body of breathing light, the furious brilliance of the faceless entity with his blue-hot eyes and star-plasma hair. Asofel had looked down silently as the woman had worked her magic, and when she was done he had departed, closing the bridge-gate behind him.

Old Ric had not seen the sentinel since, yet on each subsequent visit to World's End, it was his skywide voice that had called the gnome. The Radiant One's thunder called solely for Ric: *I, Asofel, summon you to World's End. Come at once.*

None other in the worlds below heard that voice. And by this intimacy, the gnome sensed a strange affinity with the creature of fierce light—strange because the Radiant One was a guardian and a warrior of light and the gnome was but an aged and scholarly worker of gnomish magic. Their affinity, however, was light itself, for the gnome's magic was fire, and he could sometimes see through the shapes of fire the powers of the worlds. That was how he had observed the shadow thing that had intruded upon the Lady of the Garden's dream.

"Asofel!" he dared call into the night, fearless of the shifting and murky shadows around him now that he was beside the luminous ladder of the well. "Asofel! Our lady bids me summon you."

Silence claimed the nightland. Only the tread of the gnome's heart stalked into the mute darkness, and fear tightened like a cinch about his chest.

Out of the advent of night, a throb of thunder shook the gnome and widened to words that reverberated like the very weather: "Come to the bridge-gate."

Old Ric's body obeyed before his brain could think. He leaped off the well and onto the tufty sward and began running through the amorphous dark and only then thought of the peril ahead. Quickly, he slowed his pace and stood a moment on the night-smothered lawn, pondering the wisdom of returning to the well and the long climb down from whence he had come.

But of course he had been called forth by Asofel the Radiant One and disobedience was not in him. Besides, the very fate of the universe depended upon him and this being of light. He ushered himself forward, his jaw set, his face turning darkness like a flame.

Several paces on, something sloshed in a tarn, the frogs fell silent again, funny lights ran upon the shelved horizon, and he remembered that his face was no flame but mortal flesh aquiver with fright. He ran harder and soon attained the zigzag road, its dry gravel snoring under his scampering feet.

Ahead, the brimstone lantern flared brighter from upon the bridge-gate and cast warped shadows with its lonely light. By that small glow, he stared down to either side and glimpsed the wild lands above the terraced lawns, the hunched boulders shawled in creepers. Leather-winged minions rose up from there on the vesperal wind and flashed past him with their agonized faces. He gasped the honeysuckle air and mounted the steep road faster.

At last, the path turned a final bend and placed him before the bridge-gate, with its ponderous lantern of iron fins and spikes. Thick dockweed and dense hollyhocks sprouted before the weighted gate.

"Old Ric has come," he announced in a gasp, bending over and holding his knees as he reached for breath.

At his word, the gate clanged from within, and the wormholed planks groaned upon their clawed hinges. A blinding brilliance rayed forth from the narrow crack of the budged gate, and the gnome slapped his hands over his eyes. Through his fingers, he watched the old door swing wide upon star-core radiance.

"Come forward," the voice of thunder commanded.

Through a fog of white blindness, shapes gathered form to themselves. Gradually, the gnome discerned the narrow bridge beyond the gate. Its substance seemed a phantom of the glare, and he advanced upon it by inches. By feel alone he knew it was wood, much worn and splintered.

Through his wincing eyes, he could make out only the skimpiest visual details on the bridge of light, and he moved forward with both hands pressed to his face. Averting his gaze, he glanced downward into a rocky chasm where fog floated in rings around craggy peaks.

He gingerly returned his gaze to the fiery path ahead and crept ever forward. Eventually, he found himself stepping onto a stone ledge and, by swinging his gaze side to side, saw that he stood before a great wall of stone. Its heights vanished in the abyssal darkness above.

"Asofel?" the gnome called tentatively. The brilliance required him to press the heels of his palms into his eye sockets, yet he felt no heat. "I am come as you bid."

The massive voice spoke. "I am sent into the darkness to destroy the shadow thing that trespasses our lady's Bright Worlds."

"For the sake of our lady's child," Old Ric said with head bowed.

"For the sake of the child."

The glare dimmed, and when the gnome dared remove his palms and squint through his fingers, he saw a large human figure shaped of white fire striding away. The Radiant One approached the colossal pylons of the vast wall. White flames splashed over the stone blocks and swirled up the immense pillars beside the titanic portal.

Slowly, the giant gateway opened outward on darkness and the smoke of stars. A vista of stellar fumes and planetary orbs in gibbous and crescent phases loomed into view.

"Behold the Bright Shore," the cataclysmic voice announced.

Old Ric backed away from the widening panorama of nebular vapors and the orbs of far-flung worlds.

"To the brink, gnome," the stupendous voice commanded.

"Not I!" Old Ric protested. "I am as you say—a gnome. I dare not place my frail self before the abyss."

"Our lady requires you to go before me and find this shadow thing," Asofel boomed. "Come to the brink."

"Nay!" Old Ric backed several paces. "Let me return to the Bright Shore by the ladder of magic that I have always before used to come and go from World's End."

"Obey! I have a more direct route to the worlds below than the ladder you climbed."

The big voice shook the very meat on Old Ric's bones, and he scuttled forward with his hands against his ears.

Asofel stood aside, and as the gnome passed within the Radiant One's shaking blue aura, a now gentler voice, neither large nor vibrant but mortal and close to soothing, said, "Fear not, Old Ric. The way is long, and our destination is darkness. But I will never be far from you. Go now and obey our lady."

The gnome peeked around the barrier of his arm and saw a luminous face slant of bone as a lynx's. Its long and devilish eyes, both humorous and wicked at once, peered at him. Its lips were small as petals, and the complexion of its visage looked like bluish powder tinged pink, a face of ash still cooling from a fallen star. Blond, almost white, hair, long and massy with curls, seemed to float like sunlight swarming on water.

Asofel pointed into the gulf of star vapors and moons. "Go forth now."

Old Ric dared not hesitate before such a compelling vision of good enjambed to evil. Resignedly, he dropped his arms, gazed full upon the incandescent depths before him, and stepped forward.

Instantly, he fell into the void and knew he fell only because as he turned about in his plunge he saw above him a great wall lifting rapidly away. Among the huge open pylons, a star burned. That was Asofel, his skin of pale oxides burned within the hearth of stars.

Darkness hung in webs of light. Planets, in various conjugations of reflection and shadow, breathed smoke in the cold of space. Yet the gnome felt no chill. Looking at himself, he saw that his body shimmered faintly blue. The Radiant One had sheathed him in magical fire.

His plunge slowed and arced, and he realized then that he had not been plummeting but launched into space. And now he was falling back to World's End, to a day-struck region of that realm far from the great wall already steeped in night. He had been launched from the heights of World's End, where the lady's magic had created the garden wherein she could meet him, her dream-creature, who was too frail a being to trespass her place of origin higher yet within the Abiding Star itself. Asofel had simply flung him onto the lowest level of World's End so that he might begin his quest of the Bright Worlds from the top down.

A limb of land appeared, its weathers scrawled in feathery whorls above blue waters and ocher and green swatches of soil. He discerned the pocks of volcanic craters and the jagged slash of a rift valley. Below were the wild lands of Faerïe and Ælf, the haunts of the Undead, the stalking grounds of the slitherous squid monkeys, and the dread Forest of Wraiths. Fearful to behold where among these terrors he would descend, the gnome lifted his gaze to the heavens.

The horizon of World's End swelled against outer space, and Old Ric glimpsed fluorescent streamers of cometary exhaust. He cast a final glance at the far-flung worlds he knew: icy Nemora in her white shrouds; Hellsgate, sulfurous and veined red with living torrents of lava; and Irth, half ocean, half land, spinning at the very edge of the Bright Shore.

MEET THE ÆLVES

OLD RIC STRUCK THE ATMOSPHERE OF WORLD'S END WITH A SIZ-
zling roar that burned the sheath of blue magic from his body
in a trail of twisting flames. Mountain lakes flashed with day-
struck gasps of light as he soared over a glacial range and
swooped toward a dense, primeval forest. A scarlet flock of fire-
birds scattered with horrified shrieks as he disappeared through
the forest canopy in a leafy explosion.

The sundering boom that sheared boughs, split tree boles, and
shredded undergrowth to leaf meal gouged an immediate crater
in the loamy turf and left Old Ric stunned, his mouth and nostrils
packed with dirt and his startled eyeballs staring into the uplifted
rootweave of a toppled oak. He coughed violently, gasping for
breath. In his numb ears, he heard the echo of his impact go
from room to room of the forest and return again only slightly
diminished.

O gods and forebears show me clemency! he wailed in his mind, as
his lungs choked up gouts of peat and duff.

By the time he had cleared his air passages, the forest had
begun again its timeless fracas, and he clambered out of the

steaming crater to the chirrups of birds and the obstreperous howls of monkeys. He brushed futilely at the dirt stains on his browncord breeks and looked about for his cap.

A boisterous animal laugh craned his aching neck, and he spied among the serrate rays of daylight in the shorn canopy a blue-bottomed monkey tossing his velvet cap from paw to tail with delight.

"Give that here, you beast!" the gnome cried to the frenzied joy of the monkey.

He swiped a chunk of broken bark and heaved it at the creature. That evoked more frantic laughter, and the monkey spurted away through the upper reaches of the forest, leaving Old Ric hatless and stamping with fury.

When he had calmed enough to assess his situation, the eldern gnome's anger chilled quickly to fright. This was the Forest of Wraiths. He had never been in this dreadful region of the Bright Shore before, yet he recognized the place by the lurid descriptions of its crimson pearl mushrooms, whose poison was celebrated in song and chant. The songs decreed that all who found themselves in this grisly place were best advised to eat swiftly of the lethal fungi and suffer willingly the subsequent wracking convulsions and vein-bursting death rather than confront the further terrors indigenous to these doomful woods.

Old Ric reminded himself of Asofel's promise, *I will never be far from you,* and he trod over the crimson pearl mushrooms, seeking a suitable tree to climb from which to search for the Radiant One. A leaning behemoth sycamore ledged with scallop fungus offered easy access to the forest awning. Perched upon its sprawling crest, he scanned the verdant horizons for the bright presence of his guardian.

All that shone in that whole wide vista was the sun of the Bright Shore—the Abiding Star. World's End was the closest planet to that source of light, warmth, and magic. From his vantage, he could actually see the lachrymal cliffs known as the Labyrinth of the Undead. The cinder cones that lorded over the nitre cliffs seeped fumes that ignited under the close proximity of the Abiding Star and flared occasionally into vast ruffling auroras of infernal light. Within that convoluted cinderland, the dead offered unholy rebate to the living. It was said that this high, barren range was so charged with magic that shades could assume physical form and resume their mortal lives for so long as they had Charm to sustain them.

Charm! Old Ric wished mightily that he possessed that most concentrated form of magic. Magic itself was everywhere. It radiated forth from the Abiding Star. It flourished in the blossoms and seeds of plants. It sparked the life force in all living creatures. But it was elusive. Only certain stones, known as hex-gems, and rare alloys, called conjure-metals, could retain magic in the compact and potent form known as Charm. Charmwrights fashioned these materials into amulets and talismans, and with them humans eluded sleep, lived for days without food, and saw things from afar.

But he had no amulets or talismans. He possessed no Charm but the natural magic of his gnomish flesh and bones. And he was hungry and tired.

A thrashing movement in the distance caught his eye, and he twisted about with alarm among the topmost branches. His impact in the forest had alerted a pack of squid monkeys. His keen and bulging gray eyes distinctly perceived their tentacles lashing through the forest canopy as they swarmed toward him. Dimly, he heard their roisterous shrieks.

The gnome swiftly descended from his roost and dashed into a tunnel of the forest that led away from the advancing squid monkeys. Their whooping cries bounded closer, and he moaned to imagine how their powerful tentacles would tear his limbs from his body.

Fire! he thought. But there was no time to ignite a fire. *A hole!* he thought again, and dismissed that desperate notion with a gasped moan. Squid monkeys could easily excavate any shallow burrow he could dig.

He tripped over a root ledge and skidded across the leaf litter with a howl. As he scrambled to his feet, he dared glance back and saw with horror that the thicket where he had fled shook with the frenzied presence of the pack. Their yells struck him like physical blows.

Arms whirling wildly, knees pumping, the gnome bolted through the forest corridor. "As-o-fel!" he called, and his heaving breath barely cleared the name from the sound of his huffing fright. "As-o-umph!"

The bark of a slant tree swung wide and struck him full in the face, knocking the wind from him. He lay spraddled on his back, staring up at a young but warty blue-black face with green, nappy hair and wintertime eyes.

Two strong hands seized his shirtfront and yanked him upright and into a door in the tree. The bark slammed shut behind, and the rescuing hands spun him about so that he could stare through the knothole in the secret portal. With one agog eye he watched the orange-furred squid monkeys charge past the tree, their slaverous muzzles snarling back from black gums and massive fangs. Tentacles thudded against the tree, and a crimson-fringed sucker slapped briefly over the knothole. Then, they were gone.

"If they'd found us in here," a gruff voice spoke from directly behind his ear, "I'd have fed you to them and escaped. I warn you, I can harm as hard as I heal, so don't even think of fighting me."

The sturdy hands that had pulled him from the forest floor heaved him about, and the gnome found himself facing that blue-black face of pale, wintry eyes and flesh lumpy with growths. The youthful visage was not unkindly but feral, smudged with moss stains and scored with thorn scratches. Burrs and grass blades hung in the kinked green hair, and livid creases from the nostril wings to the mouth corners looked carved by much laugh-ter. The midnight complexion and pointed ears tipped a dusty pink informed Ric that this was an ælf.

"I'm Old Ric," the eldern gnome said, employing the common dialect of the Bright Shore that the ælf had used. "And were it not for you, I'd be in gory pieces now."

"You owe me a life then, Old Ric," the ælf replied, and re-treated a pace, revealing in the hollow tree's slim light his leaf-knit tunic and boots of vine-lashed tree bark. A warm odor from leafsmoke hung in the air cut through with a redolence of loam. "One life promised to me, Broydo, ælf-counselor in the Forest of Wraiths. And as you're a gnome, I know I will be paid back. That's why I took the risk, though the others feared me a fool. No counselor is a fool—yet as the Empty Screed tells us, 'Wis-dom is not always wise.' "

"You know of gnomes?" Ric inquired with evident surprise. "I thought I was the only gnome on World's End."

"Well you may be," Broydo said. "I've never seen another. Yet as I say, I am a counselor, and my position reqires me to collect wisdom. And in collecting wisdom one gathers a great deal of knowledge. I've heard of your kind. You have faces like bats, wear frippery, and dwell inside Nemora, the winter world. It is said that sibyls never lie, and gnomes never break their word. Is that true?"

"Aye, it is true." The gnome gazed past Broydo's large frame to the crude winding stairway carved into the living hollow of the tree. Latten braces of conjure-metal infused the pith of the tree with Charm, keeping it alive though most of its interior had been carved out. Crowding the stairwell, silhouettes backlit by an orange glow pressed closer.

"Come with me then, Old Ric," Broydo invited, and led him down the uneven steps.

The packed silhouettes gave way, and the warm odor of leaf-smoke thickened to a dense aroma of hearth ash. The gnome entered a large grotto hung with root tendrils. It was lit by numerous gourd lamps perched among squat carven figures of telluric entities in the crevices and crannies of the marly walls. A score and twelve ælves ranged about the cavern, some sitting on the stairwells and ramp ways to the forest portals, others cross-legged on the tamped ground or fern carpets, many simply standing arrayed about an old ælfen woman athwart a settle carved to the likeness of a winged sphinx. Her sea-green locks spilled like kelp over her bony shoulders and withered dugs, and her blue-black face seemed gnawed and pocked as worm-riddled wood. Yet she moved with soft grace and litheness, gesturing the gnome near to her.

"Smiddy Thea," Broydo called to the ælf crone, "I bring you the eldern gnome, Old Ric, who owes us a life."

"Do you come well into our presence, Old Ric?" the crone inquired in a whispery voice.

"Yes, ælf lady," Ric attested, "I am whole and well."

"Good," she said with a slow smile, and watched him for a moment from under droop-lidded eyes. "You alone then are well among us."

Ric took the meaning of her words with grave concern and peered about more carefully at the surrounding throng. To his dismay, he saw that all displayed the same warty nodules as Broydo, and many also had flesh grotesquely pocked with small holes. "What ails you ælves?"

"A demon has cursed our clan," Smiddy Thea confessed wearily. "We did hope to locate the conjure-metals we seek for our livelihood by conjurement of a demon."

"Against my better counsel," Broydo interjected sternly.

"For sure against my grandson Broydo's counsel," the crone acknowledged. "The one who summoned the demon, Tivel, is now worn like a garment by the evil thing. When we strove to drive the demon out, it laid upon us this cankerous curse."

"Ælves are famous through the Bright Shore for their healing talents," the gnome said to the afflicted gathering. "Can you not heal yourselves?"

"We heal the illnesses of the world, not curses of the ultra-mundane," Smiddy Thea whispered hotly. "No. There is only one cure for our clan. One cure alone. And already eighteen of our own have perished to attain that cure."

Ric glanced about nervously at the bright eager stares in the dark faces surrounding him. "Surely now, you ælves are not look-ing to me for help? I—I am but a gnome. What do I know of demons and curses?"

"There is nothing to know," Broydo spoke up, clasping a sturdy hand to the gnome's back. "You owe us a life. You said so your-self. And gnomes never break their word."

Old Ric quailed and clutched at the muddy front of his shirt. "But how can my small life be of use to you against a demon?"

"The cure we need to break this curse and survive is in the Labyrinth of the Undead," the ælf crone rasped. "You must go there and retrieve it."

"To the Labyrinth of the—Oh no!" Old Ric's knees buckled, and he dropped forward to kneel and beg for release, but Broydo held him upright. "Send me not to the Undead! I am already on a mission of utmost importance for the author of these worlds. I cannot be distracted from my task."

Broydo shook the gnome so that Ric's teeth clattered. "If not for me, you'd be in pieces now all snug in the gullets of the squid monkeys. How would that have furthered your important mission?"

"But the Undead!" Old Ric looked desperately from one ælf to the next. "The squid monkeys will have me for supper, and the Undead will own me for a long and horrid time ever after."

"Then it's the squid monkeys, you lying gnome!" Broydo hauled Ric toward the stairwell they had descended. "Your life is a lie!"

The gnome thrashed free of the ælf-counselor's grasp and stood defiant before the congregation. "I swear, I am no liar! I am a gnome!" He lifted his whiskery chin and turned toward the crone with the flared nostrils of his pug nose quivering. "All right. I will go to the Labyrinth of the Undead, even as you command." His sunken, whiskery cheeks puffed out with the irate vigor of his speech. "I will find the cure you seek and return it here to you, however inconvenient that will be for me. Then my life-debt to Broydo will be paid and you—" He swung a knobby finger around the grotto. "All of you will owe *me* a life-debt. Is that understood?"

Smiddy Thea's slow smile returned to her haggard visage. "Understood, gnome. If you bring us the cure we need to live, our entire clan will owe you a life-debt, and we shall be yours to command."

"Indeed you will!" Old Ric righteously asserted, wattles shaking. "I am a gnome and good to his word." He emphasized this with a firm nod. "Now tell me, Smiddy Thea, what is this cure I am to retrieve from the Labyrinth of the Undead?"

The crone's smile slipped from her chewed face. "The Necklace of Souls."

Old Ric sat down where he had stood and rested the misery of his head in his hands. The Necklace of Souls had been crafted by the dwarves, night-creatures, created by the devil worshipper Duppy Hob from maggots in the flesh of a world serpent. The dwarves were monstrous, carnivorous creatures with supernatural stamina, for they possessed the mania of devils fused to the single-mindedness of maggots. It was Duppy Hob who employed them to make his fiendish demon harnesses and devil cages, so that he could trap fiends and shaitans out of the ethers of the Upper Air to do his bidding on World's End. The Necklace of Souls was one such wraith-fetcher. It snatched ghosts with its crystal prisms and bound them to the will of the wearer. When the dwarves revolted and cast Duppy Hob into the Gulf and all his hellish instruments after him, the Necklace of Souls alone survived. The overeager dwarves had dropped it accidentally into the volcanic labyrinth. Its presence there was what enabled departed souls drawn into the radiance of the Abiding Star to return and briefly assume mortal form again. The Undead hovered about the Necklace, feeding off the lives of all foolish enough to enter the maze of lava tunnels and cinder cones. And the dwarves themselves, with all their wicked fervor, guarded the Necklace in the labyrinth and often enslaved the wraiths attracted to it for their own dwarvish magic.

"The Necklace of Souls is all that can trap the demon who possesses Tivel," Smiddy Thea said in her thin voice. "Unless we get it, we shall rot away. Go, old Ric, and fetch our cure from the Labyrinth of the Undead."

BROYDO

THE GNOME EXHALED A LONG, HOPELESS SIGH AND ROSE TO HIS FEET. Without saying another word, he shuffled out of the grotto and up the winding stairwell to the door of the hollow tree. Outside, numerous staves of daylight crowded the forest, and no squid monkeys were to be seen.

From numerous eyeholes in the boles of hollowed trees, the clan of ælves watched him trudge through the leaf drifts in the direction of the baleful cliffs that he had seen on his plunge to World's End, muttering to himself the whole way. "Never should I have heeded the voice of thunder," he groused. "What is a gnome to know of World's End? Why me? Had I not completed my labors for the gnomish kith of Nemora? Am I not eldern? Have I not outlived two wives and too sadly three of my own children? All I crave is a warm burrow and my pipe. But I broke my beautiful pipe! Ai-grief! I smashed it to pieces when I first heard that voice of thunder and thought it was the blue smoke finally addling my brains. Ai-grief, what a blunder! Why me? Why should the blind god Chance pluck me from my happy seclusion to be a thirsty ear to the author of worlds? No one believes me in Nemora or even here at World's End. Why me?"

He kicked at a cluster of crimson pearl mushrooms, and a puff of pink spore billowed. Quickly he danced away, afraid to breathe the toxic smoke, and collided with a barbthorn shrub. A sharp yell escaped him as the razorous hedge pierced his breeks and stabbed his haunches.

Fearfully, he crouched, listening for an answering cry from the prowling swarm of squid monkeys. But there was no surcease in the rattling songs of the forest birds, and after a moment the eldern gnome dared right himself and rub his aching flanks. Morosely, he scanned the enclosing trees, seeking landmarks by which to find his way back to this clan who held his life-debt.

Nothing distinctive offered itself, and he briefly considered pounding upon one of the hollow trees and requesting further instruction. But then the hopelessness of his quest reasserted itself, and the unlikelihood of his returning at all urged him onward with his muttersome trek, "Why me? Two impossible tasks! Is it not enough that I serve the greater powers? Must I now also accomplish heroic deeds for the sorry likes of ælves?"

The honor of the gnomish kith depended upon him, and he would not be remembered throughout time as the one gnome who broke his word. *Time!* The word rang hollow. If he failed the Lady of the Garden, there would be no more time. She would dissolve her dream-magic and World's End, Nemora, Irth—all the Bright Worlds—would disappear. Sullenly, he continued his hike. The journey, tedious for its many enclosing dangers, required all his stamina. The forest was so dense that frequently he had to climb trees to scout the terrain and make certain that he was moving in the correct direction toward the grim cliffs he had viewed during his fall from the garden, and by night he was exhausted. As he curled about himself in a root cove with only his upturned nose and weary eyes uncovered by leaves, he strove to calculate how long a time remained for him—and for all the worlds—before a full day elapsed in the garden at the heights of World's End. There time meant something other than it did outside the great walls and in the bright planets below.

Dreamless sleep found him before he completed his calculations, and he woke to an emerald dawn and the first twitterings from the forest awning. "Ælves!" he hissed with the vehemence of a curse and brushed leaf dust from his mud-caked clothes. "For the likes of ælves I, an eldern gnome, am sleeping on the forest floor and foraging berries!"

While he poked his bald, freckled head among the underbrush, searching for anything edible, he pondered the nature of ælves. Like gnomes and dwarves, they lived underground. Like gnomes but unlike dwarves, they were natural creatures and enjoyed the light of the Abiding Star. But unlike gnomes and very like dwarves, they devised clever ways to trap the magic of daylight in hex-gems and conjure-metals, and they employed this Charm to manipulate their realms. Gnomes prided themselves on their charmless lives. They were not averse to utilizing amulets and talismans when they chanced upon them, but they preferred to live without such appurtenances. Gnomes did not need Charm. Their bodies, like the animals and plants of the natural world they revered, possessed sufficient magic to sustain them without Charm. That could not be said for ælves, dwarves, or people. Lacking devices of Charm for ballast, all these creatures would drift away into the Gulf on the nocturnal tide if they dared to sleep. And by this distinction, gnomes considered themselves the most superior of the sapient inhabitants of the Bright Shore.

"If I'm so superior," the gnome chided himself, "then why am I risking certain doom for an ælf? Asofel!" he called aloud but not too loudly, for the squid monkeys roamed nearby. "Asofel, why have you abandoned me? You said you would never be far. Yet where are you?"

No reply came.

He advanced through the day to another night in a leaf-strewn root cove. And two more days and two more nights passed as he struggled through the forest.

In the green dawn of the fifth day since falling from the pylons of the great wall, the eldern gnome lay exhausted in his latest root cove, entirely bewildered by hunger and the terrors of the night. Sleek flame vipers stalking monkeys had crawled past him in the dark, and their shining paths, like molten trickles of lava, and the terrified screams of their prey had deprived him of all rest.

"Da?" a small voice piped from the morning mist. "Da—where are you?"

Old Ric sat up rigidly. He recognized that child's voice by its wet lisp. It was Amara, his youngest daughter. She had died many, many years ago, when he was young and married to his first wife.

"Amara?" he called tentatively.

"Da!" Out of the dawn vapors, a frail form appeared. The sight of her pallid face and her slim shoulders draped in braided loops of russet hair yanked him upright.

The eldern gnome staggered three full paces, arms outstretched, before reason seized him. "Amara!" he cried, as her body dissolved to fumes in his grasp.

He fell weeping to his knees, and the next instant lifted an angry, blotched face streaked with tears. "May flame consume this damnable Forest of Wraiths!"

Heavy-hearted, Old Ric twisted upright and continued his ponderous march. Not far on, he found more sugar stalks gnawed only a little by the monkey troops, and he foraged them but had no willingness to eat. He had loved Amara as he had loved all his eight children and all the more the three whom he had outlived. They were here in this forest, he knew, because his memories created them—memories he had stored away with locks of forgetfulness broken now by days of hunger.

Avidly, he searched the corridors of trees for food, predators, and wraiths. He found none until midday, when he came upon giant droppings steaming on the river shales—tarry excrement packed with anonymous bones. A bull lizard prowled the purlieus of the forest. Its clawprints scaled the riverbank and disappeared in the leaf drifts.

Searching for spoor of the large beast so that he could avoid a confrontation, Old Ric noticed a mica glint in the river bracken. He approached to inspect what glimmered, and a silver spark flurried out of the ferns and spun upon the tail of the wind. When it spiraled past him, he observed that it was a faerïe, a wee burnished figure with a bleared visage and neither raiment nor genitals, and he yelped with glee. The faerïe knew the way between the worlds.

The gnome followed the flitting flight of the faerïe up the riverbank. It would likely lead him to a shaft that dropped off World's End and slid through the middle air to another of the Bright Worlds. If he could find that, he would have a way to proceed with his quest of the dark thing after he had retrieved the Necklace of Souls for the ælves. Otherwise, he would be obliged to seek passage with wayfaring humans on an ether ship. Gnomes were not much welcomed among humans, and he would have to find some charmful object to buy his passage.

The faerïe led him scrambling up a rill, between boulders splotched with lichen. Pool to pool he mounted the watercourse, sloshing among trickling rivulets, slipping across mossy ledges. Dark scraggly trees fell away to bounding slopes of heather. Ravens soared across the wide high country, and the forest below hung tattered in mists.

More faerïes appeared. They swirled in the chill air like snow motes. Among rocks ferned with ice, he found a sinkhole, where hordes of the tiny beings blustered. He knelt on the rock plates and peered down into the pit. Filaments of hot light twisted like slow lightning. Suddenly, teeming millions of faerïe packed the chute, gyring up and down the corridor of worlds.

As the gossamer beings twirled past his head their chill music laved his brains. And he heard them singing in miniscule cadences that blurred to one speech: "Go down—go down to what loves you."

Da! his youngest daughter's voice called from the luminous depths. *Da—where are you?*

"Amara!" he shouted into the hole, and then remembered she was but a wraith of his mournful memory.

"Not a memory," the cold voices sang. "Time folds backward through this chasm. Go down—go down to what loves you."

I'm here, Da! Amara called plaintively. *Where are you?*

Amara's slim figure drifted into view far below. She stood upon a green turf meadow among shredded fog, her arms upraised. Rags of fiery daylight blew past and illuminated her reddish brown hair.

"Are you really there?" the gnome asked, amazed. "You are not a wraith?"

"Time folds backward through this chasm," the whispering voices promised. "Go down—go down to what loves you."

Old Ric climbed into the hole and began to descend, and the faerïes sang with melodious glee. "You have found your way down to an old time made new. Down—down to what loves you."

A strong hand grabbed the collar of the gnome's shirt and hauled him up out of the hole. He spun about and brushed noses with Broydo's smudged and warty countenance. "Where do you think you're crawling, foolish gnome?" the ælf shouted into his startled face.

"Release me, ælf!" Ric shouted back. "Release me! The faerïe have shown me a way back through time. I can save my youngest. I can keep her from death's grasp. Let me go! I'll return, I swear, as soon as I save her."

"Enough!" Broydo shook the distraught gnome to silence. "That's a ghost hole you're crawling into. There's no escape from that. Behold!"

The ælf unslung a string of four dead hares from his back and dropped Old Ric to the ground. Deftly, Broydo unknotted the twine from a hare and dropped the animal into the hole. It fell a short way among a gust of faerïelights billowing like windblown sparks, and then a pugnacious face of fangs jumped from a root-shrouded niche and devoured the hare in two bites.

"A troll!" Old Ric gasped.

"Without a doubt, it would have chewed you to a ghost and you'd have met your dead kin in the afterlife," Broydo said fiercely.

"But the faerïe—" The gnome stared aghast as the slitherous troll retracted into its hiding place. "The faerïe deceived me! Why?"

"You must remember, faerïes thrive on the light of the Abiding Star," Broydo said, taking the gnome's arm and pulling him away from the ghost hole. "That is sufficient to sustain them. But blood-light—aye, that is a drug to them. The trolls offer them bloodlight from every prey they lure to the ghost hole. You would have fed troll and faerïe alike had you crawled in there seeking the wraith that lured you."

"Then, my poor Amara is—" The gnome chewed his lower lip.

". . . but a ghost of your memory." Broydo led Old Ric to the leeside of a scarp overlooking the misty Forest of Wraiths. "All can see now how prudent it was that I followed you or there'd be no hope at all for my clan." He shook his head accusingly.

The gnome stared up from under his tufted eyebrows. "You did not trust me."

"I am an ælf-*counselor*," Broydo proclaimed. "I trust no one. Neither ælf, nor ogre, nor human, nor even a gnome. All have their foibles. And yours would have made you a tasty tidbit for a troll."

"Then I, too, am grateful you followed me, Broydo," Old Ric admitted, and turned a hungry eye on the three remaining hares. "Would that you had revealed yourself earlier. I might have eaten better."

"But I had to be certain that gnomes do keep their word," the ælf explained. "I've heard of gnomes and their veracity. But hearing and knowing from experience—well, you know." He slapped a callused hand upon the gnome's bony shoulder. "You could have fled. And for a while I thought you might, especially after your windy speech about the superiority of gnomes and the futility of accomplishing heroic deeds for the sorry likes of ælves."

"Forgive my wicked tongue, Broydo," the gnome spoke contritely. "I grouse to quell my fear and soothe my anguish. I have much respect for ælves, for they know the craft of Charm. And would that we had some Charm for this quest."

"*We?*" Broydo queried with a skeptical eyebrow cocked. "I have shadowed you to test your merit. And you have not been found wanting, Old Ric. But this is not *my* quest. Oh no. I would not be foolish enough to enter the Labyrinth of the Undead."

"Foolish?" the gnome asked with a huff. "Is it less foolish to await your doom passively in the forest hollows?"

"That is a doom I regret but can bear better than the claws of the demon." Broydo unsheathed a curved flensing knife. "Gather kindling, Old Ric. You deserve a worthy meal before you enter the Labyrinth—a destination that awaits you beyond this scarp."

The gnome obligingly marched up the long slope of gorse among pulpy clusters of mushrooms and stood upon the mighty shoulder of the highlands gazing out at black volcanic hills and lava tunnels, ridged, crevassed, and jammed together as the lobes of a brain. No life stirred among those burned-out ranges. Yet beyond them, immense reptilian birds soared on sulfurous thermals exhaled by a pocked row of cinder cones.

Old Ric came down the slope weary with despair, absently gathering dried twigs of mountain shrubs. He dropped the kindling into the small pit Broydo had carved in the heath and sat down with his back against a stunted spruce.

"Don't look so grim," Broydo counseled, snapping a spark with flint-and-steel in one hand and catching it in leaf duff held in the other. "If you go into the Labyrinth with that black mood, you're sure to join the wraiths."

Old Ric hung his bald head between his knees. "Unless you have an amulet to protect me, what chance have I among the Undead?"

"Very little, it is true," Broydo agreed, fanning the flame in the pit with a threadworn cap of crushed blue velvet. "Little chance, indeed, for I have no amulets. All the Charm that my clan possesses it uses now to stay alive under the demon's curse."

"My cap!" the gnome blurted. "That is my cap you have there, ælf!"

"Oh, is it?" Broydo brushed the velvet nap. "I found a meal sitting in it some days ago." He displayed the armbands he wore of blue monkey fur, a simian visage glaring eyeless from one, its leathern snout locked in a permanent fanged snarl. "Makes a handy fan to ward cooking smoke and flies."

Old Ric snatched the hat from Broydo's grasp. "This is no flyswat. This is my hat."

"Well, you're welcome then, Old Ric," Broydo said, and turned his attention to the hares he had flensed, gutted, and impaled on a spit of spruce wood. "Wear it in good health."

Ric glumly fit the hat to his head. It smelled of monkey fur and woodsmoke, yet he was glad to have it back, for without it, he had felt naked.

As fearful as he was of what lay ahead, the eldern gnome ate heartily. Broydo produced a sack of varied nuts, which he placed in the fire and shucked as the heat cracked them. Berries, too, came forth from another pouch. And moss wine from a flagon embossed with ælvish sigils. The minty green wine frosted their insides with a euphoric chill, and soon they were smiling and lauding each other—the gnome for his life spared from the squid monkeys and his hat restored, and the ælf for the hope, however slim, that Ric offered the stricken clan.

INTO THE DARK LABYRINTH

IN THE MIDST OF THEIR THIRD TOAST, A FEROCIOUS ROAR SCALDED the uplands, and the two squatters leaped to their feet. A bull lizard, huge as a horse, loped toward them, drawn by the scent of the braised hares. Its rut-warped muzzle aimed straight at them, razor jaws flanged wide, while its heaving shoulder muscles rippled with the force of its attack, serrate tail lashing behind.

The ælf and gnome abandoned their meal and ran up the rocky scarp. The gnome knew better than to look back and instead fixed his attention on the crest and its grove of dwarf spruce. But Broydo dared a backward glance. The sight of the giant fanged lizard elicited a cry of terror, and instantly he lost his footing on the tangled heath and fell hard to his stomach with a mournful gasp.

Old Ric heard the ælf's frightened scream and turned in time to see the lizard descend upon him. Its talons pinned Broydo squirming to the ground, and its dagger fangs slashed. The ælf's vest and bodice flayed open, and Broydo's shriek rode high above the triumphant growl of the bull lizard.

With a despairing yell, Old Ric wrenched a fist-sized rock

from the ground and hurled it with all his gnomish strength. It whistled as it flew and smote the beast in the socket of its swivel eye.

An anguished yowl slashed from the lizard, and it reared back, claws flailing and a black ichor drooling from the struck eye.

Ric darted forward, grabbed Broydo under his shoulders, and dragged the stunned ælf out of the shadow of the beast. "Get up!" he bawled. "Get up, ælf, and flee to live!"

Broydo twisted upright and stood agog before the giant lizard clawing at the sky in its agony.

The gnome snagged the ælf's arm and pulled him along. They ran hard, heads wagging, legs gulping wide strides as they crashed through the brittle branches of spruce at the crest of the bluff. Only then did they risk a look back at the beast.

But the lizard had forgotten them. It slouched down the scarp, lolling its horned and wounded head.

Broydo's hands slapped his naked torso, astonished to find himself intact. Only a thin crimson welt from his clavicle to his navel marked the path of the lizard's claw. He burped a disbelieving laugh and slapped his belly again to be certain that he was whole.

"You saved my life," the ælf gasped.

"Aye, so I did." The gnome beamed, hands on his wobbly knees, heaving for breath. "So I did."

Broydo sat down hard on a tuffet knobby with quartz. "Well then, your life-debt is paid!"

"Aye, so it is." The gnome sucked a deep breath through his teeth. "So it is."

The ælf gazed about with eyes that looked bruised with grief. "It were better then that you had left me to the bull lizard."

"Was it?" The gnome straightened painfully, still panting.

"Oh, yes. For now you're free to go your own way—and my clan—" Broydo took in a harsh gulp of air. "What hope has my clan now of lifting the demon's curse?"

Old Ric plopped down beside him and cast him a sidelong look of incredulity. "What hope did your clan ever have with me, an eldern gnome, as your so-called champion?"

"All of us have failed to retrieve the Necklace of Souls," Broydo spoke hollowly. "But we are only ælves. You, at least, are a gnome. You were our best hope."

"Me?" He pulled back his head in disbelief. "I have no Charm, no amulets or talismans, no weapons of any kind. What hope could you possibly invest in me?"

"But you're a gnome!" Broydo returned Ric's skeptical look. "Gnomes are clever enough to live and live well, *without Charm*, on the ice world of Nemora! If you can do that, then stealing jewelry from dwarves would be little challenge, I'm sure."

"From dwarves, perhaps," the gnome conceded, sitting taller with pride. "But a demon—what hope against a demon?"

"Help us, Old Ric." Broydo fell to his knees before the gnome, and his curly brows bent piteously. "I will accompany you into the Labyrinth."

"My debt is paid, Broydo," Old Ric said gently. "Believe me, if I had no other task before me, I would help you. I am old and have no family that expect my return. The plight of your clan moves me. And you have been not unkind to me. But I have been summoned by the author of these worlds."

"Author?" Broydo squatted on his calves. "What author of these worlds?"

"She has not divulged her name to me," Old Ric said thoughtfully. "But she is of another, wider order. There, beyond the cloud mountains, she dwells guarded by her sentinels, the Radiant Ones."

"There is naught beyond the cloud mountains, gnome, but the Abiding Star itself."

Ric removed his hat and wiped the glinting sweat from his brow. "So I myself thought. Then, the voice came. The thunder voice of Asofel, the Radiant One. He had been sent to summon me to her garden. I followed his voice to a ladder of twine." A laugh wheezed from him. "*Twine!* But how luminous, lit with a cold fire! The ladder ascended into a rock wall among the ice-veined crags of Nemora, where I had lived nearly my whole life until then. I climbed it. It did not seem a long way. But when I emerged, I found myself atop a massive well of ancient origin. The lady was there. She said she had bid me into her presence for a talk."

"A talk?" The ælf canted his head skeptically.

"Aye, a talk," the gnome repeated, and fit his cap back on. "She would talk with the dream itself, she said. The dream—that's us, you see. All the Bright Worlds, a dream of hers, hung here in the void by her magic."

"Who was this lady?" Broydo pressed, his interest piqued. He pulled his legs out from under to sit more comfortably. "How did she refer to herself?"

"That she did not." Old Ric put his knobby hands on his thighs and bent forward under the weight of what he had to impart. "She is of the Nameless Ones. I know of them from my own fire magic. I have been trained to see into flames. And in those torn veils of light, I saw a shadow thing trespass our Bright Worlds from the Dark Shore. I was not the only one to see this, of course. But the blind god Chance led the Lady of the Garden to me among all her subjects who had witnessed this evil. It is an evil that I and others believe was Hu'dre Vra, the Dark Lord who brought cacodemons to Irth from beyond the Gulf. He is dead, but he has left behind another, a magus whose presence injures our lady. And that injury may well invoke the wrath of the child's father and other Nameless Ones."

"I know of no such Nameless Ones." Broydo lidded one eye. "Were you perhaps dreaming this yourself?"

"No!" The gnome sat straight. "What I say is true."

The ælf rubbed his warty, dented chin. "Have you any proof?"

"None that would satisfy a counselor such as yourself, Broydo."

"Then why am I to believe this?" Broydo heaved himself impatiently to his feet and began tying together the loose shreds of his torn bodice and vest. "I think this is a handy story by which to evade a terrible journey. You needn't bother, gnome. Your life-debt is paid. A simple 'no' would have sufficed."

Old Ric sighed heavily. "Whether you believe, I care not at all. I am bound to serve the nameless lady. She has sent me back into the Bright Worlds on a dire mission. I must accomplish it in short order. I fear that I have little time left, and none to devote to your quest."

"A day!" Broydo cried, hands outheld beseechingly. "The Labyrinth of the Undead is before us. We will go in this very afternoon and be out by tomorrow's dusk, I promise you. One day of your time, and you will have saved my clan and won our fealty."

"How can you say one day?" The gnome cast a fearful glance toward the cankerous horizon. "There is a demon in there, not to mention vile dwarves and wraiths voracious for bloodlight. We may never get out."

"But my clan!" Broydo fixed him with a piercing stare. "What will become of us?"

"Ælf, listen well to me." Old Ric stood and drew a deep breath. "If I do not complete my mission for the nameless lady, then all the worlds will cease to be. Everyone will die!"

"Bosh!" Broydo waved him away in disgust and strode down the far side of the bluff toward the badlands. "Go serve your author of the worlds. I must find salvation for my people."

"Farewell, Broydo!" Old Ric called, but the ælf did not bother to respond. The gnome watched after him a short while, his chest clogged with grief for the ælf's suffering. Then, he looked about him at the wind-bent spruce trees and the boulders splashed with lichen under the sky's blue, and he wondered how he would find his way down from here to continue his quest among the Bright Worlds.

Possessing no charmful object to barter, he could not book passage on the human's ether ships. Yet, even if he had possessed such a charmful object, he knew not the way to the nearest human enclave or even if such enclaves existed here on far-flung World's End. He crouched on the scarp ledge and peered down at the pitch-green depths of the Forest of Wraiths. There, the wounded bull lizard roamed among flame vipers and squid monkeys and other horrors.

He glanced back at the retreating figure of Broydo and realized with dread resignation that the path into the Labyrinth of the Undead was in truth no more perilous than any other direction he might follow in his trackless journey across World's End. And there, in the diminishing figure of Broydo, was his one and only ally in this fierce nether realm.

"If I succeed in retrieving the Necklace of Souls," the gnome reasoned aloud to himself, "I will have a clan of ælves and all their charmful things to help me find my way to the Bright Worlds beyond. And if I fail"—he puffed his cheeks out and shrugged—"I will be no more, and what concern will I have then that all the worlds have followed me into oblivion?"

Shaking his head at the implacable course of fate, Old Ric rose from his crouch and shambled after Broydo.

The ælf blinked hard when he turned to see the gnome striding downhill, waving his cap, and calling his name heartily. "What, may I ask, changed your mind?" Broydo inquired suspiciously.

"I need allies for my quest," Ric admitted with candor. "I must find a dark thing that has come into the Bright Worlds, and I cannot accomplish this without charmful tools. If I help you save your clan, will your clan help me find this dark thing?"

"If you help me in the Labyrinth and we emerge alive with the Necklace of Souls," Broydo said, breaking into a lavish smile, "your quest will be ours, assuredly."

"Done!" The gnome extended both hands, right arm crossed atop the left, palms down.

The ælf likewise crossed his arms in front of him, palms up, and clasped Old Ric's hands in the timeless grasp of ælvish covenant. "How do you, a gnome, know the ælfen embrace?"

"There are ælves on Nemora, you know," Old Ric explained as they continued their walk through the heather toward the infernal horizon. "On my world, gnomes and ælves are not unkindly toward each other."

"On this world, too, then," Broydo said past a sudden tightening in his throat, "we shall be friends."

"We shall need to be friends if we are to survive what lies ahead," the gnome said, attention fixed upon the unruly terrain. In a short time they were slogging through reddish black sand among stobs of whitethorn cactus. Ridges of albino sand rose before them, too steep to climb.

They wended among the gypsum hills, using the Abiding Star as a guide through the convoluted gravel paths. Gradually, the white walls darkened to barren granite above which a stark promontory of cinder cones came into view. Slurry and volcanic ash crunched underfoot.

Broydo offered refreshing sips from his flagon of minty wine, but by nightfall both of them would have preferred to slake their implacable thirsts with simple water.

"It did not look so far from back there," the ælf defended his reason for carrying wine.

Old Ric said nothing. His alertness was devoted entirely to the terrible twilight above the black hills. Blood red clouds shone as a backdrop for the zigzag flights of bat-winged asps.

Soon, dark filled the crevasses of the volcanic maze, and the narrow sky above swarmed with planet light, cometary vapors, and star smoke. By that illumination, the two wanderers decided, despite the daunting odds, they would nevertheless press on.

"We are within the maze as it is," the ælf-counselor repeated each time they reached a fork among the rocky passages. "Best we continue on."

The gnome kept his silence, all senses strained to their limits. Above, swift-flitting shapes played darkly against the cope of heaven, and below, among the tarnished silver shadows, frightful noises abounded—the crunch of gravel, the scrape of sand, the growl of a predator on the far side of the walled granite.

The only weapon between them was Broydo's flensing knife, which he kept unsheathed and wavering before him. Ric thought to warn him to put it away lest he trip and fall on it, but he was too afraid to speak. All his focus was invested on finding their way through the dark Labyrinth. The star patterns provided directional clues, and they managed to continue their approach toward the dread cinder cones where the Undead lurked.

The sizzle of coils rasping against gravel sounded from a nearby corridor. The immensity and nearness of the perilous noise coaxed Broydo to a run, and he slammed into a stone abutment and dropped his knife. While he fetched about on the dark ground trying to retrieve it, the slitherous scraping drew closer, accompanied by an ominous brattle of claws.

"Forget the knife!" Old Ric whispered hotly. "We must flee!"

Broydo found the blade, but before he could stand up the air quaked with the grating of granite and the crushing of gravel. From out of a side passage, a gruesomely massive face shoved, its undershot jaw wide, exposing rows of needle-thin teeth. Eyes aslant with wicked fervor gleamed in the starlight under a ledged brow of cracked shale.

The gnome seized Broydo by the back of his pants and hauled him backward into another corridor. A moment later, the giant jaws clacked closed on the ælf's shadow, and Broydo stood a hand breadth from the meshed fangs and bonepit eyes of the huge beast. A fetid stink jetted from its nostrils and choked the ælf's scream in his lungs.

Broydo stabbed his knife into the scaly hide, and the roar that burst from the gaping jaws blew the ælf and gnome deeper into the corridor. They rolled to their feet and fled howling, Ric's hat flying from his head and disappearing into the dark. Heavy claws scratched rock, and the big face lurched up and out of the trace only to rear above them, a reptilian colossus scuttling across the ridge crests.

Talons swooped over them, and Ric and Broydo pressed themselves against the rock walls whimpering. The stupendous visage peered down on its prey, snapping the air and bellowing with rage, unable to wedge its mammoth head into the narrow defile. Again, it struck with its claws, scratching rock dust from the walls. In moments, it would shear away enough rock to scoop them into its ravening maw.

Old Ric and Broydo looked for escape, but the passage only widened in either direction. Cries of hopelessness leaped from them and were swallowed up entire by the roaring of the beast.

Then, from the wide end of the passage ahead, a cowled figure separated from the shadows. It beckoned them urgently and signed toward a hole in the rock wall. The gnome and the ælf clutched at each other, looking to see if either could surmise who this stranger might be. But they saw only terror in each other's faces as the behemoth above tore at the rocks protecting them.

Frantically, Ric and Broydo locked arms and ran bent over. The air around them shook with the rage of the beast and the scything nearness of its claws. The figure ahead had vanished. But the hole in the wall remained, and Broydo dived in first. Ric swiftly followed, and the two crawled through the narrow chute a long way, the frustrated roars of the predator echoing dimmer behind them and an amber glow brightening ahead.

THE WITCH

EVENTUALLY, AFTER MUCH HUFFING EXERTION AND SHOUTED ENCOURagement to one another, Old Ric and Broydo crawled out onto an alkali pan whereon blazed a warm, welcoming fire. The cowled figure sat before it and silently summoned them into the light.

Broydo pulled his companion closer and chattered nervously into his doughy ear, "Behold, gnome, that fire burns without kindling!"

"Aye, but it's warm and bright nonetheless," Old Ric replied bravely. "Surely, we'd be chewed meat now in the dark belly of the beast if not for that one who has led us here and who now must be considered a friend."

Firmly grasping one another, the ælf and gnome approached the fire, their entrails shaking like the shuddering shadows cast by the blaze.

"Don't be afraid." A woman's gentle voice spoke from within the hood. "Come to the fire and warm yourselves. There are no creatures nearby who will harm you."

"Thank you, kind lady, for offering us escape from the beast," Old Ric said, and sat opposite the cowled woman. "I am Old Ric, an eldern gnome of Nemora. And this is my fellow traveler—"

"Broydo, ælf-counselor of Smiddy Thea's clan in the Forest of Wraiths." The ælf bowed deeply and squatted beside the gnome.

"You nearly forsook your lives back there," the woman said, turning her cowl toward the bunched ridges beyond the pan where the black tethers of night bound the jumbled land to the most obscure reaches of the starry horizon. "I know you are not ghosts, for the beast does not stalk ghosts. Why are a living ælf and gnome trespassing the Labyrinth of the Undead?"

Old Ric and Broydo assessed each other and found no reason between them to keep their quest secret from the woman who had saved their lives. "We seek the Necklace of Souls," Broydo answered simply. "That alone shall lift the curse that a demon has set upon my clan."

"Duppy Hob's Necklace is well guarded," the stranger cautioned. "It is what enables wraiths to wander the Labyrinth as well as the Forest of Wraiths. They will defend their anchor to World's End. And then there are the dwarves. They are the ones who made the Necklace of Souls. It is their property now that Duppy Hob is fallen into the Gulf. Even if you retrieve it from the wraiths, the dwarves will stalk you across World's End to take it from you."

"I mean not to steal the Necklace," Broydo added, his brow furrowed contritely. "I mean to borrow it only long enough to heal my clan. Then I will return it personally."

"Dwarves are not as reasonable as ælves," the cowled woman said. "After all, they are but maggots of a world serpent granted simian shape by Duppy Hob."

Old Ric cleared his throat. "Forgive my impertinence, kind and knowledgeable lady—but may I inquire who you are?"

The voice that came from the dark hood spoke softly, barely audible above the thrashing fire. "I am a witch."

"A witch?" Broydo echoed with fright. "A human?"

"Yes."

"And this fire that burns without kindling—" Old Ric inquired, "this is your magic?"

The witch gestured, and gusts of flame jetted from the naked ground behind them. She motioned again, and the fires vanished, leaving no scorch at all upon the blanched ground.

"Why have you saved us from the beast, mistress witch?" the gnome asked.

"Then you admit that I have saved you?" She leaned closer, and two eye glints sparked under her cowl. "You acknowledge that you owe me a life-debt, the two of you?"

Broydo and Ric exchanged fearful glances, and the gnome nodded. "We cannot deny it, gentle witch."

"I am not gentle," the dulcet voice said. "But I am needy. Will you help me with my need?"

"If it is within our power," Broydo agreed.

"It shall be," the witch breathed hotly, "when we retrieve the Necklace of Souls."

"*We?*" Broydo noted, tufty eyebrows lifted. "You will help us?"

"I can take you directly to the Necklace of Souls," the witch promised. "I can lead you safely past all horrors and obstacles. Except the demon."

"But the demon is the worst of our foes," Broydo interrupted. "It occupies the body of my clansman, Tivel, and will know all the secret ways into my soul. I will have no defense against it but the Necklace itself."

"You will have the Necklace," the vague voice from within the hood assured him. "I cannot lead you past the demon, but I can distract this terrible thing. If you are intrepid, you will have a chance to seize the Necklace of Souls and exorcise the demon from your clansman Tivel."

"What do you want from us?" the gnome asked trepidatiously.

The witch held up one pale finger freckled with blood. "One crystal prism from the Necklace shall be mine."

The gnome and the ælf retracted at the sight of the gory finger. "Who are you?" Old Ric cried out in horror. "Whose blood is this we see upon you?"

"It is my own," the witch answered without emotion. "I bear wounds that will never heal. And only a crystal prism from the Necklace of Souls can sustain me long in this world. I have been sustained thus far by the proximity of the Abiding Star that allows wraiths to wander this wilderness. But I am trapped here unless I get a crystal prism to give me the strength to wander farther from the Abiding Star. I have not the stamina to go on from here without it." She drew back her hood and exposed a human visage welded with rays of blood, a cut face disfigured with puncture wounds and ripped gashes that had flayed open the cheeks and exposed jawbone and teeth. "Behold my suffering!" Bruised eyes gazed forlornly from behind the rags of torn lids.

Broydo stifled a cry, and Ric upheld a hand to block the horrid vision. "Who did this to you?" the gnome asked.

The witch covered her living wounds. "Those who feared me."

"Show us the way to the Necklace, hapless witch," the gnome said. "If we succeed, you shall have your crystal prism."

The cowl faced Broydo, and the ælf said, "You are a witch. You have magic. Why do you need us to get the Necklace?"

"The dwarves have taken precautions against witches and my ilk. Only those without magic can hope to get close enough to the Necklace to take it from the dwarves."

Broydo nodded. "Then I am agreed. You shall have your prism from the Necklace if we succeed. Lead us directly to where it is, witch, and let us be away from this frightful place."

The witch rose to her feet, straight upward, as though her cloak held no more than hot air, and the blazing fire vanished.

The gnome and ælf squinted in the abrupt dark and found the witch's starlit shadow drifting across the alkali pan. Ahead, against the clotted starlight, the cinder cones loomed. Ric and Broydo hurried after their guide, their feet falling mutely on the ashen surface.

The terrain dipped, and they traipsed among alien stones, menhirs and dolmens that had been knocked askew. Fireflicker eyes peered at them from the seamless dark of the alcoves, but no creatures came forth. Soon, the threesome had so utterly immersed themselves in the meander of leaning rocks that even the cinder cones had dropped from sight. Above the jagged slates set edgewise in the ground, the stars in their fluorescent webs were barely visible.

Only the wispy shadow of the witch offered direction in this confounding land. Broydo and Ric shuffled quickly to keep her in sight, for she floated effortlessly over the pebbly paths. The harder they strove to keep up with her, the faster she moved. Before long, they began jogging and then running to keep her in view. Yet, strangely, they experienced no weariness from their exertion.

All night long they ran. Occasionally they threw feverish glances to one another but saw little in the dark but the glimmer of reflected star shine in each other's startled eyes. The dread of losing the witch held their attentions firmly forward until dawn. Pink clouds erased the stars, and a brisk wind sprang from ahead and swept away the darkness among twisting weeds and heeling fumes of dust.

In the gray light, they became aware that they were not running alone. A third figure loped between the gnome and the ælf. Grinning maniacally at them in the empurpled haze was another ælf, bison-shouldered with a block of a brow, and a cuff of mossy hair under a bald pate.

"Tivel!" Broydo recognized his comrade instantly and screamed with alarm. He waved fervidly at Old Ric. "It is the demon!"

They ran harder to catch up with the witch, but she had disappeared. Effortlessly, the demon Tivel kept pace with them, grinning insanely. "Greetings, Brother Broydo!" a harsh voice rasped from the leering ælf, and his eyes lit up in the gloaming like rays from a gourd lantern. "Have you come to the Labyrinth of the Undead to join the others?"

The ground bulged in front of them, and the runners skidded to a stop as the crust cracked and necrotic hands sprouted from below. Broydo and Ric crouched with horror as skeleton figures draped in rags of flesh lifted themselves from their graves. Arms of wet-looking bones reached out, and torn faces, their empty sockets lit with votive flames, swayed above tottering carcasses.

Broydo sobbed, "They are the eighteen!" He fell to his knees and covered his face with his hands. "They are my clan! The ones who came to this terrible place before me."

Old Ric pulled Broydo upright and away from the morbid assembly.

"Where are you two going?" Tivel asked through a molar-wide grin, and sidled closer. "This is where you belong. This is where you shall reside for all time to come."

The ælf and the gnome turned to flee, but a slab of slate blocked their way. From either side, the Undead slouched closer, their tattered fingers reaching out, the chamfers of their eye sockets inflamed with burning filaments. The demon came forward clothed in a caustic green smoke and putrid stench. His chalk face sweated ruby points of blood. Out of his open mouth, the genital head of a viper emerged, unmeshing its treacherous fangs.

"Tivel—sleep—" a sultry voice suddenly called from the darkness beyond.

A shower of stars folded around the shambling Undead, and
they immediately collapsed to a fuming stack of bones and peel-
ings of hide.

"Sleep, Tivel, sleep," the soothing voice spoke, and the cowled
witch stepped from out of the dark of the leaning stones. "Your
flesh awakes a fog. Your bones awake a rain. The lightning in
your eyes begins a thunder in your brain."

The witch clapped her hands, and a bolt of electric fire hissed
vibrantly in the space between Tivel and the shuddering gnome
and ælf. The demon staggered, then stood unmoving in deeper
darkness as the lightning sizzled away.

"Be quick!" the witch called. "The demon and its Undead will
wake in moments. Be quick!"

The gnome leaped over the smoldering bones and ducked
under the demon's grasping arms. But the ælf could not budge.
He squatted terrified before the evil countenance of Tivel, dizzy
with the rotted stink of his dead clansmen. The bald white eyes
of the demon gazed sightlessly, yet the viper remained writhing
in the jarred mouth, twisting with lethal intent.

"Broydo!" Old Ric shouted. "Come along! Jump the bones!"

The ælf would not move. He sat mesmerized by his frightened
reflections in Tivel's white eyes.

Ric turned to retrieve his companion, and the witch sang with
alarm, "No! You will break the spell."

Too late the warning came, for the eldern gnome had already
flung himself back over the steaming slag of melted flesh and
bones. No sooner did he grasp the ælf and yank him upright
than a bestial cry descended on them.

"Broydo would not abandon his brethren," a sibilant voice
spoke from all directions, "and so you both shall remain faithful
as the dead!"

Tivel lurched over them, his chalky, asp-tongued face hideous
with a fearsome glee, drops of blood sweat flying like sparks. He
seized Broydo and Old Ric, one in each supernally powerful
hand, and hoisted them off their feet.

They bawled like babies and searched frenziedly for the witch.
Already, she had fled, and the two knew then that they were
doomed to an ignominious death.

The viper stabbed forth from the demon's gaping jaws and
struck first Broydo, biting into his naked chest and burrowing

into his flesh, gnawing for his heart. The ælf yodeled his agony, writhing futilely in Tivel's unrelenting grip. Blood jetted, and the crunch of cracking ribs resounded above the demon's screeching laughter and the ælf's anguished shrieks.

"Asofel!" the gnome cried in desperation. "Asofel!"

The demon shook Old Ric to a blur. "What are you calling for, fool? Your gnomish gods cannot save you. You are mine! Your bones will melt in the heat of your suffering. You will know . . ."

His exultation broke off when, out of nowhere, a shaft of blue-white radiance fell upon them, and the viper unclasped from Broydo's chest and curled into the demon's maw. Tivel staggered backward blindly, with his prey yet in his hands. A rank, steamy smell of rain wafted from the ground where the brilliant beam of light illuminated the heaped bones of the Undead. The corpses rose up whole—eighteen ælves intact, unmarred by lesions or wounds; though their eyes were but paling stars, their faces were joyfully surprised. And in the next instant, they bleared away on the wind, vanishing within the dazzling lightshaft like a heat mirage of wrinkled air.

"Nay!" the demon bellowed, squinting, holding the ælf and gnome to shield its blood-runneled countenance from the blinding light. "Nay!"

The pillar of blue-white luminosity gradually condensed to a figure with two legs, two arms, and a head like the naked core of a star. At the sight of this, Tivel released the creatures in his grasp and backed away so swiftly he seemed blown by a gale wind. An inchoate cry spooled from him, and as he whirled about to flee, his leather wings spontaneously shredded to rags upon his back.

The being of star fire pointed its left arm. There was no ray, nothing visible that projected from its hand. Yet, the brown wings of the demon burst into flames at once as if naphtha-doused and torched. Tivel howled and thudded to the ground under a hot crackle of burning membranes. Limned in blue flame, the demon wrenched himself upright. He gazed with abject terror at the entity of light that had granted annihilation with one gesture. Then, he pitched forward, wailed horrendously, and shriveled into a blackened husk beneath a twist of acrid smoke.

Broydo sat up startled, slapping his body, feeling for wounds.

There were none. He squinted at the radiant being who had saved them and could discern no features save a dazzling outline. "Ric?" He groped for his companion.

Old Ric did not reply. He knelt abjectly before the Radiant One. "All blessings on you, Asofel!"

"Get up, Old Ric. It's over now." The shape of stellar radiance stepped closer, and the enclosing slate monuments revealed every pith and spall, lucid as under a microscope. "You found the dark thing swiftly and now our work is done. Let's get out of this dream."

"No, no! Asofel, you are mistaken." The gnome raised both his hands to guard his sight from the burning presence. "This is not the dark thing I was sent to find. This is but a demon. A wicked spirit of the ethers. A dream thing such as myself."

"What?" The intensity of the Radiant One dimmed, and his bodily characteristics became recognizable. Asofel wore a cuirass atop a tunic and the thongs of his sandals crisscrossed his shins. A luminous mane of hair billowed from a lion's face. "You summoned me for that?"

"Forgive me, Asofel." Ric spoke with his arm over his eyes as much to protect his gaze as to avoid facing the supernal being's wrath. "It would have slain me. Our mission would have been lost. I needed your help."

Asofel's aura flared, erasing his features. "I am not your servant, gnome."

Old Ric pressed his face to the ground. "What was I to do, Radiant One?"

"Find the dark thing," Asofel said, stepping backward. "Go at once."

The gnome reared upright, face averted. "But—you see, it's not my fault, Radiant One. You dropped me into the Forest of Wraiths—and Broydo"—he motioned to where Broydo squatted with his hands on his head peeking through the cleft between his arms—"this ælf you see here before you—he saved my life from the squid monkeys and then—"

"Silence, gnome!" Asofel had brightened to a blue-hot shaft of light, and his voice called from far away, "I am a Radiant One— a sentinel of the Nameless. My mission is to save the lady's child, not pander to you. Do not summon me to this flimsy dream again until you have found the dark thing."

The radiance faded and blurred into the orange glow of dawn.
Old Ric rose and walked unsteadily to where Asofel had stood.
No trace of the Radiant One remained.

Broydo gaped at the scorched remains of Tivel. The ashen
shape of the dead ælf trickled away in the bright morning wind.
"You spoke the truth," the ælf-counselor whispered. "You *are* on
a mission for the Nameless Ones."

Ric said nothing. He turned around in the space where Asofel
had walked and felt nothing special.

"Gnome, you should get on with your mission at once,"
Broydo remarked.

"How?" Old Ric asked, palms up, feeling the air for some
lingering sense of the overwhelming power that had occupied
this space only moments before. "We owe our lives to the witch."

Broydo put his finger over his heart, where the demon-asp had
bored for his heart. "Behold, gnome! I am whole. We owe our
lives to Asofel." The ælf put his hands on the gnome's bony
shoulders. "You were right all along, Old Ric. I did not believe
you. But I surely do now. We must obey the greater being."

"Yes." The eldern gnome shook his head in agreement. "I will
obey the lady who sent *me* to find the dark thing. She is the
author of these worlds. She is the greater being. I do not have
to obey Asofel. What does he know of our Bright Shore? You
heard him. This is but a flimsy dream to him. That is why the
lady sent me. I must find the way, best I can. And so, I declare
that we fulfill our vow to the witch." He reached out and put his
hands on Broydo's thick shoulders. "And we will heal your clan."

The ælf's warty face composed itself to a sage smile. "Ah, Ric,
you have the clarity of a counselor. I am sorry I ever doubted
you."

"Reserve your praise for when the deed is done," Ric advised
soberly, and gazed about among the tall slates of shale. "First we
must find our way."

THE NECKLACE OF SOULS

BY THE DAWNING LIGHT OF THE ABIDING STAR, THEY ORIENTED themselves in the direction they had been running when Tivel first appeared and continued on their way. They adhered to the bearing that the witch had set for them.

Their stamina wore thin without the witch's magic to bolster them. Soon Old Ric wheezed for breath, and his stride faltered. They slowed to a brisk walk. Around them, fireflies jittered.

"*Where is Tivel?*" a tiny voice called out.

Old Ric, through his labored breathing, thought that Broydo had addressed him. "What did you say?"

Broydo swatted at the thickening haze of fireflies. "I said naught."

"*Tivel—Tivel!*" came the chant out of the sparkling air.

The gnome peered anxiously at the sparks flickering about their heads like shattered halos and saw that each tiny light was a faerïe. But they were not ordinary faerïes. Each possessed a spiderous shape.

"Demons!" Broydo yelped. "The demon host that Tivel convoked from the ethers! Run, Old Ric, before they enter the small holes of our heads! Run!"

Lungs churning, the gnome fled after Broydo, alarm feeding
him the strength he needed to sprint. Still, the sparkling legion
of demons streamed behind, chanting in their eerily thin voices,
"Tivel—Tivel—where are you? Tivel—Tivel—where are you?"

Broydo paused for Old Ric to catch up, and the demon sparks
flurried about his head, darting for his earholes and nostrils. He
batted them away deliriously. "Don't let them in!" he cried, and
a mote of cold fire flew into his mouth. He spat it out at once,
and the poisonous taste of it filled the hollows of his head with
a rancid stink that nearly doubled him over with vomiting.

Old Ric's breath mangled in his chest with exhaustion as he
batted the demons away. Arms waving wildly, the two of them
ran around a shale plate blocking their way and flared suddenly
downhill along a quartz-studded slope. The tall rocks fell away
behind them, and they found themselves on a vast shale maze.
It was situated beneath a sheer basalt wall topped with turrets and
stone cairns. Far above them, the Abiding Star, rising through a
cloudless sky, contorted their shadows among the shattered
stones like creatures of another form.

The gnome spun about, arms still waving to ward off the
demonic swarm. But they were gone.

"The Necklace of Souls must be nearby!" the ælf announced
with delight. "Only its presence could drive off a host of devils."

Old Ric bent over to catch his breath, his blood burning hotly
through its loops.

"There!" Broydo shouted.

Old Ric squinted into the Abiding Star toward where the ælf
pointed, spectra raying through his lashes. Out of the glare, he
discerned an anvil rock upon which lay a heap of clear gems
clasped by interlocking glyphs of gold. "The Necklace!" he
bawled with relief, and his echoes, too, tumbled over themselves
on the climb up the cliff wall to the wind that swept them to
silence. "The Necklace of Souls!"

"Who goes there?" A heavy voice startled them from high up
on the rampart. A pure white entity, squat and creased with
obesity, waddled into view from a crevice in the wall. It had a
slash of a mouth and two red beads for eyes and otherwise no
features at all, only stubby arms with immense hands. No raiment, only pinguid folds of marble flesh shaped its glossy appearance. "Who goes there?"

"By the Scrolls!" Broydo squealed. "It's a dwarf!"

"The witch has led us directly into the courtyard of the dwarf fastness!" Old Ric whispered sharply.

"You two!" the dwarf shouted in a squealing, high-pitched voice, holding up a thick hand to shield its featureless face from the light. "Who are you? How did you elude the guardians in the Labyrinth of the Undead? How came you here?"

"Old Ric, seize the Necklace and get away, quickly!" Broydo ordered. "The dwarves cannot abide daylight. That is why the witch has led us here at this hour. Come!"

Broydo and Ric rushed toward the anvil stone, squinting into the level rays of the Abiding Star.

"Stop!" the dwarf spat. At its side other white beings appeared, emerging from crevices in the granite wall. "You two, stop!"

The gnome and the ælf paused before the anvil stone, gazing in amazement at the Necklace of Souls. Frayed rainbows spilled about the heap of gems—each stone bigger than a big thumb and pellucid as air. Old Ric lifted the gold-clasped jewels, astonished at their beauty.

Suddenly, a searing pain penetrated him, and blood sprayed onto the empty anvil stone. Horrified, he looked down at himself and saw the barbed tip of an arrow impaled through his chest.

Broydo gasped with shared pain. "By the gods, Ric, you are killed!"

Old Ric agreed. The arrow had slammed directly through his heart. The pain ate like flames through his whole torso.

More arrows whistled past and clattered against the anvil rock. Quickly, Broydo swept Ric into his arms, careful not to jar the embedded shaft, and ran with him into the cleft of the rampart wall, toward the Abiding Star. Feathered shafts wobbled past them, and others clacked at the ælf's heels.

"I am killed!" Old Ric moaned, and fisted his hands about the gems that had cost him his life.

"Be silent, gnome." Broydo cleared a flinty bluff and came in view of the giant cinder cones. Above them, sulfur clouds boiled with poisonous shades of citrine and puce, and the morning light fanned to fierce spikes of radiance. The ælf clattered mightily over gravel banks until he no longer heard the slicing sound of arrows.

Under a weathered bluff embedded with immense arcs of petri-

fied bone—the huge hull of some dragon's rib cage—Broydo
lowered Old Ric. Blood trickled from the gnome's mouth, and
his eyeballs rolled loosely in their sockets.

"By the gods!" Broydo groaned. "By the very gods!" He fretted
helplessly over the mortally wounded gnome, until a long morning shadow fell over them. With a cry, he lunged about, ready
to fight, and fell to his knees with relief when he saw the cowled
figure of the witch approaching.

"Place the Necklace of Souls about him," she ordered. "He will
go forth now as one of the undead."

Broydo obeyed, and the instant he touched the Necklace, the
warts vanished from his young and not unhandsome face. When
he draped the gems over the gnome's head and around his neck,
Old Ric's eyes focused at once, and his breathing calmed. The
gnome sat up taller, surprised to feel no pain whatsoever. He put
a tentative hand to the arrow.

"Leave it be," the witch said. "It has killed you. And if you
remove it, you may well lose your body and become a wraith."

Broydo wailed piteously.

"Hush." Old Ric laid a blood-streaked hand on his companion.
"I am not suffering. I feel no hurt at all. What is this wonder I
have become?"

"You are now a deadwalker, Old Ric," the witch informed him.
"So long as you wear the Necklace of Souls, your life goes on.
But when it is removed—you will die."

The gnome peered down quizzically at the rainbow-shot gems
linked with gold. "I have been killed, yet I feel no pain, no fear.
Is this good?"

"Is your mission for the Nameless One good?" the witch replied
brusquely. "Without the Necklace of Souls, your mission cannot
be accomplished."

"My mission—" Old Ric gawked, remembering at once his
promise to the Lady of the Garden. "I must not die yet!"

"Then it is good that you live," the witch agreed with a slight
smile visible beneath her cowl. "And there is more good yet. For
now that you are a deadwalker, you will have no further need
of food, water, or air."

Ric put a finger to the barbed arrowhead varnished with his
blood. It felt firmly lodged. "I am ready to join my wives and my
Amara—but first, I must fulfill the bidding of the nameless lady."

"We must hurry then, Old Ric," Broydo said nervously. "The dwarves will be upon us. Only the daylight impedes them. But they will don shrouds and pursue us. The Necklace of Souls is the last of Duppy Hob's magical implements. They will chase us into the Gulf itself to recover it."

"But why?" The eldern gnome scowled. "Smiddy Thea said that it was the dwarves themselves who overthrew Duppy Hob and cast all his magical devices into the Gulf. The Necklace of Souls fell by accident into this blighted place. Why should they want it back?"

"The fervor of their rage toward their old master has cooled," Broydo replied, casting an anxious glance at the witch, who stood silently in the narrow shade under a ledge of rock. "If they could, I do believe the dwarves would retrieve Duppy Hob himself from the abyss, for without his magic they have been reduced to mere caretakers of the ancient fastness where once he ruled. His magic alone gave them the wit to create charmworks. The Necklace of Souls is their last object of power. It is the Charm that summons the wraiths from the Bright Worlds and the great souls from the Abiding Star. The wraiths pay the dwarves homage and grace them with portions of their Charm. Without this great amulet, the dwarves are quite literally no more than maggots with arms and legs."

"The ælf is correct," the witch spoke, and her blood-freckled hand pointed to the giant bones encased in the bluff. "And here, it might interest you to know, is what remains of the world serpent from whose flesh those maggots fed before Duppy Hob cast them into simian shapes."

Broydo's ice-pale eyes widened. "*This?* This is a world serpent?" He reached out and stroked the yellowed surface of a rib. "Have you any notion how valuable this material would be to charmwrights across the Bright Worlds?"

"Or how valuable it would be to you against the dwarves," added the witch knowingly. "A talisman fashioned from bone of this world serpent will surely keep the dwarves at bay."

"Of course!" Broydo agreed excitedly. "They rightly fear it. If they are touched by a world serpent, Duppy Hob's magic is broken, and they revert to their maggot origins." The ælf looked about with a thrilled attentiveness, searching for a rock large enough to hack at the embedded ribs.

"Stop, Broydo. There is little time for such manual labor," the witch stated. "The dwarves will be upon us soon. Stand away."

Broydo took Old Ric under his arms and helped him up. As soon as they had stepped back, the witch raised her arms abruptly, snapping the robes of her cowl. A stab of lightning branded their vision, and they averted their faces. When they looked again, an arm's length of slivered bone had cleaved from a stone-locked rib and lay on the ground in a sparkle of retinal afterglow.

Broydo warily approached the long sliver, hands out, feeling for heat. The sharp bone was not hot but cold to the touch. He hefted it with a flourish and turned with a grateful smile to the witch. Making no motion to acknowledge him, she stepped out of the shadow of the ledge and disappeared in the morning light.

"By the blood of drakes!" Broydo blinked. "The witch is a wraith!"

"As I will be soon," Ric moaned, "if the dwarves catch us. Come, Broydo. We must flee this place at once."

"What direction?" the ælf asked, pivoting to scan the flinty slopes.

In the distance, the cowled figure of the witch appeared in the shadows at the stony bottom of an extinct stream. The eldern gnome was delighted at how fluidly he moved with an arrow through his chest that now pointed his way ahead. The Charm from the dwarves' gems filled him with a supernatural strength, and he was not even breathing hard when he ran along the benchland above the empty channel of the dried stream.

"Wait up!" Broydo called after him, huffing to follow.

"Who would think that I, a gnome, would stride so mightily in the sway of Charm!" Old Ric exulted.

The ælf staggered to his side, clutching his ribs with one hand and with the other stabbing the bone sliver into the ground and leaning heavily upon it. He gasped, "Then why is it—that you gnomes—are famous for—avoiding Charm?"

"Charm is not the gnomish way." Old Ric tapped his finger against the arrow jammed through his chest, amazed to feel so little hurt. "It has ever been thus. Our very bones possess enough Charm to sustain us. What need for amulets and talismans?" He tapped the arrow shaft. "Until now."

In the dark of the gorge, the witch walked on, and the ælf

and gnome followed along the ridgelines. "Yet you are a prac-
titioner of magic, eh, Ric?"

"Gnomish magic, aye." The gnome cast furtive glances over
his shoulder, searching for dwarves among the cobbled piles of
rocks that reared like smelter chimneys against the ashen sky. "I
am the first in my family of textile workers to learn the gnomish
magic of elemental fire. I served my people for many years as a
firemaker, hearth-builder, flue-cleaner, and reader of flames. That
was how I first saw the shadow thing. A mere glimpse, mind you.
A glimpse of something dark intruding upon the Bright Shore."

"And that is why the Nameless Ones summoned you, for your
magic?" the ælf queried, hurrying to keep up with the spry
gnome.

"The blind god Chance plucked me from my den." He stopped,
then walked backward several paces, reviewing the evil landscape
behind. "When I asked the great lady why I was chosen of all
the gnomes versed in magic, that is what she told me. She needed
a figure from her dream to tell her why the child in her womb
had gone still. And blind Chance chose me."

The witch waited ahead in the slurred shadows of talus boulders fallen from the hellish cinder cones that reared above among
fumes of brimstone. She motioned them closer.

"Where are you leading us, witch?" Broydo asked. "Ahead are
the Gates of the Underworld. Must we trespass that dread
territory?"

"Yes," her voice whispered from within the dark of her hood.
"Before we part, I must have what you promised me—one crystal
prism of the Necklace of Souls."

The gnome clutched at the gems. "But you said I will die if
the Necklace of Souls is removed." He backed away a pace.
"Wait until my mission is complete. Then you may have the
Necklace entire."

"I cannot wait, gnome." The witch spoke firmly. "I must have
my crystal prism at once. And so we shall seek a charmwright
who can remove my crystal without disturbing the others. That
is why we are entering the Gates of the Underworld—to find
Blue Tipoo, the one dwarf who may help us."

"A dwarf?" Old Ric clacked his jaw with alarm. "He will seize
the Necklace!"

"No." The witch turned and walked on, disappearing into the

slanted rays of early morning and appearing again in the next
swatch of shadows cast by the large, scorched boulders. "Blue
Tipoo has gone mad. He alone of the dwarves defended Duppy
Hob, and for that he was exiled beyond the Gates of the Underworld. He may help us—if we can calm his madness."

"How will we do that?" Broydo squawked, gazing timorously
ahead to the fuming summits of the black volcanoes.

"With the serpent sword," the witch answered.

"Serpent sword?" the ælf repeated before recognizing that he
was holding the weapon in his hand. As he ran to keep up with
the witch and the Charm-powered gnome, he studied the length
of sharp bone in his hand. Indeed, it had the slender shape and
sturdy heft of a sword, and he brandished it with vigor.

THE SERPENT SWORD

SOON BROYDO WAS BREATHING HARD TO KEEP UP WITH HIS SWIFT companions, and he had no strength for questions. He concentrated instead on his clambering stride over the dry, blistered land. Each cumbersome stride shattered plates of volcanic glass or gray, brittle tar bubbles. The Abiding Star had bleached and cracked the ground like old porcelain, and shards lay strewn among the talus rocks, where no life moved all the way to the foot of the cinder cones.

Old Ric slowed his pace to allow Broydo to come abreast of him. The gnome felt lithe and strong as the wind itself, and he beamed at the ælf, "I never felt so good alive! I think I like being a deadwalker."

"Aye—" Broydo huffed, jogging as fast as he could across the broken land, "but will you—like it much—in there!"

They stared glumly ahead at the Gates of the Underworld, the steep calderas on whose black slopes sulfur fumes leaked into the wind and whirled away like dervishes in dementia.

"I like it not," the gnome admitted ruefully.

Broydo thought to protest going any farther, but he lacked

breath as well as courage. The talus boulders had fallen behind
them, and they scampered into the full glare of the ascendant
Abiding Star, where no promontory offered shade. The witch
was invisible. Obedient to their promise, the ælf and gnome
climbed the cracked slopes among molten shapes of hardened
lava that had less the appearance of geology than black-
shawled figures.

At the verge of exhaustion, Broydo gasped that he could not
trudge another step. He quaffed the last of his green wine, and
his parched throat burned for water. The gnome turned back for
him and pulled him up the broken slope.

The witch beckoned from a cave fanged with rime.

Old Ric dragged Broydo to the crusted entrance of the dark
cavern, and the ælf lay exhausted, unable to move.

"Leave him," the witch instructed. She bent close to the spent
ælf and ran a gory hand through the nape of his green hair. At
her touch, he sat up taller. "Keep a watch, Broydo." She pointed
across the huge vista of slag fields and ashen plains that the cave
commanded. The sprawling panorama revealed the cinderland
they had crossed, with its brittle tracts of sharp black glass and
flinty rocks. At the jagged horizon, the fastness of the dwarves
and the maze beyond stood visible, crusted and discolored as a
chancre. "When the dwarves do appear, give shout. Will you
obey me, ælf?"

Broydo croaked an affirmative sound. He sat with his legs
spraddled out before him and his head leaning back against the
glistening rock with his mouth ajar and his lips laced white
with salt.

"Now take the serpent sword," the witch commanded Old Ric.

The gnome pried the long sliver of bone from the ælf's locked
grip. "Don't fear, Broydo. We'll bring you water." His own words
sounded foolish to him, yet he spoke them anyway. "Rest here
now. We will return shortly."

The witch entered the cave, a shimmering green presence in
the dark. Old Ric gave Broydo a last wary glance and entered
the black maw. Within the darkness, he saw that he, too, shone
with an ethereal glow. The Necklace of Souls hoarded light, like
embers, only blue and fiery as day-struck sapphires.

The relentless dark continued a long way. Stalactites and
glossy silica columns glimmered with ghostlight reflected from

the cowled witch and the eldern gnome. They descended among
grottoes and caverns ornate with natural pillars and crusted gems.

From deeper yet came a silver tapping. Presently, a red eye
blinked from the far end of a lava tube, through which they had
to proceed hunched over. Old Ric discerned that the scarlet
flickering came from an open forge with anvil rocks set before
it and gold and silver implements arrayed upon the rocks.

The witch stopped and turned. The dark within her hood
suffused an eerie shine with the skullish contours of her maimed
visage. "Go in there, gnome, and tell Blue Tipoo to fashion this
bone to a sword with a proper haft or you will skewer him
upon it."

"Me?" The gnome peeked past the witch's silhouette at the
breathing crimson pulse of the forge. "What about you?"

"Say no word of me," she cautioned. "Go quickly now and do
as I have said. Go!"

The ghastly face of smoke within the hood propelled Old Ric
past the witch and into the glowing red chamber. Once within,
he stood upright and quickly and frightfully surveyed his sur-
roundings. The foundry crypt was large, with a soaring ceiling
that dimmed beyond sight. Tiers of galleries shelved the naked
rock walls, a honeycomb of balconies, alcoves, and niches that
flashed with talismanic weapons, embossed armor, and heaps of
jewel-studded amulets. This was a huge treasure trove of Charm,
and the gnome could feel its power thrumming in the shining air.

He looked closer and saw that the large forge was but a vent
that had been stove through the rock to a molten interior, and
it gushed with planet fire. He searched for the smithy dwarf and
found no one in the vault save his own tremulous shadows.

His eyes played over the anvil stones draped with glittering
works-in-progress—armbands woven with magical sigils, daggers
bound by conjure-wire to hilts of fused hex-gems, and a cuirass
etched all over by magical script fine as spiderwork. With a
marveling hand he reached out to touch the slick dagger blade
that was throbbing with fiery reflections.

"Touch and be touched!" a deep bass voice boomed from behind him.

Old Ric spun about, bone sliver wagging in his frightened
grip. Out of a smoky side passage a dwarf came hurtling, hairless
and red-eyed as any dwarf but with white flesh scorched blue-

black across its featureless face and over its immense hands. A large faceted hammer in a raised fist shook threateningly. Old Ric gulped and summoned forth all his courage.

"Halt, Blue Tipoo!" the gnome managed to scream at the charging dwarf, and slashed the bright air with the bone sliver. "Halt or be pierced by the bone of the world serpent!"

Blue Tipoo pulled up short, the red beads of its eyes brilliant in the singed mask of its face. It scrutinized the trespasser. "You wear the Master's . . . Necklace of Souls!" Its thick body quaked, and its heavy apron of blackened hide bulged as if about to split apart. "You—you—"

"I am Old Ric, an eldern gnome of Nemora," he announced to the apoplectic dwarf. "And I am dead." With his free hand he plucked at the arrow piercing his chest.

The swollen dwarf deflated with a surprised gasp. "You are a gnomish deadwalker!" Its slash of a mouth gaped like a toad's. "How came you to take the Necklace of Souls from the fastness of the dwarves?"

"Never mind," Old Ric said, remembering the witch's admonition. "I am here to have this bone shaped to a sword. Do it or . . ."

"Or what?"

". . . or I will pierce you with it—and Blue Tipoo will craft no more amulets," the gnome added with as much threat as he could muster.

"Hah!" Blue Tipoo swung the ponderous hammer over its blunt head. "I see it all now. The dwarves have sent you to slay me! Ingrates! Rebels! They cannot stop me from preparing for the Master's return! I must make his weapons. They will not stop me!"

With one eye on the swinging hammer, Old Ric nudged closer and jabbed with the bone sliver. "Hush, Blue Tipoo! I am Old Ric, a gnomish magician of Nemora. I do not serve dwarves! You will make this bone of the world serpent into a sword, and I will let you live to continue working for your master's return. Deny me and die!"

"Bah!" Blue Tipoo lunged and the sweeping arc of the hammer brushed past the gnome's pug nose.

Old Ric skipped backward with a yelp, banged into an anvil stone, scattering hex-gems and springs of conjure-wire, and toppled to his back. The arrow shoved farther through him with a mortal pang that cut a scream from the bottom of his lungs. His face and eyes stretched wide with hurt, and he saw the big hammer flying toward him at the instant Blue Tipoo released it. He hauled himself after his scream as if it were a taut wire strung into the sightless heights where he had hurled it, and his body dodged the heavy projectile by a fraction so narrow its thunderous impact shoved him aside. Again the impaled arrow rammed agonizingly in him, this time backward, twisting a blinding shriek from his depths.

In a daze of suffering, the gnome pulled around to confront his assailant and blew bubbles of blood from his gaping mouth. The scorched dwarf did not move. It stared past him, thick hands reaching out nervously to where the witch stood. Unseen, she had entered swiftly and seized the big hammer. Lifting it with both her bloody hands, she stood poised to drop it into the forge flames.

"Stop!" The dwarf pranced in horror.

"Blue Tipoo," the soft, insistent voice of the witch rose above the surf noise of the blazing forge. "You will do exactly as I say, or I will drop your hammer into the fire."

"You must not!" The dwarf edged forward and stopped with a jolt when the witch suspended the hammer closer to the fire. "Why do this to me?"

"Because I know that this hammer is your power, Blue Tipoo. It is the strength that Duppy Hob has granted you. With it, you need neither food nor drink and may work endlessly creating the weapons for the host that your master will bring with him out of the Gulf. But without it—" She swayed the hammer through the fireglow, and the dwarf groaned with fright. "Without it, you are no more than a common dwarf. One touch of the bone from the world serpent and you will fall to the ground for what you are—a maggot starved for dragon's flesh."

"Give back my hammer!" the dwarf demanded, this time pleading.

"If you do as I tell you, you shall have your hammer back and we shall leave you as we found you," the witch assured the dwarf.

The dwarf's oversize hands fell submissively to its sides. "What do you want of me?"

"Two simple deeds for one of your magical skills." The witch passed the hammer close to the forge flames to keep the dwarf's attention sharp. "Remove one crystal prism from the Necklace of Souls while keeping the Necklace intact and in place about this gnome."

"A moment's work," the dwarf promised. "And the second deed?"

"Work this whittled bone of the world serpent into a magical sword with a Charmed haft and handguard."

"That is all?" the gnome asked incredulous. "You will return my hammer for these two small deeds?"

"Gnome—" The witch motioned with the sway of her hooded head for him to rise. "The world serpent's rib. Give it to Blue Tipoo."

Old Ric did as he was told, and the dwarf received the lethal bone gingerly with tongs from a nearby anvil stone. Blue Tipoo carried it to a workbench across the chamber. "In the Master's arsenal are many swords. It is but a moment's work to replace any one of their blades of conjure-steel with this wicked bone," he muttered as he went.

He bent to the task, shaping the long bone with hasps and chisels. From a cranny in his cave, he retrieved a gold sword with a curved blade. "Who are you?" he asked as he worked. "Who are you to trespass my smithy?"

"I am the one who holds your hammer above the forge fires," the witch replied tersely. "And my arms grow weary."

"Done!" the dwarf barked in triumph and upheld an ivory yellow sword fitted to a haft of gold coils. "The serpent's sword!"

"Now the crystal prism," the witch demanded. "And be swift. My grip is failing."

Blue Tipoo approached Old Ric with a pliers in one hand and a coil of iridescent conjure-wire in the other. The dwarf remained perfectly still as the dwarf coiled the wire about three of the gems. A burnt smell lingered about the smith, a carbon stench of something charred. The gnome watched its tiny red eyes directing its big and surprisingly nimble fingers. Metal snicked and the pliers twisted, its ends magically incandescent, fusing metal and reshaping it like wax.

The dwarf talked while working: "It is good you take the Master's Necklace away from the rebels. It is good, for I have made sufficient weapons for the Master—enough to conquer this world and all the Bright Worlds." Its red eyes stole a glance at Old

Ric's watchful face. "The days of murder are yet to come. And the Master's warriors shall be merry with pain and cold and disaster. Nothing shall thwart them when the time comes. And it comes soon, gnome. Oh yes. Soon, Duppy Hob shall return, and his lightest word shall again be unbreakable law!"

"My arms are weary, Blue Tipoo!" the witch admonished. "Be quick—or your master loses his smith."

"I *am* swift!" the dwarf declared, and stepped back, tossing aside the glowing pliers and unspooling the conjure-wire. "Behold!" It upheld one crystal prism between its blackened fingers.

Old Ric touched the Necklace to be sure it remained intact and was pleased to see that it fit more securely across his chest and no longer dangled against the piercing arrow. He stepped toward the workbench where the serpent sword lay.

The dwarf stopped him by putting one finger against the tip of the impaled arrow. "My hammer first."

The witch cast the hammer into a gloomy corner of the chamber. "Take the crystal prism and get the sword, gnome."

The gnome snatched the crystal prism from the dwarf's big fingers, and Blue Tipoo shoved him aside to get at its hammer.

Obediently, Old Ric hurried to the workbench. When he put his hands to the sword, it felt Charmed—airy and nimble. The gold-coil haft seemed to shape itself to his grip, and he felt a luminosity course through his bones as he hefted it.

"Stop marveling, gnome!" the witch called sternly. "Come away!"

Old Ric hurried to the witch's side, and she shoved him into the lava tube by which they had entered. He turned and looked back to see the dwarf retrieve its hammer. With a furious yell, it thudded the ponderous tool against the rock wall, and the mountain itself shook, drizzling sand and pebbles over the gnome.

"Ha! Who says you may go?" the dwarf called out belligerently. "You who invaded the Master's keep and disturbed the Master's work must die!"

Blue Tipoo attacked, hammer swinging, and Old Ric yelled with incoherent alarm, for there was no place for the witch to flee. The gnome cringed with fright—and the large hammer slashed through the witch's vaporous body and clanged vibrantly against the rock wall.

Like smoke, the witch healed, and clapped her hands. Small lightnings crackled over the hammer's faceted head, electric blue writhings crawling along the shaft and biting the dwarf's hands. It released the hammer with a yelp, and the phantom witch seized the implement before it hit the ground. With a deft twist of her body that flung the hood back from her mangled head and exposed her slashed features, she tossed the hammer. It arced past the cringing dwarf and, with a gust of sparks, plunged into the blazing forge.

"My soul's own creature is slain!" Blue Tipoo blathered, then screamed like sheet metal ripping. "The work of the Master is undone!"

The witch had vanished, and Old Ric did not strive to search further because the smithy gushed with spinning sparks and clots of green flame. A rumbling shook the walls of the lava tube, and the gnome launched forward with all his strength, clutching the serpent sword in one hand and the solitary crystal prism in the other. Once only he glanced back, at the end of the cramped tunnel. A crimson fireball veined with green lightning swelled toward him.

Old Ric heaved himself into the grotto ahead. Blowtorch heat filled the cavern and jags of lightning stabbed among the stalactites and mineral stumps. Livid colors leaped from the glossy walls, and the ground shook, heaving the gnome off his feet.

Hands lifted him by the back of his vest and jerked him upright. Broydo's green hair, icy eyes, and blue-tinged black skin shone brightly in the glow of the conflagration. "I've been searching the bowels of this volcano for you!" his gruff voice shouted above the gushing flames and the peal of bursting rocks. "This way out!"

The ælf pulled the gnome after him into a cleft of shuddering walls. The shaking rock scraped at them, squeezed so tightly upon them there was no room to heave a cry, then pulled apart before a blue shaft of dayshine. They collapsed into the open under a plutonic cloud of black smoke. Under their bodies, the ground shivered like a beast.

Broydo led their charge downhill until exhaustion reclaimed him. When he fell to his knees, Old Ric pressed the serpent sword into the ælf's hand. The sword itself seemed to lift Broydo to his feet. Its Charm coursed through his limbs and fitted him with the strength to continue his flight. Again, he took the lead, casting fearful looks over his shoulder to gauge the slide of rock slabs behind them. He veered, and the gnome followed, as a fuming avalanche swept away the slope they had occupied.

Cracks appeared in the flanks of the cinder cone, jetting steam and green flares of Charmed fire. Empowered by the serpent sword, Broydo leaped fissures with Old Ric at his side. The two ran only paces ahead of the collapsing mountainside, the deafening tumult carrying them as on a wave.

A column of twisting green energy spiraled into the sky, shattering the volcano and hurling swarms of rocks like an exploding hive. Giant harps of electricity twanged out of the billowing sky to the crests of the surrounding hills, and the clamor made the very horizon shiver.

PURSUED BY DWARVES

FROM THE LAVA BED OF GLASSY SAND, THE TWO RUNNERS PAUSED and looked back. Where the cinder cone had stood only a vast crater remained exhaling a torrent of churning smoke. Green flames danced upon the summits of the surrounding crags, and a din of subterranean thunder vibrated underfoot.

"We are alive!" Broydo announced with loud disbelief.

"*You* yet live," Old Ric agreed, then tapped with his finger the arrowhead of the shaft lodged in his chest. "But I remain a deadwalker."

"Would you rather be back there?" Broydo swept an arm at the cataclysmic landscape where sheets of green fire flapped among the boiling smoke of the pit. "Let us away, gnome, and swiftly."

Old Ric scanned the ruinous land. "Which way shall we go?"

"Away from this evil place and away from the dwarves' fastness." The ælf pointed toward the shale ridges beyond the talus slopes. "We must get the Necklace of Souls to my clan as quickly as possible. That direction takes us farther away from the Forest of Wraiths, but it avoids the Labyrinth of the Undead."

"And where is the witch?" The gnome held the crystal prism

to the sky, hoping to alert the witch to their presence. But no cowled figure appeared among the stony land's broken shadows.

"Perhaps she perished with Blue Tipoo," Broydo said pensively, and pressed the serpent sword to his chest, grateful for its Charm. "There is no water in Labyrinth, and without the witch we may never find our way through. I can live on Charm for a while, but I must drink eventually—unless I am to become a dead-walker, too."

Old Ric agreed, and they began their trek toward the shale ridges. Nightfall found them climbing the stony ledges. As the witch had foretold, the gnome needed no sleep, and Broydo, too, was able to continue drawing strength from the serpent sword and to continue marching. Luminescent chains of stars lit their way, and by midnight they crested the ridge and stood under the cold faces of the planets.

Looking back the way they had come, they saw the collapsed cinder cone glowing with a green nethershine amid the dense vapors from the underground blaze. Phosphorescent sparks eerily flurried across the wide volcanic plain, sifting toward them through the dark.

"What are they?" Old Ric asked, the slim light about his arrow-pierced body shining suddenly brighter.

"I don't know," the ælf replied, "but they are following us—and they are moving fast."

"They are dwarves," a silken voice said from behind them. The witch drifted from out of the dark of a crevasse as if carried by the wind.

"Witch!" Broydo gasped, and the serpent sword quavered in his grip.

"You abandoned us in Blue Tipoo's mountain!" Old Ric accused.

The witch seemed woven of the night's own fabric. "I could not stay—not in the presence of the green fire."

"Charmfire," Broydo said. "Why did you leave *us* to the charm fire then?"

"I trusted you to save yourselves," the witch answered forth-rightly. "And you did. But if I had remained, I would have perished."

"Why?" the gnome asked puzzled. "What of your magic?"

"Surely, you know," the witch said. "I am less substantial than you, and the green fire would have wafted me away no matter my magic."

"Insubstantial?" Old Ric scowled without understanding. "I saw you lift and throw the smith's hammer."

"The magic of the hammer gave me strength," she answered simply. "But once the Charm was broken, I had to escape."

Broydo nodded with dawning comprehension. "You are a wraith."

"Certainly, you must have known all along," the witch insisted and drifted closer. "Why else would I require a crystal prism from the Necklace of Souls?"

"But what will you do with the prism?" the gnome asked, stepping back a pace.

"That is no concern of yours, gnome." The witch stood in silhouette against the stellar fires. "You have your own work to do. I will show you the way from here to the clan of ælves in the Forest of Wraiths. And then, we shall part. But we must hurry." Her cowl nodded toward the swarming phosphorescent lights upon the shale cliffs below. "The dwarves pursue. They will not relent until they retrieve the Necklace of Souls."

"You seek vengeance upon the ones who maimed you so horribly," Broydo ventured, glancing nervously down at the dwarves.

"That is a reasonable supposition, ælf. But no, I seek no vengeance upon them, for they are far beyond my reach." The witch held out her bloodstained hand. "Give me the crystal prism that is mine."

The gnome looked to the ælf, and Broydo nodded. Old Ric stepped forward but did not remove his hands from where he had stuffed them in his pockets. "You abandoned us on the mountain. Before I will give you the crystal prism, you must lead us away from this dismal place and the dwarves who stalk us. You must take us back to Broydo's clan in the Forest of Wraiths."

The witch seemed to shrink. "Very well. We are not far from your destination. Follow me closely."

Shining a spectral green in the dark, the witch and the gnome lit the slag terrain one step ahead, and Broydo had no trouble finding his footing. The serpent sword continued to provide him strength, though his throat felt parched as leather and the flesh of his hands and face became drawn and desiccated. But whenever the thought of rest intruded, he glanced behind and was

driven on by the sight of numerous incandescent sparks cutting
their own paths through the darkness.

Dawn arrived colorless, gray as a slug's underbelly above the
desert of lava dust and rimrock. Onward they drifted, speechless
and vagrant as sand devils. Late in the day, before a urinous
twilight, they climbed ledges of slick black rock where trickles
of water inspired the perilous growth of rock orchids and hairy
scarlet air plants.

At last, Broydo had water to sip, if not to fully quench his
thirst. He licked the rock walls and kissed the crevices, gnawing
at the scabby lichen and chewing wads of moss. Gradually, his
near-mummified flesh began to relax, and his eyes lost their
dull glaze.

In the night, the ground leveled and became soft and damp.
Creepers and grass mats covered the volcanic ash, and the starry
vista grew smaller, screened by tall cane and feather-leafed saplings. Monkeys cried. Birds sang morning up out of the darkness,
and the wanderers penetrated the dense and steamy margins of
the Forest of Wraiths.

Golden salamanders flurried through the underbrush, and trumpet lilies breathed intoxicating fumes. Broydo knew these paths,
and he exultantly took the lead, hacking through ivy curtains
and looping vines with his serpent sword.

The witch called, "Stop!"

The ælf and the gnome paused and looked for the witch
among the forest's buttresses of light. They found her standing
in the shadow of a leaning oak.

"I have fulfilled what I promised," she said. "You are now in
the Forest of Wraiths and will soon be among the ælves. Give
me the crystal prism."

"Give it to her, Ric," the ælf agreed. "We are not far from my
clan, and I know the way well from here."

Old Ric conceded with a nod and produced the crystal prism
from the pocket of his vest. "Here it is, witch. You have kept
your word. I now keep mine." He held out the prism, and a
filament of daylight threaded through it and wove a small rainbow in the air.

The witch's transparent hand reached out of the shadows and
plucked the crystal prism from his fingers. The instant she

touched it, her hand firmed and became opaque. The blood that had covered it vanished.

A gentle laugh came from the witch. "Thank you, gnome. You have proved a worthy champion for me." She drew back her hood and revealed a lovely face unmarked by wounds. Sable tresses sinuously framed a pale and smiling countenance of dark eyes and broad cheekbones.

"You are whole again!" Broydo marveled.

"Yes, indeed I appear whole again, thanks to the Charm of the crystal prism. Yet I remain a wraith, an insubstantial being given form by Charm alone."

"What will you do now?" Old Ric asked.

"I have a mission to fulfill, the same as you have, gnome." She turned to go and watched them sidelong across the pixie slant of her now-unmarred face. "Perhaps we will meet again among the Bright Worlds."

The gnome motioned to speak, but she was already gone. She stepped into a hot slant of dayshine and vanished, leaving behind only a few motes of charmshine that settled like snowflakes on the grass and melted wholly away.

"Come along, gnome," Broydo beckoned. "My clan is not far."

Old Ric turned quickly and followed the ælf through the ferns, but the image of the beautiful witch lingered. And her words haunted him. *I have a mission to fulfill, the same as you have* . . .

"What did she mean?" Ric asked the ælf. "A mission the same as I have?"

Broydo hacked strenuously at the dense growth of bracken, cutting a trail for them. "She is a witch, how am I to know?" He shrugged and grunted with the force of his slashing blows. "But rest assured, she did not descend from the Abiding Star and risk annihilation by green fire at the Gates of the Underworld on a whim. She is about some witchly task."

"Not *some* witchly task, Broydo," the gnome pressed. "Think on this like the counselor you are. She said *the same* as I. *The same.*"

"She is on a similar mission to the Bright Worlds," Broydo speculated. "She is searching for someone, obviously."

"Then why did she not simply say, 'I have a mission to fulfill, even as you do'? Why say, *the same* as I? Does that not strike you as of a particular meaning?"

"And what would that be, gnome?" Broydo cut through the fern screen to a wide avenue of the forest and paused in his efforts.

"Do you think—" Old Ric scratched his bald head and wished he had his cap to wring. "Could it be?"

"What?" Broydo urged. "Could what be?"

"Maybe I am not alone on my mission?" the gnome speculated. "Perhaps the Nameless Ones have sent another."

"A redundant searcher? To be certain you achieved your mission." The ælf nodded ruminatively. "That may be. And it would explain why she sought us out in the Labyrinth of the Undead. But there's no knowing now. She is gone."

"Unless, as she herself said, we meet again." The gnome shrugged and put a finger to the shaft piercing his torso. "Whatever happens, this arrow shall point the way."

Broydo dared a laugh, and Old Ric joined him. They proceeded down the lane of interlocking trees, conversing with good cheer, glad to be away from the desolate rimland and once more in the midst of life's verdant frenzy.

Before long, swart visages with vivid green hair and astounded ice eyes peeked from tree hollows and the tunnels of the underbrush. Broydo trilled a triumphant ælvish cry, and the peeking faces accepted that Broydo was not a wraith in the presence of this gnomish deadwalker, and they rushed from their coverts.

As each of them came running through the leaf litter, laughing and shouting welcomes, the fungoidal warts fell away from their ravaged features, drizzling away like so much ash. The Charmed presence of the Necklace of Souls banished their deformities before they came within arms' length of the wanderers. By the time they grasped Broydo in happy embrace and heaved him upon their shoulders, they were whole again.

None dared touch Old Ric. Pierced through with a barbed arrow and yet striding nimbly on the forest boulevard, he frightened the ælves. Not until Smiddy Thea herself stepped out from a hollow tree did anyone address him directly.

"You do not come well into our presence, Old Ric," she spoke sadly, though her gnawed-looking face had sloughed its cankerous growths and Charm already began to heal the pits and gouges in her flesh.

"I am a deadwalker, Smiddy Thea," Old Ric acknowledged

with a grim nod—then smiled widely. "Yet I feel stronger and more nimble than ever I did in my younger days."

"Alas, you sacrificed your very life to retrieve our salvation," Smiddy Thea said, stepping forward and putting her dark and smooth hands upon him. Her face, though still old, had lost all deformity and shone with a regal loveliness. "Our clan, every one of us, owes you a life-debt, Old Ric, eldern gnome of Nemora."

"I shall have to collect at some other time, lady ælf," Ric answered with a courteous nod. "I am pursued by dwarves. They would have their Necklace returned. And I fully intended to give it back to them—until they nailed my life upon this arrow you see in me. Now they will have to wait until I complete my work in the Bright Worlds beyond. But I dare not tarry here; you may well be subject to their wrath."

"Dwarves cannot travel by day," Smiddy Thea knew. "Stay and celebrate with us then, Old Ric."

Broydo agreed with a boisterous shout and waved the serpent sword. "Be not afraid, gnome. Should a dwarf show its deformity here, it will die beneath my blade."

Old Ric conceded. The journey thus far had been arduous—not physically, of course: the Necklace of Souls gave him indomitable stamina. But his soul, the feeling pith of him, suffered from all that had happened at World's End, and he would be glad for a happy respite.

He followed the ælves into a hollowed tree and descended among song and cheers to their grottoes of luminous moss. Festive music began at once, and a parade of delicacies emerged from the larders. They began with the berries and sugar stalks ready at hand while the cooks set to work preparing a proper feast.

"You intend to return the Necklace of Souls when your mission for the Nameless Ones is finished?" Smiddy Thea asked, staring with interest at the barb-tipped arrow.

"Yes, lady ælf," Old Ric responded between munches of a mint apple. Before him, burl-bowls of honey tubers and snowberries had been placed on a fern carpet. He required no feed, felt no hunger, and ate merely to show courtesy. "Gnomes are not thieves. As, I'm sure, neither are ælves."

"Ælves surely are not thieves," the crone agreed, "yet we have no compunction about keeping what we win in contest of blood."

"Yes." Old Ric wiped his mouth with a napkin of pressed moss. "But my blood is old."

Smiddy Thea ladled dandelion mead into a goblet of polished bluewood. "When you return the Necklace of Souls—you will die."

"All whom I love have gone that way already." He accepted the goblet with a gracious nod. "When this difficult task is accomplished, I shall be joyful to join them."

"You are honorable to a fault, Old Ric." Smiddy Thea nodded sadly. "It is no wonder to me that the Nameless Ones would choose you to do their bidding."

While Smiddy Thea and the gnome chatted, the clan's charm-wrights gathered around Broydo to examine the extraordinary craftsmanship of Blue Tipoo. The ælf grinned proudly at them as though this were his own handiwork. But when he passed them the serpent sword, he collapsed. The long trek without sustenance had emptied him of all strength save the Charm of the sword.

A Battle of Dwarves and Ælves

Broydo was carried to a back chamber to rest, and the clan gathered before Old Ric to hear the story of the journey through the Labyrinth of the Undead to the Gates of the Underworld. He told them in detail all that had transpired, and when he came to the account of Asofel immolating the demon, Smiddy Thea wanted to know, "Who is this being of light that comes at your call?

"Asofel does not serve me," Old Ric corrected. "He is a Radiant One, a sentinel, one of four set upon the terminals of the garden to watch over the lady and her unborn child."

The gnome explained how he had been beckoned into the presence of the nameless lady and what assignment he had been given to fulfill with the help of Asofel.

"It has long been known that we and all created things are but a dream," one of the charmwrights said thoughtfully, "but there is no notion among any of the sages—ælven, gnomish, or human—that a shadow thing would trespass our Bright Worlds and endanger our very being. What is this shadow? Whence does it come? What do you know of it, Old Ric?"

"Very little, I must admit." The gnome passed an abashed and hapless look over the gathering. "I thought perhaps it was the Dark Lord."

"The Dark Lord is dead," another charmwright called from the crowd. "If ever he was alive."

Ric placed his perplexed look upon Smiddy Thea. "What do your people mean?"

"We are denizens of World's End," the ælf crone stated. "Our charmwrights usually find their materials in the wilderness. But occasionally they trade with humans for witch-glass and hex-gems. The rumor among the humans is that some criminal of theirs who was thrown into the Gulf actually returned and brought with him cacodemons impervious to Charm."

"That was the Dark Lord," Old Ric acknowledged with a frightened nod.

"Dark Lord." Smiddy Thea snickered. "What a childish title."

"That was his flaw," Ric remembered. "He possessed a weak mind."

"You saw this Dark Lord?" the old ælf asked. "He is not a rumor?"

"No, I never saw him, thank all the beneficent gods." Old Ric addressed the group of ælves, eyes wide. "But he was no rumor. He came back out of the Gulf with a host of cacodemons from the Dark Shore."

"What befell him?" the crone asked, drawing closer with curiosity.

"He and his legions of demons ravaged Irth for a season," Ric said, "and then a magus from the Dark Shore was summoned. He slew the Dark Lord, and the cacodemons disappeared like smoke. I thought nothing more of it, snug in my den on Nemora, until the nameless lady drew me to her."

"Ah, you thought perhaps what ailed her was this invasion of shadow creatures from the Dark Shore." Smiddy Thea nodded with understanding.

"Yes. I advised her to wait for the spell to pass." The gnome shared a look of dismay with everyone. "But I was wrong. She drew me to her again and informed me that her child yet lies motionless within her."

"So if her suffering is not the result of the Dark Lord," Smiddy Thea said, eyes slimming with comprehension, "it must be the magus brought into our worlds from the Dark Shore."

"I suspect he lingers on Irth." Old Ric scratched his bald head and longed again for his lost cap to wring between his helpless hands. "No doubt he is ignorant of the Nameless Ones, as so many of their dreaming are."

"What do you know of this magus?" Smiddy Thea inquired.

"Very little." Old Ric plucked nervously at the cuff of gray hair above his large ears. "On Nemora I paid little heed to the events of Irth."

"We will find out for you." Smiddy Thea pointed a bent finger at her clan. "Charmwrights, go hence to your scrying crystals and far-seeing mirrors and look to Irth."

"It will exhaust our Charm to peer so far from World's End," a charmwright groused.

"That is why we know little more than rumor of that world," the ælf crone muttered to Old Ric, admonishing the others with a frown. "Our lives were about to be exhausted by the demon before this gnome saved us." Smiddy Thea gazed sternly at the charmwrights. "Exhaust our Charm and look to Irth."

"That is not necessary, dame ælf," Old Ric demurred. "With the Necklace of Souls, I will learn to scry, and I will find the shadow thing wherever . . ."

A bone-juddering gong sounded, and the crowd of ælves surged to their feet as one.

"The war alarm!" Smiddy Thea informed the startled gnome. "We are under attack!"

The throng seethed toward the exits. Several brutish guards immediately formed a protective barrier around the sphinx throne.

"The dwarves!" Old Ric realized. "Is it yet night?"

"I fear so," the crone admitted, accepting the serpent sword from one of the guards. Her venerable face brightened at the touch of the remarkable weapon. "There is more Charm here in this blade than in all the clan's amulets and talismans combined."

"Give the serpent sword to your best warrior," the gnome counseled.

"Spoken like a gnome!" The crone hacked a laugh. "Your kind do not much use charmworks, so you are to be forgiven your ignorance. A weapon of Charm makes the warrior."

"*You* are going to fight the dwarves?" Old Ric stood back

amazed to watch the old clan chieftess brandish the sword with flourishes of lethal speed and precision.

"I am the leader of my ælves." Her blue eyes stared proudly from their bonepits. "Swordplay is not unknown to me. I regret that you suffered so much to bring us healing only to have the dwarves snatch our lives from us."

"It is my fault," Old Ric moaned. "I should never have lingered."

"Call down your Radiant One," Smiddy Thea said, the sword-light casting her aged features to stern shadows. "If you die here, the Bright Worlds are forfeit."

"Asofel told me not to call him until I found the shadow thing." Old Ric spoke to the crone's back as she hurried across the grotto to a stairwell. "Can we not dispatch these dwarves ourselves?"

"Dispatch dwarves?" a gruff voice despaired, and Broydo, clutching a club strapped with conjure-wire, jolted from out of the chamber where he had been roused from his slumber by the alarm. He brandished the club and gazed nervously at the arrow piercing Ric's chest. "Gnome—behold your own woeful fate at the hands of the dwarves."

Ric clutched at Broydo while they climbed the tight stairwell behind the crone, screams and deathly cries crashing from above. "Perhaps we can reason with them. They will die, too, if the Nameless Ones end the Bright Worlds."

"Reason will not avail!" Smiddy Thea shouted in the doorway to the forest. "These are maggots!"

The night shone with green blurs of light—the ethereal glow of the dwarves in the trees, firing arrows at the ælves who emerged from the grottoes. Many ælves stood nailed to trees by arrow shafts, some squirming, others limp in death. Through the underbrush came a wave of dwarves radiant with green fire. In their big hands they wielded pikes and hatchets, and their red eyes glinted like drops of blood.

Old Ric shivered with fright though he was already dead. He knew that dwarves were endowed with supernatural stamina. Every gnome knew that. How dare the ælves regard these foes as mere maggots? Desperately, he tried to warn the crone, "Retreat, my lady! Call a retreat! We will negotiate with the dwarves for the Necklace."

But his words were snatched away in a tempest of howls and screams. A whistling wind of arrows threw Broydo off his feet, and he collided with the gnome. The two collapsed over a root ledge as barbed shafts swarmed past. The serpent sword in Smiddy Thea's hands whirled and deflected the hail of arrows. The next moment, she danced lethally into the midst of the charging dwarves.

"My clan is doomed!" Broydo wailed from behind the root ledge where he crouched with Old Ric. He peered through a cluster of arrows embedded in the tree root and watched as the dark tunnels of the woods disgorged an army of dwarves. "Every maggot on World's End is here!".

Old Ric saw that this was true. The dwarves had positioned themselves with uncanny accuracy among the numerous exits of the hollow trees. They had discerned the major passageways into the ælven grottoes and had stationed snipers clever enough to wait until all the clan had emerged.

"Old Ric!" Broydo shouted in despair. "Call Asofel!"

The gnome did not hesitate. He shouted for his guardian. But his breath would not come. His fright had constricted his voice.

Broydo saw at once what had happened and began to shout, "Asofel! Asofel!"

An arrow buried itself to the fletching in the tree bark beside the ælf's face, and he fell silent. His cries had only alerted the dwarves to their presence.

The name of the Radiant One had to be shouted by the eldern gnome to be effective. But Ric could not quell his fear sufficiently to muster a cry. And the sight of armored dwarves on a root shelf above them withered him to a whisper.

"Ric!" Broydo bounded to Old Ric's side and shook him. "Call for Asofel!"

"No—voice!" Ric croaked, clutching at his throat.

The ælf gaped with disbelief. "Calm yourself, gnome! You're a deadwalker. Look!" Broydo grasped the Necklace of Souls and held a crystal prism to Old Ric's terrified face. "Look! What do you see within?"

At the first glimpse into the crystal, the gnome's world deepened as though he had passed into a long, echoing valley. The war whoops and death shrieks of the battle dimmed and yet sounded more distinct. Peacefulness enclosed him as in a harbored remembrance of childhood, far gone among the ice caverns on Nemora manyfold winters ago. The gnome watched Broydo heave about and fling his wire-wrapped club at the advancing dwarves. Beyond the ælf, Ric saw the horde of archers taking position on the root terraces above and dwarvish lancers running through the smoky shadows among the trees.

"Asofel!" Old Ric shouted strongly.

Shafts of star fire pierced the forest night as though a vast moon veered overhead. Silence washed away the din of the battle and left sobs and groans palpitating from the alleys of the forest but little other sound. A keening cry crooned from Smiddy Thea, and the serpent sword rose skyward in her grasp. A tangle of small, hot lightnings lashed from the tip of the white-bone blade, and strokes of this sizzling energy flashed among the branches and struck the archers.

The Radiant One floated overhead. He grasped the wide scope of peril that threatened the gnome and their mission. He saw Old Ric and Broydo quailing among the root steps of a giant tree, and a squad of lancers and hatchet troopers assailing them. With mortal precision, he stabbed the dwarves with lightning.

The bursts of charmfire that Asofel shot at the invaders arced from the serpent sword upheld in Smiddy Thea's rigid grip. She focused the power of the Radiant One. Her frail, aged self became distant, and she rose to her toetips strong with dreamstrength. She could see what Asofel perceived.

Across the forest slopes and down the mountain ranges, the nation of dwarves milled destructively. All the vile maggot-manikins on World's End had gathered in the Forest of Wraiths to reclaim the Necklace of Souls.

"They can have it!" Smiddy Thea could hear the gnome bawling. And she could feel the Radiant One not listening. His energies flowed rapidly, coursing from him through her and the sword in wider and longer whip strokes of lightning. He reached out through her across the forest, striking at the throngs of dwarves that staggered blindly through the dazzling forest.

Scores fell and writhed into dying larvae—large, twitching curls of segmented flesh waxy white and spiked with tiny stiff hairs. The effluvial mists of broken magic pooled into fog shoals and ringed the trees.

But Asofel could not slay the dwarves fast enough. Smiddy Thea felt his power waning first. The force pouring through her faltered. She looked upward. Overhead, the lunar glare muted.

Lightning still uncoiled from the sword but more fitfully. And soon even those jolting spurts stopped.

Night closed in darkly, and Smiddy Thea's arm went slack. The suddenly heavy sword weighed her to the ground, and she stooped and then knelt in the trampled mud. Her last shared thought with the Radiant One was the awareness that more dwarves remained. They were far off on the mountainside, for all the near squads were dead.

Broydo crossed to where his grandmother sagged and took her weight in his arms. She clasped the serpent sword to her body, and it burned against both of them, cold as ice.

Old Ric stood and gawked at the dead maggots everywhere. On every root shelf, the thick, white, humid bodies lay inert. At dawn, the rays of the Abiding Star would shrivel their pale remains to crisp husks.

"Asofel?" the gnome called tentatively to the still night.

The moans of the wounded and dying answered him.

"There—" Smiddy Thea flung a limp arm toward a thicket where the ectoplasmic fumes of the dead dwarves shimmered brighter.

The gnome stepped toward the thicket, where a glaucous light sputtered. Like a piece of green morning, the saplings and spindle trees separated from the darkness, then dimmed again into night shadows. Several ælf fighters staggered out of the gloom, eyes glowing with fright.

"There's a burning man in there!" one of them shouted.

"He fell out of the sky!" another cried. "He fell *burning* out of the sky!"

Broydo's heart banged like a bat in his rib cage as he hugged Smiddy Thea to him and hurried to follow Old Ric into the thicket.

"The Radiant One could not slay them all," Smiddy Thea muttered. "The others are coming. They will not stop—until they take back the Necklace of Souls."

Old Ric shoved through the thin trees, mindless of the flinching pain from the arrow through his chest that the branches wrenched. He heaved himself toward the smoldering luminosity at the interior of the dense undergrowth.

Abruptly the branches and thin boles of the bunched trees became brittle, then ashen. Under the gnome's swatting arms, a

whole wall of vegetation collapsed into a dusty cloud. Within its
rolling darkness, a dull red light pulsed like a heart.

Broydo pressed Smiddy Thea's face to his chest to protect her
from the flying cinders and ash. He squinted at the still-glowing
center of the thicket and discerned a human form standing upright at the base of a crater aswirl with mists. Asofel's countenance of curved eyes, long straight nose, and petal-small mouth
shone with a brown light. The angelically demonic features appeared pressed into metal still cooling from the forge.

"Asofel?" Old Ric stepped closer, awed by the mortal dimensions of the supernal entity. "Asofel? Can you hear me? Are
you alive?"

The figure stood naked, throbbing with dark energy, setting
rigidly to a statue.

"He lives—he lives . . ." Smiddy Thea mumbled and writhed
in Broydo's arms until he set her upon her feet. She stepped into
the crater and pointed the serpent sword at the lithic figure of
Asofel. "He gave everything he had. He killed all he could. He
gave everything . . ."

At the touch of the sword tip, the statue broke into caked
ash. Clots fell away in crumbly spills of smoking dust. Beneath
the outer shell of his former aspect, his new body crawled
with sparks.

A shriveled being breathed light within the broken casing of
cinders. Then the light went out, and all that remained was a
bald, salamander-skinny manikin, blotchy and still steaming.

Old Ric caught the shrunken entity as it fell forward from the
brace of its cracked shell. In his arms, Asofel had the weight of
smoke. Shivering, the Radiant One appeared no larger than a
withered old man and barely as substantial.

"He lives—he lives," the crone chanted, and handed the serpent sword to Broydo. A crisp look returned to her gaze. "Take
the gnome and the Radiant One to their destiny, grandson. Serve
them as they have served us. Go now and take the Necklace of
Souls far from our clan so that the dwarves will kill no more of
our folk."

Broydo accepted the serpent sword, and the instant he took
it, Smiddy Thea turned away. Many had died—but all would
have died had not the gnome and the Radiant One broken the
curse of the demon Tivel. The price was dear, but it had bought

salvation for the clan. She did not look back at her saviors, for she did not want to steal one moment from their vital mission. Instead, she waited until she had clambered out of the crater before she offered her blessing under her breath: "Go forth, grandson, and soar above all obstacles, your enemies far below green with bruises and you on the great wing."

PART TWO

Down the Well
of Spiders

"Love is its own justice."

—THE GIBBET SCROLLS, SCREED 4:31

LARA

DOWN THE WELL OF SPIDERS, THE COWLED WITCH MOVED. AS A wraith, she did not climb along the root tendrils that matted the walls of the Well, nor did she grasp at the rock walls that gleamed with seepings and mineral glazes. She simply floated down the wide shaft, her cowl blown back by her descent, her black hair streaming from her ripped face. In the misty blue light that shone from above, her torn flesh gleamed with blood and the bone white swatches of her skull showed through shredded skin.

As she descended, she glimpsed herself reflected in the thick nodules of quartz that the passage of the spiders had buffed to mirror clarity. She was not appalled by her gory visage. Yet she remembered with bitterness how once she was whole.

Long ago and far away from the original light of the Abiding Star, deep in the Gulf on a planet in a void of shadowy worlds known as the Dark Shore, she had been a living woman. Her name was Lara.

From her first days, her life had been strangely cursed. At her birth, her mother, an aboriginal woman outcast from the tribe for bearing the child of a drifter, abandoned her at a station where the forest ended and the desert began. But before the station manager could find her, a wild dog carried her off. She would have been devoured, a not-uncommon fate for unwanted infants. But she was found first by a muttersome crone, another exile of the tribe, festooned in the bones of animals and renowned for her long, rambling chants to the stars.

The hag tended the baby in her small hut carved from a lightning-struck tree. She fed the girl root milk and mashed tubers until the child grew strong enough to walk. Then old age pulled the crone to the ground, and she would not get up when the child tugged at her.

The toddler wandered off to find food for the motionless crone. In the forest, wild dogs watched her hungrily. Again, she would have been devoured but for the next strange twist of her fate. The old woman's songs to the stars had been heard by an entity from another reality, a brighter realm close to the Abiding Star. Drawn to the Dark Shore to seek magical implements, a sorcerer from the luminous worlds had taken up residence in the forest. His name was Caval.

Caval's assistant found her bruised and starving in a bog where the dogs had chased her. Insect bites had disfigured her, but under the care of the sorcerer Caval and his apprentice, she recovered quickly and eventually grew to become a beautiful woman with dark aboriginal hair, dusky skin, and night-deep eyes.

The sorcerer lived in the sky. Caval's magic had built him a blue mansion whose many rooms were the milky chambers of clouds. There he gathered the rare stuff he had come to the Dark Shore to collect. She did not understand his work. She barely understood him, the way his words always slipped away downwind. And light seemed to bend oddly around him, tiny prisms ever glinting from the orange whiskers that precisely trimmed his long jaw. Whenever he spoke to her, her attention drifted inevitably to the wee sparks in his bristly red hair.

Caval's assistant was easier to understand. Like herself, he was a denizen of the Dark Shore. He came from the city beyond the forest and was sophisticated in the ways of their world as well as adept at the magic the sorcerer worked. His name was Reece Morgan. It was he who had named her Lara and who had reared her and trained her to be a witch. Kindly, playfully, he had taught her how to work for Caval, how to draw energy out of the solemn trees with her dances, how to gather the moon's white ink and write upon the night's darkness the talismanic sigils that directed the forest energy to the purposes of the sorcerer.

Lara did not understand those purposes. The energy she drew forth from the trees and spun from moonfire rose into the sky, into Caval's celestial estate. What little was left she played with. She made poppets dance, animals talk, and flowers sing. Her mentors delighted in her games, and sometimes they gave her magic simply so they could watch her call down the boiling twilights and transform the forest shadows into a radiant garden tumbling with fiery acrobats.

Caval laughed like wind torn by rocks, and the still center of his eyes burned like stars. She feared him. Though he never hurt her or even so much as scowled at her, she feared the way he came on black wing out of the cloud shadows and so casually walked down the sky. Several times, he took her with him to his blue mansion and showed her the glassware he used to purify the energy she sent him from the trees. But every time he carried her there and tried to explain his work, she lost her attention to the fluent clouds below masking the emerald horizons of forest and the desert's long, blistered body.

Lara was happiest with Reece Morgan. He wore a magic skin of shaggy fur to frighten away the nomadic aboriginals that sometimes wandered into their corner of the woods, but he was himself a handsome man. He had hair the color of fresh cut wood, a soft, pale beard, and hooded eyes, gray as mist. With care, he had provided her with everything she needed. He had built her tree houses throughout the forest and a cabin in the desert with its own well. Out of the city he brought her fabrics and jewelry, and sometimes he even took her back with him to see the giant towers of glass, the endless storefronts displaying their fabulous wares.

As alluring as the city was, the wilderness was her home. The city was enjoyable only because Reece was there. She loved him and was most content wherever he was. He had a blue scent, a smell like the windy sky that has rubbed its fragrance from mountaintops and glacial lakes. The placid odor of him was enough to comfort her, but she yearned deeper for him. She

wanted to hold him and embrace him not just with her dances
but with her body.

Sadly for her, Reece cared for her as though she were his
child. He watched after her as closely as his magic would allow
and protected her from beasts and nomads alike. Lara resented
that. With her own energy collected from the trees, she could
easily control all the creatures she encountered. As for the nomads, she did not fear them. She was one of them, she felt.
Hidden by leaf screens at the riverbank, she watched them gather
water, splashing each other and laughing. Only when they were
injured or ill did she reveal herself, and then only long enough
to use her energy and her knowledge of the forest to help them.

Reece warned her to stay away from the aboriginals. Vexed at
him for treating her like a child, she ignored him. She met with
the people who had settled along the river in small shanty villages. Because the wind talked to the sky and the trees talked to
the wind, she heard from the trees all that was happening up and
down the river, and she shared these secrets with whoever asked.

This frightened some of the townsfolk. The most unhappy
among them gathered into a small gang, and on a moonless night
they took her from her tree house and hacked at her with their
blades. Her magic was helpless against their fear.

Horror jolted through Lara at the memory of that murderous
night, and, aroused from her reminiscence, she came alert to the
Well into which she descended. As she floated down the shaft
of hazy sapphire light she saw in its illuminated stone walls the
burnished reflections of her mangled face and the painful memory
of her death.

Her last thoughts in her physical body had been screams. Then
blood from her stabbed lungs choked her cries and drowned her.
The wrathful faces of her murderers stenciled her vision as darkness seized her.

She woke inside the brilliance of the Abiding Star. Caval had
carried her marred soul there after he had found her dead body
and buried her remains among the trees she had loved. From
within the luminosity of the Abiding Star, whose rays shone
across time, she had actually watched the sorcerer carry her soul
up into the sky and away from the Dark Shore.

Her soul had seemed such a small thing, a diminutive glassy
sphere. Caval had stood at the highest rung of the Upper Air,

among the star fumes and planet smoke, and used his magic to propel her soul away from him and into the glare of the Abiding Star. His actions were reflected in the clear round surface of her soul. The whole cosmos was reflected there so long as she remained within the Abiding Star.

Enwombed within that light, she listened to silence. And silence listened to everything. She heard flowing and eddying and splashing against the worlds of the Bright Shore and, farther away and more dimly, the thunder of surf against the cold planets of the Dark Shore. And in that sound was the music of those spheres—the orbital chimes of creation tolling rhythms that canceled to silence.

The silence would have carried her deeper into the Abiding Star, away from darkness, away from memory, to an eternity of brilliance with no time left to kill. But a thin, distant voice stopped her.

"Lara—"

The sound of her name pulled her away from the promise of heaven. Memories thickened. She recognized that tiny yet distinct voice.

"Lara—come to me!"

The sonorous, commanding voice of Caval summoned her away from the dazzling realm of light. And as she retreated from serenity and returned once more to the color and riot of memory, she realized that the sorcerer had not carried her soul up from the Dark Shore to the Abiding Star to deliver her to heaven.

"Lara—come to me! I need you!"

Caval had steeped Lara's soul in the Charm of the Abiding Star, the source of all Charm, to heal her. And the source of all worlds had indeed done that.

Drifting down the Well of Spiders, Lara remembered the horror of her murder but was not haunted by it. The Abiding Star had cured the trauma of her brutal death. The shock of knives piercing her body floated like a dream inside her. Saturated with Charm, she experienced no anguish at returning to creation as a ghost. Direct exposure to the interior of the Abiding Star had purged her of all shock and mourning.

But she was now little more than a wraith. And as a wraith she had fluttered insubstantially through the Upper Air to World's End. The presence of the Necklace of Souls had enabled her to assume a form that others could see, and in that form she had deftly manipulated Old Ric and Broydo to provide her with a crystal prism from the Necklace itself. Without that, she would have been unable to leave the Labyrinth of the Undead and the Forest of Wraiths.

Briefly, she pined for the listening silence within the Abiding Star, beyond time, far past remembrance. But the call had come from her master, the one who had made her a witch. In the round reflecting surface of her soul, his cry was the merest mote, yet she responded. The sorcerer had created her for this. She was his servant, even in death.

Within the high vantage of the Abiding Star, Lara had seen all of Caval's life. The infinite country of time wrapped its reflections around Lara's spherical soul, and when she had been inside the Abiding Star she could have seen anywhere and anytime. It was Caval's call that had drawn her awareness to him, and so she had witnessed all of his life, from his youth in the Brood of Assassins, to his training by the Sisterhood of Witches, and his service to the Brood of Odawl. Even his death was not withheld from her gaze. And she saw him stabbed by a rival warlock and his corpse torn to pieces among cacodemons.

Caval's soul had not ascended to the Abiding Star and the listening silence of eternity. Instead, he had drifted off on the nocturnal tide and floated away across the Gulf and into the anonymous depths of the Dark Shore. And yet—his cry could reach her!

Lara could not see Caval in the darkness, though she sensed him. Vaguely, she became aware that he was warning her, that he was calling to her to help avert a terrible calamity. What that was, she did not know. Beyond the stars, above the suns of the night and just within the corona of the Abiding Star, beings of a supernal order dwelled. While she herself was in the fierce light of the Beginning, she had felt the calamity emerging from there. It had been a feeling like a never-guessed fear, an unknowable dread.

The Nameless Ones. That was what they were called by those few of the Bright Shore who knew of their existence. The knowledge came to Lara like everything else in the Abiding Star, as if already known, as if remembered. But when she tried to know more, she pushed against sudden sleepiness.

Some terrible thing was about to happen. This she felt with a certainty. Caval's cry was but a splinter of this truth. She had been called back into time by an urgency that was only gradually coming clear. Though it was the sorcerer Caval who brought her soul to the Abiding Star and who called her forth from it, she became ever more convinced that it was not he who dwelled at the focus of the coming calamity. Listening to the silence she carried within her soul from the Beginning, she grew increasingly sure that the one who needed her help was the man she loved—Reece Morgan.

Lara put a hand to the crystal prism about her neck. Its Charm gave her phantom form substance, but it could not give her understanding. The farther she moved from the Abiding Star, the less clearly she could recall all that she knew while in its radiance. Even Caval's voice had vanished. And the Nameless Ones seemed an odd notion to her now.

Down the Well of Spiders, she floated. The deeper she went, the more her wounds ached and the less clearly she could think. She was becoming her former self—a slain witch reanimated by Charm.

Caval had called her. She distinctly remembered that. And she knew without knowing somehow that Reece was in danger. She had to go to him. By then she was sure she would understand why she had been called forth from the listening silence.

Faeries twinkled in the dark niches of the Well, and a giant spider scuttled past, rasping against the rocks. This was no arachnid as she had known in the forest of her first life. Those were small creatures that could grow only so large before their chitinous exoskeletons restrained them. But the spiders of the Well were actually huge assemblages of mites, hundreds of miniscule creatures bound together by Charm and hunger.

Lara kept her mind outside of herself, on the glossy rocks with their side chutes and tunnels, most of them veiled with cobwebs and spider nests. Bioluminescent tendrils illuminated the spiral path downward and the obscure depths to which she had committed herself. Pain flashed in her all the brighter as her descent grew darker.

After a while, she forgot how she had found this Well at World's End. The knowledge had come with her from the Abiding Star, but it would go no farther among the inchoate shadows. She sailed through the lightless shaft thriving with pain. And just when she had almost forgotten her mission and was contemplating turning around and climbing back up to World's End and from there to the joy of the Beginning, she emerged on Irth.

Lara arrived in the Spiderlands, a sere terrain of thorn trees and scattered boulders, many shawled with the webworks of arachnids. She sat down on the sandy ground and lifted her torn face toward the firecore of the Abiding Star. Understanding flowed into her, and she remembered once more all that she had known before.

Her pain had not diminished, but her mind had grown more clear. The Nameless Ones were unhappy. Reece Morgan had climbed into the sky after Caval and come to Irth carrying shadows with him from the Dark Shore. Those shadows were somehow poisoning the Nameless Ones, and in turn those supernal beings were intent on destroying Reece.

"Old Ric knew," she said aloud to the spider-festering land. "The gnome knew. I saw that. And if he finds Reece first, we will be ghosts together, Reece and I."

She did not want that for him. He had been too good to her, and she was determined to defy her suffering and find him, warn him, protect him as he had once protected her.

Weightless, she rose to her feet and scanned the horizon. Scraggy brush and broken rocks swept in every direction. She lifted the crystal prism and gazed into its depths while chanting, "Reece—Reece Morgan—"

A direction came clear, and she willed herself to rush toward him. But her phantom body would not fly. She had journeyed too far from the Abiding Star to enjoy the powers she had possessed at World's End. Here on Irth at the very brink of the Gulf, her form possessed a nearly corporeal solidity. And the pain of her old wounds throbbed miserably.

To calm herself, she fixed her stare again on the Abiding Star and drew strength from its warmth. The leagues of distance between her and the man she loved trembled before her, reflecting the heat of noon in wrinkly mirages. Even they were more actual than she—though she was real enough to feel pain.

She walked south, toward where the crystal had indicated that Reece dwelled. Each step inflamed her with hurt. She cried out, and her voice startled the spiders that hung like gems in their silver webs.

Eating Shadows

"SHE WENT DOWN THERE," OLD RIC SAID WITH CONVICTION, STAND-ing at the brink of a sinkhole wide enough to admit four horses abreast. "I feel we must follow her. She has said she is on the same mission as I."

Broydo clutched at the gnarled bough of a dwarf pine to an-chor himself and peered over the crumbly rock brim. Daylight fell as a murky shaft into a darkness flimmery with distant lights. Among the colossal boulders that composed the wall of the pit, the ælf observed a troll cave with a mossy ledge strewn with bones. Closer to where he stood, viper holes riddled the flaking shale rim, and he glimpsed a crimson tail lash out of sight. "Only a wraith would dare go down there. Where does it lead?"

"Wherever she wants to go." The gnome kicked a stone into the sinkhole, and it plummeted soundlessly. "This is the famous Well of Spiders, my friend."

"Famous to gnomes mayhap, but I've never heard of it." Broydo stepped back gingerly from the edge, disappointed that their long hike had led only to this forbidding hole in the ground. He retrieved the serpent sword from where he had placed it on a flat rock, and he slashed the air with it as if driving away the cold breeze and its scent of frost. "Where does that hole in the ground go?"

"It connects the worlds," the gnome said, and studied the glittery darkness of the deep. "No one knows who created it. Few had explored it and survived in pretalismanic times. Only with the most powerful amulets may any living creature enter the Well and live."

The ælf hunkered under a fire-bald tree of blistered bark, the sword across his knees. A blaze had seared this countryside several seasons before, and now a pale wood of saplings hazed the undulant knolls. "Is this the way we will go to find the dark thing?"

"It's too dangerous." Old Ric turned abruptly from the Well and strode to where his companion sat. "He would never survive down there," he added, and indicated with a glance at where Asofel sat before a wall of red willow, too weak to leave the lady's dream.

The Radiant One looked like a doll of shriveled fruit. He watched them with pink fetal eyes, his bald head bowed chin to chest, his shrunken body bundled in shawl moss.

"I wonder he has survived this long." Broydo nervously pulled his leaf-knit tunic tighter about himself and stamped his boots of vine-lashed tree bark as if driving off the cold. The air of this high country was wintry, but the chill the ælf felt was the same clammy apprehension that had accompanied him since he departed from his clan after the battle with the dwarves.

"He would not have survived had you not accompanied us," the eldern gnome said with an appreciative nod of his bald head. A sad glance acknowledged the arrow that still impaled his chest. "With this, I could not have carried him as far so quickly. The dwarves would have found us in the low country, still bumbling through the Forest of Wraiths."

"I've done little," Broydo answered distractedly, his mind returning again to his clan and his dreadful concern for them now that the hordes of dwarves swarmed across the land. "I am merely obeying the command of my elder, Smiddy Thea."

"So you have reminded me time and again, Broydo." The gnome's thick eyebrows knitted tighter. "The life-debt between us is fulfilled. You are kind to have escorted us this far from your home. But now you must take the serpent sword and return to defend your clan."

Broydo ran a blunt-fingered hand through his tight green hair. "Our adventure should be concluded. We have destroyed the demon Tivel, retrieved the Necklace of Souls, and healed my stricken clan—and yet the dwarves give us no peace to enjoy our triumph."

"Go and give your people the protection of the serpent sword." Ric jangled the crystals that draped his pierced chest. "I have the Necklace of Souls to give me the strength I need to find my way to the dark thing."

"And how will you drive the dark thing from our worlds with Asofel—like that?" Broydo shook his head at the shrunken grotesque under the red willows. "Smiddy Thea has charged me to accompany you and serve you as you served us. I cannot return to my clan until you have accomplished your mission for the Nameless Ones."

"So you have said several times each day since we quit the Forest of Wraiths." Ric put a gentle hand on his friend's shoulder. "And each time, I tell you the same: You should be with your people."

"If I have any people—" The ælf hung his head morosely. "The dwarves may well have slain them in retribution for the many of theirs the Radiant One killed."

"And I've told you, I think not." The eldern gnome picked up the sun hat he had fashioned from vines and fronds and had taken off to peer into the Well of Spiders. "The dwarves want the Necklace. They are not thirsty for blood but for Charm, and they will not waste resources on vengeance when there is yet the chance they may track us down and retrieve the last of Duppy Hob's amulets."

"Well then, yes—" Broydo sighed heavily. "I am once more convinced that my clan is well. I am once more convinced that we must be on our way to find the shadow thing before the day of the Nameless Ones passes."

The gnome slapped the ælf's shoulder. In his torn breeks of browncord and his green blouse serrate with silk ruffles now stained with mud and blood, Ric looked ghastly—yet he smiled. "The worlds have not vanished for the moment, and so there must still be time to save creation. With you at my side, friend, I cannot fail."

"How will we continue?" Broydo twirled the serpent sword anxiously in his thick hands. "How will we leave World's End if not down the Well of Spiders?"

"We will have to book passage on an ether ship," Old Ric answered decisively, then continued less certainly, "That is, once we find our way to a city with a sky harbor."

Broydo's mouth turned downward, and he scratched at the mossy green beard that splotched his ebony cheeks. "I know of no cities on World's End."

"Then we'll have to find our way to Hellsgate." Old Ric bent and picked up Asofel. The Radiant One weighed no more than air.

"That means we will have to descend the World Wall and risk getting eaten by a roc." The ælf stabbed apprehensively at the scorched ground and continued to mutter as they strolled away from the sinkhole. "If only there were some way to be certain that my clan is well . . ."

They descended from the wild uplands into fields of flowering stalks. The cultivated plants announced the perimeter of a marsh community. Stilt huts appeared among the trees, and scaffolds and rope bridges connected the trunks. The residents, a blue-haired clan of ælves, greeted the wanderers warmly. Reed flutes heralded their arrival, and the clan elders emerged to hear Broydo recite his lineage and the story of his wanderings with the eldern gnome.

While Broydo spoke, ælves came in from the fields and down from the verandas of their tree houses. By the time he concluded, the entire clan had gathered on the tussock where the strangers stood, the weird, staring homunculus lying at their feet.

News of the nearby dwarves alarmed the clan, and Broydo swore to them that the three travelers would leave the village long before twilight. Once assured that their cousin ælf wanted nothing more than food and fresh clothing before continuing to lead the dwarves deeper into the marsh, the blue-haired brethren enthusiastically agreed to help.

Old Ric would not part with his beloved silk shirt and cord breeches in exchange for grass-woven garments, but he did strip and allow his clothes to be cleaned and himself bathed. The swamp ælves marveled at the barbed arrow that skewered him, the fletching worn away and the shaft moldy and blackening. When his garments had been cleansed, they dressed him with ceremonial solemnity to show their respect.

The victuals the bog clan served included sugar stalks and honey berries prepared in a mint sauce. These dishes reminded Broydo of the meals he had shared with his own clan, and moisture filmed his eyes. Through the blear of his sadness, the ælves around him looked oddly transparent. He blinked back his tears, and his breath slowed in his lungs when he gradually began to realize that the figures around him had changed.

At first, he did not know what he was seeing. The ælves looked somehow brighter, their plaited garb more colorful.

"Broydo!" Old Ric called out in alarm. "Look! Have you noticed? They have no shadows!"

Shock jerked Broydo to his feet when he saw that this was indeed the case: The clan's shadows had completely disappeared. As the ælves themselves began to realize their condition, screams of fright exploded from them.

Quickly, Broydo peered down at himself and saw that his shadow curiously remained, as did Old Ric's and the shadows of all other objects within the village. Only the unfortunate ælves had become transparent to the rays of the Abiding Star. Yet they felt as solid as ever before when they angrily seized Broydo and demanded to know what evil magic he had worked upon them.

While the ælves' attention was averted, Old Ric was able to grab Asofel's bundled body and scamper off into the marsh. Left to fend for himself, Broydo lifted the serpent sword and faced the loud anguish of the clan with tears glistening on his cheeks. "This is not our doing!" he shouted. "I swear upon the ghosts of our blood, this cruel magic is not our doing!"

Yet the crowd would not listen. Brandishing his serpent sword, Broydo turned and fled. As dozens of runners pursued him, shouting threatening curses and raising sticks, Broydo kept them at bay with the sword and bolted into the gloomy enclaves of the swamp.

The clan's young warriors charged after him, determined to drag him back to answer for their lost shadows. But as soon as they entered the green darkness beyond the village clearing, they vanished, their sticks and garb falling emptily in heaps to the ground.

Hearing no sounds at his heels, Broydo stopped midflight and turned about, aghast. He walked over and picked up one of the vanished men's headbands, the cloth still warm with body heat. A cry of fright flashed in him, and he flung a panic-stricken look to the gnome up ahead.

But Old Ric did not see him. His gaze had fixed instead upon Asofel, who had swollen to twice his former size. The pink of his eyes had become anthracitic black, and he stared now with wincing clarity at the shock of the ælf and the gnome.

"This is our lady's dream," Asofel whispered, his voice a rasp.

The gnome dropped to his knees before the sprawled and waxen figure of Asofel. "You—you did this?" He gestured vaguely toward the village where ælves shrieked to see their clansmen evaporated into the swamp's perpetual dusk.

"I need their Charm . . ." Asofel breathed softly. "And I need still more."

"More?" Broydo stalked closer and impaled the serpent sword in the peat beside the Radiant One. "What barbaric appetite is this? You want to kill more of my kin?"

Asofel made no reply but shut his eyes and curled tighter about himself.

"Why have you not eaten my shadow, Asofel?" Broydo demanded. "Why have you spared me?"

Old Ric pulled Broydo aside. "Waste no strength on him, ælf. He is of another order of creation. He does not answer to our laws. You heard his first words."

"This is the nameless lady's dream—" Broydo scowled, profoundly troubled by this turn of events. "To him we are just dreamstuff. Taking our lives is not murder to him—it's just energy."

"Sadly true—sadly true," the gnome mumbled. Shock had set his thoughts flurrying, and the thinning screams from the village felt like pieces of his mind flying off. "Assuredly, this was not murder. It was an exchange. The Radiant One saved your clan, and, in return, this unfortunate swamp clan was doomed."

"And yet, he wants more!" Broydo nudged Old Ric aside and yelled at Asofel, "Eat the shadows of the trees. Eat the animals. Don't eat the ælves!"

Asofel made no reply. He had become once again inert.

Ric gathered tatter moss from nearby boughs and began fashioning a blanket for the enlarged entity. "Broydo, come and carry him," he called. "We dare not tarry with dwarves asleep all around us."

"I'll not carry him," Broydo insisted.

Asofel's black eyes opened. Saying not a word, he lifted himself ponderously to his feet. Gray stubble darkened his scalp where hair had begun to grow, and a halo of midges and marsh flies smudged the air around him.

Old Ric offered his arm, and the Radiant One put his weight of feathers upon him. With Broydo slouching behind, haunted by the horrified wails of the villagers, the gnome and his withered guardian continued their journey across World's End.

THE MAGUS OF ELVRE

THE FALLEN KINGDOM OF ARWAR ODAWL FLOURISHED IN THE JUNGLES of Elvre. Only one road connected it to the rest of Irth, yet the tiny realm had already become more prosperous than much larger cities, such as the busy trading capital of Drymarch or even the vigorous industrial terraces of Saxar. That was because the remote crash site served as residence for the most powerful magus under the Abiding Star, the interloper from the Dark Shore, Reece Morgan.

Reece lived quietly in a comfortable cottage on a knoll above the sand rivers of Kazu. Arwar Odawl loomed nearby. Its ruins had been transformed from a mountain of rubble to a towering city of scaffolded spires and tiered neighborhoods. Stately palms lined the broad boulevards, and trellises of flowering vines dripped outlandish blossoms over a maze of lanes and winding byways.

The magus had used his power to rearrange the heaped debris into a lovely, verdant city vaguely shaped as a flat-topped pyramid. If he could have, he would have restored the dead themselves. But his magic was limited to manipulating the physical stuff of the Bright Worlds.

Five hundred days earlier, Arwar Odawl had been a floating kingdom. It had cruised above the clouds, traveling among the dominions of Irth, wont to drift wherever trade was good and its ruler, Margrave Keon, commanded. Then came the Dark Lord. . . .

The one road that Reece had constructed to connect with the crash site in the jungles of Elvre was a monolithic highway to Moödrun, the skyport to the north. All imports and pilgrims bound for Arwar Odawl came by that efficient route, for there was no sky bund in the fallen kingdom. No dirigibles or flyers of any kind were allowed in the airspace above Elvre. As the city itself had forsaken its place in the sky, so would all travelers to this realm.

Along the sides of the long highway through the jungle, rest stops had been designed to preserve the gruesome history of the Dark Lord's invasion and the fall of Arwar Odawl. Sculpture gardens offered visitors statues of cacodemons, a safe perspective of the monsters that had ravaged Irth. For now, little more than a hundred days since the defeat of the Dark Lord and his demons, memories remained vivid, and the gardens and museum galleries had few guests. But in time, Reece knew, people would need to see again the reptilian hulks against whose talons and fangs Charm had been useless.

Reece built for the future. He felt responsible for what had happened to Irth when the cacodemons savaged the countryside. It was he who had inadvertently left open the Door in the Air, the portal to the Dark Shore that the sorcerer Caval had revealed to him. If he had been a more humble man, he would have remained on the Dark Shore and there would have been no slaughter of innocents.

Instead, he had come to Irth searching for the lost soul of Lara. And, in his eagerness to find her, he had left the way open for the cacodemons. Lara was gone—her murdered ghost delivered into the mystery of the Abiding Star. Reece never found her. But he discovered instead the enormous magical strength he possessed in the charmful light of the Bright Shore. With that might, he helped destroy the evil he had brought with him. Since that fateful triumph, he had spent his days dedicated to making amends for his fatal trespass.

Oblivious of the Nameless Ones, Reece landscaped the world

around him to suit his vision of beauty. He thought that his work was noble, wholly opposite the brutal magic of the Dark Lord. At his insistent chant, the barren soil of Kazu's sand rivers bulged into dark mounds and sprouted desert trees thick as artichokes. In this way, he stood in their shade and regarded the stucco cottage where he lived. At his whim, its yellow tile roof turned blue.

A youthful laugh chimed from inside the cottage, and the lithe, athletic figure of the margravine appeared in the round doorway. "You're giddy as a child!" She wore an amulet-vest over a gray bodysuit tucked into cross-strapped boots. Tied in a topknot, her blond-streaked hair pulled back from a wide, freckled face. "Is that why you live so far from the city, so that you can play your fickle games without anyone seeing you?"

They kissed and laughed. During the hundred days that they had been lovers, he had grown young again. The dead in their thousands still haunted him, the ritual dead left to the mercies of the Dark Lord, the blood sacrifices that had frenzied the cacodemons—and yet, when he was with Jyoti, that all seemed false, a bad dream.

Neither of them believed what they were doing was wrong. A woman of Irth, a man of the Dark Shore: they saw only their common humanity. Charm and Reece's magic had helped Jyoti with the desolation of her life after the Dark Lord. Of late, she preferred to be with Reece without amulets and free of his splendid power, just the two of them getting to know each other as people from distant shores of humanity.

For his part, Reece had become wholly absorbed in his magic. Later, he would marvel at this foolishness. But at the time, he did not see his power to shape matter by his will as something terrible. This was the human dream. Mind over matter. He had attained the paragon of human aspiration.

At his command, the shuddering treetops flared into bloom, clouds scrawled messages, fountains spurted from the desert floor. Yet, he knew he was no god. His memory of the Dark Lord and his own culpability for those many deaths kept him humble. The statue gardens of cacodemons and the atrocity museums actually offered perpetual testimony at the roadside *for him*—so that he would never forget that his power was anything more than mortal. But he had yet to visit them.

Protected by his false modesty and his ignorance, the magus of Elvre dedicated himself to reshaping the face of Irth. He would begin here with Arwar Odawl and repair the damage that the cacodemons had inflicted on the dominions. It would take the remainder of his life to accomplish. After a hundred days of hard work, he was only a fraction of the way to restoring the fallen kingdom.

Magic was exhausting. The bulky trees he had sprouted along the sand rivers drained his strength for the moment and left him feeling torpid. He lay with Jyoti in a hammock on the patio of his cottage and confided in her, "I will never atone for the evil I've visited upon Irth."

"Posh." She poked him sternly between the ribs. "Stop blaming yourself, Reece. 'Does the stream own its water?' What happened is past. Time has moved on."

"Quoting again from the Gibbet Scrolls," Reece acknowledged. His arm tightened about her tenderly. "Is that how you overcame your grief—for your father, your brood?"

She turned in his embrace and lifted her head so that her brindled hair tented his face. "I haven't overcome my grief. But the Gibbet Scrolls have kept my grief from overcoming me."

He offered a frown. "You think my grief is mastering me?"

"Clearly." A kindly smile rayed across her freckles.

"Really?" Concern pinched the velvet space between his eyebrows. "I've tried so hard to be creative, to renew what was ruined . . ."

Jyoti laid her head on his chest and listened to the heart's ancient music. "That's how grief is using you, Reece. You never stop. Since you killed the Dark Lord, you've given all of yourself to trying to heal what he wounded. You lived for weeks in the jungle building the highway to Moödrun."

"Arwar Odawl needed a connection with the other dominions, to bring in supplies. It would take too long to use magic to make everything . . ."

"I'm not disputing that, silly." She nuzzled against his shoulder. "I just thought you'd rest after you finished the highway. But then you launched right into transforming the ruins of my city into our vision of the fallen kingdom."

"I would have rebuilt it exactly as it was before, for you, Jyo . . ."

Without looking at him, her fingers found his mouth and silenced him. "And you were caring enough to hear me when I told you then we must not go back. This is a new era. Entirely new. The terror of the cacodemons has unified the dominions more tightly than ever. And now, with your magic, an epoch of peace and prosperity can begin."

He kissed her fingertips. "Are we fools to believe this is possible?"

"If we live for nothing else—then, yes we are fools." She stifled a yawn. "But our mortal limits will keep us from attempting more than we can do. That's what I'm trying to tell you. You're doing too much."

Reece grunted with understanding. "We are not gods. I've been reminding myself of that since we won our freedom."

"And yet—here you are creating trees out of sand!" She pushed upright and sat over him. Unlike the Dark Lord, he did not use his magic to alter his appearance, and she could plainly see his fatigue: the inflamed capillaries in his flinty eyes, the disarray of his sandy hair, the gaunt hollows of his cheeks. "Look at you. You're completely exhausted."

He sat up on his elbows. "I'm just doing what has to be done."

"Like sprouting giant trees here in Kazu," she said, canting her head with skepticism.

"The skyline needed some green." He shrugged. "And there's a convenient aquifer not too far down."

"No, Reece. I know why you spent yourself to put these trees here." She stared past the fat trees and the blue-tiled cottage with its upturned eaves and read the winding dry creek bed that furled among the hills. "It was on this granite bluff that my brother Poch and I were camping when the horror began. From here, we watched the city fall."

He shook his head, and his hair fell into his eyes. "That landscape is gone now, Jyo—like the water in the stream. It's moved on."

"You reshaped this land to purge it of that painful memory." She touched the back of her hand to his whiskery cheek. "It's a beautiful detail, and I can't deny that it's healing me. A beautiful detail. But you're draining yourself. If you're not careful, you're going to need amulets to keep from drifting off on the night tide."

"It's a new era, just as you say," he replied earnestly. "I want to give the future everything that I can."

"Hush now." She gently pushed him back so that he stared up through the blossom arbor at the cloud drift and the floating hawks. "No more magic for a while. Just rest. Here in my arms, rest."

His pale eyebrows bent wearily. "There is so much to do."

"We will do it all," she assured him, and closed his eyes with a pass of her hand.

"Mirdath—" he muttered. "The city under the falls was five times as large as Arwar. How will I ever draw enough magic to rebuild that? And Floating Stone—and Dorzen—"

"Be still now." From a pocket of her amulet-vest, she removed a theriacal opal and pressed it against his brow. He sighed at the touch of Charm and slipped into sleep.

Reece dreamed, and the city of his dream rose in steel-and-glass towers on the eastern banks of a spacious natural harbor. This was Darwin, the tropical port city where he had lived on the Dark Shore. It was the home of his immediate forefathers, who had been among the founders of the settlement in the previous century, the entrepreneurs of Palmerston, who had made large fortunes in the Northern Territory.

In his dreams, the magus relived his memories of life in Darwin, where he had grown up and first learned magic. On his own at first, in the library stacks, he had read about the torn wedding veil of creation, the Big Bang of science, the Fall of legend, when light plunged into darkness, and consciousness enmired itself in matter. If the books were to be believed, then mind and light were one, awareness partook of light's legacy of infinity, its origin in compact dimensions of immeasurable energy.

Reece became a lightworker at an early age and taught himself how to collect light in the niches of his body. He began simply, with breathing intonations and visualizations that pooled energy in his bones and organs. He studied with others who had collected enough light that they could move it not only around inside their bodies but among themselves.

A lifetime of memories from the Dark Shore filled his dreams on Irth. He had trained with many masters, and all of them met him again in the dreamtime, the ancestral range where birdsong was sold to the forests, where souls were gems that had to be polished to receive and hold light, and where night was a black feather and you the white.

Among the masters who met him in the dreamtime, the one he feared the most, of course, was Caval, the wizard from Irth who had lured him into the fern forests of the Snow Range on the large wilderness island northeast of Darwin. He traveled as an ethnologist, but he had been called there by an entity from a brighter order of reality.

In his dreams of Caval, Reece most often relived the death of their witch Lara. He returned to the sleek waters of the river where her soul had melted away—or so he had thought at the time. Caval had retrieved it downstream and carried it with him across the Gulf back to the Bright Worlds, the luminous reality of the Abiding Star. . . .

Asleep in the hammock, Reece dreamed that he stood in the river and could not budge. The vacancies of Lara's soul held him there—vacancies filled with a dark music that spoke of her. The stream lapped at his legs, urging him to walk along with it. But he would not budge. He wanted to stay there listening to the floating echoes of her last cries.

And then, she stood before him on the riverbank—Lara. Defying all his previous dreams dreamed on Irth, which had been revived memories, this dream *was* a dream.

Lara's face was torn, as it had been in real life. But she stood as only this nightmare would allow, gory arms outstretched for him, face slashed open to reveal bone, and her nosehole a foam of blood bubbles . . .

Reece woke with a start.

"It was a dream," Jyoti consoled him before slipping out of the hammock.

"That's the problem." He sat up sequined with sweat. "I don't dream on Irth. I've never dreamt here before. I—I remember. That's all."

"So—what does this mean?" Jyoti brushed the sweaty hair from his furrowed brow. "I think it means you're depleted. You've used up so much of your magic that you are sleeping deeply enough to dream."

Reece agreed with her and promised to use no magic at all for the next few days. She had to leave at once to attend a city board meeting followed by a series of neighborhood conferences, but she promised to return later in the day. After admonishing him again for living so far from the city, she kissed him farewell, and flew off in her personal airfoil. Alone in the cottage, he returned to the hammock and stared at it.

"A dream—" he wondered aloud, "—or not?"

He entertained the thought that he was not dreaming on Irth, that something else was happening. *Perhaps she calls me—from the Abiding Star.*

Sitting in a cane chair on the patio, the magus closed his eyes and strove to quiet himself to the dream level where he had met Lara's mangled wraith.

"Reece—beware!"

Reece jolted so violently to hear Lara's voice that he nearly toppled from the chair. "Lara!"

Silence heightened the thudding of his heart. He breathed to calm himself and sat still, this time with his gray eyes open and staring. He watched the afternoon light darken among the bulky trees. Evening's red knife cut day from night before he heard her again, softer, far, far away: *"Reece—beware the Shadow Eater!"*

The fiery constellations of Irth rose like silent screams, and he sat listening for more. There was no more. Lara, illusion or telepathic cry, had withdrawn.

Reece paced the patio. Days would pass before his strength returned to work magic strong enough that he could listen deeper. *Is it possible she has left the Abiding Star?* he asked himself. *Can that be?*

"And why?" he went on aloud, feeling stupid with fatigue, wishing he had not drained all his magic but had left enough for a strong eye that could see from where Lara was calling—*if* she was calling.

The Shadow Eater—The name made him think of the Abiding Star, the first sun, devourer of shadows—but also the maker of shadows.

Reece slipped back into the hammock and pondered this until sleep found him again. On the dreambank of the river, Lara waited. Her face was healed. She wore a cassock with the hood drawn back and her black hair flowing over her shoulders, aboriginal features stern with alarm. "Flee the Shadow Eater!"

"Who?" Reece called to her from where he stood in the satiny river, the soft current slipping around him. "Who is the Shadow Eater?"

But she was gone. And in her place, the weedy moonlit space of the dream offered her soul's dark music.

TO THE ETHER SHIP

ASOFEL SHAMBLED THROUGH THE SOMBER AVENUES OF THE SWAMP forest. Tremulous as a shaken bough, he dared not remain still for fear that he would shake off his physical form—and he did not know what would happen then. He wondered if he would wake from his mistress's dream and find himself again at his post at the bridge-gate above World's End. Or perhaps he would simply die and become nothing. That fate seemed most appealing as he suffered to keep walking through the brown-greeniness that surrounded them, his fleshly body aching.

"I need light," he mumbled.

Old Ric, who ambled beside him, feather-light and painless within the Charm from the Necklace of Souls, pointed past hanging air plants and lianas to another corridor among the enormous tree trunks. "We go that way."

Asofel changed his direction to comply. His ponderous footfalls sank heavily into the soft ground, a dark compost of rotted leaves that gave off a dense, bitter smell. "I need the light of the dream."

Broydo, who had lagged several paces, hurried closer to hear what Asofel was mumbling. "He's too weak to climb down the Wall of the World," the ælf observed. Dismayed as he was at this cruel entity who had devoured an entire clan of ælves, he knew that Asofel alone could save the worlds. The skeletal body of the Radiant One looked as if about to collapse, and Broydo considered giving him the serpent sword to use as a crutch. But the furtive shadows around them dissuaded him. Though it was daylight, he feared the dwarves he knew were hidden in the swamp, sleeping, waiting for night.

"Be strong, Asofel," Old Ric encouraged. "Our lady has granted me the sense of our goal. I can feel our way to the shadow thing."

"I need light . . ." Asofel staggered onward in zombie rhythm, mumbling barely audibly.

"There will be no more taking of lives—" Old Ric insisted in a stern tone.

"I need the light of the dream . . ." The Radiant One looked to neither side but kept his heavy gaze on the slow seepings underfoot.

"He must eat, gnome." Broydo bent over and peered into the Radiant One's haggard face with its sharp angles of bone. "He suffers."

Old Ric shot a harsh look at the ælf. "Are you volunteering yourself as food?"

"Me?" Broydo flinched. "Not me. I have been commanded by my clan to accompany you."

"Then whose lives shall we sacrifice to the Radiant One, ælf-counselor?" Old Ric asked with an annoyed scowl. "Shall we seek out other villages of ælves?"

"Why can he not eat plants and animals as we do?"

Old Ric regarded his companion with incredulity. "He is not as we are."

"And if he dies?" the ælf inquired. "You have the sense to find the shadow thing, but do you have the strength to drive him back to the Dark Shore?"

"I will not kill innocents." Old Ric's tufty eyebrows frowned so tightly they touched. "And you would, Broydo?"

"No, no, gnome, you mistake me." Broydo shook his head vigorously. "It is obvious that the Radiant One needs food—but I would prefer he devour the shadows of dwarves."

Old Ric spat over his shoulder with disdain. "The dwarves are maggots."

"This is truly a conundrum then, isn't it, gnome?" Broydo lifted a frustrated look to the high galleries, where the light filtered down through torn places and birds fretted and clicked. "Do we sacrifice others like ourselves to save all the worlds—or do we leave the Radiant One to starve and thus fail in our mission and lose all of creation?"

"Thank you, counselor, for apprising me of our situation." Ric cast him a dark look. "I am much enlightened."

"Don't act snide with me, gnome." Broydo returned his irritation with a frown. "My concern is for the benefit of all beings."

"Then we must find a way to drive out the shadow thing in a way that benefits all beings and sacrifices none."

"I need the light of the dream . . ." Asofel murmured as he limped on.

The ælf and the gnome exchanged apprehensive stares. "Your ideals are noble, Old Ric, but I fear we will have to be more practical if we are to survive at all."

Old Ric lifted his stubbly chin, defiant of necessity. "Then perhaps it is best we do not survive."

"What?" Broydo walked backward so that he could stare full into his comrade's fisted face. "You cannot be serious."

"No?" Ric voiced his pain, "Why should creation persist? Life devours life. Existence is an endless round of horror. Let it end. Let the nameless lady conclude her dream and end the suffering of our nightmare."

"I like not your reasoning, gnome." Broydo turned back around and walked forward, rubbing his beardless jaw ruminatively. "Yes, indeed, life is suffering. That is and has ever been the foundation of existence—from birthwrack to deathwrack and all the numerous physical indignities between. And yet, gnome, and yet—"

Ric nodded with comprehension and waved one hand dismissively. "There is joy, there is pleasure, there is happiness—but all of it fleeting."

"You are bitter." Broydo placed a friendly arm across his companion's bony shoulders. "What became of the bold and daring gnome who stole the Necklace of Souls from under the snouts of the dwarves?"

Old Ric hung his head, and his cap of vines and leaves

slouched over his troubled eyes. "He witnessed the destruction of an entire clan of ælves, and it broke his spirit."

"No, it did not!" Broydo spoke this so loudly that the birds in the awning stopped fretting, and one could hear the stirring leaves. "Think with your heart for just a moment, Old Ric. Think back on your beloved daughter—Amara her name was, yes?"

"Yes," he answered in a tiny voice.

"She died in her childhood. Why did you not die then yourself?"

"Perhaps I did."

"Oh, something in your soul died, for sure. That is why you took to living alone, isn't it? And that is why the nameless lady chose you to remove from her dream." Broydo poked a finger against Ric's chest, beside the dwarf's barbed arrow. "You were empty and she could fill you with her will."

"Yes, yes, and so?" the gnome asked, annoyed. "What is your point, ælf?"

"That we are shaped by our losses. And though this feels terrible, it is not bad in the wider scope of life." He went on more softly, "It is the way of our lives to be shaped by death."

" 'Life shapes itself on the anvil of dreams—' " Ric quoted from the *Gibbet Scrolls*.

" '—and the hammer is death,' " Broydo concluded. "Yes, that is my point."

"Well taken, ælf. Well taken." The nostrils of Ric's upturned nose widened to draw a deep breath, and then he asked, "That then justifies our murdering whole clans to fulfill our mission?"

Broydo gasped a sigh, struck again by the pain of their predicament. "I could not order it myself. But what are we to do? The survival of all the worlds requires us to be strong."

"I am not that strong," the eldern gnome admitted with a narrow shake of his head. "The mistress of this dream chose the wrong gnome. I cannot slay innocents—not even to save all the worlds."

Broydo's shoulders sagged, and the blade of the serpent sword dragged along the ground with the weight of this decision. "Aye, gnome. Nor can I. Though I recognize the necessity, like you I can see my way no further. What are we to do?"

Old Ric looked to Asofel, whose space black eyes in his

starved, skullish face stared hard at the rotted ground. "The Radiant One yet lives. We will carry on."

They proceeded in silence. Under the beards of the giant trees,
they walked in the direction that Old Ric sensed until afternoon's
angular light ambered. Broydo found a covert at the groin of two
boughs on a tree veiled by creeper vines. Ric sought small pleasure from a shrub of wild sugar stalks, and they gnawed on the
sweet fibers while lying in the tree and watching darkness rise
up the smooth pale boles.

At dawn, Asofel was gone. Old Ric, who slept out of habit
not necessity, and Broydo, risen from weary slumber, blinked
groggily at each other in the gray light, looking for an answer
to his absence in each other.

On the ground, they found his trail. His wading gait was easy
enough to track, and they hurried through the green light to
catch up with him.

"The dwarves might have found him!" Ric worried. "Why did
he leave our covert in the night?"

"Food," Broydo answered, and pointed through the trees to a
clearing where butterflies crisscrossed the silence of an empty
village.

Ric and Broydo wandered among the grass huts looking for
anyone. But the entire community had vanished, leaving behind
everything—garments fallen in disarray, simmering cauldrons,
children's toys beside the cots where they had slept.

Asofel's tracks were visible at the far end of the village, where
he returned to the forest. But his step was lighter, his stride
longer.

"We won't catch him," Old Ric knew. "He's stronger now. And
he's going to get stronger yet."

"What will we do?" Broydo asked in a fright, turning in a slow
circle to take in the ghost village.

"Take as many amulets as we can carry," Ric answered. "The
villagers have no use for them now, and we will need them to
book passage on an ether ship when we get to Hellsgate."

"We're going down the Wall of the World without Asofel?"
Broydo shook his head fretfully. "How will we drive out the
shadow thing when we find it?"

"It is a *him*, a magus from the Dark Shore." Old Ric spoke as
he entered the healer's hut and began collecting the necklaces

of theriacal opals and headbands set with rat-star gems. "I saw him first in the torn veils of flames during my fire meditations on Nemora. And I sense him now by the power that the Lady of the Garden has granted me in this dream of hers. I don't know what we'll do when we confront him. We'll just have to do what we can."

Grumbling grouchily, the gnome packed the amulets in a twine sack and returned to the forest to continue their trek. Three more days they journeyed before the marshy woods thinned to the rocky moraine that led to the Wall of the World.

Long before the immense precipice came into view among the boulder-strewn steppes, the wind surging out of the abyss became audible, moaning like surf. Broydo removed the amulets from the twine sack and draped himself with their Charm. The calm they inspired in him quelled his fright when they did behold the jagged cliffs that curved along the rim of World's End for as far as they could see.

The descent was easier than they had feared. Pilgrim trails switchbacked down the steep rock face and steps had been carved by these holy wanderers at the most dangerous bends. Soon, they were among the clouds and could see nothing. There, Broydo took the lead, using the rat-star headbands to see through the dense fog.

Below the clouds, they emerged on a windy crag set with religious banners and whirling pinwheels. Several worshippers in elaborate tinsel windings offered ashen libations to their gods. Old Ric noted the fear in their eyes when they saw his wound, and he covered the arrow that pierced him with sheet moss that he had used as a blanket in the marsh. After that, the pilgrims ignored the ælf and gnome as they passed their shrines of eroded rocks and snapping flags.

Hellsgate ranged below—a motley landscape of sulfur sands, red and green oxides, and black swirls of soot. Volcanic mountains cluttered the horizon. Their cinder towers gusted with blue, almost invisible, flames.

"Thank the gods we don't have to cross that burning land," Broydo sang with relief. "There dwell giants. It's good indeed that we have not far to travel." He motioned down the gravel trail toward a city of scorched, squat buildings. This was a religious destination, the terminal of the Bright Shore. From here, pilgrims began their hike to World's End, to worship their gods in the wilds above, under the direct glare of the Abiding Star.

This pilgrimage had been far more popular in pretalismanic times, and the settlement of charred temples and dingy houses appeared dilapidated. Beggars roamed the broad streets, and the few pilgrims in their brilliant tinsel wrappings seemed garish among the filthy, rag-draped mendicants.

The sky harbor, too, appeared run-down. Many of the glass windows that had fronted the passenger station had been boarded over, and the interior stank of stale smoke from burnt offerings that smoldered in numerous alcove shrines. Broydo gawked about at the dimly lit statuary of deities from every faith—animal gods, mortal divinities, abstract symbols—and Ric bartered their amulets for passage to Irth.

Unlike the ticket agent, most of the passengers who milled about the station were not human. A burly crew of ogres, their tiny faces stained black, were on their way home to Sharna-Bambara after completing a work tour as miners on Hellsgate. Most of the pilgrims returning to Irth were beastfolk—fox-furred people—and none paid any heed to the gnome and the ælf.

The ether ship looked old where it squatted like a giant platinum toad on the cracked tarmac of the landing field. Its gray hull was dented and blotched with lime streaks where stellar debris had struck it in flight. The glass nacelles were scratched and clouded. And the sphinx's face pressed into the prow had a spalled nose and chipped wings. But the crew were friendly and made no objection to Broydo carrying the serpent sword on board so long as he kept it secured in a compartment of his berth.

Old Ric pressed his scrawny body as deep between the crimson squabs of his seat as the lodged arrow would allow. After the juddering ascent ended and the stained surface of Hellsgate diminished to an ugly sore in the black of space, he allowed himself a deep breath of relief. "We have escaped the dwarves."

Broydo made no response. He was enthralled by the view of space through the transparent nacelle of their berth. Stars pulsed from within cocoons of planet dust, and comets trailed long scarves of cold fire. He had never seen such a celestial panorama, and for most of their days-long flight he sat in the window bays watching planetoids and suns drift past, all aglow inside their firework-flowers of burning gas.

Late in the flight, as Irth's blue orb gradually expanded among the star webs, Old Ric gripped Broydo's shoulder and forcibly pulled him away from the viewport where he watched their approach. "Wau!" Broydo wailed in protest at the gnome's gruff hold on him. But his cry choked in his throat when he saw what the gnome was pointing to.

The ogres drinking mead in the sunken pit of the lounge had no shadows. They had not yet noticed and carried on boisterously with their celebration.

"He's on board!" Broydo realized, his heart slamming in him.

"We must alert the crew," Old Ric declared, and hurried out of the recreation suite and along the companionway that led forward.

"But how?" Broydo asked as he followed. "How could Asofel have gotten on board?"

"He's a being of light," the gnome replied. "What can't he do—if he's strong enough?"

The front of the ship was empty. The berths whose sliding doors stood ajar were unoccupied. Broydo yelped at the sight of empty green garments strewn along the companionway—the collapsed uniforms of the ship's stewards.

Ric pounded on the portal to the ship's bridge, and the hatchway budged open. Inside, the control panels still glimmered beneath a wraparound viewport. The cockpit indeed appeared inhabited, but in the pilot's and navigator's seats there were only the crumpled uniforms of the vanished officers.

"No one's flying the ship!" Broydo cried, looking about in a panic.

From behind the open hatch, they sensed movement. Trepidatiously, they entered, suspecting the worst.

"I am flying the ship," they heard a deep voice announce. It was Asofel, as they had feared. He emerged wearing a pilot's tunic and square-toed boots of gray leather, and his angular face shone like a lantern.

Old Ric held a bony hand to his face to cut the glare. "Asofel! What have you done?"

"I have taken the light of all on board save the two of you." His dark eyes appeared long and wicked with glee. "I have taken the light of the dream for myself. I am not yet strong enough to depart the dream, and so I remain in this physical form for now."

"Why have you not eaten us?" Broydo moaned.

"I need Old Ric to find the shadow thing," Asofel replied. "And I spare you because you are his friend. You see, I am not cruel, though you believe I am."

"Cruel?" Broydo squeaked from behind Old Ric, squinting with pain at the glowing figure. "We did not say you were cruel, though it certainly appears that you are."

"I must partake of the light of the dream to restore my strength," Asofel said simply as he turned to look out the wide viewport. "I will need all my strength to meet what awaits us there—on Irth."

Neither ælf nor gnome moved. The Radiant One had a smell of morning that eased their fears to hapless resignation, and they stood motionless, watching him bend over the controls and guide them to their shared fate.

WRAITH

REECE LAY ASLEEP IN HIS HAMMOCK, DAPPLED DAYLIGHT ON HIS SLACK face. The flowers that dangled from the trellis above him began to fret in a sudden breeze. His name echoed from down a long corridor. The afternoon light pierced a slim figure, who paused for a moment, then stepped through the arbor gate of the patio. The specter watched him with fixed stars in her dark eyes, her sable tresses falling along a narrow body the color of air.

With a groaned curse, Reece broke the dream and thrashed awake, unwilling to face this phantom again. He rolled out of the hammock, his brown trousers and white, collarless shirt bunched with sleep wrinkles.

He did not notice immediately that Lara stood at the edge of the patio with her hood drawn back and her proud face unmarred. Afternoon light slipped through her feral features and revealed the shrubberies behind.

When Reece did catch sight of her finally, he staggered two steps toward her, then stopped. Amazement stole his voice for a moment, and he wondered if she were a true apparition or some illusion perpetrated by his exhausted magic and weary brain.

The phantom approached, countenance gleaming with withheld tears of joy. "I embrace you in my soul, young master, for I cannot with my arms."

"Lara—is it truly you?" He held out his hand and touched emptiness. "Am I still dreaming? You seem so real! It can't be you. I held your soul in my hands—in the river—after we found your body—"

"You drowned me," she remembered with a shining smile. "But indeed, I return . . ."

Reece's face clouded with grief, and his searching eyes played over her happy features, finding again the traces memory had lost. "You were so horribly deformed by the murder . . ."

"Shh, be calm. For assuredly, I don't blame you, Reece." She extended both hands comfortingly, and they disappeared inside him. "You did what was best for me at the moment. Then Caval retrieved me. He brought me into the radiance of the Abiding Star."

"Yes," Reece acknowledged, staring into the widening dark of her expanding pupils. "An act that changed me forever. I climbed to Irth to find you. You were the beginning of my new life, Lara."

Her flat face held sorrow. "And now I fear I am herald of the end." She withdrew her hands and crossed her arms forbiddingly. "Master, I've come to warn you—"

"Of the Shadow Eater." He met the surprise in her gaze with a nod. "Yes, I know. You've reached me in my dreams already. But I never guessed that you would actually come for me." He beckoned her closer. "Let me look at you. You're still as beautiful as when you danced for us among the trees. The Abiding Star has healed you."

"Yes." She lifted her chin for him to behold the clean line of her jaw. "I am healed within the wholeness of the Abiding Star. But I confess, young master, out here, there is pain. The farther I go from the Beginning, the more I suffer. Soon I will go back, must go back. But something stays me—it is terrible what is going to happen. I must warn you."

Reece sat on the patio bench while the ghost related to him all that had happened to her since the settlers of the Snow Range hacked her soul free of her body. He wept to hear of the rapture she had abandoned in the Abiding Star and the pain she endured

coming down through the cold layers of ether in the Upper Air
to find him.

"Let me see your wounds," he asked.

She declined by lifting her hood. "My wounds are the amulets
given me by my enemies. I show them only to those I wish to
keep at a distance. Not you, young master."

"Then show me the crystal prism you won from the dwarves,"
he requested, and she obediently put in his hand the gem in
whose cloudy core a piece of noon glowed. Winds of light turned
within the clear stone, small as the galaxies strewn across the
Dark Shore. Staring into those distances, he heard the bloody
cries of the damned echoing outward to the cold worlds. These
were the souls that the Necklace had captured. Their compacted
lives powered the crystal prism—lives shrunk to screams.

"It is an evil thing," Lara agreed. "But it was the only way I
could come down from the Abiding Star."

Reece wished he could crush the prism and free the souls, let
them skitter like water drops in a hot pan, flashing to nothing
with one last hysterical scream. But he stopped himself. This
was his only connection to Lara, the one he had loved as his
own child.

"It is an evil thing," the young witch repeated softly.

Reece regarded her sadly. The Abiding Star had healed the
trauma of her murder but not the fact of it. She was but a
phantom, a changeless image of what had once lived—and tortured souls gave her form.

"It was Duppy Hob who made it," she continued. "Duppy Hob
pulled fiends and shaitans out of the ethers of the Upper Air to
do his bidding on World's End." She pressed so close to him, he
could see through the peepholes of her eyes into the black crypt
of her head. Small lights wormed there: reflections from the prism
in his hand, the ravenous devils that wove the shape of his beloved Lara.

"If what I've done offends you, young master, crush this evil
thing with your magic." She bowed her head contritely. "Only
heed what I have told you and flee the Shadow Eater. His arrival
here promises evil, that much I am sure of."

Reece bowed down to look into her face. "I'm not offended.
You have come to me out of love—the same love that made me
climb up to find you." He looked with disdain at the dazzling

crystal. "But clearly we must free you from this wicked thing and get you back to the Abiding Star."

"No." She moved as if to seize him, and the hood fell back and revealed her worried aspect. "The Shadow Eater descends from there. No, you must escape in another direction."

"But to where?" Reece set his jaw and decided, "I will confront him."

"No—Caval has warned us." Lara looked frantic. "I saw it in the light of the Beginning. Something disastrous is stalking you. Caval sent me to warn you."

"Caval is dead," he said distractedly, peering into the diamond distances. "We can't trust what his wraith calls out from the Dark Shore. The old master is gone."

"Am I not also?" she reminded him, and moved to catch his eye. "Yet even in this bodiless state, my love for you remains."

Reece returned the prism to the ghost. For a moment, as the physical object passed from him to her, a tangible but fleeting vibration connected them, like a ripple of electric current. He met her beseeching look and held it. "I came to this world to find you, Lara. And now that I have found you, I'll not leave you to suffer anymore. I swear, I will get you back to the Abiding Star."

"What of the Shadow Eater?"

"I don't fear the Shadow Eater . . ."

"Who is the Shadow Eater?" Jyoti interjected unexpectedly and stepped onto the patio. "I heard you talking." She strode to Reece's side, removing her flight helmet and shaking loose her blond-streaked hair. "I thought someone was here with you."

Reece passed a baffled looked between Lara's ghost and Jyoti. "There is, and I'm speaking with her."

"Who?" Jyoti gave Reece an anxious look, then searched around the light-stippled patio and saw no one else.

"She stands right here beside me," Reece insisted, and swung his hand through the wraith. "Do you not see her? She's ghostly pale, I'll admit, but as clearly defined as you and I."

Jyoti fingered the niello eye charms on the shoulders of her amulet-vest. "Reece, there's no one anywhere nearby in my eye charms. Not even ghosts." Her brow tensed with concern. "You've just woken up. You must have been dreaming."

"I'm not dreaming now. She's right here." He faced Lara. "Tell her."

Lara smiled sadly. "Only you can see me, young master. I am a wraith from the Dark Shore. This far from the Abiding Star, only those from our world can see me unless I show myself."

"She says you can't see her," Reece muttered unhappily.

"Can't see *who?*" Jyoti asked impatiently

Reece met the margravine's skeptical expression with a hard line between his eyes. "It's Lara—the young witch Caval and I reared to serve us on the Dark Shore."

Jyoti studied the magus's face deeply before answering, "Yes, you've told me about Lara before." She gently turned him back toward the hammock. "Come, lie down, and we'll talk about her."

"She's right here. We can talk with her."

"Reece, if she were here, I'd see her in my eye charms." She pulled the hammock open. "Lie down. You're exhausted, and you've been dreaming."

"I'm not dreaming now, Jyo. She's right here, even if you can't see her. She says she's too far from the Abiding Star for you to see her."

"And yet, you can? Please, lie down."

He twisted free of her grip. "I don't want to lie down." He looked to Lara. "Let her see the crystal prism."

"Young master, I dare not." Lara spoke with alarm. "You could hold it for you are of the Dark Shore. But I dare not expose it to her. If I lose it, I will fall into the Gulf."

"Let me hold it and show her," he said but saw her helpless expression and relented. He faced Jyoti with a frown. "There's no use. I think you'd best leave me alone with her for now."

"Alone?" Jyoti gave him a puzzled smile. "I just canceled two neighborhood conferences to be with you. Don't send me away."

Reece rubbed the sudden tension from his forehead, wondering if he was hallucinating. He peeked sidelong at the phantom, and she was still there, watching him with worry. "I'm sorry, Jyo. You're just going to have to believe me. Lara is here."

Jyoti agreed with a conciliatory nod and motioned to the elegant wooden chairs stained by daylight. "Sit down with me and tell me about her."

They sat, and Lara drifted bodiless through a rhomboid of

daylight to the darker, herringbone shadows under the arbor and stood there watching.

"I'm taking her back to the Abiding Star," Reece announced firmly.

Jyoti blinked with surprise. "You're leaving Irth?"

"To bring her back to where she belongs," he answered, and stared at the ghost even as she began to protest. "She came here to warn me."

"You must flee, young master." Lara beckoned to him beseechingly. "Please, heed me. I have seen the Shadow Eater, and he cannot be faced."

"Warn you about what, Reece?" Jyoti searched the dark corner of the dazzled patio where he focused so ardently, and still she saw no one.

"Caval has called her out of the Abiding Star," he said, "because a radiant being is stalking me. She calls it the Shadow Eater."

"You told me about troubling dreams you've had about her," Jyoti reminded him. "Is it possible that your brain is playing tricks on you? You've worked so hard these many days. Perhaps you have worked too hard."

Reece's lips paled as they tightened over his teeth, holding back a cry of frustration.

Jyoti wanted to touch him with Charm and gentle his overwrought mind, and she took his hand in her strong grip. "Just think this through with me, Reece. Caval is dead. He was ripped apart by cacodemons, and his soul was swept away into the Gulf. Even he, master wizard that he was, cannot call across such an abyss."

Briefly, Reece entertained the thought that she was right, that he was addled. His magic had been depleted, and he felt hollow within. And yet, there was Lara, watching him with her bright stare.

"The Dark Lord and all his cacodemons are gone," Jyoti continued, her voice pitched to comfort him. "You slew them all when you killed the Dark Lord. We have no more enemies among the worlds, Reece."

"Tell her that the Shadow Eater comes from World's End," Lara spoke.

"Do you know of World's End?" Reece asked, and studied her face for reaction.

"It is the world closest to the Abiding Star," she answered matter-of-factly. "It is a wilderness fraught with dangerous creatures—squid monkeys, bull lizards, more dangers than any other world. No one lives there. Only ælves. Sometimes pilgrims go there for religious rites."

"Lara says that the Shadow Eater comes from there," Reece reported.

"Ask her who sent this Shadow Eater," Jyoti suggested.

"Even in the Abiding Star, I did not know," Lara admitted to Reece. "I know less now. The farther I descend from that radiance, the less I remember. Memory is dimmed. Only pain is sharp and clear out here."

"Pain?" Reece stood. "You're a wraith."

"I suffer even so." She stepped back, almost vanishing in the darkness. "But that's not important, young master. I *am* dead. You yet live, and I have come to help you. Listen to me. I don't know who sent the Shadow Eater. There are two others, as well. A gnome and an ælf . . ."

Jyoti came up behind Reece and took his arm. "If only you will rest, your magic will return."

Reece ignored her and asked the ghost, "Where are this Shadow Eater and the others?"

"I have been watching them through the crystal prism," Lara replied. "They are on an ether ship out of Hellsgate bound for a city carved out of giant sea cliffs."

"Saxar!" Reece recognized at once. He told Jyoti what the ghost had said.

"And she sees this in her crystal?" Jyoti inquired dubiously.

"It is a crystal taken off the Necklace of Souls," Reece remembered from Lara's story.

"Dwarvish magic—" Jyoti mumbled, surprised to hear mention of that ancient device. "It's the charmwork of a devil worshipper."

"Duppy Hob—yes." The ghost nodded. "She knows this history."

"Duppy Hob?" Reece squinted inquiringly at Jyoti. "You know of him?"

"Every schoolchild knows," Jyoti answered. "Duppy Hob was thrown into the Gulf by the dwarves he fashioned from dragon-maggots. He used them as slaves to make demon harnesses, devil cages, and soul-catchers—like the Necklace of Souls." She tilted her head inquisitively. "You never heard that before?"

"No," he answered earnestly. "Lara just told me."

A cold finger traced a line down Jyoti's spine. "Maybe you heard and forgot—and your fatigued mind has called it forth."

"Jyo—Lara is right here, I tell you." He took Jyoti's shoulders and turned her to face a shadowy corner of the patio marbled with daylight. "Everything I've told you is true. It's not a delusion."

Jyoti backed away and sat down. "Tell me everything she told you."

Reece complied, pacing before her, shooting glances to the ghost for confirmation. When he was done, he sat and stared hard at the margravine. "Do you believe me now?"

"I believe we have to be cautious about what we cannot see," Jyoti replied. "You've pushed yourself hard, Reece. I think you should rest a few days and assess all this at a later time, when your magic is fully restored."

"There is no time!" Lara cried.

"The Shadow Eater will arrive soon in Saxar," Reece said. "Lara does not want me to wait."

Jyoti reached over and took both of Reece's hands. "Lara may well be here," she conceded. "Yet even if she is, can she be trusted?"

"I know her," Reece strongly insisted. "I've known her since she was a child."

"You knew her when she was alive." Jyoti squeezed his hands. "She's a wraith now. She can't even remember what she knew in the Abiding Star. She could be wrong."

"Wrong or not, Jyoti, this is Lara, the soul Caval and I shaped on the Dark Shore. I cannot ignore her. I am going to return her to the Abiding Star."

"And the Shadow Eater?" Jyoti pressed. "What are we to make of that?"

Reece hung his head. "I don't know."

"I think we must learn more about this party from World's End," Jyoti declared. She released his hands and sat taller. "I'm a trained diplomat. I'll go to Saxar and represent you."

"I can't let you." Reece cocked a worried eyebrow. "I told you what Lara said about this entity and what it did to the demon at World's End. It's too dangerous."

"I'm not going to attack him, Reece." She spoke confidently. "I'll contact this Asofel and the others with him—the gnome and the ælf—and find out who has sent them and why. Meanwhile, you should rest. I'll report back to you by aviso, and you'll know in a few days."

"We cannot stay here." Lara stepped out of the shadows, transparent to the shrubs behind her. "We must get away as quickly as we can. We must flee this place, for they know you are here, and they will come."

Reece stared through the ghost and out the arbor gate across the leagues of afternoon that illuminated the Kazu sand streams. "You have work to do here, Jyo. And this being is dangerous. It eats lives." Reece grabbed the back of his neck and wrestled with a decision. "Lara has seen it coming after me. Perhaps it's best that I confront it directly."

"We don't know enough yet," Jyoti countered. "How real is this threat? Let me find out. I owe you, Reece."

"I don't want to be repaid with your life, Jyo." He looked to Lara. "Will Asofel let her approach?"

"I think so." Lara's pale eyes shifted, trying to see through her confusing pain to her remembrance of World's End. "The gnome and the ælf have courage and compassion. I saw that myself. With companions such as those, does this Shadow Eater not merit some respect? Trust her to go to him, and let us get away from this place."

Jyoti rose to her feet and spoke with determination. "I have my city to rebuild. And my young brother still needs me. I'm not going to die. But I will find out why you are stalked."

Reece stood and bowed his head sadly. "I can't wait here for you."

"You're determined to return her to the Abiding Star, aren't you?"

"I must."

Jyoti frowned. "But how will we stay in touch? How will I find you?"

"Between your Charm and my magic, we will not lose each other." He took her shoulders and pulled her to him. "I will never lose you, I promise."

Jyoti hugged him tighter against herself. "We have so much to share, Reece. I couldn't bear to be without you."

"I'm not so easy to misplace. I got here from the Dark Shore, remember?" He stepped back. "Go," he agreed. "But don't do anything daring."

She smiled, so full of life, vibrancy, and daring that his heart hurt.

He did not want to be apart from her, but Lara needed him. For her alone, for the history they shared and the love that had grown between them, he would use everything his magic offered, even his friends and his lover. "Get in touch with my old partner, Dogbrick," he instructed, taking her toughened hand between his soft palms. "He's established in Saxar now. He'll help you. But remember, don't endanger yourself or him."

"Where will you go?" she asked. "How will you find your way to the Abiding Star?"

"The Spiderlands. There are caverns there that connect by charmways with all the dominions—and the other worlds." He released Jyoti's hand and took his place beside the phantom. "Lara and I will find our way back to the Abiding Star—and as soon as I can, I will return for you."

Down in Saxar

DIG DOG LTD. OCCUPIED THE PENTHOUSE SUITE OF A GLASS TOWER set into the rock face overlooking Cold Niobe Plaza. Dogbrick had selected this site in the affluent center of Saxar's commercial district because from here he could see down Everyland Street to the impoverished industrial warrens where he had grown up. This was his thirty-sixth day in his new offices, and he had not yet weaned himself from standing at the wide sheet-glass windows and gazing down into his past, ruminating philosophically about the trajectory of his fate and the demise of so many others during the brief, bloody reign of the Dark Lord.

Occasionally he turned about to overlook the long suite of comfortable, stylish furniture, where a score of operators strolled among hanging plants or sat on plump sofas sipping tea while talking on their headpiece avisos, coordinating trade orders and distribution routes for many of the largest factories in Saxar. One hundred and sixty-seven days ago, he had been a thief preying on those very factories. Now, they were his clients.

Dogbrick's friendship with the magus, Reece, slayer of the Dark Lord, had won him numerous lucrative contracts, and Dig

Dog Ltd. proved a prosperous enterprise. Yet rarely was the large, beastmarked man unaware of the many who had died during those evil times that had changed his fortune.

Jyoti found him with his back to the busy suite, dressed in the elaborate amulet-shawl of a successful businessman. At first he did not notice her. He was staring morosely at the factories that crowded the sea cliffs and daily released a pall of noxious smog over the impoverished leeward districts, where he had once lived or, more accurately, survived.

"Your honest life has made you inattentive, Dog," Jyoti greeted warmly.

Dogbrick swung his long head toward her, and his smile showed fangs. "Margravine—I didn't expect to see you until the trade conference in Moödrun next season . . ." He read the concern in her face and broke off.

"Reece needs your help," she began.

His big hand took her by the elbow and led her to a private office festooned with gem-strings of muting amulets and big rope knots connecting copper-plated talismans of silence. They sat facing each other on a circular bench at the center of the carpeted room, and she told him about Lara's wraith and the coming of the Shadow Eater.

"Assuming that Reece has not snapped and is telling the truth, when do these emissaries from World's End arrive?" he asked with a hint of malice in his gaze, piqued at the very thought of a threat to his old partner in crime.

"The ether ship docks at the sky bund later this morning." Jyoti reached over and placed a caring hand on his shaggy arm. "I have come to believe that we must trust Reece, for his sake. That being the case, it may be very dangerous. I've brought a security squad with me, but we have to avoid using firecharms if we can. Reece says the ghost has informed him that this entity can erase beings. If you'd rather not be there, I understand."

Dogbrick's amber eyes did not blink. "What can I do to help?"

She smiled and thanked him with a gentle squeeze of his thick arm. "You know Saxar far better than I. I'd be glad to have you nearby when my squad and I board the *Star of Fortune*."

Dogbrick agreed readily, and, after turning over the day's business to the office manager, they departed Dig Dog at once for the sky bund. In the air van that Jyoti had flown to Saxar from

Arawar Odawl, Dogbrick leaned over, assumed a confidential air, and asked, "Now you must let me in on everything—is she beautiful? That is, now that you've seen Lara, does it makes sense that Reece crossed over from the Dark Shore for her?"

"First of all, I've not seen her myself. But if you're asking if I'm jealous, I'm not." Jyoti gave him a stiff look across her shoulder as she pulled the air van off the roof of Dig Dog Ltd.'s glass tower.

She banked so sharply, Dogbrick's furry face pressed against the pod window, and he saw the near-vertical city tilt crazily below him. "I believe you," he grunted. "I was just curious . . ."

"What's that over there, Dog—that smoke?" Jyoti leveled the van into a slow ascent above the steep avenues and pointed to a flare of green fire billowing orange smoke. It gusted from a warehousing lot where fumes from smelters and refineries already clouded the air. "That's a charmfire!"

Dogbrick had not often seen charmfire, the green flames that erupted when concentrated Charm exploded, and he knew it meant danger of an even greater explosion among those sheds and hangars where the factories stored Charmed and volatile materials. "Get away and find out what happened on the security band."

Jyoti tried to raise a coherent signal on the van's aviso but received only static. "That's a raging charmfire down there. It's interfering with communications." She turned the van toward the column of orange smoke.

"Hey, not that way!" Dogbrick yelped. "That whole lot could go up!"

The van sliced through the factory exhaust, and the control pod's eye charms revealed the streets below. An industrial silo had collapsed into a sinkhole. Out of the hole, a host of squat, white creatures with segmented bodies strapped in amulet harnesses and motley pieces of armor swarmed among the lanes between the warehouses. Security officers fired at them from the rooftops and had slain several, but there were too many of them. The hairless humanoids had overwhelmed most of the factory guards and imploded their firecharms. Green flames licked avidly at the warehouses.

"Great Goddess, what are those things?" Jyoti asked in a voice fractured with fright. Then she remembered what Lara had said about stealing the Necklace of Souls. "Drake's blood! Those are dwarves!"

"Pull away!" Dogbrick ordered frantically, and grabbed the yoke.

The air van dipped, then rose sharply as the beastmarked man grappled for control.

A green flash inked dark shadows in the pod. An instant later, the shock wave struck, and the air van bucketed violently.

Jyoti pulled the van away from a billowing green fire cloud laced with black soot. Gravel flung upward by the explosion twanged loudly against the airframe.

When they crested and Jyoti was able to ease them into a wide circular path, they saw that the warehouses were gone. The whole flank of the cliff where the hangars nestled had collapsed onto the terrace below. Factory sirens wailed, and firefighters and security forces scrambled among the nearby winch lifts, hurrying to bring aid from other levels. A large water-bearing balloon from the seaside swung through the boiling clouds.

"Yes, those *were* dwarves," Dogbrick finally answered her, face pressed to the pod window, looking for the diminutive warriors and finding none in the rubble. "I saw a pickled one once when I was a boy. They're denizens of World's End, you know, where they are . . ."

A rattle from somewhere within the air van's ducts clattered louder and faster and quickly shrilled to a whining shriek.

"Our thrusters have taken in some debris," Jyoti grasped at once as the yoke vibrated in her grasp.

Two rapid explosions from the interior shook the pod to a blur, and Dogbrick wailed.

Jyoti cut the engine, and the vibrations quelled. She eased back on the yoke, bringing the van's nose up. "We're going down, Dog. Curl up and relax. The pod's Charm will cushion the worst of it."

Dogbrick tucked his head between his knees. "Don't drop us in the sea!" he yelped. "I can't swim!"

The van dropped into a sudden sideslip, and the smog tore away, divulging a brief tableau of factory yards with their pitched roofs and chimney stacks tucked compactly into niches of the sea cliffs. Then, the buckled landscape of broken rock and spilled brickwork swung toward them, and they glided through the acrid fumes of the smothering charmfires.

Talking fast, Jyoti relayed an emergency broadcast to the sky bund. Static from the charmfires disrupted her message and sizzled louder as the shattered rocks below swung up toward them.

Impact ripped the air van apart. Panels winged away, and the airframe splintered into toppling rails and a spewing of engine parts. The pod bounced free, and carried its whirling passengers over the fields of shattered rock. It rolled to rest against a cutaway factory of freestanding stairwells, twisted pipes, and an open interior where the forges still steamed and spat flames.

The pod hatched open, and Jyoti helped a dizzy Dogbrick climb out onto the slope of toppled boulders. Above, through shreds of vapors, Saxar's factory tiers loomed; below, curved rooftops stagger-stepped down the cliff face to the thriving dockyards. But on either side, destruction ranged.

Peripheral movement seemed just a blur of dizziness to Dogbrick until Jyoti seized his arm and tugged at him. "Quick, get down!"

Dogbrick ducked with Jyoti behind an upturned slab of masonry and watched as several dwarves strode through the seething fumes. They wielded brutish hatchets and short lances, and their thickly jointed bodies moved with surprising nimbleness though they were encumbered with heavy straps and plates of amulets. Metal helmets like insect mandibles framed featureless, glossy faces of rippling slit mouths and lidless, crimson eyespots.

From her amulet-vest, Jyoti took out her aviso and tried to call for help. Static flared from the communicator, loud interference from the charmfires that still seethed under the buried buildings, and she slapped it shut. "We're on our own, Dog."

To elude the approaching squad, Jyoti and Dogbrick crept backward, past a stone abutment fallen to its side and into the hole its collapse had exposed. At that moment, the damaged engine core of the shattered air van exploded. Though the roar was muted by the weight of heaped boulders, a thunder swelled over the cliffs, distracting the dwarves and turning aside their approach as they moved off to see what the blast portended.

Dogbrick took advantage of their absence to exit the hole and begin to scan for a way out of the fuming pit. But Jyoti called to him softly.

"Dog!" Her whisper carried urgency.

In a single bound, he was back in the hole and beside her. Immediately, he saw why she had summoned him, and he grabbed her shoulders and pulled her back and down behind old plates of upended pavement.

Through a honeycomb lattice of foundation girders and ganglia of jarred-loose cables, they watched ranks of dwarves emerging from inside the cliffs. Their bodies glowed green in the dark, and they stumbled forward, clearly blinded by the light of the outer world.

"They can't see us," Jyoti pointed out, and moved deeper into the shaft, to where it widened and she could stand.

Dogbrick gnashed his teeth at her temerity and followed, hunched over.

A stone's throw away, a steady advance of dwarves gleamed greenly among the cavern's shadows. Jyoti used her eye charms to find her way through the dark. Moving parallel to the advancing dwarves, she advanced farther into the cave. Ahead, a grotto sank among scrollworks of stalagmites, and there the dwarves were stepping out of a crevasse.

"It's a charmway, I think." Jyoti spoke over her shoulder to where Dogbrick crouched at her heels, reading his amulets with eyeballs that seemed to hum in their sockets.

"My—my eye charms say the dwarves are stepping out of nowhere!" Dogbrick stammered.

"It just looks that way." Jyoti drew a strand of conjure-wire from a utility pouch in her vest and began dexterously binding two amulets. "They're crossing from another domain of Charm. If you want to see where they're coming from, patch the niello to a rat-star. Then look."

Through the amplified eye charm she had cobbled, the grotto appeared for what it was, a threshold beyond which a corridor branched into a hive of tunnels. The dwarves shambled along several of those shafts, arriving from farther than the eye charms could probe.

Dogbrick affixed several tiny trapezoidal squares of hex-gems to the modified eye charm and he listened, past the thudding fright of his own heart and Jyoti's running pulse, to the life strength of the dwarves. He heard their slow blood, their turtle plasma winding its loops through thick bodies. He listened closer and discerned the brood talk of the dwarvish nation. It was not unlike the brood talk of his own clan—harmonics of perception and thought. But there was no variance to their talk. Their thoughts seemed frozen, a wall of ice that enclosed an image of gold-clasped gems each as big as a thumb and tufted with rainbows.

"The Necklace of Souls!" Jyoti gasped.

"Hush! Listen!" Dogbrick put a taloned finger to his ear, listening further to something enormous breathing sustenance into them from beyond.

"I hear it!" Jyoti whispered hotly, hugging close to the altered eye charm in Dogbrick's hand. It was an ashen voice, the chanted commands of their creator. "Duppy Hob!"

Somehow broadcast from the Dark Shore, the gray voice of the devil worshipper who had shaped them from maggots directed the dwarves' advance. They moved with the unison of one mind, the will of their exiled master. His magic burned in each of them with a heart pinch of pain that forced them to obey him.

"The lord they deposed has got power over them again," Jyoti mumbled almost in trance cadence. "He's sending them down from World's End. *Why?*"

Dogbrick snapped apart the conjure-wire, and the charmful perception broke. "The devil worshipper must not sense us."

Jyoti clutched at her vest's power wands, releasing more Charm to calm herself in the face of what they had witnessed. "I thought Dubby Hob was a child's fright story."

"They thought the same about cacodemons until not long ago." Dogbrick tapped at the rat-stars on the hatband that glinted under his tawny mane. "Think about it. Perhaps it is not a coincidence that this most evil of sorcerers appears now after the wave of cacodemons."

"We have to get this eye charm out of here and show it to the others." With frantic fingers, Jyoti secured in a hip pocket the niello that had peered across worlds. "The Dark Lord was just a scout!"

Dogbrick drew a blunt-nosed firelock from beneath his shawl and aimed it at the grotto. "Let's close up this rathole."

"Don't!" Jyoti seized his hand. "We could collapse more of the city and . . ."

Her grasp jolted a round from the firelock. The blue bolt

smashed into the fanged ceiling, and chunks of limestone fell like spears and anvils. The dwarves yowled and stampeded each other under the slamming collapse, their flung bodies hurtling across the cavern.

Dogbrick swept Jyoti in his arms and charged with her away from the plummeting rocks and panicked dwarves. He briskly searched with his eye charm the way back along the path they had entered. The blindness of the dwarves had kept them from noticing the wider corridor through which they trickled, but now they fanned out, impelled by the crowd surging from the din in the grotto.

Shrieks of alarm went up as the dwarves spotted the intruders. Hatchets slashed past, and Dogbrick tucked himself around Jyoti and ran close to the shadows. Sparks flew where the hatchet steel cut stone, and an enraged clamor boomed along the corridor, whipping him faster.

Ahead, several dwarves scuttled for the exit. The rumbling cataclysm masked Dogbrick's footfalls, and the dwarves did not sense him until he slammed over them.

In a bound, he lunged out of the hole beside the toppled stone abutment. Three dwarves stood with their backs to him as he released Jyoti and leveled his firelock. One shot leveled all three, and Dogbrick waved Jyoti to run toward the sheared open factory beside them. He jammed the firelock so that it would explode and dropped it into the hole before sprinting away.

The force of the rupturing firecharm set boulders scampering again. Dogbrick snatched Jyoti from behind and swept her out of the way of a tumbling, vat-shaped furnace.

Dwarves shrieked from above, their pale spongoid arms waving their hatchets wrathfully.

Dogbrick immediately wished he had kept his firelock. Then he reminded himself that he was better without it. A stray shot among these charmworks could ignite another firestorm. He looked for an escape route downward. The strewn rock spill crawled with dwarves. "We have to go up," he decided, and drew a thick, short blade from the sheath strapped to his back under his amulet-shawl. "Stay close behind me."

"Just get us out of here, Dog." Jyoti drew her utility knife and slapped his back, signaling him to go. "We have to warn Irth."

Dogbrick clambered up a slope of broken slate to the shelled

facade of a factory shop. Jyoti followed, throwing fitful glances
over her shoulder. The furious dwarves scrambled after them
across the heaped rocks, their shrill cries slicing loudly as the
sirens.

Up a ramp way to a lading yard, Dogbrick and Jyoti ran hard,
relying on their amulets to give them strength. The dwarves, too,
seemed to partake of Charmed stamina, nimbly ascending the
incline of jagged slate and whirling their hatchets above their
heads as they closed in.

Dogbrick faced Jyoti with a harsh stare. "Hold on to me,
margravine, and don't let go."

She threw her arms around his thick shoulders, and he grabbed
a nearby pulley rope with one hand and with the other used his
knife to cut it from its anchor. The cargo crate it was fastened
to hurtled downward, and Dogbrick and Jyoti flew upward. The
concrete of the pulley path blurred past, and the rush of their
ascent shoved their viscera against their ribs.

At the top, they swung onto the scaffold landing as the crate
smashed below, crushing dwarves. Dogbrick searched in vain
among the loading bays for workers or security officers. The
wailing sirens had driven everyone from the area. Below, dwarves
churned up the rungs of the pulley path's ladder. Any hope of
escape lay above.

Dogbrick climbed narrow steps behind the wooden piers of
the lading docks, and Jyoti hurried after him to the stile-lanes
that mounted the stone fences between factory levels. She
climbed the stairs bent over, using both hands and feet, her eyes
fixed on the oil-stained stone, not daring to look behind.

Along a stone ribbon-walk above the turbid black water of a
canal, they fled. The piercing cries of the dwarves dimmed, and
escape beneath the pocked brickwork of imposing walls seemed
suddenly plausible. Overhead, through shreds in the dense factory smoke, large, colorful balloons sailed, carrying to the smoldering rubble gondolas filled with water.

From the canal's towpath just below them, a hatchet blade
swung into view, splitting the pavement before them. A shrieking
dwarf pulled itself onto the ribbon-walk.

Dogbrick did not break his stride. His knife spun from his
hand and cleaved the dwarf's head between the metallic mandibles of its helmet. Deftly, he retrieved his weapon and, with a

thwack of his powerful arm, severed the blunt head of the dwarf. Howling triumphantly, he hoisted the helmeted trophy to the cloudy sky.

Jyoti grabbed his arm. "Dog, stop it!" She put her hands on his amulet-shawl and activated another power wand.

The surge of Charm calmed Dogbrick's frenzy, and his howl curved to silence. "My apologies, margravine."

"Don't apologize." She glanced up anxiously at the mazy heights of trestles, winches, buttresses, duct pipes, and cables, looking for dwarves. "Just lead us out of here—quickly!"

Dogbrick tossed the severed head into the canal and kicked the rotund corpse after it. The black murk received the body and left no trace on its oily surface.

"Well, margravine, I believe Reece's premonition was onto something," Dogbrick mused as he watched the corpse disappear.

Jyoti did not venture an answer, only pulled at him to hurry.

Dogbrick relented and guided her on a weaving route among old brick lanes between warehouses. Presently, they climbed moss-grown stairs of cobbles to a trolley station on a day-bright terrace just above the smoky industrial congestion of the city. This was Hiphigh Street, a small avenue of fishmonger stalls and vegetable stands, where crowds had gathered to gawk down at the jammed factory yards below and the steaming brash that had buried several warehouses.

Jyoti snapped open her aviso and contacted the sky bund atop the cliff city. A channel clicked open, and silence seeped through. Then, a frightened voice chattered, "Margravine! the *Star of Fortune* has docked. We've been trying to reach you."

She recognized the voice of the squad leader she assigned to oversee the arrival of the ether ship bearing the party from World's End. "Have you boarded her?"

"Yes—yes, we boarded," the frantic voice replied. "But *no one* is aboard! No one!"

"No one?" Jyoti turned a worried glower on Dogbrick. "How can that be? Who piloted the vessel? Who brought her in?"

"Something terrible is happening, my lady!" A sob choked the voice. "The whole squad—all of us! We—we don't seem to have shadows!"

GHOST SHIP

ASOFEL STRODE DOWN THE GANGWAY OF THE ETHER SHIP CLOTHED in feathers of light. His gauzy hair the color of fire snapped sparks into the stiff wind blowing through the pier buttresses and girders of the sky bund. He stood on the staging where the Charmed bollards had secured the large, gray, toadlike body of the ether ship. From here, he could see all of Saxar plummeting below in a wide curve of black and riven sea cliffs.

Old Ric and Broydo timidly emerged from the ship, afraid for what they would behold. And, indeed, there was no one visible anywhere on the multiple platforms of cable-suspended docking bays. A black dirigible floated motionless in its berth, and no sign of crew or passengers was visible. Even the stevedores who usually bustled among the tiered stagings were gone, mounds of crates and barrels left unattended.

"He ate them all!" Broydo whispered sharply to the gnome.

"Not all, ælf." Asofel pointed a shining arm past the crisscross struts of scaffolding to the cliff city. Among the scorched buildings and oxide-seared streets of the factory town, motes of people milled visibly. "I am not the monster you pretend me to be."

"Then you have restored your power?" Old Ric asked. "You'll need no more lives?"

Asofel ignored the question. Instead, his ignited eyes scanned the industrial ranges and fixed upon a district where a fleece of chimney exhaust obscured many of the slopes. "The dwarves are here."

"What?" Broydo croaked and nearly dropped the serpent sword he carried in both hands. "That cannot be. We climbed down the Wall of the World far ahead of them. And it's daytime now. How can they be about?"

"We are far from the Abiding Star, ælf," Asofel explained without budging his stare from the cliff city. "At this level, the dwarves can move actively by day and night."

"Oh by the gods!" the ælf wailed. "All is doomed! They will be everywhere, all the time!"

Asofel still wore a pilot's brown leather tunic and gray boots, though with his new strength he bulged the seams. Rays of silver light leaked through gaps in the garment. "The dwarves have found their own way through the dream."

"This may be a dream to you," Old Ric said, "but I beg you to remember, this is our reality. We must strive to proceed from here without taking any more lives."

The Radiant One turned from his scrutiny of Saxar, his angular face blue as ash. "Where is this shadow thing?"

"He is with the witch." Old Ric lifted the Necklace of Souls. "I can see her in here, because she carries a crystal prism from this soul-catcher. She has found her way to the magus we are seeking."

"And where in this world is that, gnome?" Asofel trawled a wide review of the horizon, from the steel blue horizon of the sea, across the charred vertical labyrinth of the city, to the ghostly salt hills and hardpan waste of Sky Edge, the margin of a dread wasteland called the Qaf. "How much farther must we travel to fulfill our mission?"

"You sense dwarves but not the magus of our quest?" Old Ric asked coolly. "But, of course. The dwarves are creatures from World's End, shaped from the same energy of the Abiding Star that has made you. But the magus—the shadow thing—he is a creature of darkness, risen from the abyss. You have no sense of him at all, have you?"

"None," Asofel readily conceded. "Now where is he? Let us swiftly conclude our work."

Old Ric walked down the gangway and stood in the hot aura of the Radiant One. "I won't tell you."

Asofel's ashen face darkened. "What are you saying, gnome?"

"I am saying that I will not be complicit with any more murders." Old Ric had abandoned his leaf-and-vine cap in the ship, and his bald head with its side tufts of grizzled gray hair nodded sternly. "If you want my help, Radiant One, you will take no more light from this dream."

The stars of Asofel's eyes sharpened hotly. "You would sacrifice all the worlds of this dream for a few lives?"

"Few?" Old Ric scowled angrily. "What manner of being are you, Asofel? You have slain whole clans—children included. You have stolen many lives, and I can have no part of that. Not anymore. It sickens me."

"Then you are a fool, and these worlds are doomed," Asofel declared. "My strength is only a fraction of my former vigor. Do you not remember how radiant I once was?"

"How much more strength do you need?" The gnome stabbed a gnarled finger into the Radiant One's torso, which felt like lava rock still cooling. "You have substance. You seem not weak anymore."

Asofel's petal lips tightened before he said, "I need my strength back. I *want* my strength back."

"And I am sure you shall have it—when you report our success to your mistress." Old Ric lifted his chin strongly. "Until then, we shall make do with what strength you have. Do you understand?"

Broydo edged backward, ready to dive into the ether ship to escape the wrath of the Radiant One.

But before he could move, Asofel spoke, "You would risk everything for your vanity?"

"Vanity?" The eldern gnome retreated a pace. "Compassion is not vanity."

"Compassion for whom?" The Radiant One swept a luminous arm across the vista of the fuming city. "Not for this world and all the others that will vanish entirely if we fail. No. Your so-called compassion is for the few who have given their lives for our noble cause—just as you have. It is your vanity as a small being to care for the few that you see at the expense of the multitudes you do not."

"I consented to this quest," Old Ric swiftly replied. "My doom followed upon my choice. Yet what choice had the innocents that you devoured?"

"I do not understand your gnomish logic." Asofel lifted his radiant stare to Broydo. "Ælf, what do you say to this vanity of the gnome?"

"I?" Broydo's serpent sword quavered in one hand as his other splayed over his chest. "What do I know of worlds and the Mistress of Worlds? I've never seen her. I don't know . . ."

"Broydo!" Old Ric shouted irately. "Ælf clans were destroyed. You saw that with your own eyes. Speak, counselor. Speak for the dead of your own kith."

Broydo braced himself against the jamb of the ship's portal. "Radiant One," he began reluctantly, "the eldern gnome speaks for me. There should be no more killing."

Asofel crossed his arms. "So be it then. I am strong enough now to accompany you wherever we must go. But do not think I can save you or even myself should the dwarves that are pursuing find us before we locate the shadow thing."

"Then we had better hurry away from here," Old Ric said with a satisfied jut of his jaw. "The magus is with the witch Lara far south of here."

"How far?" Asofel peered south along the winding, misty coastline.

"Far." The eldern gnome closed his wrinkled eyelids. "The sense of the magus that our lady has instilled in me is stronger than ever, yet still dim. He is many, many leagues from here, in another dominion of Irth. Also, I sense fear in him, though I know not why he should fear us. And yet, the prisms indicate so."

"If the witch is with him," Asofel noted, "then he is fully aware that we are coming. What evil person must he be that the author of worlds has sent us to retrieve him. It is for us to fear him, not the other way around."

"There is nowhere he can go that I cannot find him," Old Ric asserted. "But we must hurry."

"How will we travel so far?" Broydo asked, stepping down the gangway.

"The light of the dream that I have made my own," Asofel

said, "informs me of all that the light knew. I have the expertise
of the pilots and crews who gave of themselves for our cause. We
shall use that knowledge to fly swiftly south. There are airfoils on
another level."

A shout from an adjoining catwalk turned their heads. A large,
golden-furred beastman in a shawl dense with amulets came
charging toward them, followed by a brindle-haired woman sleek
and light-footed as a cat.

Asofel's starry eyes narrowed.

"No!" Old Ric commanded. "You have given your word. Break
it, and you betray our lady."

The Radiant One glared with frustration at Old Ric.

The gnome did not flinch. "Which way to the airfoils?"

Asofel pointed to a metal stairway that climbed a support
pylon to the top of the sky bund. He led the way, his blurred
speed streaking the air with silver light. Old Ric and Broydo
scurried to keep up. The Radiant One vanished up the stairway,
and the gnome flew after. But Broydo stumbled, and the serpent
sword clattered down the stairs. He bolted back to retrieve it,
then hurried after his companions as their pursuers banged loudly
onto the staging area before the ether ship.

From the crest of the sky bund, the world's circle encompassed
sea and desert. Asofel stood beside an airfoil, an avian span of
orange canvas wings, brace wires, struts, and fins. He had already
opened the bubble canopy and waved for the others to hurry.

Old Ric bounded to Asofel's side and turned in time to see
Broydo huffing up the stairs. Just then, a furry arm reached from
behind and grabbed Broydo's leg, throwing him forward with a
yelp at the top of the stairs. Ric jolted forward to free him, but
Asofel seized the gnome by the back of the neck.

"I cannot lose you." Asofel lifted the kicking gnome above the
wing truss and into the flight pod. "Let the ælf go. We don't
need him. Unless you want me to—"

"Broydo!" Old Ric stood in the pod and watched helplessly as
the massive beastmarked man easily disarmed the ælf and hoisted
him off his feet.

"Go!" Broydo yelled. He waved them off even as the beastmarked man shook him to silence.

Streaked hair flaring, the spry woman darted toward them,
shouting something that the brisk sea wind carried away.

Asofel climbed into the flight pod, tossed Ric into one of the four basket seats, and slammed shut the canopy. Engine thunder shook the airfoil, and the props whirled to a nearly invisible blear, driving back the woman, who waved frantically at them.

Straight upward, the craft lifted away from the sky bund and quickly dwindled into the cobalt sky.

"Who are you?" the beastmarked man asked the green-haired, purple figure squirming in his grip. "Tell me who you are and what has become of everyone here. Where is everyone?"

The ælf clamped his jaw, preparing to be struck and killed.

"Put him down, Dog." The lithe woman stood with arms crossed before the ælf, who sat quavering where the beastman had dropped him. "I am Jyoti Odawl, margravine of Arwar. And this is Dogbrick of Saxar. We mean you no harm. Do you understand me? We simply want to know what has happened here." She motioned to the berthed airfoils, many of which had been flown by her missing pilots. "Where is my security squad? What has happened to my people?"

The ælf turned his head, looking from one of his captors to the other. "They were devoured by the Radiant One."

"The Shadow Eater?" Jyoti asked, but the ælf did not know that expression.

"What is your name, ælf?" Dogbrick inquired brusquely. "And where are you from?"

"He is Broydo, the ælf that Lara told Reece about." Jyoti squatted beside the ælf and gazed in wonder at his crude apparel of woven grass. "And your companion is the gnome Old Ric, isn't he?"

"You have met the witch?" Broydo's ice-gray eyes widened. "You have seen her?"

"Then it's true—it's all true." Jyoti stood, shaken. "The Radiant One is Asofel the Shadow Eater. He has gone after Reece."

"And Duppy Hob and the dwarves?" Dogbrick ran a nervous hand through his mane. "The Necklace of Souls is what they're after. And the gnome is wearing that!"

"Duppy Hob?" Broydo's voice cracked. "The devil worshipper is here, on Irth?"

"His dwarves are here," Jyoti informed the ælf. "We found them in a grotto under the city. Somehow their master has reached across the abyss to reclaim his slaves. They obey him now."

Broydo groaned dismally. "Then all is doomed."

"What do you mean?" Jyoti helped the ælf to his feet.

"If Duppy Hob is using his magic," Broydo asked, "what chance does Old Ric have against that? The shadow thing—the magus—will never be thrown into the Gulf now if the dwarves seize Ric and take the Necklace of Souls. And then all the worlds are lost."

Dogbrick growled, "What are you babbling about, ælf?"

Broydo told them what little he knew from Old Ric about a nameless lady who had summoned the gnome some time ago. "I don't know why she dislikes Reece," the ælf confessed, "but she believes he must be done away with."

"What you say sounds like madness to my ears," Dogbrick stated flatly.

"So, too, did the Shadow Eater until we came here." Jyoti reached for the sword in Dogbrick's grasp. "What is this strange blade? Is this bone? And the haft—look at it, Dog. Have you ever seen such craftsmanship. Who is the charmwright?"

"The dwarf Blue Tipoo." Broydo regarded the sword proudly. "The witch forced him to craft this from a splinter of bone off a world serpent."

"World serpent?" Dogbrick's bearded face wrinkled with disbelief. "Soon we'll be talking of centaurs and elephants as if they were real. World serpents are myth."

"On Irth, perhaps," Broydo insisted. "But they crawl the heights of World's End. And this serpent sword is made from a slat of their bones. One touch of it and—"

"Dwarves shrivel to maggots," Jyoti finished for him, and marveled at the veracity of the child's fairy tale. "We must get back to Arwar—to Reece—before the Shadow Eater does."

"Or the dwarves do," Dogbrick added. "But we don't know where he and Lara will go."

"Yes, I do! I remember now—to the Abiding Star, to return her," Jyoti recalled, and began walking briskly toward the berthed airfoils.

"But there are endless ways to the upper worlds," Dogbrick countered. "How will we track him down to tell him that he has put all of creation in jeopardy?"

Broydo spoke up brightly as he followed Dogbrick and Jyoti,

glad to find himself in the company of allies. "Old Ric can sense the magus. If we follow him, he will surely lead us directly to Reece."

"And the Shadow Eater?" Dogbrick looked about uneasily at the empty sky bund. "Will he live up to his name and eat our shadows if we pursue?"

"Old Ric made Asofel forswear any more killing," Broydo said.

"Forswear killing?" Dogbrick looked quizzical. "What manner of enemy is this, then? Tell me, ælf, is this Shadow Eater evil? Need we fear him? Why does he stalk Reece so single-mindedly? Why does Lara warn us of danger? Out with it now!"

"Indeed, sir, I know not your answers. Sometimes, I think the Shadow Eater is indeed evil, for his appetite is voracious. Whether he can keep his word or not is yet to be seen. And yet, he is an emissary of a great lady, as is my friend Old Ric. If we can catch up with the magus and the witch, we can all work together. We want the same thing, to save the worlds."

Dogbrick and Jyoti, pondering the situation, had to agree with the ælf.

"Send out an aviso warning," Dogbrick suggested. "Tell all the dominions what is happening. Wherever Reece goes, he'll be apprehended."

Jyoti climbed the wing truss of an airfoil and opened the bubble canopy. "No! That will cause a riotous panic. And Reece may well be killed."

"Then let's use the airfoil's aviso to contact this Asofel and the gnome Old Ric," Dogbrick said. "Tell them we're friends and we've got Broydo and ultimately want what they want."

Jyoti activated the pod's aviso while the others clambered in after her. Static slashed from the speakers. "It's no good. I can't reach them. The Shadow Eater's energy must be interfering with reception. We're just going to have to catch them."

The engine revved before Broydo and Dogbrick had secured themselves in their seats, and they knocked heads when the airfoil lurched into the sky. Clouds whipped past, and the cope of the heavens darkened as Jyoti took the airfoil to its maximum altitude.

With a gnashed oath, Jyoti pounded the control panel. "I can't even lock onto them! Too much static. Unless we get a visual sighting, we're going to lose them."

The airfoil juddered at its limits, and Jyoti leveled off. Three
faces gazed out at the dizzy world below. Factory fumes from
Saxar worn by the wind thinned away over the glitter of the sea
and the cracked clay floor of the desert. Irth tilted its sky-bound
horizons as the airfoil dared climb higher yet, to the perilous
limit of its design.

"Margravine!" Dogbrick bawled when the airfoil began to shake
violently. "Don't get us killed. Even Charm can't break our fall
from this height."

"We can't catch them at their altitude." Jyoti swiveled in her
seat, searching the cloud strata below and the misty horizon.
"We have to get above them."

Dogbrick turned to Broydo, wanting to take his mind off the
risks of Jyoti's aerial maneuvers. "Tell me, ælf, is World's End as
frightful a realm as legend says?"

"How can I answer you?" Broydo replied, peeking apprehensively through the ferns of frost on the canopy. Down below,
an alkaline river spread its dry branches through the salt hills. "I
who have known only World's End cannot say. Irth seems frightful enough from this height."

"Ah, yes, fear—" Dogbrick stroked his beard and began to
expound to distract himself from the ominous creaking of the
struts and brace wires. "Fear is the mind's shadow, even as mind
itself is light personified. Don't you agree, ælf?"

"That mind is light and fear darkness?" Broydo lifted a tense
face to Dogbrick. "That seems true enough—for a mind can be
enlightened and fear certainly obscures thought."

Dogbrick smiled appreciatively. "The stronger the light, the
darker the shadow, eh? I do believe, ælf, that you are proving
to be a most agreeable conversationalist and an ally to be trusted.
Then do you agree, we must face the light and keep our shadow
behind us?"

"That sounds true to me. But how do we do that?" Broydo
managed to say, his stomach wincing when the airfoil bounced
over a pocket of cold air. "Right now, I'm ready to blind myself
with the light."

"Facing the light means discarding contrastive thinking,
Broydo, transcending egotistical involvement—"

The airfoil hit more turbulence, and Dogbrick and Broydo
shrieked together.

"Enough nattering, you two." Jyoti's blue-knuckled hands fought the shuddering yoke. "I know what I'm doing. Just sit back and . . ."

Before she could finish, the engine sputtered. With a cough of white smoke from under the cowl, the airfoil shivered to silence. For a moment, no sound violated the stillness of their celestial station. And then, the craft began to dive, and all three sang their fright loudly.

RIPCAT

THE SAND DUNES OF THE SPIDERLANDS LOOKED TIGER YELLOW UNDER stripes of black thorn trees. Nests of webs veiled those trees, and the victims of the land's ferocious arachnids hung as desiccated husks from the branches, the paper-crisp shapes of luckless dogs, birds, and monkeys.

Reece remembered this vicious dominion from his previous sojourns here while fleeing the Dark Lord. That seemed an age ago to him now that Lara had returned and pulled his world inside out. Protected from the spiders and the biting mites by his magic, he marched with determination through the sharp weeds and the blighting desert heat. He was searching for a charmway, a passage that connected remote areas of Irth.

Lara floated insubstantially beside him, her black hair adrift in the air about her like a darkness full of wind. She was glad that Reece had agreed to elude the Radiant One. Throughout the flight from Arwar Odawl to the trade port of Moödrun, she had used that joy to counter the agony that had been wracking her since she descended from World's End. Alone with him in the glider as they flew out of Moödrun into the

Spiderlands, she began to sing the old songs he had taught her on the Dark Shore.

But those chants that had once pleased her masters so well no longer gave pleasure to Reece, he discovered. Rather, they only reminded him of the servitude he had inflicted on her during her lifetime, for which he had already apologized several times: "I was wrong to leave you alone in the forest. I should have known that the people of the town feared you. I should have been there to protect you from them."

To ease him, she stopped singing, and her pain flared brighter. So amazed was he simply to see her again, to hear her voice, that he did not notice the small indications of her suffering she could not hide, the tiny tics at the edges of her face, the tense lines under her fire-blue eyes, the occasional lag in her speech.

"Tell me, Lara, what is it like inside the Abiding Star?" he asked, pausing a moment among the emblems of death dangling in their cobwebs from thorny branches. He sensed with the strong eye of his magic that the charmway he sought was nearby. The dense brush had obliged him to land the glider on the salt flats before the dunes and to hike through this terrain of death.

"Young master, I've told you, I do not want just yet to return to the Abiding Star." Lara swung around to face him and hovered just ahead of him as he walked. "I am already dead. It is you I am worried about."

"Why fear for me, Lara?" Reece opened a way through the thick scrub with his magic, and the thorns parted with a noise like rain. They walked on. "I have magic here on Irth. I am so much more powerful than ever I could have been on the Dark Shore."

"But what stalks you is even more powerful." Her eyes flinched at the memory of Asofel destroying the demon Tivel. "I want you to go to another world. I want you to keep moving until this Asofel wearies of pursuing you."

The hurt he saw in her face he mistook for concern for him. "Will he ever weary, this powerful being?"

"Perhaps. In any event, your magic is not to be underestimated, master." A shaft of daylight through the sharp trees smeared her features, yet her voice continued, "So long as you keep moving, there is hope. Think of the worlds you can explore. All of the Bright Shore lies before you."

"Yes," he said, though in truth he did not want to wander the worlds. He wanted to remain with his consort, Jyoti, with whom he shared a future, and help her rebuild her dominion. But he loved Lara, too, as he would a daughter, and he knew that the kindest, the best and only fate for her now, would be to let her go back to the rapture of the Abiding Star—even if he had to lie to achieve this. "We will wander the worlds, you and I," he said sadly. "That's why we must seek this charmway."

"But the charmways here only connect with other places on Irth." As she flitted through the shadows, her dusky face appeared even darker with dread. "If we remain on this world, Asofel is certain to find us. I tell you, we must go to the Well of Spiders."

"Won't he find us there as easily?"

"I don't believe so." Her memory lay in tatters amid her pain, and she rummaged for the threads that could convince him. "I came down the Well of Spiders, and they did not follow."

"Why would they, Lara?" He whistled at a glaring dog and sent it scampering away in fright through the twisted trees. "You said Asofel wants me."

"Yes, I know." A troubled frown flickered between her eyes. "But I wear a crystal prism from the Necklace of Souls that the gnome carries. Old Ric can sense me in his crystals as surely as I am aware of him in mine."

"Then he knows you are with me," Reece finished her thought. "So why have they not come for me as directly as you did?"

"The Well of Spiders is a fearful charmway," she reasoned. "Old Ric himself has no effective magic to ward spiders. The Necklace of Souls will not protect against that threat. So perhaps he fears losing himself in the Well."

"And my magic is strong enough for us to climb through the Well of Spiders to other worlds—is that it?"

"Yes." She passed cleanly through a wall of razor shrubs as they talked. "We can elude them forever that way—or at least until the Radiant One dims and goes away."

"If he ever does, Lara." He shrugged his hands and sighed. "All this is speculation, dear one. We know too little to stake our lives on that perilous charmway. Trust me to find a better way."

She spun gracefully to his side. "What is that better way, young master?"

"Let me use the crystal prism to speak with Old Ric and Asofel."

"You could be ensorcelled!" She placed both hands over the gem. "Asofel is powerful. He could well cast a spell through the prism if you reach through it too strongly. We must use it only to glance at them."

He frowned sadly. "Your fear limits us."

"I have seen the Radiant One kill." Her earnest gaze appealed to him. "Please, come away with me. There must be some way we can flee Irth."

"The charmway to Gabagalus," he answered with deliberate certainty. "Do you know of Gabagalus?"

"No."

"It is a continent on the far side of Irth." The cavern he sought appeared ahead, and he stopped momentarily to face his spectral companion. "It sinks into the sea each night and rises by day. Or so I am told by those who know. Gabagalus is independent of the dominions, a separate realm all to itself on Irth, yet, apparently, part of a trade empire that connects the worlds. From there, we can escape Irth and travel by ether ship across the Bright Shore."

"Forgive me, master, but that sounds more like rumor," she protested instantly. "The Well of Spiders, on the other hand, is real. I've journeyed through it myself, and I'm certain we can as well."

Reece sat down on a rock of orange rust. His jaw tensed, then he sighed, and said slowly, "I'll not lie to you anymore, Lara." He shook his head sadly. "I'm not going to spend what's left of my life running away."

"But you must." Her expression, heartbreaking in its sincerity, widened with alarm. "Or you will surely die."

His eyebrows bent kindly. "We all die. This is not a question of death but of life and how *I* will live."

"You have magic." She knelt before him, and the sand did not dimple under her weightless form. "You can live long and know joy, much joy."

"The joy you never had?" He reached out to cosset her care-worn face. "I can't, Lara. That is not my nature."

She placed her transparent hands upon his knees. "I came to Irth to help you, young master. As you and Master Caval came to my rescue once when I was a small child, so might I return that life-favor to you now."

Reece shook his head, then placed his hands over hers and yearned to feel her warm and well once again, yet not even his magic could accomplish that.

"There is nothing more I need." She stared into the back of his eyes, wanting to reach his heart. "I am a ghost."

"You *are* a ghost, and that is why you need help." He tried to touch her with the care in his voice. "Lara, listen to me. You don't belong here among the living. That is why you must carry that evil thing about your throat to remain with me. You are in jeopardy of losing your soul to the Gulf. I won't let that happen."

She stood up and stepped away. "You're taking me back to the Abiding Star, aren't you?"

"I want you to know peace. Your mission is done here." He gestured toward the silver threads of light in the needling branches. "There *is* peace in the Abiding Star, isn't there?"

"Oh yes." The tautness of her mouth relaxed. "There is fierce peace there. It seizes souls and draws them into its radiance."

"And from there?"

"Who knows?"

Reece held her fretful stare with a gentle smile. "The Sisterhood of Witches claims that souls delivered to the Abiding Star are healed, made whole, and reborn with knowledge of their past life."

"Perhaps." She seemed to fade a little at the thought of rebirth. "I did not stay long enough. Caval placed me there only to be healed of my trauma. And then he called me forth. We must consider that. The old master has called me forth from the Dark Shore."

"That I don't understand." Reece watched mites small as sand grains swarming around his ankle-strapped boots as he tried to think through what Lara claimed. "Souls that are swept into the Gulf lose sentience. They forsake all identity and blur away into the frenzy of unconscious rebirth. That *is* known. We are from the Dark Shore, and we know that cycle well."

"Then how can the old master have called me?"

"Are you sure it was the old master?"

"Now I don't know." Pain thrashed in her as she strove to think back to her first memories as a wraith. "In the Abiding

Star, everything was clear. I knew so much more then. I have forgotten so much." Her eyes winced closed around an ugliness of hurt. "So much is lost."

Reece stood up and moved toward Lara. For the first time since she appeared to him, he was struck suddenly by the obvious anguish in her face, her tightened posture. The revelation stunned him to exclaim, "Lara—you're suffering!"

"It is not so bad, young master." She stepped into a sheet of day bright as a wing of an angel, trying to hide her torment. "I—I'm fine."

"No you're not." He placed himself before her and framed her face with his hands, using the shadows to read the depth of hurt in her. "You're in pain. How blind could I have been not to see! Why didn't you tell me, child?"

"What is there to tell, young master?" She edged away. "It is you I came for, not me."

"For godsake stop it!" he shouted, feigning anger, wanting to reach past her selfless devotion to him. "You know I care for you. Don't hurt yourself for my sake."

"Master, I'm sorry." She curled about herself among the wind-varnished stones. "I'm not here to bring you my pain. I want to protect you and save you."

"Lara, please—" He crouched beside her, put a hand in her emptiness, reaching to feel the depth of her suffering. But his magic offered no disclosure. "Just tell me—how bad is it?"

"Not bad."

"Liar." He tried to reach her eyes with his, but she kept her head low, ashamed that her secret had been revealed. "You died on the Dark Shore in my care. Your pain is mine."

"I would not have come to you if I hadn't thought I could help." A sob caught her breath, and she added more quietly, "But when the old master called me, I knew that was different. He told me about the danger you are in. I had to warn you."

"You did well, child." The void of her defied all his attempts to reassure her. "But now, Lara, it's no use staying here, you know."

She lifted her face supplicatively, almost blue with sweat.

"Before we do anything, we must heal you," he told her resolutely.

"I don't want to go back to the Abiding Star," she protested again.

"Don't worry about that. I'm going to heal you here, right now."

She shook her head. "There's no time, master! Forget about me. I beg you."

He paid her no attention. Instead, he stood and with the heel of one boot traced a circle around the wraith. "Now just sit still. I'm going to focus my power on you."

"But I'm a ghost," she interrupted, and ducked again beneath the dark veil of her hair. "How can your magic touch me?"

"Are we not both from the Dark Shore, you and I?" He stood back from the circle. "If I focus strongly enough . . ." He brought his magic quickly to bear on her before she changed her mind. As he suspected, his power connected instantly with her, bonding with the same strength that had guided her to him.

Shadows quivered, though there was no breeze. The circle enclosing the wraith glimmered over as though a brighter shaft of day had found its way through the trees.

Suddenly, pain peeled away from Lara. For the first time since descending the Well of Spiders, the stifling hurt was gone. A smile widened through her, and she gazed happily at Reece who stood at the circle's edge taller, head thrown back, his eyes upturned to white.

But the pain that entered him was like nothing he had ever experienced before. At first, he saw her bedecked in her wounds, as he had seen her that last time on the Dark Shore, with the splattered blood welded in rays across her naked body.

Then, her image vanished—and the pain was his.

His teeth gnashed tightly as a cliff. Death-hurt pierced cold into his marrows as knives stabbed him and invisible fire whirled from each wound, inflaming all of him, consuming his mind, his strength, even his magic.

Reece had not expected so violent an outrush of suffering. His love for Lara had betrayed him to a miscalculation. Only briefly did he perceive his error: Lara's pain was overwhelming him. In a moment, his magic would be exhausted and his life force itself extinguished. He would die—unless he used the last of his magic to create a protective skin of light about himself. This he willed, and it took all his available strength before the afflicting onslaught cut his mind to darkness.

He collapsed as though pulled violently from behind, and then he thrashed ferociously in the sand.

Lara screamed and leaped toward him. She crossed the circle, and in that instant the shaft of pearled light illuminating the sand dimmed and became once again daylight's mosaic among the branches.

The yellow dust settled—and Reece was gone.

In his place, a beastmarked man lay spraddled among the rocks. He wore Reece's boots, gray pants, and shreds of his denim shirt that had torn open around a thicker torso—a body of blue fur.

The ghost knelt beside the beastman, and he sat up, passing right through her.

Ripcat blinked alert, green eyes sharp with surprise. "Where am I?" he mouthed aloud. Stinging bites pushed him to his feet, and he brusquely dusted away the spider mites invading his pelt and stomped a dance, kicking himself free of the tiny predators. "The Spiderlands!"

"Young master!" Lara swung close, her hands blurring through him.

Ripcat did not see her.

"Young master!" she screamed again, and tried to give back his magic. But her frantic motions offered nothing. Was this truly her Reece? The clothes alone assured her that somehow Reece had transformed into this outlandish creature. She gaped at him, trying to find some semblance of the man she knew. His round head looked entirely unfamiliar, with its tight pelage marked by rosettes of darker fur and topped at the cope of his skull by cub ears.

"Reece!" she cried. "Reece Morgan!"

Ripcat walked through her, oblivious to her presence, and stared about in alarm. He could not remember coming here. His last memory was of seeking the Dark Lord with Jyoti. *What am I doing in the Spiderlands?*

The magic that had stolen Lara's death-pain from her had sheathed him once again in the skin of light that had first protected him when he arrived on Irth to search for her. But his memories of his life as Reece Morgan were smothered by this same skin of light. He remembered neither the Dark Shore, nor the Radiant One who stalked him, nor even the return of Lara as a wraith. His memories were obsolete, of a time already past.

In desperation, Lara removed her crystal prism and held it before him.

The sudden appearance of a the shining gem floating in midair startled Ripcat, and he bounded away with a snarl. "What is this wicked charmwork?" he shouted. "Who is there?"

He hunkered like an animal, his keen eyes fixed on the floating gem, his peripheral sight searching for cacodemons and the Dark Lord.

Lara saw the fright in his beastmarked face and put the gem away.

The gem's disappearance startled Ripcat, and he dashed away from where it had hovered. He was convinced that the Dark Lord had worked some evil magic to exile him to the Spiderlands. But he would escape. He recognized the caverns ahead, the charmways he had traveled once before to find his way across Irth. He would lose the cacodemons there. Dust flew with his swift footfalls, and in a moment he slinked into the maw of a rime-crusted cave.

Lara floated after him. But in the dark of the caverns, she could not see him. He was no longer Reece, and the bond that had led her to him down the Well of Spiders was gone. Despair ripped screams from her—cries that made no echoes.

THE WELL OF SPIDERS

"HE'S GONE!" OLD RIC SAT UP STARTLED IN THE BASKET SEAT OF THE airfoil that Asofel piloted. "The magus has disappeared!"

Asofel's fiery look made the eldern gnome cringe.

"I felt him until but a moment ago," the gnome added quickly. He twisted about to press his face against the bubble canopy, wanting to see where they were, but the shaft of the arrow lancing him caught on the seat and impeded him. Below, he glimpsed the scabrous badlands of the Qaf.

"How can he be gone?" Asofel spoke to the cuff of gray hair at the back of Ric's bald pate. "Our lady has given you the sense of him. You can find him wherever he goes within her dream."

"He is not in her dream anymore." Old Ric sat back in his seat, baffled, having seen nothing in the wasteland beneath them that could possibly interfere with the gravid lady's vision entrusted to him. He did not know what he had expected to see outside the canopy, for the only power strong enough to subvert her would be another Nameless One, and such a being would not be found in a dream. "The magus has left our lady's dream— gone entirely."

"That's not possible," Asofel hissed.

"I tell you, I do not feel his presence anymore." Old Ric pressed both hands to his wrinkled brow and squinted with concentration. "He has vanished."

"What of the witch?"

"Yes—yes, the witch." The gnome held up the Necklace of Souls. "I see her!" His leathern face brightened briefly, then closed again. "But she is alone."

Asofel's baleful expression inspired terror in the eldern gnome.

"Are we too late?" Old Ric asked in a frightened voice. "Has our lady awakened the father of the child?"

"These worlds would be no more if that were true." The Radiant One's dusky blue complexion breathed pink from within as though the fire inside him had risen closer to the surface. "Our work is not yet done. There is time remaining. We must strive harder."

"Harder?" Old Ric closed his eyes and reached deeper into himself but found only darkness. "Hard as I try, I find no clue of the shadow thing whatsoever. What are we going to do, Asofel?"

The Radiant One said nothing. The long hair that floated like pink cobwebs about his faceted skull crawled with tiny sparks as if energy seeped from his brain. Momentarily, he spoke in a cold voice, "I need more light from the dream."

"More lives to be taken?" The eldern gnome crossed arms over his chest so that the barbed arrow stuck between his wrists. "How will that help us?"

"I need the strength to leave the dream," he answered, "to return to our lady. Perhaps the threat is ended. Perhaps the child in her moves again. Our task here in these depths may already be accomplished."

"But how can that be?" Old Ric's lower lip covered his upper as he considered this. "No, Asofel. I alone have been plucked from the dream to serve our lady. This she made clear when she first summoned me. It costs her much energy to commune with beings that are illusions to her, such as myself. No. Her strength must be reserved for her child. She would not have sent anyone else to do our work."

"Tell me then, eldern gnome, why the dream?" Asofel's long jaw pointed out the canopy at the cloudless blue sky where

Nemora floated like a piece of skull. "Why has she created these worlds?"

At first, Ric thought that the Radiant One was taunting him, but his fiery stare remained level and rigorously intent. "You do not know?" the gnome asked, surprised.

"I am a sentinel." Asofel squared his shoulders proudly. "I have been set upon the palace to watch over her. I myself am a dream dreamt by those who want our lady protected from all harm. I know nothing of her, her child, or her magic."

"Who then dreams you, Asofel?"

"Does the dream know the dreamer?"

"I know our lady."

Asofel shrugged. "As you say, you alone have been selected, because something terrible has gone awry with our lady's magic and she needs someone from within her dream to set it right. You have a privilege that I do not. And it is a privilege that has cost her dearly, for dreams are no easy thing to control." Not removing his hot gaze from the saw-toothed land below, he asked, "Do you know why you have been selected?"

"Of course," the gnome replied at once. "I have studied gnomish magic for a long lifetime—a magic more ancient and more subtle than Charm. But more importantly, I am old and belong to no one. My family are all gone, my wives and my beloved Amara dead, the others moved far away and as good as dead to my aged bones. There is no one who would believe what I have known in her presence—and so her dream is safe with me. Her dreamers remain blissfully unaware of her and her child, whom they serve unwittingly and so most faithfully."

"But you have not yet told me, why this dream?" With a long-fingered hand he gestured again to the barren land and the shell of Nemora hung in the blue void. "Why has she created these worlds?"

"This dream is her hope of warmth, light, and love for her child," the gnome told him, his eyes slim with remembering. "When the babe is born, these worlds will be its school, where the young one will learn the lessons of compassion, caring, and the dangers of vanity to which all conscious life is heir." His lids closed sadly. "But none of this reflection helps with the problem facing us."

"Perhaps." His small lips twisted in a curious flash of a pout.

"I am hoping you will see that this is a problem of the dream and the dreamer. Release me from my promise to take no more light for myself, and I will return to the palace and speak with our lady. You may come along, too. Together we will determine if she is whole again and the child well."

"That's a dangerous proposition, Asofel." Old Ric gnawed the corner of his lip dubiously. "The lady was impatient with me last we met. If we appear before her, and the child remains motionless in her womb, she will surely wake the father."

"The dark father—yes, the one who would regard this school of dreams for his child an unnecessary indulgence." The Radiant One seemed to ponder this, rocking his jaw side to side. "Maybe then he is right."

Old Ric's eyes narrowed. "You—you just want to get out of the dream, don't you? You care not for these worlds."

"This is true, gnome." Asofel impatiently tapped his fingers on the yoke. "I belong with the other sentinels, not here in the dark and the cold chasing after chimeras. The shadow thing is gone. Our work is done. Let us away from this illusion meant for a child."

"You don't care if these worlds vanish or not." Old Ric glared angrily. "You're not of these worlds. But our lady has given me authority over you. And so long as you are in her dream, you shall do as I command."

The Radiant One's countenance of blue ash turned slowly. "And what do you command, gnome?"

"I don't know." Old Ric sank deeper in his seat. "I think we must go back for Broydo. We abandoned him to our enemies. I feel terrible about that."

Disgust masked Asofel, and he said sharply, "I was not sent here to rescue ælves."

"But Broydo is our ally," Old Ric asserted. "Without him we would have failed before we began."

"Ally or not, we are all at risk in this mad dream." His face looked like a visage seen from the other side of smoke. "We will not imperil ourselves for him or for anyone else. I will use my power only for the mission we were sent here to fulfill."

Old Ric accepted this with a sigh of resignation. "And so, Radiant One—what do we do now?"

"Find the witch-ghost," Asofel decided. "She was the last to see the shadow thing. She may well know what has become of him."

They flew on in silence, the acid-stained landscape crawling below. Abruptly and excitedly, Old Ric spoke up, "She has moved swiftly. She is there!"

He pointed to a chain of mountains that gleamed like glass on the horizon.

"How can she move so quickly?" Asofel banked the airfoil and glided toward the icy rim of the world. "The last you saw of her she was far from here."

"These worlds are riddled with charmways, passages that connect distant points." Old Ric held a crystal prism from the Necklace of Souls close to one eye. "Ah, yes—there she is on the slope of a mountain. Still alone."

"Where is she going?"

"I cannot say." Ric's jaw slackened. "Ah, I recognize that mountain now. It is the tallest peak on the planet—the famed Calendar of Eyes."

"What does that portend, gnome?" Asofel steepened their descent so sharply, their ears whistled. "What is this Calendar of Eyes?"

"It is a crag that reaches higher than time." Old Ric filtered the snowy light of the approaching mountain through a prism and saw the ghost moving across a snowfield and leaving no tracks. "She has crossed to here through a charmway. I think she intends to leave Irth."

"For where?"

"We'll know when we find her." Old Ric indicated the direction Asofel should fly, toward a vast mountain with a shape like a shard of broken glass. "She is a ghost. All I can see is where she is now. And she is entering a cave, there on the south flank."

Asofel landed the airfoil with dainty precision on the brink of an icy slope above a glaring snowbowl. The cold did not touch either the gnome or the Radiant One, yet both stood as if frozen after they had deplaned from the flight pod. No paths wended among the fluffed drifts.

Old Ric waded through the powder white snuff, and Asofel followed, his orange hair fluttering like flames and the cold steaming off him in silver fumes. On all sides, ice mountains stood giantly.

"There is where she is." The gnome hurried gingerly past frosted boulders, anxious not to fall and stab himself again with the arrow already lodged in him. "She's gone in there." Sheaved ice glittered starkly from the lintel of a cave.

"Why do you hesitate, gnome?" Asofel threw a tuft of fire into the lightless cave and illuminated glossy rock walls unhewn by mortal hands.

"This is no ordinary charmway," he warned. "She has gone back into the Well of Spiders. If we follow, we will leave Irth for worlds beyond."

"We must capture her." Asofel stepped to the threshold of the cave, and his luminous presence revealed asp holes and viper crevices among the ill-joined rocks. "My power will protect us from what beasts we find. Lead the way, gnome. Do not let the ghost elude us."

Old Ric entered the cave, and a smell of damp stone enclosed him. Warmth radiated from ahead. And scuttling noises, scratching, clicking sounds of chitinous creatures trembling alertly to their presence. The spiders had not sensed the ghost, but they flinched excitedly at the approach of her pursuers.

Asofel's face blazed like a lamp and cast slewed shadows from the craggy walls.

The gnome's shadow stretched ahead of him like a narrow path. He crept forward, listening to the sharp sounds growing louder and nearer. From out of the dark tunnel, a spider big as the cave itself came scurrying. Its jointed legs scraped noisily against the rock walls, and a scissoring sound from its lively mandibles chewed its own echoes.

Old Ric cried in terror, yet even before his shriek unwound, a flash burned vision blind. Wincing, the gnome looked away. When he turned back, the giant spider had been blasted apart into thousands of flittering puzzle pieces. Tiny spiders unclasped from their gigantic form by Asofel's attack scattered into the dark, some burning like embers.

"Move forward," Asofel commanded. "Take us to the witch-ghost."

The gnome advanced less timidly, having experienced the force of Asofel's renewed power. The sound of the scattered spiders' metallic cries flew ahead, and the way appeared clear enough for Ric to take his nervous eyes off the shadowy path and to gaze again into the Necklace of Souls.

"She is far, far ahead of us," the eldern gnome reported. "She is a wraith, after all. She has moved on to the shaft that lies ahead and has climbed up the Well of Spiders. We will have to move quickly to keep pace with her."

"Then hurry." Asofel nudged Old Ric forward, and the two moved almost at a run through the long cavern until they arrived at the Well itself.

The sound of water searching for a deep place to rest rippled from below. Even Asofel's lucid eyes could not penetrate the darkness that plumbed depths far below Irth. But the wraith had gone not down but up. And in that direction, bats spun, spider nests dangled, and faeries twinkled like motes of gusty fire.

"How will we climb the Well?" Old Ric asked. "I have not the sight or strength to mount these rock walls."

"Get on my back, gnome." Asofel knelt, and Ric reluctantly mounted his shoulders. "Had I taken more of my light from the dream, we could fly. As it is, you must cling to me. And do not lose sight of the ghost."

The touch of Asofel was not hot as the gnome had feared. Straddling the Radiant One's shoulders, Old Ric felt suddenly wild at heart, the licking flames of Asofel's hair brushing him with a cool, musical sensation as of holy fire. He sat up tall so that the barbed tip of the arrow through his chest would not poke the sentinel's head, and he fixed his attention on the prisms that hung from his neck.

Asofel clambered with astonishing swiftness up the nitre-crusted wall, lighting the way ahead with twin rays from his flame-cored eyes. Sparks drizzled where his hands clawed at the rocks, and his boots kicked footholds into the wall as though the stone were soft clay.

Old Ric watched through the crystal prisms as the image of the witch drew nearer. She had already departed the Well of Spiders and strolled beside a shallow brook in a field yellow with small vetch. The eldern gnome immediately recognized the silhouette of the knobby mountains and the wind with its lapful

of birds under a violet sky. This was the land of his earlier life—
the summer veldt of Nemora.

"She has gone to my home world!" the gnome announced
excitedly.

Asofel made no reply.

Already, Old Ric felt that he could smell the rain of the veldt
full of freshness and the cool shadows of the great blue thunderheads trawling slowly over the land.

"Stop squirming," Asofel demanded.

The gnome clung tighter to the Radiant One, amazed that
the blind god Chance had favored him this way. The summer
veldt was where he had lived as a boy, before departing for
the frost plains and snowy tracts that dominated most of the
planet. Life on the veldt was hard, for it was the one fertile
region of Nemora, and it had to provide grains and fruits for
all the broods of gnomes in the frozen regions. His parents and
their forebears before them for many generations had served as
dyers and weavers for the gnomes of the veldt farms and orchards. He alone of his lineage had left the fecund fields and
the hard labor of veldt life to study magic in the ice caves.
And he had not returned to the green land of his ancestors—
until now.

In the rainbow light of the prisms, the witch ambled slowly
beside the slapping waters of the brook. She knew she was being
followed, for she saw in her crystal prism the sparks sizzling in
the Well of Spiders from the Radiant One's fierce hands that
clawed at the rock. She saw his fiery hair snapping brightly in
the dark, illuminating the gnome astride his shoulders, his aged,
underlit face gleefully watching her.

She was not afraid. She had accomplished what she had set
out to do, which was to lead the Shadow Eater away from the
man she loved—even though that man no longer seemed a man.
Transformed into a beastmarked amnesiac, Reece had fled into
the charmways of the Spiderlands. The witch had no idea where
on Irth those charmways had taken him. But she knew he was
somewhere on Irth, because those charmways led only among
the dominions.

Through her prism, she could see that the Shadow Eater and
Old Ric could no longer locate Reece. Changed into Ripcat, he
had become a form they could not detect. And so she had taken

a charmway to the Calendar of Eyes and then entered the Well of Spiders to lead them away from her beloved.

When they arrived, she would lead them across this lovely country to the next shaft of the Well of Spiders that she sensed not too far distant. How long she could continue to distract them from Reece she did not know. But now that he had lifted her free of pain, she could go on indefinitely.

She waded across the brook over green rocks, making not a splash as she moved atop the clear water.

PART THREE

Gabagalus

"Truth is the most necessary fiction."

—THE GIBBET SCROLLS, SCREED 3:24

ALLIANCE IN THE QAF

GABAGALUS SANK INTO THE NIGHT OCEAN. JETS OF SPUME AND VEILS of spindrift shot from its submerging peaks and shone like phosphorescent vapors under evening's planetshine. Citrine streaks of day's end marked the west as the last waves exploded over the summits. By nightfall, the swells of the sea undulated in broad amplitudes of shining darkness, lit from above by star smoke and from below by the bright lights of the sunken continent.

One of those shimmering underwater lights shone from a bubble dome attached to a cliff ledge. Kelp ribbons unfurled from the rock walls and silhouetted the lit dome and its spare interior: an oval swimming pool that cast cobbles of reflected light across the suite. Globe lanterns hung over the pool and a blue-carpeted deck.

Beneath one globe, an old, old man sat in a wire chair, his bald, mottled head gleaming. He wore green slippers and a black tunic fretted in gold. Time seemed to drip from his eyes, the flesh of his cheeks folded like melted wax. His mouth hung open, and a voice like a slow shadow emerged, "Where is Reece Morgan?"

*   *   *

Ripcat knew something was wrong his first night under the
stars. The scrolls of planet smoke and webs of star fire had
changed too much in too short a time. At first he thought perhaps he was enduring a strange dream. But the cold rock floor
and the black knife of the night wind convinced him otherwise.

Though he had been trying to reach the Cloths of Heaven in
the Reef Isles of Nhat, where he last remembered himself being,
the charmway from the Spiderlands had conveyed him unexpectedly
to the Qaf. Instead of returning immediately to the charmway
and getting more disoriented, he had lingered that afternoon.
From the crest of a rock ridge, he had seen spurs of rhubarb
and tufts of oat grass in the saddles of the tottering hills to the
south. He was at the margin of the wasteland and from there
could find his way to water and food when dawn came. And so
he had settled down between thrusts of rock that both blunted
the wind and anchored himself to Irth so that the nocturnal tide
would not carry his Charmless body into the sky. And in this
manner he had waited for sleep and dreams of the Dark Shore—
until he saw the ominous night sky so changed from what he
remembered.

Fearful thoughts rushed through him: Had a warlock cast a
spell that had stolen time from him? Or had the Dark Lord
himself entranced him so that many long days had passed
obliviously?

He compared what he saw of the luminous sky vapors now
with what he remembered their disposition had been the last
time he had surveyed the night, only a day ago it seemed to
him. In all four directions, the planetoids lay scattered far from
where he had seen them last: a comet he had viewed in the
north had carried its icy streamer to the west; the veils of star
exhaust had shifted and fluttered in the wide winds of space to
new abstractions; and even the planetary phases marked a
changed order—Hellsgate and Nemora carrying different vol-
umes of shadow in their vessels of light.

"This cannot be," he murmured to himself like a chant. "This
cannot be."

And his chant carried him to fitful sleep under the ballast of
the desert rocks.

The same dream came to him as it did every night he slept

as Ripcat, a dream of a peculiar world without Charm. As on
Irth, the sky there shone blue and clouds moved in herds on the
migratory paths of the wind. But unlike Irth, in these dreams he
never glimpsed basilisks, griffins, or dragons in the air.

The city of his dreams did not float in the sky as did the
greatest cities on Irth. This metropolis rose directly out of the
ground in steel-and-glass towers, and houses sprawled for many
leagues in grids of streets and avenues among tropic vegetation.
He glimpsed road signs, and the name Darwin chimed in his
dream-held memory—a meaningless name to him. Darwin of the
Northern Territory in the Southern Realm that his dream
named Australia.

On a tree-lined street of that town, in a pink house with white
trim and a sloping lawn of hedges and shrubs, he stood before
a discreet sign that read: *Boarders Welcome* in large calligraphic
lettering.

Infuriatingly, this repetitious dream seemed more than a dream
and throbbed in him with the insistence of memory—but a memory that kept eluding him.

The people in the boardinghouse seemed to know him, but
he could call forth no names. He saw them only briefly as he
entered the house and climbed the left-hand stairway, his footfalls silent on the burgundy carpet. As he approached the landing
where a dark doorway of solid mahogany stood at the end of a
corridor, the dream became ponderous. He moved slowly, with
near paralysis. He sensed that this heavy, glass-knobbed door
opened upon his room.

His hand reached for the knob with excruciating slowness. At
its touch, the cold glass startled him with a jolt like an electric
sting, almost too real for the dream, almost shuddering him
awake. But he clung to the knob and, with great effort, turned
it. And slowly the door opened.

Inside, heavy crimson drapes covered the wndows. On the
walls, precise circles were painted, each containing intricate geometric patterns—magic sigils. The sight of each one smote him
like a drum, and his insides quavered resonantly, echoing through
him with bold recollections of himself naked, sky-clad, dancing
with precision and vigor about the room. His limbs felt sheathed
in cold fire; his voice chanted words that came not from his
throat but his bones.

He looked away from the magical sigils and noticed that the room was bare, empty of all furniture save a long, shrouded table. Looking closer, he recognized that this was no ordinary table but an altar that carried a magician's implements—a rod of amber glass, a dagger with a green blade etched in serpent scales, a chalice of blackened silver, and a metal plate burnished to mirror brightness.

Slowly, he pushed himself through the dream's viscosity and stood before the altar. When he looked down, he saw himself reflected in the buffed plate. It was a stranger's face, with storm gray eyes set deep in a boxer's block brow, a blunt nose, hard-set mouth, flat ears, and bristly sun-bleached hair that at first he thought was gray but for the youthfully taut and clean-shaven cheeks.

The dream changed at the sight of this stranger, and suddenly he stood in a forest with a naked, sable-tressed woman—a dancer with footsteps so light no sound rose from the strewn leaves. But something else rose out of the ground under the rhythm of her dancing feet, a soundless tension like a gathering storm. And watching her, he felt as though he were standing at the end of time.

"Lara—" he heard himself calling to her. "Dance for us, Lara."

Us? he wondered in the dream and looked among the trees for others.

Night held the forest. The light by which he watched the dancer Lara filtered through the branches in threads of starlight. And the wind rose up with a ghost in it. A figure of moonlight came flying through the woods—a man shape with long limbs and a countenance like a fish hawk, hooked and predatory. Its fierce eyes fixed upon him with an intensity that set the fact of his existence into the fable of a dream.

"Caval," he heard himself call. "The power rises! The witch has danced us the power and it rises like the tidal paths of the sea."

Caval—the name filled him with an urgency of something that wanted to be said. But he did not know what.

Like a story with no beginning or end, the dream rushed on, turned to confusion, and things unseen and unspoken occupied him, magical things he did not comprehend. He danced with Lara. The storm energy ran deep in his veins. The ghost called Caval became more solid, heavy as a rain-soaked garment. He stood at the center of their dancing, motionless, suddenly wholly real and rooted in his six senses.

"I've come back to the dream to warn you," Caval spoke with the immediacy of waking reality. "You will remember this when you wake. I have used the last of my strength to reach you here, and you will remember this when you wake. Remember—" The shadow raised from the moss appeared both young and old. In the starlight and night shadows, his red hair appeared like dried blood caked to his long skull, his bone-sharp face intent. "I thought I came here alone—on my own—by the power I had won from the Brotherhood of Wizards, the Sisterhood of Witches. I was wrong. Listen to me now. I was wrong. Terribly wrong. I was summoned here. Do you understand me? I was summoned to the Dark Shore by a far greater magic, an evil magic. I was called here to participate in a strategy beyond my ken. Do you hear me? Listen! I was called here by Duppy Hob."

The name struck him like a blow. It knocked him out of the dream.

He woke to the copper hairstreaks of dawn. The Qaf looked blue in the early light. Its gypsum hills were ghost shrouds, re-mindful of the dream, whose taint clung to him like the stink of brimstone.

Lara—Caval—The names shook him alert. Caval the wizard, the weapons master of the House of Odawl, was engaged this moment in a battle with the Dark Lord. *Or is he?* Confusion eclipsed his dream. Time had turned back on itself. Was this the past or the future?

Before he could ponder the mystery further, his keen ears heard gravel crunching from within the Qaf—several bodies large as trolls moving directly toward him. He slapped his body, reach-ing for a knife that was not there before he remembered that he did not remember. He wore strange clothes—a ripped denim shirt, gray trousers that fit too tight, and ankle boots that hurt his feet.

He curled into the shadows of the rocks and circled through the muted light toward the approaching sounds, seeking higher ground from where to observe what came his way. Belly-crawling up a sand hill, he contemplated how he could defend himself with-out a weapon against trolls. But at the top of the dune, his anxiety evaporated.

"Ripcat!" Dogbrick's big voice boomed. "I know you're out there! I know you can hear me! I have a seeker!"

Ripcat stood. He raised a hand in greeting to the three figures marching out of the morning radiance, night's last stars whistling silently in the green air above them. He scrutinized the short, stocky fellow beside Dogbrick and noted his crude boots of chewed tree bark, grass tunic, burnt-looking face, mossy green hair, and pointed, pink-tipped ears. He carried a sword that shone white as a moonbeam in the gloaming. *Is he an enemy? Does he hold the others in thrall?*

Jyoti broke from the group and spurted toward him, mauve dust at her heels. Charm had protected her and the others when their airfoil crash-landed, yet she had thought Dogbrick traumatized when he claimed he detected Ripcat under the empty sky. He had shown her the seeker, and she had touched the Charmed hum of his presence. But she thought the amulet damaged and had not allowed herself to dare hope until now.

Ripcat squinted into the bronze haze of early day as into an antique world, trying to discern the margravine's expression. The last time he remembered seeing her, they stood together in the Palace of Abominations, obscene living corpses flayed of their flesh in tanks on either side, their exposed hearts throbbing with the Dark Lord's magic. She appeared changed. Something quieter about her visage soaked in dawnlight instead of dread.

What mischief is this? he wondered as he slid down the dune face on his heels.

"You've changed back!" she huffed with alarm and the exertion of her run and stopped just short of throwing her arms around him. He had assumed again the beastmarks he had worn in their struggle against the Dark Lord, and the sight of him transformed thrilled and frightened her. She fumbled with her amulet-vest while looking him over, glad to find no wounds. A power wand came free, and she pressed it against his chest.

"Jyoti—" At the touch of the amber wand, the sullen anxiety in him dispersed, and he reached for her.

She clasped his arms and felt night's chill on his fur, saw bewilderment in his slant stare.

"What's happened to us?" he asked, avidly searching her face for clues and finding consolation in her sad regard. "Has the

Dark Lord defeated us? Why are we here—in the Qaf? And why are you looking at me like that?"

"Defeated us?" Dogbrick snarled, coming up behind Jyoti. "The Dark Lord is dead! You killed him yourself."

The tan smell of him, the tree-sour scent of her, both baked by a day's Charmed hike through the Qaf convinced him this was no magical deception. It was too real. "I don't remember," he admitted. "I don't remember anything about my past."

"Give him your rat-stars, Dog." She brushed the marked velvet of Ripcat's cheek. "Maybe they'll brighten your memory. Meanwhile, we'll tell you everything."

"Why are you here?" he wanted to know.

"We crash-landed yesterday, some leagues away," she told him, while helping loop a strand of rat-stars into a headband.

"We thought we were alone out here with the trolls," Dogbrick added. "And then, this activated and made all my hackles stand on end."

In his large hand, Dogbrick presented a seeker amulet—a round case of conjure-metal and witch-glass with a lock of blue fur sandwiched within it.

"I kept this as a memento of our partnership in Saxar," Dogbrick explained, and indicated with his thumb where on his shawl of amulets he had stowed it. "I never thought it would be of use again. Remember when I used to need it to find you in the cliff lanes the morning after a job? All night, I could barely get myself to believe it was really detecting you."

"We thought perhaps it was broken or, worse—a trick," Jyoti said. "Something the Shadow Eater had worked to deceive us."

"Shadow Eater?" Ripcat's round face turned to the stranger, who cringed under his feral gaze.

"We will explain everything," Dogbrick promised. "But first— this is Broydo, an ælf from World's End. With his help, we will remind you of what you already know."

Broydo bowed deferentially. "Dogbrick and Jyoti have told me of you and how you risked everything to save Irth from the Dark Lord."

"Then you'd best tell me." Ripcat's oblique green eyes looked frightened. "I remember nothing."

"We will help you." Jyoti put her arms around him again, and

they walked to the leeside of the dune and sat where the rising
light would not smite them.

By turns, they told him all that had happened, Dogbrick in-
forming him of his life as Reece Morgan, Jyoti recounting to him
the exhausting magic he had worked to rebuild Arwar Odawl,
which had led to her mistaken belief that he had suffered a
breakdown, and Broydo relating what had transpired at World's
End with Old Ric, Asofel, and the wraith Lara.

When they finished, the morning had advanced and the Abiding Star blazed above the tilted rocks of the Qaf. Ripcat rose,
stunned by the revelations. He walked a wobbly circle, his mind
indrawn, trying to reason through a strategy. "I think I understand
my dream now . . ." he ventured aloud. His mind ranged dizzily
to the limits of his comprehension. "Last night, I met Caval again.
His ghost called to me from the Dark Shore. He told me—he
told me that when I met him on the Dark Shore all those years
ago, he had gone there not of his own will as he had thought."
Ripcat muttered more to himself than the others, "Caval had
come to my world without realizing that he had been called
there by a greater being—called there for some plan he didn't
know. But he did know the name of that being." He stopped
pacing and faced the others. "It was the same name that you say
you heard in the grottoes under Saxar—the same devil worshipper that is believed to control the dwarves."

"Duppy Hob," Dogbrick snarled, and his big teeth snapped
fiercely.

"Something larger is going on than we know," Jyoti said, and
rose to go to Ripcat. She put a hand to his furred chest and felt
his heart hammering. "Much more is at stake than Irth alone,
I fear."

"Old Ric said the worlds will end," Broydo piped up, "unless
you are driven into the Gulf."

"Can that be so?" Ripcat asked, his desperate eyes searching
his comrades' faces beseechingly. "The Door in the Air through
which I came from the Dark Shore is closed, though. I can't
open it as Ripcat, only as Reece. The only way back for me now
is to kill myself!"

Dogbrick and Jyoti protested at once, and Broydo said, "There
is time. The eldern gnome said that time moves differently for

the Nameless Ones. There is time yet to restore yourself to Reece Morgan."

"How?" Ripcat asked with a twang of despair in his voice. "Caval is dead."

"There are other wizards," said Dogbrick. "We will travel with you to the wizarduke himself in the capital of Dorzen if we must."

Jyoti shook her head doubtfully. "Caval had knowledge gleaned from the Dark Shore. I doubt any other wizard on Irth can remove this skin of light from Reece."

An oppressive silence fell upon the group, until finally the ælf thought to speak up. "The Necklace of Souls will restore you," Broydo announced in a small voice. He had been closely observing the beastmarked man—the shadow thing that Old Ric had brought the Radiant One to destroy—and he detected nothing evil about the magus. He became convinced that if the gnome met this Ripcat, understanding would pass between them. He went on in a larger voice, "That is the power of the Necklace. It is a soul-catcher. It will catch your soul as surely as it caught the souls of my clan and restored them from the curse of Tivel the demon. If we go to Old Ric, he will see that you are not a bad man and gladly use the Necklace to remove your beastmarks and make you once more a man."

"But where is this eldern gnome?" Ripcat asked. "You say he and the Shadow Eater had left Saxar ahead of you to find me. They should have located me by now."

"Not as Ripcat," Dogbrick realized. "My seeker found you because it holds a tuft of your fur. But the eldern gnome is searching for Reece. He has no notion of Ripcat. You are invisible to him."

"And then perhaps I am invisible to this nameless lady above World's End as well," Ripcat hoped. "Perhaps so long as I remain in this form, I can stay here on Irth."

"Maybe—maybe not," Broydo pondered. "We cannot know for sure and it is far too great a risk to take."

"Then we must find Old Ric," Jyoti concluded.

"Or Lara." Ripcat's eyes brightened. "She, too, has a crystal prism."

"But she is a ghost." Broydo rested his chin on the hilt of the serpent sword, whose tip he had embedded in the sand. "She will be even harder to find."

"Wait!" Dogbrick jumped to his feet. "There is a way! We are not the only ones seeking the Necklace of Souls."

"The dwarves!" Jyoti gripped Ripcat's arm excitedly. "If we can locate them in the charmways, they will lead us to the Necklace of Souls."

"We will do better than follow them." Dogbrick's lips curled back from his fangs with a clever grin. "Ha-ha! We will become again the thieves we once were, Ripcat and I. We will use our cunning and sneak up on the dwarves. And then with Broydo's sword, we will kidnap one and use it to guide us to the Necklace!"

"It is a bold plan," Jyoti acknowledged. "And dangerous."

"Our destiny now calls for nothing less," Dogbrick stated with conviction.

"All the worlds are at stake," Broydo acknowledged, and raised the serpent sword above his head. "We must not fail."

"The charmways are there." Ripcat pointed across the broken land to the cave from which he had emerged the day before. "Let us go take a dwarf."

MASSACRE ON NEMORA

OLD RIC KEPT TO THE HIGH TRAILS WHERE HE AND THE RADIANT One would not be seen by the gnomes of Nemora's summer veldt. The open country below bustled with activity. Numerous cobbled roads crisscrossed over mossy turf and through groves of tall staghorn ferns. The quaint peat houses and grassy knolls stirred profound nostalgia in Ric, and he yearned to walk again the mushroom-banked paths he had frolicked along as a child. But he dared not, for the presence of Asofel would alarm the residents.

Even though the Radiant One had expended considerable energy climbing the Well of Spiders, he had grown stronger than ever, because Nemora's close proximity to the Abiding Star saturated him with Charm. He was not yet powerful enough to assume again his invisible station adjacent to the nameless lady's dream. But he had changed. His hair billowed like thermal smoke. And his eyes—slits of crushed light—burned dense as stars.

The hills carried old forests swarming with creatures, and it was easy to stay out of sight among the walls of ivy and veil

moss when hunters approached. Those gnomes wandered the
hills tracking specific beasts for the breeding yards of the villages.
The veldt's economy depended on providing beastfolk as laborers
to the gnomish communities in the icy vastness that dominated
most of Nemora.

From a high bough in a lightning-scarred cedar, Old Ric satisfied his wistfulness by watching unobserved as the gnomes below
fulfilled their labors for the gnomish kith. Some toiled in the
orchards and gardens laid out in spoke-wheel patterns on the
open plains. Others tended the water wells and the cider presses.
But the majority worked in the breeding yards.

Unlike most mortals on the Bright Shore, gnomes had no need
of amulets or talismans. The Charm they carried naturally in
their bones was sufficient to keep them grounded when Nemora
faced into the night. Deprived of the charmwind that blew from
the Abiding Star and held them in place, ælves, ogres, humans,
dwarves, and all mortal beings but gnomes were at jeopardy of
lifting away from the ground like smoke: If they lost the ballast
of consciousness, they would drift away during the dark hours,
floating first into the sky and then into the Gulf beyond.

Gnomes enjoyed not only the stability of their charmful bones
but also an uncanny ability to use that internal Charm to work
gnomish magic. That magic included the ability to fuse the ga-
metes—the seeds—of disparate animals *and* mortals. Combining
birds and humans or ælves produced a beastfolk useful to the
textile mills in the ice caves. Their keen beastmarked eyes and
swift, dextrous handiwork made them the best tailors and seam-
stresses in all the worlds. Gnomes themselves were famous for
their fine apparel and lavish style of dress.

The avian beastfolk were also superb at gathering snail-linen
threads from the snowy crags where the slugs excreted their fine
colorful filaments to cross crevices. For gathering spidersilk, the
gnomes had melded mortals and rats. The nimble ratfolk proved
useful to the textile industry for their ability not only to harvest
the spider-nest fabric swiftly but also for their nonpareil skill
at loomwork.

There was a perpetual demand from the garment shops of the
ice caverns for specialized workers, and that day he watched the
villagers training a group of young harefolk. Their sleek polar-
furred bodies ran obstacle courses among the corrals and stock-

ades of the breeding yards. When they were strong and fast enough, they would be sold to ice-girt communities as sled drivers and messengers.

Over the ages, beastfolk had been traded for goods from other worlds, and the descendants of those beastmarked mortals could be found everywhere. Only ogres openly protested the gnomish magic that made beastfolk. Both œlvish and human communities openly offered their indigent young men and women to the breeding yards in exchange for the excellent textiles and fashions of Nemora. The gnomes paid these genetic participants well: After siring or birthing just one or two beastmarked children for the gnomish magicians, the youths had earned funds enough to buy their freedom and live well another thousand days. There was no dearth of eager participants.

As a child, Ric had anticipated learning the breeders' trade, but his family had moved to the ice caves before he had grown old enough to apprentice. For a moment, he speculated what his life would have been like had he fulfilled his labors for the gnomish kith in the stalls. Would he have enjoyed that tedious magic tinkering with all its percolating beakers full of crimson jellies and yolks?

Instead of seed-magic, however, he had apprenticed to a fire magician in the frost fields when his family moved there to continue their labors as dyers and pattern cutters. He had no love for garment work and was glad he had spent his days serving the gnomish kith with warmth and light. Whenever forges faltered or ovens malfunctioned, he brought remedies, for he had learned all the mysteries of fire and how to use the Charm of his bones to control the flames.

His lifetime's work providing fire to his kith gave him some small empathy for the nature of the Radiant One. He watched Asofel sitting patiently at the base of the tree, shining blue-white as quicksilver. He climbed down the cedar, and said, "Returning to Nemora fills me with memories of my life's days."

"You are indulging in memories?" Asofel asked, annoyed, coldly removing his gaze from the ancient stairways of daylight deep in the woods. "I thought you were up there searching for the wraith Lara."

Old Ric's nose wrinkled. "I've no need to search for her. I see her clearly in the Necklace. She thinks she can lead us merrily on and on. But she is in for a surprise quite soon. Now that she is here on Nemora, I can use my gnomish magic to reach from the Charm in my bones, through the Necklace of Souls, and into her crystal prism. And I can hold her fast."

"Then why have you not done so?" Asofel groused. "I've been miserable for days in this cold dream. Let us find this wraith and learn what she knows about the shadow thing. Why are you dawdling, gnome?"

"Dawdling?" The eldern gnome blew a cold laugh from his pierced lungs. "I am well aware of the peril that threatens all creation. I would not waste an instant, I assure you. But I do not have your radiance. And gnomish magic is not as swift as talismans and amulets. It takes more time. Yet it is effective. Patience, Asofel. My magic reaches out, and soon the ghost will stand before us, fixed solid as a tree."

The luminous being rose before him glittering in tiny stuttering rainbows. "Well, how *much* longer?" he snapped.

Quickly, the gnome tried to think of a way to distract the unhappy being as the magic worked.

"Long enough for you to tell me what your world is like," the gnome responded, eyes bright with reflected luminance. "Is it as beautiful as Nemora?"

Startled at first by the question, Asofel answered in a voice slow with disdain, "I do not come from a world. Where I originate, there are no rocks hung in the void spinning through light and dark ceaselessly." His chromatic body swelled with pride of his origin. "I come from the light. It is a realm of energy within the corolla of the Abiding Star."

"This I know." The gnome's eyes slimmed with curiosity. "But what is it *like* there? Do you have trees? The nameless lady has revealed to me her garden, with its climbing blossoms and sunken pool."

"So it appeared to you, gnome." Asofel turned aside and paced through the chipped light of the forest as he spoke. "In the realm I come from, all form is made of thought. Life does not devour life there. This indignity to which you have reduced me in this cold creation, where I must devour pieces of our lady's dream to regain my strength, has no place in the light. We do not eat. Therefore, we have no need to void ourselves."

"And yet you war," the eldern gnome inserted. "Why else would the lady need sentinels? From what do they guard her?"

Asofel's hot stare rayed through the pollen smoke adrift in the daylight. "Good and evil are not exclusive to these chill worlds. Nor is mortality. I guard our lady against those that would harm her."

"And who are they?"

The Radiant One's laugh sounded empty as a cough. "What concern is that of yours, little gnome? You belong in this cold dream. Not I. I do not have to explain anything to you." Wrapped in ribbons of light, he spun away and stalked restively through the trees. "Take us to the witch."

Old Ric tossed his hands up, frustrated with his companion's surliness. "Very well. My gnomish magic is beginning to have something of a hold on her. Follow me then."

They marched out of the trees, and for a moment one could see green horizons folding into lavender distances and snow peaks far away. Then the slope carried them down root steps and slate stairs maintained by local hunters. Smoke from lodges rose thinly above the trees behind them. Ahead, riprap crossed a creek where faun prints poked the mud. A cobbled path began in a glade of club moss and led to a stone bridge over dark knots of water and a family of blue-haired ælves washing their laundry.

On the far side of the bridge, a party of farmers from the high fields charged toward them with pitchforks and scythes. They had seen Asofel's prismatic shining from afar and, alarmed, had come running to protect the village below. As they drew closer, their pace slackened, slowed, then stopped entirely at the sight of the Radiant One's wicked beauty, burning stardust shaped to a demonic angel moving toward them with the agility of music. And behind him—the eldern gnome run through the breastbone with a hooked shaft.

The sight sent snakes slithering through their hearts, and the gnomish farmers backed off onto the tussocks at the side of the cobbled path and did not challenge the intruder. Only one dared call out, "Ho, eldern gnome! Ho!"

Old Ric made no response. He had determined earlier not to reveal himself to his fellow gnomes until he was ready to seize the wraith, and then to do so swiftly and with little interaction. He wanted to minimize the fright he and the Radiant One were

certain to inspire. And so he strode forward entranced by his
bone-deep Charm, which he had threaded through the crystals
of the Necklace of Souls and had affixed to the prism that bound
the ghost to her form.

The eldern gnome held tight his threads of Charm and paid
no heed whatever to the children who came running to see the
frightful glory of Asofel, or their screaming mothers charging
after them. He moved steadily along the stone road past garden
gates and cottage fences. Most of the startled gnomes were silent,
though some called out greetings, warnings, frightened gibberish.
He heard none of it. Threads of Charm fastened him to Lara,
and they drew tighter with each step.

The witch felt the constriction at once. She had drifted toward
the peat village, with its grassy rooves and bracken fences. The
breeding yards had intrigued her, and, thinking herself beyond
reach of her pursuers, she had intended to explore the sights
before returning to the Well of Spiders and luring the Shadow
Eater and the gnome farther yet from her young master. Her
fascination with the white-furred children running hay-sheaf obstacles, their laughter like birdsongs, kept her attention diverted
from her crystal prism. She did not sense Old Ric's approach
until her movement began to slow.

She pushed harder, and the invisible threads tightened. With
a hand to her chest, she sensed their convergence on her prism.
But there was nothing that she could do. She was helpless to
sever the taut threads, though she tried, twisting her fingers to
mudras and gesticulating every exorcising sign she knew. The
astral cords tightened further yet, and soon she could not budge
from the roadway where she stood, locked like a boulder.

Trailing a throng of farm couples and their children, Old Ric
came into view. He descended the pilgrim road from the wooded
hills, and behind him strode the Shadow Eater, glowing like stone
shed from the moon. Lara knew there was no escaping them
short of removing the crystal prism and forfeiting her phantom
existence. But her young master still needed her, she felt, and
she would not abandon him no matter the consequence.

The eldern gnome strode toward her, eyes glazed. He stopped
a single pace away, and his crinkled face snapped to alertness.
With a slow and careful hand, he reached and took her crystal
prism. At his touch, her wraith form shimmered into view, and

the crowd flinched backward and cried out at the sight of her gory wounds.

She lifted her smashed chin so that everyone could see the decisions pain had made for her.

"Where is the shadow thing?" Old Ric asked flatly. "I saw you with him in the Necklace before he disappeared. Where has he gone?"

Lara would not speak, and so the eldern gnome reached through her prism and took her memories.

Gingerly, Old Ric's Charm touched her motionless soul, careful not to disturb the memories near her wounds. That pain would break his threads of Charm. He reached only for thoughts of the shadow thing—and he learned then of Reece Morgan, the magus from the Dark Shore, apprentice to the Wizard Caval, young master of this witch unburdened now of flesh.

Ric retreated three paces, and said to Asofel in a voice barely audible above the excited chattering of the crowd, "We cannot find the shadow thing because he has abandoned his original form and his magic for the aspect of a man with the beastmarks of a cat."

"Why have you sent him away from us?" Asofel asked the ghost.

"You eat shadows . . ." she mumbled in reply. "You intend to harm him."

"You thought we were going to kill him?" Old Ric asked in surprise. "You are sadly mistaken, witch. We don't intend to kill him. Never have. We have simply come to remove him from the Bright Shore, for his magic troubles the author of these worlds." The eldern gnome touched the Necklace of Souls to Lara's prism and gave to her all that he knew of the nameless lady and his mission.

Lara trembled like a fern, shocked. "It can't be that I—I misunderstood! Caval told me that my young master was in dire trouble."

"It is the worlds that are in trouble!" Old Ric corrected her with exasperation. He gave Asofel a hapless look and saw that the Radiant One was clearly not amused by the witch's meddling.

Lara's whole being throbbed with fright at her blunder. "Caval told me . . ."

"How could Caval speak at all to you in the Abiding Star?"

the gnome asked sharply. "His soul has flown into the Gulf. No voice can cross that abyss."

"Yet I heard him," she began, but before she could say more, screams blundered out of the crowd.

"Dwarves!" a voice yelled, and curdled to a shriek.

Out of the hills, squat white bodies flurried like unraveling snow. The dwarves had tracked the Necklace of Souls to Nemora and the summer veldt, to this brookside village, and now they came hurtling down the slopes, whirling hatchets and firing volleys of arrows.

The crowd of gnomes broke apart as the first hail of arrows whistled among them. Anguished cries seared the air as many went down under the attack. Like a sweeping curtain of rain, another volley darkened the sky.

"Asofel!" the gnome wailed. "Asofel! Stop them! They're killing my kith!"

The Radiant One turned his back on the legion of dwarves in their hundreds. "I have no power to waste defending gnomes," he stated flatly. "Mount my back, gnome, and we'll outrun them."

"My kith!" Old Ric cried as more arrows slashed among the scattering gnomes. "Save my kith!"

"On my back, gnome!" Asofel commanded. "Quickly! They want the Necklace of Souls. We'll lead them away from the village and your kith."

Old Ric leaped onto Asofel's back, and the arrow that impaled him jabbed the Radiant One.

"Hey—watch out!" Asofel scolded. "If you panic, we are doomed."

The eldern gnome clutched his legs about the Radiant One's warm shoulders. "Run! Carry us far from . . ."

Before he could mouth *the village*, Asofel sprinted away, and the gnome nearly toppled from his back. His head snapped back, and the prism pulled away from his fingers. The last thing that he glimpsed was the wraith Lara still fixed where he had rooted her. Arrows glided through her transparent body.

A pang of remorse winced through him that he had not held more firmly to her prism and set her soul free. In moments, the dwarves would be upon her, and with the crystal prism in their hands, her fate belonged to them.

Asofel bolted along a rutted dirt road that ran aslant the advancing dwarves. The army of maggot-warriors shifted the line of their attack away from the village and toward the glowing being with the gnome on his back, the gnome who carried the Necklace of Souls.

Broydo Blunders

"Let me have the serpent sword," Ripcat ordered Broydo.

They stood with Dogbrick and Jyoti under a tall rubble of clouds at the moss-grown brim of a small sinkhole. The muffled drum of march steps resounded from within the lightless shaft.

Broydo shook his head.

"The sword—" Ripcat extended a black-palmed hand, whose thick fingers each bore a retracted claw. "I need the sword if I'm to go in there and face those dwarves."

"I can't give it to you," Broydo stated flatly. He stood with the sword in both hands, pressed against his tunic of woven grass. "Smiddy Thea entrusted it to me. I will have to answer to her if I relinquish it to any other."

Ripcat appealed to the others with an exasperated look. "I need a weapon in there."

"The serpent sword is the only effective weapon we have against the dwarves," Jyoti gently reminded the ælf. "It's the only hope we have of capturing a dwarf and making it work for us. We are not your enemy. Let Ripcat have the sword."

"He has the fastest reflexes of us all," Dogbrick pointed out.

"If anyone should carry the serpent sword against the dwarves, it should be the Cat."

Broydo shifted his weight apprehensively and looked each of his captors squarely in the eyes. "Forgive me, I cannot relinquish this sword placed in my care. The lives of my clan may yet depend on it."

During the hike through the dark charmways that had led them out of the Qaf, Broydo had said little and had dutifully followed the others. When, after groping their way through dank rock corridors lit only by the wan glow of hex-gems, they asked to make a dwarf-seeker of the sword, he did not object. He even helped Dogbrick braid conjure-wire and affix lozenges of black crystal called niello eye charms to the haft. A net of linked rat-star gems formed a makeshift glove. When it was completed, Broydo grasped the hilt, the rat-stars and eye charms touched, and, as Dogbrick had predicted, the ælf felt the presence of dwarves in the grip of his blade. By waving the sword around, he was able to sense a direction toward the dwarves through the maze of charmways.

"We trusted you to lead us here," Ripcat persisted, his fur-backed hand still extended. "Now you have to trust me to use the sword correctly. I'll give it back, I promise."

"Old Ric and I suffered to get this sword." Broydo's hands tightened on it. "I cannot let you have it."

Ripcat's arm dropped to his side. "I'm not going down there without a weapon."

"Is this reluctance your attempt to serve your gnomish friend— Old Ric?" Dogbrick approached, stepping through a mushroom circle on the forest floor. "Are your loyalties so skewed, ælf, that you do not yet realize that we are trustworthy. We want what you want."

"You want to save the worlds?" Broydo asked with a taint of acid. "You do not even believe that the worlds are in peril."

"Why should I believe your hearsay?" Dogbrick snarled briefly with indignation. "A nameless lady has dreamed our worlds into being? A likely story."

The ælf squared his stance with doughty defiance of the beastmarked man. "Old Ric told me so."

"And who told him?" Dogbrick chided. His hand flashed out and snatched the serpent sword from Broydo's grip. "Ha! Enough of rumor. Let us catch a dwarf and see what it has to say about all this."

Broydo jumped to retrieve the blade, but Dogbrick pushed him away with one hand and glared menacingly at him until the ælf was forced to back off, stamping and huffing, crestfallen to have lost so valuable a tool that was vouchsafed him by the leader of his clan.

Ripcat quickly seized the sword from Dogbrick and, leveling at his friend a sidelong stare tight with disapproval, handed it back to its rightful owner. "We're not thieves anymore," he admonished the beastmarked man. "So take back your blade, Broydo. If you're brave enough to stand against this bully, then you're worthy of holding your own weapon against the dwarves. Will you lead us?"

Considerably buoyed by this act, Broydo affirmed this with a shake of the sword. "The bone of the world serpent will protect us!" He strode to the sinkhole, to the side shaft from the Well of Spiders that opened upon the dwarves' route from World's End.

Jyoti put a cautionary hand on Ripcat's shoulder and bent to his ear. "Is this wise? Our only effective weapon in the hands of an ælf with no battle experience?"

"I just hope his sword does what he says it will." Dogbrick tossed his head ruefully as Broydo descended feetfirst into the hole.

"Let him carry his own weapon," Ripcat reiterated. "If we thwart him, we will have to watch our backs. This way, he serves us."

"No matter how poorly," Dogbrick added sourly, and lowered himself into the hole where Broydo had just vanished. "I'll watch his back now to be sure we do not lose our one defense."

As Jyoti and Ripcat waited by the sinkhole, the margravine paused to regard her companion for a moment. She had not dared to look at him fully since he reverted to his beastmarks. It bothered her to see him like this, for she had come to love him as Reece, and the sight of his beastmarks was too much to bear, and she was grateful yet again for her amulets, which eased her disquiet.

She stopped Reece before he descended into the sinkhole. "We were there for a while weren't we? In Arwar, I mean. We had each other, and the world was beginning to look new."

"We still have it." Ripcat held up his tufted hands. "This will change back. I believe the ælf. The Necklace of Souls is powerful. Lara showed me her prism, and from what I saw, I know it can make me Reece again. The world will be new for us once more—after this."

"And if this ælf is right?" Jyoti asked, a hook of uncertainty in her voice. "If the Shadow Eater has been sent after you by nameless gods and the worlds are in jeopardy because of you—what then?"

"We don't know that." He brushed the velvet fur at the back of his hand against her cheek. "Don't worry. We found our way together against the Dark Lord. You and I, remember? We will prevail again."

Jyoti nodded valiantly, though her heart felt hollow with fear. The sound of the dwarvish marchers in the caverns below throbbed ominously. "We better hurry now, to stay close to Broydo. We don't dare let him lose that sword."

Ripcat entered the sinkhole headfirst, and Jyoti climbed down after him. The shaft descended narrowly, and they kept from falling by pressing against the damp enclosing rock with their arms and legs. The hole dropped them eventually into a grotto pulsing with the green glow of their dwarvish hosts.

They huddled together behind a glossy wall of stalagmites only paces from where the eerily shining dwarves filed. Emerging from a crevasse that connected them to a labyrinth of other charmways leading back to World's End, the dwarves then departed through a similar rift in the wall of the stadiumwide cavern. Where they disappeared to Ripcat could not tell—perhaps to another dominion, summoned by the mysterious Duppy Hob.

Jyoti and Dogbrick recalled the evil presence they had sensed in the grotto under Saxar, and in her fright she pressed closer against him. Together they watched Ripcat pad noiselessly among the mineral stumps and ringed cones deposited by seepings. He crept to a notch in the stone wall, where he stood behind the flow of dwarves.

With a slow roll of his wrist, Ripcat summoned Broydo forth. The ælf hurried to his side, kicking gravel and scraping grit loudly under his heels. He cringed. None of the dwarves seemed to notice. Their red eyespots, brown in the green shine, gazed forward entranced by some inward voice or music. Their husky, plate-armored bodies clattered and thumped and smothered the sounds Broydo made hurrying to Ripcat's side.

"I'll pull one in," the beastman whispered, "and you hold it at sword point."

Ripcat bent to the ground, spying the squat legs of the army, reading the rhythms of their advance. He noticed some marchers were momentarily out of view of the others when they turned the bend around the sheet of dripped rock where he hid. With predatory swiftness, he pounced, seized a dwarf by the leather strop that secured its breastplate and yanked it behind the stone partition.

The dwarf eked the first whine of an alarmed cry, then saw the sword of shining bone pointed at thumb's length from its visored face, bright with freezing air. Its promise of death swiftly silenced the abhorrent creature.

Dogbrick slouched over the dwarf, swiped the hatchet from its grip, and deftly looped its wrists together with braids of conjure-wire. He tugged off the sharp-jawed helmet, exposing the pointed, faceless head of the dwarf, with its lidless retinal patches for eyes and fibrillose slit of a mouth.

Jyoti dragged it by its cleated boots, and Dogbrick held it by its breastplate as they hoisted it toward the pillar of blue light from the exit hole.

Ripcat grinned at the ælf. "Well done, ælvish sword!"

Broydo dismissed this praise with a wary glimpse over his shoulder. The drumming march of dwarves throbbed like pain in his ears, he was so tense with fear. How many hordes of dwarves were there? During their search through the charmways, he had felt others in the hilt of the serpent sword—many corridors of maggot-soldiers through the caverns that connected one part of the Well of Spiders with the next. Where were they all going?

After the Necklace of Souls? he said to himself with livid doubt. *This vast army all to fetch a necklace from a gnome?*

"Something terrible and big is happening," Broydo whispered to Ripcat. "We must find Old Ric quickly."

Ripcat froze. Broydo bumped into him before he saw what Ripcat did and bit back a cry. Dogbrick, in his eagerness to shove the captured dwarf up the shaft, had exposed himself: His shaggy head stood taller than the screen of stalagmites. Before

Ripcat could hiss a warning, a searing cry went up among the dwarves.

In the next instant, the rush of outraged dwarves shattered the mineral wall like crockery, and a dozen warriors swept over Dogbrick.

"Broydo!" Ripcat pulled the ælf forward. Between them and the exit, a crowd of dwarves surged.

Broydo swung the serpent sword, startled at the lightness with which it cut through the pressing throng. On contact, the warriors shriveled away to twisting coils of maggots and a clatter of hatchets and armor. But these deaths did not deter the attack, and another wave of shrieking, helmeted bodies advanced, battle-axes raised.

Ripcat ducked behind Broydo, shouting directives to him. "Strike lower! You'll hit more. Watch your left! Your left!"

Serpent sword flailing before him, Broydo cut a path toward the day shaft. Briefly, despair shot through him at the sight of Dogbrick hauled away howling, his large vigorous body swallowed whole by the seething mass of dwarves. Then the rabid warriors were hacking toward him again with their brute weapons, and he had to watch his sword to keep it from getting shattered.

"Give me the sword!" Ripcat swung about with a violent hiss, driving back the grasping hands of the dwarves. "Watch our back! They're going to cut us!"

The crush of the crowd prevented hatchets from flying, but the blades still slashed dangerously close. Broydo tried to slash and turn in a wide arc and nearly tripped over Ripcat.

Hands clasped the Cat's shirt and tore the last shreds of it from him. "The sword!" he called out as his ankles jerked away and he slid boots first into the throng.

Broydo tried chopping a path after him, but it was hopeless. The oncoming dwarves had no end. His courage collapsed to find himself alone underground in the green pulsing mass of dwarves. Screaming maniacally, he beat his way toward the luminous column of daylight.

Jyoti's hands grabbed him as he clambered backward up the wall ledges and pulled him into the shaft. Legs pumping, the ælf squirmed up and out of the sinkhole, knocking Jyoti to her back

with the ferocity of his exit. Immediately, he swung about and
jabbed the serpent sword into the hole.

The dwarves' screaming attack dulled. They had taken coup,
and their ululating cries sounded jubilant.

"Where's Reece?" Jyoti asked, leaving the captured and bound
dwarf on its back to rush to the moss-clotted brink. "What's
happened to Ripcat? And Dogbrick? Where's Dogbrick?"

On his knees, Broydo dropped the sword and buried his shivering face in his hands. His wracking sobs gave Jyoti the painful answer.

She grabbed the sword and dropped herself into the hole.
Landing in a crouch, she swung the blade before her, and its flat
breadth dazzled with dayshine. But the edge cut nothing. The
cavern stood empty.

Bootsteps clopping hollowly on the rock floor, Jyoti advanced
toward the rift in the cave wall where the dwarves had just been
marching. The sound of their retreat muttered like surf. She
started in, then stopped herself. The charmways were extensive
and intricate, and she had witnessed hosts here and in the charmway near Saxar. She would lose herself underground if she entered without a guide. And were they yet alive? She made herself
believe they were, or their bodies would have been destroyed in
this cavern. Her belief wavered briefly at the weirding yowls from
the dark, but she shut her ears to them and turned quickly away.

Broydo still sat on his knees sobbing into his palms when she
pulled herself out of the shaft.

"Get up," she ordered. "Stop bawling."

The ælf obeyed, chewing at his lower lip, pressing the heel
of one hand into an eye socket. "I tried to hold them back. There
were too many."

"I don't want to hear it." Jyoti held him with her angry stare
and restrained herself from speaking for a moment while she
concentrated on breathing away her panic. Momentarily, she
said, "We just lost the most important person in these worlds to
me." She edged a step closer, the serpent sword vibrant in her
grip. "And, if we're to believe you, he's the most important person
to all the worlds." She stepped close enough to stare past the
blear of his tears. "We're going to get him back, you and I."

"Kill me." Broydo spread his arms wide. "I deserve to die. I
failed us all."

"No!" Jyoti snapped. "I told you, I don't want to hear this. No crying. No pity. Not now. We have to move swiftly. We're going to get him back. That's all I want to hear." She handed him the sword. "Now you hold on to this. I need both hands."

She removed her two niello eye charms from her vest and pressed their flat sides together, doubling their range. In their inky depths, she searched for Ripcat and Dogbrick and saw neither one.

"They're gone." Jyoti fit the amulets back into their shoulder sleeves and looked to where the captive dwarf lay squirming in the grass. She nudged it with her boot tip. "You—where have they taken our partners?"

The red eyespots stared impassively at her.

Jyoti's hands reached for her amulet-vest, intending to use Charm to learn what she wanted from the dwarf, but Broydo spoke up, "That won't do any good." He pushed himself to his feet and swung the serpent sword. "Let me have a try."

The dwarf jolted upright.

"Tell us what we want to know," was all Broydo had to ask, holding the bone sword in both hands and pointed at the captive's pudgy body.

Its slit mouth opened, and the cry that had been dwelling inside since its capture flapped out in raspy dwarvish sobs.

Jyoti waved an amber wand around the narrow head of the dwarf, and it calmed to silence. "Where have you come from?"

A small voice flickered, "World's End."

Jyoti touched the wand to the dwarf's brow for reward, and ease visibly passed through the tense creature, loosening the tightness in its sloped shoulders. "And where are you going?"

"Earth."

"You are on Irth." Jyoti passed the wand before its eyespots. "Where on Irth? Which dominion?"

"No dominion."

With a perplexed tug at her ear, Jyoti stepped back. "You are hiding underground?"

"No." The dwarf squirmed, agitating for more Charm. "We are bound for Earth—on the . . ."

"Maggot, *this* is Irth!" Broydo shouted. His pent-up anger at himself for failing to save the others earlier propelled him forward in a stomping stride. "You have arrived!" He swung the sword to

alarm the dwarf, but under the sedation of Charm the wrist-tied warrior moved too slowly. The sword tip grazed the padded flesh
of its forearm, and its sudden piercing cry sizzled almost instantly
to silence.

With an acid hiss, the dwarf deflated to a writhing dragon
maggot large as an ælf's thigh. It squirmed behind its fallen
breastplate to hide from the light of day.

Broydo gasped and swung toward Jyoti, who blinked away her
surprise, then shrugged resignedly and fit her power wand back
into her vest. "We have to work on your sword technique, ælf."

"Lady Jyoti—margravine—I—I am sorry. Again, I am sorry!"
Broydo bent helplessly over the armor plates and leathern straps
of the transformed warrior. "It was an accident. Oh, here, take
this sword away from me. I know that Smiddy Thea would herself have it no other way."

Jyoti shot him a disgusted look and waved him off. The ælf
had lost their one hope of locating Ripcat and Dogbrick. But she
had no time for remorse or pity. She had to find another way
to get them back. She began to talk aloud as she moved briskly
into the woods, Broydo anxiously following. "They may yet be
alive, but they're nowhere near here. They must have passed
through another charmway, maybe into another dominion or
maybe back to the Well of Spiders and on to another world.
Even though this dwarf said they were bound for Irth, we don't
know. He might have lied. Though I doubt it. The Charm had
softened him easily. They could well be here on Irth. Still, we
can't know until we find out. And the only way I can think to
find out is to use Dogbrick's seeker, to track Ripcat like he did
in the Qaf. But he has the seeker. We have nothing. We have
the sword. It can track dwarves. Not good enough. There are
too many of them."

The sword felt heavy in Broydo's grasp, and he let its blade
trail on the ground after him. He followed silently through the
dense woods, pondering if he were cursed. He had brought doom
to those who had helped him—the beastmarked men, before
them the eldern gnome Ric, and even his own clan, which was
why he found himself in this alien land to begin with. Perhaps
Tivel or his demon had cursed him.

After they wandered far among the forest cloisters, he began
to fear that Tivel's curse had begun its dread work on his present

companion. Jyoti appeared pale with rage. The ælf feared her, because of him, she had lost her lover, Reece disguised as Ripcat. And her friend Dogbrick had been his responsibility as well. His arrogance had led to their deaths. And his stupidity had deprived them of the dwarf captive who could have led to the others. Surely, this warrior woman had not killed him yet because that would have been too swift a retribution for the pain he had inflicted on her and everyone else.

As the enclaves of the woods darkened and Jyoti continued advancing down small lanes and byways among the mammoth trees and ivy draperies, he finally mustered the voice to ask, "Where are we going?"

"To find a sibyl," she muttered just loud enough to be heard. Her vigorous advance through the underbrush disturbed a barred owl, and it broke away through the gloom with a loud thrash of its wings.

Broydo cringed and gazed at the shadowy upper storeys of the forest. Eye glints twinkled in those dark galleries, and bat-winged vipers darted through the vine-looped spaces. "Sibyls are prophecy creatures, aren't they?"

"If we can find one, we may yet learn if Reece and Dogbrick are alive." She pulled away a curtain of shawl moss obstructing an alley between rows of titanic trees and bulging root buttresses puddled with mist. At the alley's far end, ferns tasseled a hidden cove. There, night itself had curled up and lay unburdened by light.

Abruptly, two tiny sharp-eyes opened far back in that darkness and burned like serene flames.

"Come, Broydo," Jyoti commanded, and moved forward. "From her we may learn, too, if we can expect to stay alive."

RIPCAT IN GABAGALUS

ABOVE THE CHITTERING JOY OF THE DWARVES AND THE STOMPING and scuffling of their brisk march, Dogbrick's howls curled. By those howls, Ripcat knew his friend was alive, and his fear of being immediately hacked to pieces dimmed enough for him to stop thrashing. He hung limply, suspended above the dwarves' squabby white bodies, one boot and two corners of his pants hooked on the tines of their hatchets.

His mind focused beyond wondering if a butchering floor lay ahead, and he noticed by the bioluminescent glow of the swarm that crawl holes riddled the slick rock walls. A honeycomb of vents had perforated this chamber.

The opportunity these vents presented whipped his blood faster, but he did not tense his body. He dangled slackly, using the jouncing rhythms of the march to work his ankle free of the hooked boot. Then, with a sudden full-body twist, he tore loose of one pant leg, slit the other, and dropped to the cavern floor. His legs scissored among the frenzied dwarves, and he toppled two and snatched their hatchets.

Swatting and spinning, Ripcat sprang upright and cut a path

to the perforated wall. His blades clanged off helmets and sliced cleanly through the small albino bodies. At the wall, he hurled the hatchets behind and somersaulted into a tunnel just large enough to admit him.

Darkness clapped around him. Dogbrick's howls and the clangor of the wounded and enraged dwarves wobbled louder and softer as if shunted by a stiff wind. When he rolled around to face the way he had entered, the shine of the throng had shrunk to a point of green fire. He scrambled back in that direction, intent on finding a way to free Dogbrick before the dwarves inflicted their anger on him.

With each step, the light at the far end of the tunnel fluttered like a wind-struck flame. Ripcat paused. He knew by the way sounds and vision drifted that he stood at the juncture of a charmway. Whatever direction he moved would hurtle him thousands of leagues into another dominion. He remained perfectly still, knowing that, to get back to Dogbrick, he would have to advance with the precision of a high-wire walker.

He dared a step, and the sparkpoint whirled out of sight. A maritime gust brushed his pelt and filled his sinuses with the salty tang of tide pools shrinking in the heat. Webs of chlorine shadows billowed on the cave walls. Water lapped loudly and gulls cried wild with greed.

Ripcat followed the marine reflections and sounds around a curtain of rock and winced in the glare of the Abiding Star rising over a churning sea. Ocean froth streamed from pinnacles of rock thrusting through the waves. Cascades of kelp gleamed under the charmfire and clouds of the dawn sky.

Wearing one boot and shredded pants, he leaned in the mouth of the cavern, peering through streaming sheets of seawater at the sunken continent of Gabagalus. It rose from under the night sea to bask another day beneath the Abiding Star. The coraline crags of ancient iron mountains ranged as far as he could see from his own high perch atop such a peak. Brine coursed in immense rivers over broad continental shelves slick with sea plants.

Even in far Saxar, Ripcat had heard tales of Gabagalus, an amphibious domain on the far side of Irth that sank each night beneath the waves after gathering Charm from the Abiding Star throughout the day. But he recalled hearing next to nothing of

the ocean kingdom's denizens other than that they were a colony
of an interplanetary utopia wholly indifferent to the other dominions of Irth.

As the curtain of water thinned before the cave mouth, Ripcat
stared with fascination at the blotched hues of Gabagalus. Slime
covered everything, from the mountain peaks to the coastal cliffs
steaming with cataracts. The heat of the Abiding Star dried the
motley of brown slime to buff and beige leathers. The fields of
drying sea mold blistered and cracked, giving way to wort farms
crisscrossed with roads, quilted terraces of lichen, and emerald
cress paddies. Among the mountain ranges, glass towers and
golden spires of cities flashed with morning light.

Ripcat stepped out of the charmway cave, and dried slime
crunched underfoot. He stood on the ledge of a mountain summit
that commanded a vista of highways and farms. A rocket pad
occupied a bluff in the middle distance surrounded by the green
spines of eroded mountains. Derrick towers caged the slender
silver body of a cargo rocket. Tiny with distance, winches loaded
bales of wort and lichen onto the ship.

Closer to Ripcat, a hermit's shelter occupied an adjacent ledge
of the pinnacle, and before this ramshackle lean-to a salamandrine
man stood. Mists whispered out of the deep gorge that separated
them, but Ripcat could clearly distinguish the hairless, purple-
skinned man's tinsel windings. Caval had worn such devotional
apparel in his attempt to lift his soul to the Abiding Star, and
Ripcat had seen several such holy pilgrims wander into the Qaf,
never to return. But this man had glistering skin shining through
the bindings of silver-blue tinsel, and the hand that waved was
webbed.

"Stranger!" the hermit called. "Can you hear me over there?
Who are you?"

"Is this Gabagalus?" Ripcat removed his one boot and stood
with clawed toes curled on the rocky brink of the cave lip. Small
lightnings twinkled in the dense morning haze far away, where
the burn-off and spindrift augmented horizons of clouds.

The hermit nodded, bobbing his whole body up and down.
"Who are you, stranger?"

"I am Ripcat of Saxar." In two quick strides, he lunged from
the cave ledge to the hermit's terrace. "I came through that
charmway."

The round speckled head of the hermit retracted in amazement at Ripcat's leap. "You're the first to come through that cave in all the time I've practiced here—more than eighteen thousand days."

"And you are?" Ripcat noted the gill slits behind the hermit's earholes.

"I am nobody. An eremite come to surrender my soul to the eternal glory of the Abiding Star." He spoke to the blistered ground. "I eat humble krill by night and spend my days entranced in Charm."

"Perhaps you can help me." Ripcat began tying off the shredded lengths of his pants to a thong. "I'm lost. This is my first time in Gabagalus, and I'm wondering if I should stay or return to the charmway. What do you suggest?"

Interest sparkled in the hermit's rectangular pupils. "Gabagalus is a good place to make a fortune. Do you want a fortune?"

"I've had fortunes." Ripcat finished securing the waistcloth and laid his problem open to the holy man. "I seek knowledge. I want to know about dwarves, the Shadow Eater, and Duppy Hob."

"Gabagalus is a good place for knowledge, Ripcat of Saxar. We are a society of science. Not like the crude dominions of Irth. Ha!" He gasped a laugh. "They try to tame a wilderness with Charm. While we have built an empire of science!"

"Can your science teach me about dwarves?" The beastmarked wanderer faced the umber expanse of Gabagalus and watched the world waking: windmills unfurled, kites and chrome balloons soared aloft along thermal currents on their way to harvest Charm directly from the rays of the Abiding Star. Solar carriages crawled over highways, some trailing wagons of farm goods bound for the cities. "Tell me about dwarves and their creator, Duppy Hob."

"When I was somebody, I had a fortune." The hermit's round, chinless face smiled thinly and heavy lids lowered, remembering the pleasures of a former existence. "I can tell you how to make a fortune. But I don't know anything about dwarves." He slouched away dejectedly, returning to his crude stone hut.

"Well, if short ugly slugs in helmets come out of that cave, you stay hidden." Ripcat thought to ask for directions down the mountain, but the hermit had disappeared quickly, perhaps not wanting to expose himself long to the desiccating rays of day—or perhaps unhappy with mention of the infamous devil worshipper.

The way down proved treacherous. Misty winds buffeted him and obscured his footing. Twice he clung to overhangs with no toeholds at all, vapors clawing at him in the brisk seawind. He had wished then he had stayed in the charmways. Clawholds inching slowly, he gradually made his way down the rock face to the upland meadows.

Salamandrine shepherds herding flocks of blue-wooled beasts paused in their labors to watch the beastmarked stranger. He saluted them as he descended the dewy slopes, and a cur pranced barking at his heels.

Suddenly, a gruesome yodeling cry lifted faces to the heights. At the mist-spun peak where Ripcat had emerged from the charmway, dwarves packed tiny as motes. Yet distant as they were, Ripcat's keen sight identified the hermit's body impaled and convulsing on the hatchets' sharpened pikes.

In a dash, Ripcat bounded across the upland meadows. A meander of oyster-shell roadway wriggled across an expansive range of red wort. Behind him, the dwarves came tumbling like snowballs over the cliffsides and down the meadow slopes, hundreds strong.

A rocket pad hovered above misty gorges, too far away to run to. He needed a weapon. Or a shield. The flat land offered no sanctuary, and he jumped off the road, skidded down the embankment, and along the chute of a fuming spillway into the tossing waters crashing among boulders.

Dwarves gathered along the titanic rocks of the embankment, nearly invisible in the roaring mists. They watched for Ripcat to resurface bludgeoned by streambed boulders. But no body darkened the white foam.

Ripcat spun with the pouring water, and the heaving currents swept him along a rushing cascade and into the sea. Lungs locked, eyes burning for light, he shot through a dazzling fog of thrashing currents and foam, his body buffeted, slapped by giant hands.

Then, a blaze of morning burst over him, and he sucked air and flopped to his back in the bobbing sea. The cliffs of Gabagalus carried balconies of uncoiling ferns and terrace steps of farmland high above angry tusks of rockspray.

As Ripcat backstroked away from the inbound current, drifting alone under the morning clouds, he thought back on all the events that had maneuvered him into this cold green water. His effort kept his mind off the possibility of sharks and razormouth eels. It also frustrated him to touch the emptiness in his memory where Reece belonged. He tried to piece together the confusing tumult of events that had happened to him over the past few days.

First, Jyoti had told him they were lovers—and envy soured like nausea in him when he tried to imagine what Reece was able to share with her, what passion passed between them. His envy felt near to madness, and, cursing his beastmarks, he decided he had to put Jyoti out of his mind.

His thoughts turned to Lara—her almost blind devotion to him—and a paralyzing wave of confusion and guilt washed over him. What *were* his feelings for her? What *should* they be? He had made his peace over her death—or so he had thought.

His mind reeled. To center himself, he attempted to focus his attention on figuring out what manner of magic Reece possessed that some nameless and pregnant giantess at World's End would accuse him of poisoning her unborn child.

What a preposterous story! It was so outlandish he would have dismissed it readily, but he could not, for he knew how Lara's ghost had sought out Reece at great peril to warn him of the Shadow Eater. He could not fathom why a ghost would suffer to travel so far unless the message were true. Nor could he imagine her lying to him. Yet if what she said was fact . . .

And so, there was also this to consider: He himself had not heard her say anything about this Shadow Eater firsthand. The information was thirdhand, filtered through Reece, then Jyoti. He considered what advantage he would have had if he could have spoken with Lara directly instead of as Reece. What insights would he have gleaned if he were able to assess her with his keener feline senses?

His mind swerved back to his predicament, afloat in the sea off the sea-smashed cliffs of Gabagalus. He had never heard Lara say anything except in his dreams. And there she only spoke of the trees she danced among and the power they gave so freely.

"And what has become of Lara?" he asked the soaring clouds. He ruminated about his dreams and her place in them—the feral woman with her dance of feathery turnings, her wing of black hair. Grief and longing tainted him when he thought of her, and he wondered what Reece understood about her that he did not.

A tug at his foot snapped his forlorn reverie. He rolled over and saw in the clear water a smiling nymph of tilted eyebrows and silver eyes. Her blue fingers tangled with his blue fur and pulled him toward her. He moved to swim away, but she grasped his arms firmly and tethered him to a strength his beating limbs could not defeat.

The nymph's fishtail torso rippled powerfully and thrust them through the water under the sparkling surface. Her violet lips sealed his and breathed cold, magnetic air into his lungs. His body brightened like a blown trumpet, and his vision sharpened. He saw several blue-tinted mermaids floating beneath him and heard their singing, a dark sparkling inside his head.

The mermaids slowly carried him deeper, to where light drowned in the murky shadows of a kelp forest. Among the maroon fronds, she breathed her chill breath into him again. Time thickened. He saw through the flickering keyways of the weeds to diamond glints of a glass city—blister domes, bubble canopies, transparent pods clustered on the submarine slopes of Gabagalus.

Curtains of kelp parted before a transparent airlock sealed with valves of baked red enamel. Blue hands spun the wheel hatch, and incandescent sprays of laughter veiled the smiling faces in tiny bubbles. A thump of a fishtail flipped him into the open hatchway, and the round portal swung shut behind him.

Ripcat's breath exhausted itself as the water drained from the airlock in a frothy whirl, and he pushed gasping through the inner hatch as it unlocked. Dripping brine, he stood in a spacious seaview chamber. The glass enclosure displayed the mermaids who had kidnapped him, swerving among themselves more supple than fish.

A small old man sat in a wire chair. Time dripped out of his eyes. His open mouth hung darker yet.

Sodden with seawater, Ripcat stepped toward the bald and shriveled man, who sat dressed in black tunic and green felt slippers, his square knee bones pressed together.

"Don't wet the carpet, beast!" an emaciated voice ordered from the shrunken body, and Ripcat stepped back onto the red tiles before the airlock. "Use the towels behind you. And do a good job of it. I don't like the stink of wet fur."

Green towels stood stacked on wire shelves beside the airlock. Ripcat took one in each hand and began drying himself. "Who are you, old man?"

"I?" His eyes were brilliant as porcelain in a face of sad crumpled skin. "Don't you know?" The old man stiffened with surprise, and a feeble hand trembled against his sunken chest. "I am Duppy Hob."

PRISONERS OF ZUL

IN A CAVERN DAMP WITH SEA MIST, DOGBRICK SAT SHACKLED BY wrists and ankles to the salt-bleached wall. He had pulled the length of his chains to their limit, and now he squatted in the mouth of the cave. From there, he could gaze out over the sea at the gray end of day. The pulsebeat of two green stars marked the first station of night.

The dwarves who had imprisoned him here had removed his shawl of amulets, and he wore only a breechcloth. His shoulders still ached from where the hatchet spikes had jabbed him. The theriacal opals from his shawl had closed the wounds, but the amulets had been removed from him before they had completed their healing.

Without Charm to protect him, he felt the cold reaching through his fur. His pelage, a dense shag the color of cedar, brushed back from the stiff wind and exposed a grievous face, dark eyes silently screaming in their bonepits, packed jaw muscles slack but exposing a glint of fang. The nocturnal tide lightened his bones, and the absence of his rat-star headband left him prone to an oppressive gloom.

"Why do we say that night falls?" He spoke to the empty cavern, and his deep voice resounded hollowly. "Night does not fall. It rises. Look at it there, seeping out of the ocean—the lusters of darkness, mollusk stains in the sea . . ."

He ran both hands through his thick mane, and the clank of chains thickened his despair. "This is the neap tide of my Charm, my strength, my blood. I don't have the mind to know why we are here."

His great head turned and scanned the stone socket. He saw no one, but he sensed a ghost. His hackles had fluffed the moment the dwarves had dragged him here. Her electrifying muteness, her prickling nothingness stirred something unhappy in his deeps. If he had his eye charms, he might see her. Yet even without amulets, her presence touched him with a vacancy, the sole shape of placelessness that the solitary twilight only heightened.

"These chains hold me," said Dogbrick to the unseen presence. "But what holds you?"

Far down the cliff, the tide seethed.

Dogbrick let his gaze roam out the cave mouth to the tarnished shine of the sea reflecting the luminous paraphernalia of night. He thought he knew these cliffs. Their stone draperies and numerous islets reminded him of the cordillera north of Saxar, where he had journeyed as an adolescent. He had hoped then to find employment as a stevedore in the dockyards at the polar palace of Zul. But the palace did not hire men with beastmarks.

"Yes, I believe I camped down there as a boy," Dogbrick remarked. "I'd been stewing three days over my rejection from Zul. Beastmarks! Forever they mark me as less than human and more than a man."

He watched long ripples of surf cooling in the darkness far below. "I might have become a dock manager or even a wharf foreman. Who knows? Instead, I returned to Saxar and learned the trade of a thief."

As blunt fingers tangled in his hair and his beast-slanted brow furrowed, he wondered aloud, "What would that hurt young man think of himself now if he could see me here years later in shackles awaiting what indignity? Torture? Enslavement to dwarves? Slow death?"

Chains clanked as he rose and paced to the back wall of the
cave. "I need Charm to soften the hardness of these thoughts,
this dread."

In the middle of the cave, he sat cross-legged, with his chains
coiled in his lap, trying to think of nothing, hoping nothing
would take his worries and his heavy mood away from him. But
after a few moments, he lowered his brow to the cave floor and
moaned piteously, mourning his lost Charm.

Lara watched him from where she crouched invisibly in a corner. The crystal prism that gave her form so far from the Abiding
Star lay hidden under her cassock. The dwarves had seen it and
stood mesmerized by their own green auras reflected in its rainbow depths. She had feared then that they were going to rip it
away from her.

Since they had delivered her here early in the day, she had
almost wished they had taken the prism from her. She had sat
too long with herself, thinking. Once pain had kept her thoughts
simple. But Reece had taken her pain away, taken the whole of
her suffering into himself, and the shock of it had transformed
him into Ripcat.

She brooded about this. She had seen the white of his terrified
animal eyes when the transformation was done. The good she
had hoped to work for him had been lost. She consoled herself
with the fact that even when she had presented what she knew
to him, before he had dared to take her pain from her, he had
been skeptical.

Am I wrong? she had time and clarity to consider. The Shadow
Eater that she had so feared was not an enemy; rather, he had
been sent to spare Reece from doing harm that could end the
worlds! She had misunderstood the intent of the Radiant One.
The message from Caval that she had received while a dreamful
soul in the Abiding Star had faded too quickly, and now she
could indeed sing with this beastmarked prisoner, *This is the neap
tide of my memory* . . .

What was her purpose if she could not trust even her own
recollection? *Better the dwarves had taken the crystal prism from me—*
she thought, and tried to imagine dying again. The first time had
been so horrible that only the Abiding Star itself could heal her
from its pain, but she imagined that giving up the prism would
feel different.

The stars glinted like knife points. Darkness, amnesiac anonymity, eternal silence were all myths. Her first death had proved
that to her. What lay in the abyss of the Gulf for her soul if she
were cut free of her crystal prism was surely a great diminish-
ment. There would be intermittent consciousness but never again
of the lucidity and tranquillity she had known in the Abiding
Star.

She did not want to die. She wanted to return to the Abiding
Star and the warm, sustaining radiance of the Beginning. But
there was no way back now that the dwarves had seized her.
No hope—save this man of shaggy beastmarks.

"What is your name?" Lara asked.

In a frightened clatter of chains, Dogbrick lunged upright.
"Waug!" he shouted. Disoriented without Charm, his startled
senses ran him in a tight circle before he grabbed control of
himself again.

"Don't be afraid." The ghost showed her healed face, her placid
face meant to quiet him, and he sprang to the far end of the
cavern and hunched there with ears flat, fangs bared. "I thought
you were aware I was here."

Dogbrick reminded himself this was a phantom. The thought
carried no reassurance without Charm, and he remained crouched
around a growl.

"Look, Dog!" She revealed the crystal prism, and its spectral
edges spun nimbly in her fingers, casting Charm and radiance
across the cave. "There is Charm here for you. I know you need
it. Come closer, and I'll share it with you."

Dogbrick's tense mind relaxed. On her outstretched palm, the
universal sapphires, emeralds, and rubies glittered from their secret kingdom, where everything of the cold world had its coun-
terpart shaped of pure light. A shiver of warmth whirred through
him as he edged closer to the spinning crystal.

"There, Dog, there—" Lara extended a phantom hand and at
her touch images fluttered through her of the blue-furred man
shape Reece had become. The whirling charmlight revealed
flickerflash scenes of Cat and Dog together on the steep avenues
of Saxar. "You must be Dogbrick."

"I am," he growled softly, content to curl up in the shining
Charm.

"Sleep, then, Dogbrick—sleep." She lowered her hand over his glistening, watchful eyes, and he slept.

At a touch of the prism to his furred brow, Dogbrick's memories expanded across the slewed facets of the gem. If she wanted to, she could draw his entire soul out of him with this Charmed rock. But she meant him no such harm. She wanted only to see who this Dogbrick was.

Shaking her long hair over his slumbering face, she used the crystal prism to sift his memories into herself. She discarded his childhood traumas. She looked past his recent struggles and triumphs with Dig Dog Ltd. and restricted herself to draw forth remembrances of Reece disguised with beastmarks.

Ripcat—She mouthed the name, fathoming its associations for Dogbrick. Ripcat had lived as a thief in Saxar after he had left the Dark Shore and forgotten he was Reece. But he had kept none of the factory-pilfered goods for himself. He had retained only what he had needed to eat and to prevent himself from drifting off on the nocturnal tide. The rest he had given away, buying goodwill in the impoverished districts of Saxar and the sanctuaries where he could sleep and dream—of her.

Lara had loved Reece as long as she could remember, had loved him with more than filial caring. When she was alive in the forests of the Snow Range on the Dark Shore, she had possessed dreams, too. She had wanted Reece for her own—witch and magus united as a family.

But the murdering knives had killed that dream with her body. As a ghost, she laughed at her romantic prayers for love and children. Now she prayed for the freedom of the Abiding Star, free of pain, free of all shapes, for she had died to see that fate was form. She keened for the formless, the rapture beyond surfaces and masks.

Dogbrick shivered awake. Eyeballs rolled into place, and he sat up alertly, not afraid but astonished to find himself in the comforting presence of the Charmed wraith, all bite and bark in him diminished, his mouth working soundlessly, flustered as a fond fool flattered.

"That's what your teacher Wise Fish used to say to you, isn't it?" The woman of clove complexion and dark eyes smiled with crooked, white teeth and an impish dimple. "I saw her in your memories when I went looking for Ripcat. He is my master, you know."

"He is?" Dogbrick extended an amazed hand toward the luminous stone, and the ghost withdrew her palm.

"You've had enough Charm." She returned the crystal prism behind the folds of her cassock. "We need to stay clearheaded to get out of here."

Dogbrick's attentiveness sharpened. Pale blue Nemora showed its long horns atop the third station of the night, and he shivered to realize how long he had been ensorcelled. "Who are you?"

"I am the witch who served Caval and Reece on the Dark Shore."

"Lara—" Dogbrick sat up alertly. "Ripcat has often spoken of you. You lived in his dreams all our days in Saxar."

"Where is my master now?"

Dogbrick stared disappointedly at her neck chain. "Can you not scry for him in your amulet?"

"Only when he is Reece." Her rapt look faltered with her hope of learning more from Dogbrick. "I cannot see him as Ripcat. I searched your memories, but I did not view them all."

He covered his eyes in shame. "Thank you for preserving some scrap of my dignity."

"You have nothing to hide, Dogbrick." The wraith brushed his mane again and saw him with Ripcat once more in vertical Saxar. "In a certain regard, you have lived a life of dignity."

"Perhaps you did not look deep enough," he said through his fingers. "I was a thief."

She smiled at his contrite self-assessment. "You stole only from factory surplus, to survive."

"I made it a profession." He addressed his knees. "I could have sought other gainful work."

"You survived in Saxar." Lara bent closer. "Can you help us survive here?"

Dogbrick shook his chains and did not raise his head. He was still buzzing with the realization that he was speaking with Lara . . . a ghost.

"You are a thief." She followed that with a note of silence before chiding him, "You're not going to let something as elemental as these chains stop you."

"The elemental is often the most powerful."

She snorted derisively. "Is that comfort from the Gibbet Scrolls?"

"No." Dogbrick looked up sharply. "You should learn the Gibbet Scrolls. They offer more than comfort."

Lara engaged his challenging stare with the chill dark in her eyes. "What do they offer us here?"

Dogbrick lowered his stare, said quietly, "That gem that you hold—"

"The crystal prism." She removed it again, and its light smeared back the darkness.

"Can it help us?"

"We may look inside it." Lara felt comfortable enough to hold the prism close to him, where he could see the rainbows folding upon themselves like an inward music. "Look—there are the dwarves."

The compact warriors flowed like green corpuscles through black arteries of tunnels. "The charmways are packed with them," Dogbrick whined. "There's no escape."

"Not that way." The ghost tilted the crystal, and the vista shifted from the green-glowing marchers in the cave tunnels to the empty beach below. Salt waves sang on the rocks, casting silver nets of spray. Under the fiery night sky, the long wet strand beneath the cliffs gleamed like black silver dinted with bright things thrown up from the sea.

"The tide is going out," Dogbrick said, broad nose almost touching the crystal, eyes crossed to watch the loom of waters tossing its tide wrack onto the sand. "Even if we could get down there, we'd be swept out beyond the sea, into the night sky— into the Gulf."

"That would be death for you." She rose to her full height, black hair disheveled across the cowled shoulders of her cassock. "But for me, with this crystal-gem, the Gulf offers escape not even the dwarves can thwart."

Dogbrick jutted his jaw, impressed. "With the crystal prism to protect you, you could cross the Gulf and return to the Dark Shore."

"Will you help me?" she asked fervidly, looking for some glimmer of commitment in his deep-set eyes. "If I cannot return to the Abiding Star, let me fall back from whence I've come. Maybe from there, I can find Caval. After all, he is the one who summoned me to this quest."

Dogbrick rattled his chains again.

"Can't you yank them from the walls?" She followed the black chains to bolts wide as her wrists driven cleanly into the stone and found her answer.

"What holds you here?" Dogbrick gestured graciously to the black sea, where auroras shimmered lividly, enclosing planets and stars in curtained colors. "Why not stride on down to the beach and ride the tide?"

Lara shuffled to the brink of the cave and stood translucent against the star vapors. When he blinked or moved his head, she wasn't there at all, only her voice, beneath his skin, like a map of rivers, like his blood, "I can't carry the crystal prism out of this cave. Since the dwarves have captured me, I don't have the strength. They have placed a binding spell on me that keeps me here. But you could go—if you were free."

Like a jester, Dogbrick rattled his chains once more and wagged his big head.

"You already know we can't escape from here," she realized from his silence. "Why didn't you say so? Do you think you're humoring me?"

His eyes glowed cider brown in the lucent rays of the crystal. "I thought you had magic."

"I'm a *ghost!*" She tucked the crystal prism away with impatience. "Even if I had magic like Reece, it wouldn't do us any good. I cannot touch the living."

"Well, don't twist yourself into a knot over this." Dogbrick followed her across the cavern, seeking the comfort of the charmlight. "At least we're talking now and have each other for company."

"Shared misery is twice as futile." Lara flitted back and forth, irately. "That's a saying from my grandmother. Let's keep our pains to ourselves."

"A hopeless ideal." Dogbrick clanked beside her. "We can't hide ourselves from each other. The truth always comes out. 'No mystery between human beings.' That's what the Gibbet Scrolls say."

The wraith slowed down. "What do you think is going to happen to us?"

"I don't know." Dogbrick stopped and crossed his arms, reconsidering. "Well, I know something." He turned reluctantly to point outside to the black sheets of rock that sliced into the phosphorescent surf. "I've been here before. On my way to the polar palace at Zul. It's at the very edge of the world. I went to work there as a stevedore, on wharves that touch the abyss. I think the dwarves are taking us there."

"Why do you think that?"

"That's where exiles are cast into the Gulf."

Lara asked no more questions. She touched Dogbrick with the crystal-gem, and he watched her side eyed with soft pleasure.

Together, they sagged at the back of the cave, out of the wind, and Dogbrick curled up within her ghostlight. In moments, he sunk into a Charmed sleep. And she sat over him in her eternal wakefulness, her dreamless eyes watching planets and comets mark the stations of the night, troubled but less frightened for his presence.

HELLSGATE

ASOFEL CARRIED OLD RIC THROUGH A CHARMWAY TO A CRACKED lake bed of lava, a vast pan of rifts and ledges devoid of all flora. "Where are we?" the Radiant One asked, and looked about at the odd shapes of wind-fashioned marl on the bluff where they stood. Sulfur fumes carried a stench up from the rifted and cracked floor of the bleak caldera. "Do you know this place?"

"Hellsgate," Old Ric replied tersely, and peeked over the brim to the burned-out plain below. "I told you not to take that charm-way. Now look where we are."

Asofel's yellow eyes glared. "How did you know not to take this charmway?"

"It was not the cave that the ghost Lara used." Old Ric kicked a pebble over the side, and it plunged soundlessly off one of the dead dwarves. "She came up the Well of Spiders. That's the only reliable charmway among the worlds. The others are unpredict-able—like this one."

Asofel ignored the gnome's grouchy stare. "Then we will return the way we came."

"And go back to those hatchets?" Old Ric rolled his eyes. "Not

a wise strategy, O Radiant One." He lifted the Necklace of Souls
and rattled the prisms vigorously. "*This* is what those maggots
want. And they'll follow us here to claim it soon as they feel
their numbers are large enough to challenge us. Be sure of that."

"Then we will find another charmway within that cave and
leave this place." Asofel appeared annoyed, livid colors moving
like flame shadows beneath his skin.

"Lead the way—lead the way," the gnome mocked. "Where in
the worlds will we end our day?"

"Rebuke me if you will," Asofel complained. The pilot's tunic
and slippers he wore had thinned to translucent membranes on
his luminous body, and he lit up the black rocks around him.
"You cannot even find the shadow thing in your strong eye.
What good are you to the nameless lady?"

"What good?" Old Ric jutted his chest out so that the barbed
arrow pointed directly at Asofel. "Behold this shaft that pierces
me. I have given my life to serve our lady. What more good can
I offer?"

"May I suggest patience?" Asofel moved toward the cave hole
that had admitted them. "Is that an attribute known among the
gnomes?"

"Patience?" Ric threw his bent hands toward the lowering skies.
"The worlds are ending! Patience has lost its virtue to apocalypse
and become a vice."

"Why am I arguing with you—a gnome!" Asofel shook his
head in disgust and approached the cave.

"And why should a gnome be excluded from a good argument?"
Old Ric followed, rigid with indignation. "You should know,
gnomes of all mortals carry their own Charm and are . . ."

The eldern gnome broke off at the sound of rock grating
against itself. Sand drizzled across the mouth of the cave, and
the two wanderers stepped back just before shingles of stone
crashed where they had been standing.

Over the roof of the cave slid a massive, three-fingered hand
glossed black as tar and as wide as Asofel stood tall.

Old Ric flicked a cry to his partner as he danced backward,
"By the Goddess—it's a giant!"

Asofel, who had never seen or even heard of a giant, did not
budge. He stood dumbfounded as cobbles of rock crashed around

him when the arm connected to the giant hand shoved into view on the scorched hillside above them.

Old Ric grabbed Asofel's arm and pulled him back to the edge of the cliff. "Stand back! This is a giant! They're malicious creatures!"

"Malicious?" A voice wide as the burning sky vibrated pebbles out of crevices. From above the scarp that enclosed the cave, a giant, lying on its belly, rose to its elbows. Its hairless face, fire-blackened and rugged as scoria, rose like a wall. Its long mouth flexed angrily, revealing teeth gray as iron ingots.

"Leave us be, giant!" Old Ric's voice squeaked timidly. "We offer you no harm."

A laugh like a brattle of thunder crashed over them. "What *harm* could you little things offer me, Krakaz, master of the Blister Plains?"

"Do not judge us by size alone, Krakaz!" Old Ric gestured expansively to his comrade. "This is Asofel, a Radiant One visiting our Bright Shore from beyond World's End."

"Oh, I quake!" Rocks spilled down the escarpment as the giant feigned terror.

Old Ric threw arms over his head, but Asofel did not flinch though stones pelted the ground around him and one thudded off his shoulder and half turned his body.

"I am Krakaz, master of the Blister Plains!" The giant lifted his craggy head triumphantly toward the black vapors that passed for clouds on Hellsgate. "What manner of creatures are you to stand before me?"

"I am but a gnome." Ric ducked his head lower with self-abnegation. "But this—this is a Radiant One. He comes from beyond the dream of these worlds. You would be wise to show him respect, Krakaz."

"I am already wise," the giant declared, and rested its faceted black chin in its hand. "I am over seventy-six thousand days old. I know all the ways of giants, and I have learned much of the worlds from the little things that dare to trespass my domain."

"Yet you have not heard of a Radiant One, have you, Krakaz?" Old Ric dared a step closer. "I tell you, this is a powerful being. Remove your hand from the cave entrance and let us depart the way we arrived."

"Depart?" Another laugh sent more hail of gravel and rocks

down the slope. "None of the little things who have trespassed my domain ever depart. You will be no exception."

"Are you going to kill us?" Old Ric asked, appalled. "Then you *are* malicious!"

"To all but my own kind." The giant reached out a cracked and scaly hand. "I enjoy watching the little things burn in the lava pools. Their screams are like music to me. Only too brief."

Old Ric threw both arms straight up. "Wait now, Krakaz. You're making a terrible and fatal mistake. You don't know what you're doing!"

The giant's hand paused. "True. You disturbed my nap, and I have behaved like a grouchy child. Forgive me. Before I kill you, I would hear your story."

"Uhm—certainly. If it be your desire. May it please you, great one, originally I hail from Nemora," Old Ric launched nervously into his history, eager to mollify the giant and win passage out of Hellsgate. "There I was born into the kith of . . ."

"Not you!" The giant's finger, its black skin cracked and exposing a dully glowing crimson interior, pointed at Asofel. "I want to hear his story!"

"Of course!" Old Ric bowed apologetically. "This is Asofel, sentinel from . . ."

"I will hear from Asofel himself." The giant returned his cleft chin to his hand, and his fulgent eyes brightened. "Speak."

"I have been sent here by the author of these worlds," Asofel replied calmly and truthfully. "My mission is to remove an interloper from the Dark Shore."

"You are indeed interlopers, whom I will remove," Krakaz stated. "That is how we giants keep our domains private to ourselves."

"But if you fail," Old Ric interceded, "you are frustrated. If we fail, these worlds will cease to exist!"

Another quaking laugh rained pebbles. "You are the most amusing interlopers I have ever encountered in my many days." The giant half lidded his furnace eyes. "These worlds cannot end, gnome. They are eternal. Every giant knows that. For *we* are eternal. Look about you. Do you see those distant mountains? Giants all!"

"Yes, yes, as you grow older, you lithify—you become as rock." The gnome knew.

"*Living* rock, gnome!" Krakaz's eyes flared wider. "We grow slower as we grow older, sustained by the Charm of the Abiding Star, until we become slow enough to join the planetary host, the chorus of Old Ones, who lie together, sharing the music of the planets."

"If you want to hear that music," the gnome warned, "you'd best let us depart so we may save these worlds."

"I am no ignorant stone-child," Krakaz growled. "These worlds were not made by an author. They cooled from the fiery origin of all worlds, from the first fire, the blaze of the Abiding Star that forged creation."

"The author of worlds lives within the light of the Abiding Star," Asofel spoke up. "The Bright Shore and all its planets belong to her dream. And if she should stop dreaming, these worlds will vanish."

"And you, Asofel?" The giant jutted a rocky lip and squinted with curiosity. "Does the author of these worlds dream you as well?"

"I am of another dream." Asofel crossed his arms, and his head canted to one side as he remembered the life he once lived. "There are Nameless Ones who exist deeper in the light of the Abiding Star, and they are greater than the author of these worlds. I belong to the dreamer who dreams the author."

"And no doubt there are greater dreamers yet, am I right?" Krakaz twisted its long mouth smugly. "Dreams within dreams, yes?"

"That may be so," Asofel admitted. "I know only of the dream from which I come."

"Tell us of that dream, Asofel. Do you live there as I do here, waiting for time to build a future large enough for a mate, for children, and eventually for a comfortable place of recline among the Old Ones?"

"The dream I lived beyond World's End is very different. None here among the worlds would recognize it, for it is a dream without worlds. All is light there. But I was born where the light was most dim. My forebears had dwelled in that dull corner of our reality as far back as the generations could count themselves. They were unwilling to seek anything brighter."

"But you were different," Krakaz added snidely.

"Not different, doomed." Asofel's luminosity had dimmed, and his long features saddened. "There was not brightness enough to sustain me. I would have died then, as a child. But I was sold as a servant. And I have served since, that I might live and know the light."

"A thrall! Ha!" Karkaz's cliff-face smirked. "You put the lie to your own story. If creation were in peril, the author would not send a mere thrall."

"Actually, she sent me," Old Ric piped up. "Asofel is but my escort."

Krakaz's rugged head pulled back with surprise. "Enough of this nonsense!" His hand lifted toward them, its three crusted fingers spreading wide to grasp them both. "Now we'll hear you sing."

"No, wait!" Old Ric waved his arms urgently. "Your world is in danger. You must believe us!"

The shadow of the giant's hand fell over them as he chortled, "I believe you will both sing loudly in the lava!"

"Turn away!" Asofel commanded Old Ric.

The eldern gnome slapped his hands to his face and curled around, nearly bending double.

Asofel's tunic shredded like ash as his radiance glared from him in a fiery whirlblast so bright that, for a moment, the black lava rocks looked white.

Old Ric saw the bulbous bones in his hands. But he felt no heat. When darkness enclosed him again, he peeled away his hands and saw Asofel naked and ablaze with paisleys of flame. The giant was gone.

"I apologize." Asofel dazzled. "I ate again of the dream."

This time, Old Ric lifted a grateful face to the figure of flame. "Are you still hungry? I'm certain we can find more giants."

THE SIBYL

THE SIBYL WAS LITTLE MORE THAN A WHITE SHADOW HIDING AMONG the lacework of tendrils and vines in a dark forest cove. When Jyoti and Broydo happened upon her, her outraged cry sent riled birds shooting out of the dense canopy. Her curved eyes, smoky as quartz, flashed ire at the margravine for ripping away the leaf screen that concealed her.

"Sibyl, forgive me!" Jyoti blurted even as the creature stretched her crimson-and-green wings to fly away. "I am desperate for your help, or I would never intrude on you in so rude a manner. Please, do not abandon me to my plight, you who have shared prophecy with me in the past."

The bright wings relaxed and covered again the small, marble-pure nakedness of the diminutive creature. A blue tongue of flame flickered in the round hole of her mouth. "I am hungry."

Jyoti twisted from her waist and called to her companion, "Broydo—the maggot. Bring it here." Then she faced the sibyl. "I have flesh for you from World's End."

"Rare meat." The flame burned brighter in the circle of the sibyl's mouth. "Is it fresh?"

"Very."

Broydo ran back through the forest and found the maggot still hiding beneath the dwarf's dented breastplate. The ælf picked it up with the flat of the sword's blade and carried it quickly through the trees. It curled blindly around the sharpened bone yet slid off easily when he presented the writhing animal to the sibyl.

Her clawed hands flayed the maggot and her tongue of fire licked its moistly gelatinous interior with a hiss of burnt flesh. In moments, the maggot was reduced to a crisp husk emptied of its vitality.

When she was done, the sibyl's vivid, inhuman face peered up through inky streaks of hair, and her quartz eyes blinked slowly with satisfaction. The blue flame sparked in her mouth's gaping hole. "Ask me what you would know."

"Where is Reece Morgan?" Jyoti asked, kneeling in the dewy grass before the pale icon folded in her colorful wings.

"Locked in his fated self."

"Where?"

"On Irth—" The crystalline eyes fluttered, and the silken voice of the small being continued, "On Irth's far side—in Gabagalus."

"Is that far?" Broydo asked.

"Perhaps too far," Jyoti worried. "Gabagalus is an autonomous realm separate from the dominions. They do not readily welcome visitors."

Broydo only partly heard Jyoti, for his attention was distracted by the appearance of the strange little creature before him, perched in her shadowy socket of the forest. Her mortal-shaped body gave a familiar semblance that her stark face—with its rigid mouth hole, flame-tongue, and clouded eyes—belied.

"Ask, ælf." A blue spark spit from the sibyl's mouth hole. "Ask me what you would know."

"Smiddy Thea and those of my clan—" Broydo drew a long breath before daring to ask, "Are they well?"

"Under the high walk of the wind, they cower." The sibyl's wings trembled. "They must live thinly now. Dwarves stalk the Forest of Wraiths seeking vengeance upon ælves for the pain of their loss—the Necklace of Souls."

Broydo's hands tugged at his nappy green hair while the other upheld the serpent sword. "I must bring this sword to them! They need me!"

"*I* need you." Jyoti put a firm hand on his arm and lowered the sword. "If we are to find our way to Reece and free him, we're going to have to get through a lot of dwarves. I can't lose you now."

"But my people—"

Jyoti squeezed his arm reassuringly. "The sibyl says they live."

"They *cower*." Broydo shook his head ruefully. "And they live thinly. It's all my fault. I should never, never have led the dwarves to them."

"You and the gnome were brave," Jyoti reminded him from the story he had told of his adventures on World's End with Old Ric and Asofel. "Do you forget—if you had not brought the Necklace of Souls to your clan, they would have died horrible deaths under the curse of the demon Tivel."

"True—" Broydo's cheeks puffed out with an emptying of air that tried to drain the dread he felt. "I spared them one misery for another." He grasped Jyoti's hand. "I must go back. This sword is all that can save them."

"And the worlds, Broydo?" Jyoti's hard stare held him sternly. "What good if you save your clan and all the Bright Shore disappear?"

"The true is known to few." The sibyl stirred in her folded cloak of feathers. "For leagues and leagues, the day is empty. But in Gabagalus, the day is shaped—to be made or lost. The true is known to few."

"What does that mean?" Broydo gnashed his teeth with frustration. "I don't understand. Speak to us plainly, sibyl. Are the worlds truly doomed? Has Old Ric spoken truthfully of the nameless lady and the child unmoving in her womb?"

"To know this places you among the few." The sibyl closed her eyes. "But listen—"

Broydo cocked his head and heard grass birds fluting down the long, winding trails of the forest.

The sibyl's eyes eased open and shone as if lit from within. "For now, all the worlds are a singing tree, alive in a dead place."

"I don't understa . . ."

Jyoti stopped him with a thumb to his grimacing lips. "She is telling us she doesn't know what will happen. The fate of the

worlds is being shaped right now in Gabagalus. Are you coming
with me to decide the outcome?"

Broydo mumbled grouchily, his mind preoccupied with images
of Smiddy Thea and the many ælves he knew and loved. "Have
I a choice?"

Jyoti firmly held his wintry stare. "If you think it through—no."

"I am an ælf-counselor," Broydo stated aloud, more for his own
benefit than Jyoti's. "Smiddy Thea had me specially trained, not
just by the elders of our clan but by long days' servitude to the
elders of three adjacent clans. I am supposed to be skilled at
offering sage counsel to my people. So, why can't I give myself
good advice now?"

"This is a unique problem," Jyoti agreed. "But there is really
only one realistic solution. If your people are to survive at all—
if any people are to survive—we must go at once to Gabagalus."

"Is that so, sibyl?" Broydo gazed down at the little figure of a
sable-haired woman wrapped in livid wings. "Should Jyoti and I
go to Gabagalus?"

"Go as far as one can go." The sibyl shivered and stepped back
into the shadowed niche of her cove. "Past and future merge like
paths. And where they cross—oh, yes, where they cross, *there* is
destiny. And there, our life is sweet, even the very pain."

Broydo's purpled face flinched. "That doesn't tell us anything!"

The sibyl had stepped back into darkness, eyes shut, wings
shivering, unresponsive to the ælf's embittered glowering.

Jyoti carefully lowered the ivy veils she had torn aside and
restored the sibyl's secrecy. "Are you coming with me to Gabagalus or not?"

Broydo stared at the sword in his hand, and the white of the
blade gleamed like hushed snowlight. This was his clan's salvation—and in the hand of an ælf who had lost the worlds' salvation to the dwarves. Anger flexed in him. He would save Smiddy
Thea and his clan. But first he would take back what the dwarves
had stolen from him. "How do we get to Gabagalus?" he relented.

Jyoti smiled and clasped an arm across the ælf's shoulders.
"There is no easy way. Journey by airship will take too long,
and, because travelers are not welcome in that realm, no approved route exists to get there."

"It might as well be on another planet," Broydo complained

and swung the sword, swiping the head off a thistly flower. "Tell me, what is this place called Gabagalus?"

"It is a continent that rises from the sea each dawn and sinks again each dusk." Jyoti strolled with the ælf through the woods' cryptic shadows. "With my aviso and amulets, we can get there through the charmways. But the journey will be a difficult one."

"Why?" Broydo gave her a startled look. "Are we going down that Well of Spiders?"

Jyoti allowed herself a gentle laugh. "No, Broydo. That would take us off Irth to other worlds. We are simply going to cross to the other side of Irth, to where it is night now. The difficulty will be in arriving there unannounced. I believe if there's any hope at all of freeing Reece from the dwarves, we have to surprise them."

"Who lives in Gabagalus?" Broydo irately kicked a toadstool, spilling its spores. "Are there ælves there?"

"I think not." Jyoti reached through her memory for what little was known of the mysterious continent. "Salamandrines live there. I am told that they are just one outpost of a trade empire that spans worlds far distant from the familiar planets of Irth, Nemora, and Hellsgate. And most strange of all, they think our use of Charm is primitive."

"Truly?" Broydo cocked a wispy eyebrow. "What do they use? What holds them to Irth when the night tide pulls?"

"The ocean, I guess, for they sink beneath the waves by dark." The margravine's brow tightened as she recited the hearsay: "Gabagalus does not use Charm. They have mastered the discipline of science."

"Science?" A gasp of disbelief escaped the ælf. "You mean the child's game?"

Jyoti nodded with shared amazement. "Yes, the one where children learn secrets of nature by observation alone. My grandfather was a fanatic about science. He thought Charm weakened us and that we should let nature teach us by what it reveals of itself. He was the one who taught me how to defend myself without Charm."

"Science may be a happy distraction for children and good for teaching them traits of weather and wind," Broydo allowed. "But Charmed kites fly higher and farmers serve their crops best by reading weather with far-seeing amulets instead of barometers and wind vanes."

"I agree." Jyoti climbed over a fallen tree. "Yet bear in mind, science is simply a toy for us. That is why Gabagalus has little to do with us. They believe, from what I understand, that we are primitives dwelling in a wilderness."

"Sibyls do not lie." Broydo pronounced this common truth like a revelation. "If this sibyl had not told us that the one we seek is there in Gabagalus, I would never have thought to search so alien a place."

"Let's hope we will have the privilege of searching there." She tugged at her ear, trying to visualize in her mind a route through the charmways that would lead to the antipodes. "We have to get there first."

While the margravine thought, Broydo swatted the grass with his weapon, hoping to improve his sword skills.

"I can show you how to use that if you like." Jyoti closed her aviso and returned it to her vest. "My grandfather instructed me in all manner of hand weapons—including long-sword technique."

"I am just a counselor." Broydo presented the weapon to her hilt first. "You should carry the serpent sword into Gabagalus."

Jyoti waved the hilt aside. "It's best you learn. When you return to the Forest of Wraiths, you may need this sword to help your clan."

"I will not cleave to this weapon when the dwarves are upon us again, margravine." Broydo's shoulders slumped. "I was wrong to deny Ripcat the sword. He would be with us now if I had not insisted on holding the blade myself."

"Please, stop berating yourself, Broydo." She stepped behind him and reached around to adjust his grip on the hilt. "You will have another chance against the dwarves, and this time you will be prepared."

"What did your charmwrights tell you of the way to Gabagalus?" The sword reached longer now that he no longer choked the grip, and he swung it with more authority. "Will guides arrive to lead us?"

"The Dark Lord left me few enough subjects." Jyoti stepped to a holm oak dangling with white-blossomed creepers, and she tied to those vines by its leathern straps the dwarf's breastplate. She set it swinging. "I instructed my people to stay in Arwar

Odawl and continue the rebuilding. The fewer we are, the less chance of exposing ourselves before we're ready."

"But they have given you directions?" The ælf approached the swinging breastplate, swung, and missed. "You know how to lead us through the charmways?"

"Gabagalus is a continent." She stood at his side and showed him how to change the placement of his feet so that the sword's weight did not make him lean forward. "There are several charmways that lead there. But once we arrive, we'll have to rely on Charm to find Reece."

With a loud gong, Broydo struck the swinging breastplate and leaped back, startled. "I hit it!"

"Remember your foot placement, that's the key to sword technique." Jyoti demonstrated for him how to step as he advanced and retreated. "Keep your elbows in and your weight on your heels."

They practiced again and again until Broydo became proficient at striking moving targets: tossed fruits, swinging vines, and the stick Jyoti used to fence with him. By then, the Abiding Star stood shattered among the tree boughs and flocks of birds wheeled through the orange sky seeking their roosts.

"It will be dawn in Gabagalus soon," Jyoti announced. "Time to go. Are you ready?"

Broydo pirouetted with the sword inverted and deftly swung it around as his body completed turning. The tip of the blade cleanly sliced a leaf from a swaying branch. "Away then!" he shouted zealously. "To Gabagalus and Reece, so that I can return to World's End and cut the dwarves there to maggots!"

Jyoti climbed down the sinkhole first. By light from lux-gems on her amulet-vest, she saw that the cavern where Ripcat and Dogbrick had been seized by dwarves remained empty. Through a rift in the wall, they edged sideways and out a damp stone gullet to a wider corridor tall and spired as a basilica. Liquid drippings ticked from the slow seepings of the forest above, clocking the aeons that built the mineral columns and pillars upholding the world.

Through a region of skewered rock floors and fanged ceilings, they advanced, their footsteps returning soft stone echoes. The honeycombed wall where Ripcat had escaped the dwarves shimmered in the blue radiance of the lux-gems.

"This is where the charmway to Gabagalus is located," Jyoti

whispered, and her voice sounded loud against the dull chimes of dark leachings dribbling incessantly from the planet's undersides. "Once we enter, we may find ourselves among dwarves. Prepare yourself."

Broydo answered by turning the flat of the blade so that it rebated the shine of Jyoti's amulet-vest.

They crunched over coral-like flutings of limestone, and the rays from the lux-gems extended into lightless depths.

Jyoti grabbed at Broydo, and the ground beneath them fell away.

The ælf yelled with alarm. No echoes answered.

The next instant, they lay together in darkness. A tang of sea scent tainted the cool air, and the muffled shuffling of the tide came and went.

A sour odor as of bloodcurd sifted out of the nether dark. Jyoti angled her lux-gems so that their radiance fanned over Broydo's anxious face and illuminated a bandy-winged basilisk, a predator crouched at the back of the cavern, surprised by the abrupt arrival of two warm-scented prey.

Jyoti gasped at the sight of the voracious mask whose drawstrung mouth grinned fiendishly. Frantically, she scrambled away from the mutely screaming fangs yet knew that she could not outpace those razorous teeth. Its leather wings snapped, and its spiked head shot forward.

With a gut-twisting cry and eyes squeezed shut, Broydo leaped upright, sword outthrust. The impact smashed him against the cave wall, ramming all breath from his lungs. He did not expect to breathe again.

But when his next breath burned through his gaping mouth and his eyes peeked open, he stared into the golden eye of the basilisk, death dilating the darkness at its core. The serpent sword had pierced it through the top of its mouth and pithed its brain. The burning in his throat was the putrid stink of its filthy maw.

Jyoti stood beside Broydo and, with her back to the wall, kicked aside the slain monster. The sword came away oiled with basilisk blood.

"I killed it . . ." Broydo's voice arose from far away inside him. "I killed a basilisk!"

Jyoti cuffed him on the shoulder and grinned at him. "It seems you did—because we're still alive!"

DEVOURING GIANTS

ASOFEL WANDERED THE FIRE-CHEWED HILLS OF HELLSGATE DE-
vouring giants. Flames sawed in the wind around him as he strode
as if in a fever dream through the shimmering lens of that hot
world. He ate the Old Ones, the giants who had lain down ages
ago among the mountains to listen to the planetary music that
seeped through the carbonized crust from the magnetic pulse of
the core.

None rose up to defy him. Over the unruly ground, the Radiant One moved nimbly. The giants lay motionless as the stark
promontories they appeared to be. Yet they pulsed with the
firebeat of the planet, partaking of the living dream of the nameless lady.

With each of the black volcanic entities he absorbed, Asofel
grew brighter and more dazzling. They collapsed to pure light
before him, their personal memories burned away, their very lives
federated with the energy of the Radiant One. No cries went
up. No convolutions quaked the land. The dreamers in their
rapture simply disappeared into the unspeakable, leaving behind
the moon-blanched dunes where they had lain for ages.

Throughout that smoky day well into banded twilight, Asofel traversed the seared hills. Strength swelled in him. His skin sloughed away in cinders and a brighter self emerged, with a heart of fire, brilliant as the eye of the mind.

Old Ric, who once refused to countenance Asofel's slaughter of any mortals, found the massacre of the giants less objectionable, so despicable were they to him. Stunned by the renewed glory of Asofel, the eldern gnome closed his eyes and imagined what it was like for the imperiled giants, for the crew of the *Star of Fortune*, and the elf clans on World's End, for all who had been devoured by the Shadow Eater. Was there rapture in being rent from the dream? Or was there just simply nothing? Transformed into pure light, pure beyond identity, seemed a strangely happy fate to the gnome.

He shut his eyes to mere slits, trying to discern features in the starfire that webbed the blunt hills. Sharp rays of silver light lanced his brain with kaleidoscopic motes of eyes aslant with wicked glee, sun dogs, ball lightnings, and chimerical imps ajog across the incandescent furrows of his brain casting embers of day's end, twilight's murky fire.

The gnome blinked strongly, trying to shiver himself alert. He had slouched to the ground beside the cave of the charmway. Light clicked in his staring eyes, and he had sat mesmerized, gazing into the arc-fire at the rim of Hellsgate that blazed white as the coring of a star.

With effort, he averted his slack face. Retinal shadows danced like squalid ghosts, and everything he looked at stood embroided with stars. Boulders, gravel flats, black clouds glinting with gempoints. He shook his head. The magnificence of Charm sunk him deeper where he sat, to the very seat of his soul.

He realized then, though he felt no weariness at all, that he was tired. Fatigue, physical need, and most of his bodily pain had ended when the dwarvish arrow pierced him. As a deadwalker, he partook of the inexhaustible energy of the Necklace of Souls that drew its power from the Abiding Star. And yet, he knew by his yearning for nothingness that he was more deeply tired than he could feel.

The fate of the worlds was a burden whose magnitude had subsumed all of him, moral, magical, natural. Basking in the Charmed glow from the Radiant One, he found enough strength to admit to himself that he had nothing left. Everything he was had been subsumed to this cause.

This thought countered his weariness sufficiently for him to contemplate this one particular irony: that with the death of his beloved daughter Amara, he had withdrawn so completely from gnomish society that he had been more of a deadwalker *then*. Now, he truly knew what it meant to give of oneself. After Amara died, the pain had been so great it had pulled him into himself, and he could not get out.

"Thank you, lady," the eldern gnome whispered to the Nameless One who had called him out of that dire selfishness. He had lost his life in her service, yet he wore the barbed arrow proudly, for it pointed him to his freedom.

He opened his eyes, refreshed by the Radiant One's Charm.

The Abiding Star watched him across the chiseled plains like a tiger's eye. Asofel passed before the setting disc as a silver-blue spark, spectral will-o'-wisp, acetylene spore dream-hung against the bright vermilion blear of dusk. Old Ric waved, and a jet of flame saluted him.

Asofel grinned giddily at the eldern gnome though he knew he could not be seen within the glare of himself. The pandemonium of twilight matched perfectly the wonder, the brash colors of his bliss at absorbing the light of the dream. He was becoming strong again, and this vigor fed his hope that soon now, he would locate the shadow thing, wherever it had hidden, and drive it from the Bright Shore.

Then, he could return home. That was all he had ever wanted since this task began: to return to the light.

Compared to the scarlet demise of day on Hellsgate, the remembered light of his own home shone with an intensity at a higher order of being. There was none of the chaos of drifting stars and life-forms ruled by Chance, the blind god of these worlds. There was no blindness at home. Chance had no place there. The dream and the dreamer were one. And though he existed at home as a mere sentinel, a guard for other luminous dreamers, he knew from rapport with his own dreamer, his own greater self, that his radiance would eventually be magnified by longing and he would not always be a sentinel but in the glory of election and by the agency of his own dream, he would eventually change toward the brighter and the better.

All that, however, was enshadowed when the nameless lady enlisted him into her dream. At first, he had hated the eldern gnome for requesting him as an escort and for putting the idea into the lady's mind to begin with. Now, though, restored to his former power, he felt surprisingly magnanimous toward Old Ric. Was not the gnome himself but a shard of the lady's dream and, therefore, unable to help his obeisance to his dreamer, Asofel reasoned to himself? All the pain that Asofel had experienced because the gnome had pulled him deeper into these cold worlds was, he decided, forgiven if not totally forgotten. And the conjectural destiny of the worlds themselves seemed hopeful once more. He would find the shadow thing. Then he would go home—to the light.

At home all this *would* seem a strange dream. All these lives, all under indictment of death—as was he. But at least his death was known. He would grow brighter, like all did in the light, until his brilliance outshone the shadows that were his thoughts; then, the I at the center of the shadows would blaze with an intensity greater than could be held within the premises of space-time. Other dimensions awaited beyond the jurisdiction of I. Someday, he would go there.

But these unfortunate beings, woven of the lady's dreamstuff and subject to blind reckoning, had such doubtful fates. Thinking of the earnest, dutiful eldern gnome broken to emptiness saddened him. And that sadness surprised him. Why, suddenly, should he care for these illusions? And yet he did. The ingenuous gnome did not himself care that he was part of a mere dream. To him, this world was as real as the light itself, as real as Asofel's own home.

Bumbling Broydo, too, moved unfamiliar feelings in Asofel. Who was this ælf exiled within the largeness of his heart? Why had he forsaken his clan to serve a gnome? Love alone answered those questions. Love for this dream of rocks spinning through the cold of space warmed by the feeble rays of smoldering stars. *Love for the darkness*, he realized, stunned that anyone could favor these tiny, fanciful lives. And he began to realize that he felt pity for those caught inside the nameless lady's creation, hungering in her mind's tenements.

The homing force in him competed with these empathic

thoughts. He wanted to find the shadow thing, remove it from the dream, and return home.

Light.

The energy from the consumed giants enlivened him so fully that if he wanted to, he could rise and go inside the light again. He could wait there, just outside the dream, the way that he had before Old Ric called him down. He could leave behind these fictive lives that had insinuated themselves into his caring. Why should he care for these semblances?

The awareness that these creatures struggled in the wreckage of their existence with as much passionate faithfulness as he thrived in the light awed him. A simultaneously antic and urgently profound desire whelmed up in him to speak to the eldern gnome, this creature of darkness.

Old Ric sprang to his feet at the approach of the Radiant One. The shadows of the night loosened. Frostfire in the shape of a mortal stood in the cave mouth. The shape cooled, its heat luffing into the cold wind with billowy gusts of chromatic smoke. A visage of heat-blotched shadows darkened to Asofel's demonically angelic countenance.

"Radiant One!" Old Ric hailed, vivid with the excess Charm blustering in the air. "You have slain giants!"

"I've slain nothing." Asofel stood at the threshold of the cave, and its interior burned bright as a cauldron of lava. "Their very nature is illusion. As are you."

"And yourself!" the gnome cried jubilantly, drunk with vitality. He was able to face the sentinel, for Asofel had chilled to a figure of blue snow. "We are all spun from the eternal and the Nameless. All dreams!"

"I'm not a dream," the Radiant One averred strongly. "I am the light."

"A different dream and yet a dream nonetheless." Old Ric felt almost drunk with happiness to see the Radiant One empowered once again, and he energetically bantered with the being of light. "We are all spun on the loom of nothingness. Waves of light on the black surface of nothingness. Atoms of matter swarming in the nothingness. We fall apart. You blur away. Ha! We all change."

"Then why do you suffer this quest?" Flamespun hair floating like strange filaments down the eye's film, Asofel stepped closer.

"Leave the shadow thing. Let the lady wake the child's father. This dream will end and you and all these deceptions of matter and energy will be no more."

"That won't do, Asofel." The eldern gnome fixed a bold stare on the mica seams of Asofel's eyes. "Something greater is at stake here. Surely, you see that?"

"I do not." Asofel looked about disdainfully at the molten shapes of wasteland. "But I have come to tell you that I do feel something—for you, for that fool Broydo. I understand better, now that I am strong again, what it means to be weak. You are weak. And Broydo weaker yet. Nonetheless, you both strive with all that you have. Why?"

"The child!" The shrunken, pug-nosed face lit up gleefully. "These worlds were created not by whim. They exist for the lady's child. The interplay of light and darkness, of void and substance, and—yes!—of good and evil, these are the forces that will shape the child. These will anoint it with awareness of suffering and compassion. That is why these worlds must go on. We serve what is greater."

Asofel crossed his arms, diamond eyes watching, assessing. "How do you know this?"

"I am a gnomish magician." Old Ric spoke as if this fact were evident. "My magic is fire. I know why there is no malign thing in the light and why the darkness triumphs time and again. I know someone old is stitching them together by victory and loss. Each of our lives is one small stitch among the countless that will heal this wound—this wreckage of existence as you call it. By our suffering—by our willingness to suffer for what is good— by that we will make of darkness a light."

"Grand notions from a little being," Asofel replied, lowering his chin dubiously.

Old Ric plucked the stuck arrow. "I've given everything I have to holding together my stitch of light and dark. What about you, Asofel?"

"I am of the light." His face shone calm as glass. "I am faithful to the one who sent me here."

"I know that." Old Ric waved an impatient hand. "I'm talking about your soul. And by that I mean, what of *your* feelings? How are you holding together your great light with the vast darkness of this creation?"

Asofel shook his head, unhappy with the gnome's questions. "I want to go home."

"To the light. I know." Old Ric's cheeks gleamed with joy. "I have tasted of your Charm this night, and I myself would go with you if I could."

"You can." Asofel smiled, and a lightning flash stained the underbellies of the night clouds. "I will carry you to the Abiding Star. From there, your radiant body will grow. Maybe in time I will even see you in the fields of light where I dwell."

"Not likely." The gnome thumbed his knobby chin and spoke what he had seen in his trance while Asofel ate giants. "You'll have brightened by then beyond those fields into distances of the soul's going, brightening toward infinity."

"You know of my home."

"I know of fire."

Asofel offered a white hand shining from within. "Let me take you to the Abiding Star."

"Forget me." The eldern gnome stepped back with an annoyed grimace. "Think of the child. Think of the ages to come. You feel it. I know you do. Why else would you have come back to speak with me? You feel my striving—and Broydo's, too. If you looked into any of our mortal hearts, you'd find that same striving. This is no dream to us. We are each of us striving for what we believe is real. But we don't all strive for the same thing. Some want more light—"

"Others, more darkness." Asofel nodded with understanding: there would be no going home until the work was done. "I will step outside the dream and find the shadow thing."

The Radiant One faded quickly away, and darkness recharged the landscape with mystery and threat. Old Ric stumbled blindly toward the cave, seeking sanctuary in the sudden night.

Asofel, too, sought asylum from the wrought feelings that the gnome evoked in him. The nameless lady had set Old Ric a task to which Asofel acceded to help. Now he could do nothing but aid the eldern gnome, because the Radiant One was a being of light, and in the realm of light there was no blindness, no death, no chance, and justice lived there with her eyes open.

Outside the dream, in the realm of light within the aura of the Abiding Star where he had originated, the Radiant One stood sentinel. He felt peace here and was glad that, at last, he had reclaimed the strength to return to where he belonged. He had come here to find the shadow thing, and he began to search.

Far and near merged in him like wind and fire. Sparks blustered—snippets of distances he had crossed while down there. He saw again the Labyrinth of the Dead on World's End, and there was Broydo doubled over with grief before the eighteen corpses of his clan raised from their graves by the demon Tivel. The mourning in the ælf's body throbbed like a physical hurt.

He brushed the sparks of timefire away, not wanting to see any more of that grievous place. Not that his reality was any less grievous. The powerful stole light from the weak, and the weak dimmed. Some darkened to shadows and fell from sight, many gathered more light to themselves and brightened toward radiance, and most lingered in their bitter dimness. Perhaps death and oblivion would be kinder, he wondered.

It took a while for his eyes to adjust, he had been so long in the shadow world. When he could see, he noticed that he had emerged not far from his station at the south wall of the garden, upon the Gate of Outer Darkness.

By the nightglow of luminous plants and insects he found sufficient illumination to view the terraced lawns with their fishponds and tarns, upon whose mirrored surfaces drifted black swans. Beyond them was the bridge-gate with the brimstone light of its one lantern. Upon the far side of that gate awaited his own station as sentinel of the Beginning.

With blithe exhilaration to be back at his post, he stared down to either side of the entry ramp and glimpsed the wild lands above the terraced lawns, the hunched boulders shawled in creepers. Leather-winged minions rose up from there on the vesperal wind and flashed past him with their agonized faces. He gasped happily to see that nothing had changed, and he mounted the steep, zigzagging road faster.

At the final bend in the path, he stood proudly before the bridge-gate with its ponderous lantern of iron fins and spikes. Thick dockweed and dense hollyhocks sprouted before the weighted gate, yet even so the massive timbers obeyed his touch.

Light.

The portal opened on a dazzling luminosity—the radiance of himself. From here, he could look into the dream and find the shadow thing.

Azure water cast its fluttering webs of reflected light across a wall of tesselated dolphins. Diamond froth off a sparkling swimming pool underlit a man with feline beastmarks—blue fur and slant green eyes.

DUPPY HOB

RIPCAT FINISHED DRYING HIMSELF, AND HIS FUR FLUFFED UPON HIS lean frame. He glanced about for a place to set the wet towels. Then, he looked again at the old man sitting in the wire chair watching him through a mask of tired flesh with eyes like perforations.

"Drop them on the floor," the aged man instructed, his slack mouth barely moving. "And sit here." His veined hand wavered toward an empty wire chair beside a swimming pool.

The beastmarked man obeyed and sat among reflections of rambling morning light from the pool. He could smell the ferment of the decrepit body across from him. "*You* are Duppy Hob?—the devil worshipper?"

"Once I worshipped devils." The old man sat perfectly still in his black tunic of gold trim, the feet in his green slippers inert, his dried flesh spiced with age marks and blebs. "Now, devils worship me."

Ripcat shifted in the comfortless wire seat, searching the undersea chamber for signs of devils. Outside the belled, transparent walls, mermaids spun. Inside, an oval swimming pool framed in red tiles revealed more mermaids through its transparent bottom. "This is a tranquil place for a devil worshipper. You live here?"

The flesh under the old man's tired eyes looked like dripped wax, and it twitched this time before he spoke: "Don't you want to know why I have brought you to me?"

"If you are Duppy Hob, I'm afraid to find out." Ripcat watched the old man with a surly curiosity and tapped a claw on the seat's wire grille. "I thought you would look—well, more imposing."

"I am old. Very old."

Movement caught Ripcat's eye in an open hatchway beyond more wire chairs on the far side of the pool. Veiled figures passed in and out of sight. "Then why not use Charm to make yourself young again?"

"I have." A vague puzzlement, a gray shadow troubled the old man's features. "This is as young as Charm can make me."

"I don't follow." Ripcat mistrusted the mummied body before him and did not disguise this in his voice. "You look like you're about to drop dead at any moment."

"I might well," the crackled voice agreed. "That is why I need continuous care. This body is over two million days old."

Ripcat regarded more closely the waxen flesh, the spider hairs on the bald pate, the oily eyes.

"What do you know of me?" Duppy Hob asked, his voice full of sibilance and clicks, sifting through crisp lungs.

"Only hearsay."

"What have you heard?"

"That dwarves you made from maggots deposed you and threw you into the Gulf." Ripcat shrugged. "That is, assuming you're telling the truth and you *are* Duppy Hob and not some grotesque joke. Everyone believed Duppy Hob was a legend. But when dwarves arrived in Saxar, the margravine of Odawl detected you commanding them—and the dwarves were chanting one thing over and over—'Duppy Hob.'"

"Detected me?" Viscous eyelids drooped. "How?"

"With her eye charms—her amulets—" Ripcat answered frankly, seeing no reason to withhold or lie. "She saw that you had somehow regained command over the mutinous dwarves. How *did* you do that?" He perched himself on the edge of the wire chair. "And why?"

"Tell me."

With one swipe, one backhanded slap, Ripcat could snap the old man's frail neck. But that seemed far too easy, and he put the thought out of his mind for the moment and concentrated on why Duppy Hob, or whoever this dying soul was, would be asking the questions he did. Clearly, he was fishing, trying to learn what his captive knew. "Why don't you use your charmware to read my mind?"

"That's too messy." His curled hands fluttered in his lap, agitated at the thought. "If I do that, your skin of light may tear. That's not good."

"Why?" Ripcat stood. "Are you afraid I will use my magic on you?"

"Your magic?" Duppy Hob laughed eerily, his breaths sharp as bird screams. "Your magic? Oh, I see. I see." His rigid body seemed to shrink with relief.

"I know far less than you thought I did, don't I?" Ripcat realized, suddenly angry at his ignorance.

"You are clever, Ripcat—but, ah, not as clever as I had feared." The heel of one tremulous hand pressed against a wet eye. "Sit down. Go ahead, sit on the carpet if you like. But sit, sit. Tell me everything you do know. Be open with me, and I will return that kindness."

Ripcat did not sit. His ignorance before this laughing old man enraged him. He did not know what to do or what to make of this frail being, and he seethed with frustration. Yet he held himself in check and paced slowly around the seated figure. "Kindness? From a devil worshipper?"

"Sit down." Duppy Hob's voice spurted like a flame, all laughter gone. "Do not think to defy me, creature."

"Why not, old man?" Ripcat addressed the back of his host's bald head, the large ears waxily translucent. "Are you going to make me sit—like a trained pet?"

"If I must."

"Oh really?" Ripcat bent over the doll-like figure and smelled more strongly the sour redolence of the aged flesh. "I don't want to be treated like a trained animal. I don't want to obey you at all."

"You are a bewildered creature, Ripcat." The old man's eroded profile did not flinch or his black eyes avert from their vapid focus. He looked too tired to care about the fanged grin beside him. "You do not know enough to act. Sit down."

"No." Ripcat strolled around to the front of the small, seated man and crouched to meet those depthless black eyes. "I want you to tell me why I'm here."

"You serve me." Duppy Hob pointed a bent finger at him, his gaze black as the eyes of a squid. "And I need your service now."

"Serve you?" Ripcat straightened and continued walking around the seated man. "I won't serve you."

"You already have." The crepey skin of his jowls trembled with silent laughter. "You are how I communicate with my dwarves."

"Explain."

A weary breath asked, "Must I?"

"The dwarves cast you into the Gulf." Ripcat dared poke the sere and shrunken man's shoulder. It felt fragile under his claw, loose ligaments and wobbly bones. "How could *you* have survived? Look at you. You're about to fall apart."

"I survived the fall to the Dark Shore," Duppy Hob rasped. "Oh, I was so much younger then and full of fire. Even so, I barely survived. It took me hundreds of thousands of days to regain my strength."

Two veiled figures breezed into the chamber through the open hatch. They were healers from the Sisterhood of Witches, garbed in traditional gray-and-black robes, like the witches Ripcat had seen tending the sick and homeless in the gutters of Saxar. They went directly to the old man and began to press feather amulets and theriacal opals onto his brow, calming him down.

Duppy Hob waved them off, and they lingered, flustering around him until he waved again. Then the veiled ladies retreated in a rustle of scarves and hems.

"My story is too long," said Duppy Hob quietly, soothed by the ministrations of his healers. "Know this. Exiled on the Dark Shore, I needed a way to reach across the Gulf and regain control of my dwarves. It took me hundreds of thousands of days and much hard work on the Dark Shore to make the magic that could reach across the Gulf."

Ripcat stood directly behind Duppy Hob, and the speckled pate tempted him to strike. He continued to restrain himself and asked, "Why would the dwarves who overthrew you take your commands?"

"They wouldn't. They wanted nothing more to do with me. I had to amplify my strength. So I found another. Your teacher—Caval. I used my hard-won magic to influence him from the Dark Shore. Oh, I didn't know then it would be him—just someone, anyone intrepid enough to imagine they could reach the Dark Shore and return. There were others. They failed. Caval succeeded."

The name "Caval" startled Ripcat, because he had greatly admired that wizard. Caval had served Jyoti's father and had sacrificed his life and the possibility of rapture in the Abiding Star so that his death would buy time for the others to attack the Dark Lord. The thought that Caval had been used by this shriveled man was untenable. "I don't believe you. I don't believe anyone can reach across the Gulf with their minds."

"You climbed from the Dark Shore yourself, pursuing Caval." Merry wrinkles cracked the flesh of his gray cheeks. "Don't you see? I called Caval to the Dark Shore intending that you or someone like you would ultimately follow him back to Irth." A laugh hissed through his caked lungs. "Your training as a magus under Caval—that was my strategy. And the death of Lara. Who do you think inspired the townsfolk to kill her?"

"You want me to believe an old wreck like you has shaped all our destinies?" Ripcat walked to Duppy Hob's side and placed his snout close to the old man's yellowed ear. "Ha!"

"I am old here on Gabagalus, but on the Dark Shore I am much stronger." Duppy Hob's head turned with a sound of crinkling cartilage, and his puncture-hole eyes stared impassively at the beastmarked face. "To control my dwarves, I needed to put in place on Irth someone from the Dark Shore where I was exiled—an antenna, if you will."

"Really? So I'm an antenna now." Ripcat continued circling, snout wrinkled before the ghastly smell of curdled flesh. "You duped Caval and killed Lara to send me to Irth so that I would serve as your antenna. You exploited me to broadcast messages to your dwarves. Is that right?" His sharp teeth flashed. "Well, your antenna left the Door in the Air open out of ignorance. And through that Door came the Dark Lord. All this time I thought his arrival was my fault. But now you'll tell me that it was you who sent him. You are ultimately responsible for the Dark Lord."

"No." Duppy Hob lidded his eyes like a turtle, reflecting back. "The Dark Lord himself was of Irth. His name was Wrat, though he preferred to call himself Hu'dre Vra." More sharp, chirping laughter whistled from his chest. "No, no, no, I did not send that pompous idiot. I sent the gremlin inside Wrat and the caco-demons that obeyed the gremlin."

Ripcat cringed at the memory of the cacodemons. "Then you really are responsible for all those deaths, all that destruction?"

"It was necessary," his rib-scrubbed voice whispered. "Every great achievement requires blood sacrifice."

Ripcat suppressed a shiver of revulsion and stood before the old man with his claws tightened to fists. "What great achieve-ment did you sacrifice so many for?"

"I sent you first to be my antenna. Reece Morgan of the Dark Shore." Another breath of mirth tangled in his lungs, and the veiled witches hovered in the hatchway. "But when you arrived, the shock of confronting the Abiding Star overcame you. Your magic—*my* magic—created a skin of light to protect you from those rays in the desert where you landed. I admit that as Ripcat, you were useless to me. So I was forced to send the gremlin. When you eventually destroyed it, you had shed your skin of light. You were Reece again, and I didn't need the gremlin any-more. I had you to serve as my antenna. You enabled me to communicate with my dwarves. That's all that mattered to me—reclaiming my dwarves." He gasped for breath, a gnarled hand to his throat. "And don't you dare ask me why. You will find out in time, in time, in time. We must use our time very wisely now."

The witches hovered closer, chiding their master for getting overworked. Through their gauzy masks, they cast disapproving frowns at Ripcat.

"Enough!" Ripcat snarled, and they stood back, their hands casting warding signs at him. "Who is this old man? Answer me!"

The witches backed off silently.

"They answer only to me," Duppy Hob whispered.

"I don't like you, old man." With a tiger's slouch, Ripcat placed himself in front of the frail figure. "You say you killed my Lara. I want to know about that. I want to know just who you are." Stars of malice glinted in his long eyes, and he reached out and took the front of the old man's tunic in his claws. "And you're going to tell me everything."

As Ripcat lifted the birdweight man out of his chair, the floor disappeared underfoot, and he hung helpless in the talons of a furry, thick-shouldered man with adder green eyes. He was staring at his own beastmarks from inside Duppy Hob's body. And behind those tapered animal eyes, he sensed Duppy Hob staring back at him with malefic glee.

"Now you are mine, Reece Morgan." Ripcat's voice spoke Duppy Hob's words, and the old body flailed bonelessly in the clawed grasp of the Cat. "Wake—and remember!"

The shout deafened to a roar. Ripcat felt his consciousness shredding away from the withered body that had clasped him. Flung into the Great Silence out of which all things had come, Ripcat remembered Reece. All his memories returned to him from where dreams were woven, and he recalled trying to heal Lara of her pain—of the wounds he had felt responsible for. The pain had made him Ripcat again.

Memories congealed like a wave sludging to shore. The joined awareness of Ripcat and Reece trembled in the Great Silence before the black darkness of Duppy Hob. With telepathic ardor, the devil worshipper's life revealed itself.

He remembered now that he had grown up here in Gabagalus, well over two million days ago, the son of a wort farmer. As a young man he had trained to become a rocket pilot, and he had sought his fortune offworld, exploring the perilous planets closest to the Abiding Star, where few dared journey. Treacherous stellar currents marooned him on World's End among squid monkeys and poison-spore mushrooms. He would have perished then as so many other luckless wanderers had before him, except for a demon from the Upper Air. The ether-devil took up residence in the smashed wreckage of the rocket. By accident—by the deft hand of the blind god Chance—the mess of shattered lenses in the navigation pod proved an excellent receptor of charmlight from the Abiding Star and of ether forms from the Upper Air— the corona—of the Star.

It was this demon who had taught Duppy Hob how to make soul-catchers from the lens shards of the crashed rocket. Listening to the voice that opened in his head when he stared into the prismatic splinters, the salamandrine explorer from Gabagalus stranded at World's End became possessed by a demon from the Upper Air.

Ether-devils partook of both the Abiding Star's Charm and the
darkness that received its light. They swirled among and through
each other with bodiless intelligence. But once they found their
way to physical shapes, their hungers overwhelmed them.

That was what had happened to Duppy Hob. And in one
instant, Reece experienced all the rapacious hunger of the demon,
the insatiable appetite of darkness for light, of emptiness for
substance. The ether-devil had taken Duppy Hob for his own,
and together they had become one.

Reece recognized this demon. Floating in the Great Silence,
he sensed its vivid, evil presence as the wicked intelligence of
the Dark Shore. There it was known by many names: Ahriman,
Belial, Shaitan. Duppy Hob had brought it with him when the
dwarves heaved him into the Gulf. They were not overthrowing
their master but the demon who controlled their master.

Reece writhed with Duppy Hob's demonic voracity, wanting
to devour all four mystic worlds—the Dark Shore, the Bright
Worlds, the Upper Air, and the Abiding Star. He wanted to eat
it all, to chew everything down to its inmost name.

The demon felt destined to eat all the worlds, but so far he
had not been able to get past the one dark world where the
dwarves had thrown him. For two million days, he had squatted
in Duppy Hob's body on the Dark Shore, devouring human lives,
using mass graves for his cesspools. He ate pain and created
cities to help him—huge talismanic lenses framed in concrete
and steel to better house his bloated greed, vast as the world-
stone itself.

He ate pain, two million days of pain, to build the magical
strength in himself so that he could reach across the Gulf and
begin to devour the Bright Worlds . . .

The spell broke, and Ripcat staggered back into his body,
releasing the old man in his claws. He looked at his sable palms
and clawed fingers. He was Ripcat again—yet he remembered
everything about his life as Reece Morgan. All those memories
seemed infinitesimal in the cloud of horror that billowed from
his vision of Duppy Hob. "You—you're Satan!"

The small, geriatric salamandrine, head to his shoulder, body
slumped, watched him from the seat where Ripcat had dropped
him.

Ripcat shivered with an underlying thunder of terror. To hold his mind together, to keep from quaking into a panic, he spoke a comforting thought aloud, "The magic that pollutes these worlds—the magic is not mine but yours."

"Your magic *is* mine, Reece Morgan." The old man lifted a blood-webbed hand and pointed to himself. "*I* sent you to Irth." He gasped and struggled to sit upright. "Your presence is part of my grand magic. And you have served me well—albeit unwittingly." He motioned for the witches, and they bent and helped him to rise to his slippered feet. "Knowing that you are not at all responsible for the gremlin and its cacodemons ravaging Irth should be reward enough for the pain I've caused you, yes?"

Ripcat's mind felt like a shape of fire, burning him with its lucidity. The thought that he was the pawn of a monstrous demiurge, a demon who haunted worlds and devoured lives, was numbing. He forced his mind to work, to form a thought that might help him comprehend the enormity of what he confronted. "What of the author of the worlds?" he asked almost soundless. "What of her child unmoving in her womb?" He peered at perdition in its disguise of shriveled flesh. "Is this true?"

"More true than we."

"Then this is her dream?" Ripcat felt warmed by the thought of a being greater than the demon and its hunger. "The universe as we know it is the dream of a pregnant woman?"

"Dreams within dreams, Reece Morgan." Bent and stiff, the old one hobbled toward the hatchway escorted by the witches. "Come along now. We have chatted enough of me. Now I have something of your own to show you."

The hatch admitted them to a capacious anteroom appointed with wall-fixed benches and chairs of chamois. Oblong portholes shone blue with crazed reflections from the mermaids' realm. Not until the veiled women strapped Duppy Hob into one of the chairs did Ripcat realize that they were in a vehicle. A moment later, the ratcheting hum of engine noise came through the cork floor.

Ripcat secured a red amulet cord across his lap as he saw the witches do, and Charm held them in place when the ship disengaged from the undersea suite. Waving mermaids blurred past, and moments later sea-foam washed the portholes and the day sky burst into view. The fabled countryside of Gabagalus sprawled under the Abiding Star, and puffs of cloud filled the sky like white roses.

The heat of the day had burned off the last of the brown algal caul from night under the sea. High fields of red lichen tilted above slick yellow farmlands of wort and green paddies of cress. Peaceful windmill villages stood like islands on the wet plains. Their garden purlieus adjoined compact orchards and country lanes that rayed across the glistening land for leagues before touching other hamlets.

"These worts induce telepathic trances and are cherished in all the worlds," the old man said softly, eyes hooded, small frame shivering with the flight's vibrations as he remembered back a lifetime. "But this wort only sprouts here in Gabagalus. That is the reason why empire has come to this remote edge of creation."

"Where are we going?" Ripcat pressed his face against the porthole and saw a rocket pad with a silver liner erect on its pillowblocks, ready to launch.

"To the Dark Shore."

Ripcat moved to get out of his seat, and the red cord snaked tightly against his waist and held him fast. "I don't want to leave Irth."

The old man said nothing. He gazed out the porthole at a distant city of crystal filigree. "You know Irth is a wild planet. Civilization has never really touched it, not even here in Gabagalus. There is too much reliance on Charm for any genuine achievement to occur." A mild glittering in his eyeholes signaled humor. "But the Dark Shore—ah, there without Charm, where the cold darkness is as plausible as the light, great achievements are indeed possible."

Knobby, coral-like mountains reared outside the portholes. Gummy green mucilage stained the perforated rocks and crevices. Atop a roughly faceted limestone cliff rose an air pier replete with mooring trestles and berthing stanchions. They docked there with loud metallic gonging and a shudder that droned to silence with the dying engine noise.

The witches unstrapped the old man, and he laboriously stood upright. "Come along, Reece Morgan. It's time to go back home."

"I don't want to leave Irth." Ripcat removed the red cord and climbed through the hatch after Duppy Hob and his witches. "Why are you sending me back?"

"Always the why." Duppy Hob's voice echoed from far away.

Ripcat stepped onto a ledge of charcoal and nitre. At the brink of a blue abyss, muscular, shaggy Dogbrick stood beside the shimmering transparency of Lara.

Startled, Ripcat blinked—and they were gone. In a bound he rushed to the brink and saw them dropping through the empty air, flailing like eels.

He spun furiously about, glaring for Duppy Hob. And the old man stood directly behind him. With a soft push, he sent the startled Ripcat over the edge. Wind snatched him away in its great hand, and Duppy Hob vanished above him. The green knobby mountain peaks disappeared, too, and the blue sky widened, darkened, dissolved to night—and he fell into a cold, shoreless vista of fluorescent star smoke and comet veils.

PART FOUR

Empire of Darkness

"There is no freedom from our freedom."

—THE GIBBET SCROLLS, SCREED 2:16

Devil's Work

Empire of Darkness in red letters encircled a stylized goat's head, stenciling a pavement slab in front of a converted warehouse in lower Manhattan. A homeless squatter slept on the metal stoop, wrapped in cardboard beneath the black steel-sheeted double doors. No signs marked this entrance save a tiny reverse pentagram painted in fine scarlet razor lines. A staring eyeball covered the peephole at the center of the inverted star, and if one could peer back through that lens, the exposed interior would stand empty: bare concrete floor and fluted iron columns gloomy with alley light let down from caged windows.

By night here, several hundred revelers milled to thundering music played by live bands on wire-mesh platforms suspended directly over the dancers. Floor and ceiling strobes ripped light and flung shadows through the crowd. The din shook rust from the ceiling's exposed girders.

To Ripcat, the place stank of sourness—an acid mix of rancid sweat, stale urine, and brick mold. He climbed stone steps up out of the darkness where Duppy Hob had pushed him. A moment ago, he had tumbled helplessly through the starry Upper

Air into the void of the Gulf. Lightless cold wrenched him. Then, he had tumbled onto a stone floor with a startled groan like a dreamer falling out of bed.

He had glimpsed Duppy Hob's green slippers winking up the stone steps: That was his last remembrance. Traffic noise churned from outside, and an acrid stench of motor smoke burned his sinuses. But he did not stop to investigate. He rolled out of the darkness and scampered up the stairs after the green slippers.

Ripcat stopped at the head of the steps and blinked into an open space of morning light grilled with shadows. A loft of metallic screens hung from a molded ceiling. The man in green slippers who stood hashed in these shadows smiled with a strangely youthful exuberance. Tousled hair stiff as wild rye capped a round, clean, adolescent face.

"Remember me?" the young man said in a spry version of Duppy Hob's voice. He leaned casually against an iron column, arms crossed over his black tunic fretted in gold. His small, jet-black eyes said in a less-than-friendly way that he was far older and wiser than he looked. Those fixed, staring holes of darkness shimmered with an almost ultraviolet sheen. "This is my human guise. What do you think? Too young perhaps? I look inexperienced. But that's the advantage of youth. It's disarming."

The young man had no more odor than a mirage, and this perplexed the Cat. "You're—Duppy Hob?"

"Yes, I'm stronger on the Dark Shore, as I told you." He smiled warmly. "I don't like going to Gabagalus, because I'm so old there. But it was worth it, to get you."

"Why?"

"Again, the why." The youth, swinging by one arm, spun his compact body around the column of molded iron. "It feels divine to come back. Do you know where we are?"

Ripcat advanced into the capacious hall, staring up through a lattice of catwalks and scaffolds at the high windows. Morning sunlight stood like a golden angel against the pitted, time-stained brickwork of an adjacent building. "This is the Dark Shore," he said with grim realization.

Duppy Hob's puncture-hole eyes never left Ripcat as he walked across the wide room to a metal ladder. "Oh yes, this is the Dark Shore—the planet Earth, as unlike Irth's dominions as you can imagine." He pulled the ladder toward him, and a pulley let it down at the angle of a stairway. "But you don't have to imagine. You're from this cold rock, aren't you? And now you *remember*. Even though you still wear the skin of Ripcat, you remember."

Up the iron steps Duppy stepped briskly, and Ripcat followed. "What is this place?"

"It's a club—a dance hall—a useful facade." The metal stairs clanged under the weight of the climbers. "At night, the musicians and the crowds make so much noise no one can hear the chanting of my acolytes."

"Acolytes—you mean, ritual helpers?" Ripcat stood on a scaffold before Duppy Hob and a barred window. Even this close, where the Cat could feel the man's body heat, he had no detectable odor. "You work magic at nights, here on the Dark Shore—"

"Here in Tribeca. Reade Street, in the shadow of the civilized world's most concentrated power." He jerked a thumb out the window. An alley framed two identical platinum towers shining with rose-pale light. "The World Trade Center. Beacons of affluence. Symbol of my power."

Ripcat cocked an eye tuft. "*Your* power?"

"Why are you surprised that my interest in this world is proprietary? I've lived here long enough." Duppy Hob strolled watchfully along the platform beside the windows. "You saw that in our shared trance back in Gabagalus, didn't you? When my dwarves cast me into the Gulf, *this* is the planet where I landed. Over two million days ago—six thousand Earth years. When I arrived, this was but a world of animal-hide tents and mud cities. The science I brought here from Gabagalus changed everything. So, yes, this city, those towers of commerce, the very civilization on this cold rock, these are symbols of *my* power."

Leaning over the railing, Ripcat drew a line of sight through the open trapdoor and down the stone stairwell he had climbed. Absolute black squatted below. "You have a charmway in the cellar," he observed.

"I have built many charmways in this city alone." Duppy Hob gripped the rails of a wall ladder with hands and green slippers and slid down to the floor. "I can return to Gabagalus whenever I choose—though you saw the price I must pay to feel again the Charm of the Abiding Star. I don't go back often. It's much healthier for me to remain here on the Dark Shore, where the

Charm of my own bones is enough to live as a god. Not quite
the god you were at Arwar Odawl, mind you. My, my—you not
only were drawing water from rocks but sprouting whole forests
from those minerals! Nothing of that sort for us. Here on this
Earth, I've had to live a far more meager existence. But an influ-
ential one, as you can see."

Ripcat tossed a glance over his shoulder, through the dusty,
caged window at the chewed bricks of the alley and a keyhole
glimpse of the flat, purely geometric towers. "Your magic rules a
dim and cold world, Duppy Hob."

"The Dark Shore has none of the Charm of Irth. I agree with
you." He kicked the trapdoor shut over the cellar hole. "That is
why my acolytes work their chanting rituals down there every
night, drawing what vague Charm they can from this massive
array of amulets I've built—each city a talisman—Manhattan, Los
Angeles, Tokyo, Dhaka, London—a world of giant amulets gathering dilute Charm out of the planet itself." He waved for Ripcat
to come down from the scaffold and opened a side door under
a smashed exit sign. "Combined, those devices have garnered me
enough power to live forever as lord of this world."

Ripcat slid down the ladder, drawn by the draft of outdoor
scents. He stood in the exit, pushing his face into the columnar
light that fell into the alley, tasting the gutter stench and engine
exhaust. "This pitiful place?"

"Believe me, Reece, I've devoted my whole life to getting out
of here." Duppy Hob stepped into the alley, ushered Ripcat
ahead of him, and let the unmarked, knobless door wheeze shut.
Their breaths smoked in the chill air. "This is a warm period on
this planet, mind you. I got here some time after the last glacial
epoch. There'll be another onslaught of ice soon enough, and I
want out before then."

They stood in a tight alley littered with windblown newspapers.
Passersby bundled against the wintry morning moved at the street
end and, beyond them, glossy metallic vehicles identical to those
he had seen in his dreams of Darwin—cars, buses, trucks.

That was a life he remembered in total now. And all of it, the
whole transit of his life, seemed infinitesimal, consigned to fleet
anonymity in the shadow of this greater being. He gazed forlornly at the busy street and wished he enjoyed the ignorance
shared among those drifting lives.

"Want to run free—escape from me?" Duppy Hob swept an arm toward the mouth of the alley. "Go ahead. I won't try to stop you. I won't have to. The whole world is like this city. Roads everywhere. Radio waves everywhere. Nothing is hidden from me, because this whole planet has become my talisman."

A blare of horns and the growling of engines kept Ripcat from moving. He read river scents on the iced wind and beyond that the sea, pelagic, ancient just as on Irth. If he closed his eyes, he would think he was standing in a factory lane on the sea cliffs of Saxar. But the cold spoiled that dream. The wind that brushed his fur whisked away blood warmth and left him shivering. His nostrils dilated before a fragrant hint of grilled meat.

"Hungry?" Duppy Hob read Ripcat's beastmarks accurately. "Out here there is not enough Charm for common amulets to sustain life. You have to eat to live. You were a vegetarian as Reece Morgan, when you last lived here on Earth. But with those beastmarks and the metabolism that goes with them, you're carrying one big appetite. And I don't think vegetables will satisfy."

"Now that you've given me back my memories of Reece, remove this skin of light." Ripcat huddled his shoulders against the cold. "This body doesn't belong in this world. I want to return to my own form again. Give me back my original body."

"Oh no, Ripcat. You are far more useful to me as you are." The youthful face smiled but not those cheerless, oil black eyes. "Follow me, and I'll show you why I went to such peril to take you from Gabagalus myself."

At the back of the alley, a metal plate in the ground yielded to Duppy Hob's grip and slid aside. They descended down bellied steps patched with gray ice into the lightless chamber of the charmway. A flame like a bright petal opened in Duppy Hob's hand, and he set it upon the darkness.

The vault lit up, revealing a stone altar carved from the bedrock itself. A bowl scooped from the center of the altar top wobbled with liquid silver light.

Ripcat paid it little heed. His attention went directly to the alcove of the charmway, and he bolted into that shadowed niche, seizing a chance to escape back to Irth. He smacked hard into a rock wall and sat down in a drizzle of stars.

"Come out of there, Reece." Duppy Hob's laughter raked the

chamber with giddy echoes. "It's just an empty vault. I keep the charmway closed until I need it."

Ripcat emerged, rubbing his bruised snout. He surveyed the ritual chamber, the stairwell to the dance hall, the iced steps to the alley. The throb of his nose convinced him escape was unlikely, and he moved toward the anvil-shaped altar with its inset bowl of quicksilver.

Duppy Hob invited him closer and sat on the edge of the altar stone. "At night, while the eternal party rages above, my acolytes chant a cadence that carries my influence through the charmway to Gabagalus. Using Reece as an antenna—and, before him, the gremlin and his cacodemons—my will reached across Irth to direct my dwarves. Such a terrible bother. But my goal was a great one. It has taken all these two million days for me to get this far, this close to greatness."

In the silvery light, Ripcat's long eyes gleamed coldly. "What greatness can come of maggots?"

"Obedience," Duppy Hob answered at once. "They followed my commands without ever realizing they were again under my control. I used them to set up a soul-catcher under the Abiding Star itself. They thought that the fall of the Necklace of Souls into the Labyrinth of the Undead on World's End was a blunder, an accident of their eagerness to depose me. But that was no accident. Rather it was a last, desperate ploy to reclaim my power—and with a vengeance. It took hundreds of thousands of days, two million days actually, but my soul-catcher eventually absorbed sufficient Charm to catch a truly enormous soul."

"The child's soul—" Ripcat gasped, and all at once he felt understanding shaping itself like an ice form, hardening to something he could grasp. And the cold of it burned him. "You caught the soul of the nameless lady's child. You captured it with the Necklace of Souls!"

"Where it safely abides even as we speak." Flesh crinkled mirthfully around the holes of Duppy Hob's eyes.

"That's why the child doesn't move in her womb." Ripcat stepped within claw strike of the smug youth, who sat on the altar with his ankles crossed, relishing Ripcat's reaction. "You've captured its life, haven't you?"

"And I control it, too," he announced triumphantly. "If the nameless lady who has authored our universe wants her child to live, she will give me power over all the worlds. She will make me a god! Once she agrees to that, she may have the Necklace and her child's soul. *I* will be the master of all creation! Isn't it delicious? All this is possible because I possess the soul of our maker's child!" Then his face dropped as he added, "Or I did— until a gnome stole it from me."

Claws clicked in Ripcat's palms as his body flexed with under-standing. "Old Ric—he stole it from your dwarves to heal an ælven clan."

A shouted laugh lifted Duppy Hob off his haunches. "The fool carries the very purpose of his quest about his neck and has no notion!" Weary with amusement, he slapped a square, practical hand over his chest. "The irony has been a blister on my heart since I found out. But what can I do? That idiot gnome is running around the Bright Shore with a Radiant One who devours every-one who gets near."

"You're scared of the Shadow Eater."

"Even the Nameless Ones who dream these worlds fear the sentinels. That is why they *are* sentinels. They are powerful." Duppy Hob fixed Ripcat with a narrow stare. "You should be scared, too. If he absorbs your light, you—whichever form you are, man or beast—you are finished. Forever. Radiant Ones are too hot for us. Our souls melt like snowflakes in their light." He sagged, elbows on knees, shrinking at the very thought. "To keep as much distance between that monster and me, I've been direct-ing my dwarves from here, trying to reclaim the Necklace that is mine, what I worked two million days to make mine."

Ripcat shook his head defiantly. "Looks to me like it belongs to Old Ric right now."

"Not for long." Duppy Hob slipped down from the altar with the anvil stone between them. "That's why you're here on the Dark Shore with me. You're going to help me." He reached across and took Ripcat by his shoulder. "Look with me into this eyepool. It holds just enough power from last night's chanting to transmit one command. You must see this."

The youth's strength was immense and could have lifted Ripcat bodily if he resisted. But Ripcat did not resist, for he wanted to see into the eyepool, to learn as much as he could of this demon's plan. He slowly advanced until he saw himself in the mirroring liquid. Blue spectra floated across his reflected face.

Elusive as an optical illusion, the spectra rearranged to the image of Dogbrick and Lara together. Shackles bound Dogbrick to the salt-stained wall of a sea cave.

"This is an illusion, like you used to trick me with on Gabagalus, to get me to the cliff edge—" Ripcat spoke hotly to himself, trying to talk himself away from the altar. As much as he feared to look, he knew he had to see more of these two lost friends.

"This is different," Duppy Hob assured him, their brows nearly touching. "You are seeing this through an eye charm. It is most real. Watch—"

A burly dwarf approached Lara and snatched the crystal prism from her throat. Instantly, her image wavered, assumed spasmodic postures, then blinked away entirely. The dwarf fit the prism to the latex pouch of a sling and snapped it quickly out the mouth of the sea cave.

The crystal prism winked like a star, then fell into darkness.

"What have you done?" Ripcat cried. "Her soul is bound to that prism!"

"So it is." Duppy Hob stepped back with a satisfied sigh. "At last I have a piece of the Necklace in hand again. I didn't dare bring it across until you were here. It is useless to me without you."

Ripcat hissed with fright. "She can't survive a fall through the abyss!"

"She falls through a Door in the Air, just as you did." The fingers of one hand tapped his chin with mock surprise: "Oh, and look where she is landing—"

The quicksilver fluttered, and the blue spectra formed the gray, key-toothed skyline of Manhattan and an iron bridge across the wintry Hudson. A streak of light fled down the sky from above the city. It burned across the gray river and its ice cakes, slanted over the turnpike, and slammed into a catkin meadow among a few brown trees. The frozen ground erupted in a mucky explosion that tossed clods of peat high into the frosted sky. Moments later, out of the canebrakes, a mud woman lurched, covered scalp to sole in algal slime and industrial ooze.

"Not very dignified," Duppy Hob chuckled, "but I would have been foolish to use the charmway here twice in one day. I don't want any pesky wizards or clever charmwrights discovering my secret corridors between our shores. Not just yet." He slapped

the bowl of quicksilver, and it splashed to nothing. "Follow me—
our work has moved upstairs."

Excitedly, Duppy Hob ran around the altar and up the curved
stairwell and through the trapdoor to the empty dance hall. From
there, he opened a fire door and bounded up steel flights, pulling
himself along by the knurled iron banisters, chatting without
losing breath. "Now that one piece of the Necklace of Souls has
arrived on the Dark Shore, I may use it to find that larcenous
gnome and my Necklace. But to do so, I need you."

A heavy door opened onto the roof, and they stepped out,
the iced tar paper crunching underfoot. Winter morning offered
a gray smoky vista of chimney pipes and ventilator sheds. Blackened steel trusses upholding rooftop water towers etched Tribeca
in a visionary despondency.

Duppy Hob climbed onto the ledge and waved Ripcat to the
brink of the building. The Cat hopped nimbly to his side and
shared with him the teetering prospect of parapet-squatters.
Dauntlessly, he peered down five storeys past air-shaft windows
to the littered alley where they had stood earlier.

"I need for you to stand here—on the edge." He took Ripcat's
shoulders in a strong grip and turned him to face a wedge of
sooty sky. "You're agile. You're a Cat, right? You can do this in
your sleep. Now don't move."

Ripcat scowled. "Why should I help you?"

"I need you." Duppy Hob jumped down from the ledge and
held his arms out to signal Ripcat to stay. "Just stand there. As
Ripcat, you carry Charm from Irth, and your internal core of
Reece Morgan grounds it perfectly on the Dark Shore." He
backed away and left the beastmarked man with his fur shimmering in the wind. "I need you beside me as my antenna, so
that I can direct my dwarves to the Necklace of Souls. Help me,
and I will be generous with you."

The youth grinned warmly, yet his stare retained the bolt
blackness of a shark's eyeholes. "Look, Reece—" He pointed up,
into the hoar gray sky. "Look there with me—across the sky, to
the far shore, to the Bright Worlds—"

DEADWALKER

Asofel gazed back at Duppy Hob and Ripcat staring into the sky, across the dream, directly at him. They did not actually see him, only the radiance of the Bright Shore, the light of the Abiding Star, chilled across time and enormous spans of darkness. That they could see this energy at all demonstrated the astonishing power that the devil worshipper had accumulated while marooned on the Dark Shore.

The Radiant One marveled at Duppy Hob's evil ingenuity: Using Ripcat as a conductor for receiving and broadcasting Charm, the devil worshipper had found a way to communicate with Irth. A little piece of the dream could now manipulate the larger pieces. Yet still, it was no more than a dream.

Dwarves continued to march out of World's End, streaming through the subterranean charmways and the central Well of Spiders. Asofel watched them with cool fascination, like a child studying an ant farm. Duppy Hob had generated millions over the ages, and he had set them all marching, descending through the worlds with one intent—to seize the Necklace of Souls.

Asofel did not question why. He himself did not care. The

Necklace of Souls served Old Ric, and the dwarves would not have it. They would be left to wander aimlessly through the dark soon enough now that the shadow thing had crossed the Gulf and left the Bright Shore.

From afar, Ripcat sensed the Radiant One watching them, and he wanted to wave, shout, jump up and down for help. But he did not move. The sentinel was too distant, his presence vague and disinterested as some cosmic observer. Once, he had feared the very thought of the Radiant One, but now Ripcat stood rigid with hopelessness on the rooftop, fearing only the luminous being's silence, his detachment. With frustration, the beastmarked man felt powerless as the smoke he saw twisting along the cold streets below, seeping through manhole covers from the city's infernal depths.

But Ripcat's despair did reach Asofel; yet, even so, he ignored it. The shadow thing would naturally be disgruntled, having lost a godlike mastery among the Bright Worlds. The Radiant One did not dwell on it. His mind was already calculating how much longer he would have to endure the indignity of serving a gnome inside a dream.

The expectation that this would be his last foray into the cold moved him with exuberance. He sought out Old Ric and found the eldern gnome on Nemora. Ric had left Hellsgate after the slaughter of the giants to return to the ice caves and snowfields where he had lived most of his life.

Through the chill fog, Old Ric mounted the stiles that led from the frost fern banks of the frozen river to Knolls Brae, the cave community where his parents had brought him as a child and where he had reared his children. The sinuous curves of the rooftops stirred emotional depths in him, and he nearly sat down in the blue snow sobbing. The threads of peat smoke rising from flue holes in the ice domes carried sumptuous scents of meals shared with loved ones who were now all ghosts—two wives, three children, including his beloved Amara—

So befuddled by awakened grief was the gnome that he did not see the fisherfolk climbing down the stiles toward him, saws and axes strapped to their backs.

"That there is Old Ric for sure, I told you!" an excited voice announced from above.

The eldern gnome started, lifted from his dismal trance by the sound of his name. He saw gnomes in eel-skin slickers and squid-leather boots on their way to the river, and he recognized the oldest, a net-weaver and fishmonger who had once employed Ric to build a hearth in the far-gone days when he did such firework. The eldern gnome lifted both arms in greeting.

The fisherfolk returned the greeting, then paused in their descent. They had drawn close enough to see that the eldern gnome wore rags of grass and vine and a necklace of rainbows. He was bareheaded, his bald pate scalded by exposure. And—was that some kind of gory prankster's prop?—a barbed arrow pierced his torso.

"Ric?" a nervous voice called out. "Are you Old Ric of Knolls Brae?"

"The same!" Old Ric clambered toward them half-naked and aswirl in pale vapors. "I have been to World's End, brothers and sisters!"

Two of the fisherfolk began to climb hurriedly back up the stiles. The third crouched in amazement. "Goddess forfend, it really is you! Old Ric! But what is that arrow—by the gods themselves, you're wounded!"

"An old wound." Old Ric dismissed it with a curt laugh even as he had to twist his body to keep the arrowhead from catching on the embankment as he climbed. "A dwarfish arrow found me when I found the Necklace of Souls—" He chuckled as he ascended. "I was lucky I was holding the Necklace. It's a soul-catcher, you see."

"You're a deadwalker!" the fishmonger yelled, seeing more sharply the ripped flesh and the crimson arrow shaft, its varnish of blood undried. He skidded in his abrupt eagerness to flee and shouted with fright as he slid down the embankment to within grasp of the eldern gnome.

"Calm down—I'll not hurt you." Old Ric bent forward to help the fishmonger to his feet.

The fallen gnome kicked and lurched about. "Get away!" he cried, and charged up the embankment, his ice-cutting tools sent clattering.

Old Ric proceeded climbing the stiles, hurt by the foolish reaction of the fisherfolk. "I'm no monster!" he called. "I'm Old Ric, I tell you!"

Before Ric reached the top of the embankment, several squat

figures in the white and gold raiment of elders blocked his way. "Go back, Old Ric."

Two of the elders were so old he remembered them as children, and he called out their names, beseeching them for mercy accorded the venerable.

"Get away, deadwalker!" They waved staves threateningly. "In life you kept to yourself. Now that you are dead, you dare return among us? Get away quickly before we bring the fire knives from the forges."

Old Ric moaned with disbelief. "I've died to save you—to save all the worlds!"

"You're mad! Begone!" The elders flapped their ivory robes and beat their staves violently. "Bring the fire knives! Bring the knives!"

Old Ric stuck out his tongue and waved away the distraught elders. Angrily, he showed them his back and walked down the stiles kicking chunks of ice with each step and muttering, "Ignorant gnomes!"

Before him, the gray river swerved to where the Abiding Star floated in a cold haze above broken plates of ice. Frost gardens tufted the banks. Morosely, he thought to go there and lose himself among the brittle, ice-webbed drifts that wind and hail had sculpted.

Amara used to play there—as his other children had. The frost gardens signaled thick, strong ice, ideal frolic sites. Of course there was always the danger of them gouging out an eye on the jagged ice rays. The children enjoyed smashing shapes out of the frosted lattices, building mazes, playhouses, icicle palaces. There was always danger. Amara knew that.

But what good did all our care do for you, Amara? Old Ric moved like a shade down the stiles, toward the frail, glass stems and branches. Surrounded by ice flowers, enclosed by fragility, at the very center of vulnerability, he thought he could remove the Necklace of Souls.

What good does care do when by our very natures we are doomed? If he removed the soul-catcher, death would lift away the heavy burden the nameless lady had pressed upon him. Like Amara, he would find freedom.

He lifted the Necklace and saw Lara within the crystal facets. Her body was bruised, a battered vegetable.

"The witch—" He shuddered to see her face so battered, wall-eyed with concussion and gobbed in mud. "Lara—" The wise witch who had outwitted Blue Tipoo, who had come down from the Abiding Star for love—what had reduced her to this atrocity? A wail of indignation and pity started from deep inside him.

Noonlight shrunk shadows, and Asofel strode to Ric's side from behind, shining exuberantly. "It's finished, Old Ric."

The eldern gnome held a hand to his brow to shield his aching eyes from the glare. "What's finished? What are you talking about? I haven't called you."

"There's no need to call me anymore." Asofel dimmed his luminosity and took a silver shape that reflected the glacial slopes and the hazy river. "It's over. The shadow thing is no longer among the Bright Worlds."

Old Ric lurched about excitedly and nearly slipped. "What happened?"

"Duppy Hob seized Reece Morgan in his beastmarks and threw him into the Gulf."

"The devil worshipper?" The eldern gnome gaped. "You've seen Duppy Hob?"

"I have. He is very old."

Old Ric crashed hastily through a wall of ice ferns toward the radiant being, reasoning aloud, "If he threw the shadow thing into the Gulf, Duppy Hob has to be here—on the Bright Shore."

"On Irth—in Gabagalus."

The gnome tapped his forehead, trying to nudge his memory. "I don't know that dominion."

Asofel paced with him beside turquoise fins of ice at the riverside. "Duppy Hob is from Gabagalus originally, a continent on the far side of Irth. But he has crossed the Gulf with the intruder. They are both on the Dark Shore. Our work is done."

Old Ric stopped in his tracks. "I think not."

"The shadows are where they belong." The Radiant One almost growled with frustration. *Is this dreamwork interminable?* "We should at least return to World's End and report to our lady."

"And what of Broydo?"

Asofel's silver surface dulled a moment as he trance-blinked, then brightened again when he reported what he saw, "I have seen him. He is in Gabagalus with the margravine."

The gnome stamped his foot with determination. "Then we

are going to Gabagalus. And if we have to, we're going beyond. We'll cross the Gulf if we must."

"What are you ranting about, gnome?" Asofel flushed gold-red. "I will not squander my power in this dream again."

"We must go to Lara." Ric lifted the Necklace of Souls with both hands. "Look at her!"

Prismatic shadows shook and became wind tossing cattails and a mud woman staggering across spongy ground, crashing through the canes.

"She's on the Dark Shore." Asofel stepped back. "We can't go there."

"Why not?"

Out of a white aura, Asofel's face cooled, his mischievous donkey eyes widening with fear. "It's too deep into the dream, too close to the dark strata of cold matter. It will take a lot of power to do anything down there. And if my light is spent in that darkness, it will be extinguished forever. You realize, I will never get out of the dream—ever."

The gnome accepted this with a pensive look as he considered what to do. "Then at least let us go to Broydo and assure his safety." He held the Necklace of Souls to the anxious visage of the Radiant One. "But before we go, look again at Lara. See her here in the Necklace, Asofel—the woman the magus loved— the love that brought him here to trouble our lives—see her in the crystals . . ."

Stenciled in mud, she was dragging herself through swales of frozen grass, past neon green chemical pools, along rutted, gravel roads. Staring faces swept past in the flow of traffic along the viaduct above her. Impassive faces sweeping across the dull sky disappeared as she passed among the concrete piers supporting the highway.

Crows broke away from the clattering reeds like rumpled pieces of sorrow. She paid them no heed, the witch inside her asleep and reading no omens. Up a gravel revetment she leaned and tilted across railroad tracks. A commuter train slashed by and more faces turned, watching the mud woman wander stiff-kneed through the switching yard like the zombie she was.

Eventually, transit police would pick her up weaving through a boggy field in a restricted zone under high-tension cables. Trampling circles in the marsh grass, she was found dancing

power up out of the earth. Light spangled inside her head—
flashes of who she was, sky witch, ghost, messenger of
apocalypse . . .

The arresting officers left the engine of their brown car running where they stopped on the access road near the madcap
dancer. Pepper spray and hand shackles ready, the officers gingerly approached the twirling woman, calling to her and receiving no response. She appeared entranced, drugged. Most
bizarrely, for all her frenzied exertion, no breath clouded the
cold air.

The crazed woman came away from the field without resistance, the report would later show. But there would be no mention of how the air appeared brighter around her. Static
electricity from the high-tension lines, they figured. At their
touch, no spark, only a sudden passivity. They cuffed her wrists
behind her back quickly and patted her torn and mud-plastered
robes for weapons.

The crystal prism was not found until later, at the state clinic
where she was delivered for medical evaluation and care. The
admitting team stood baffled around her gurney in the examining
bay. She had no pulse and was not breathing, yet her pupils
responded to light—and she spoke, "I am the Dog—I am the
Dog."

The crystal prism threaded by a coiled gold filament had no
clasp and was carefully lifted over her bruised head when the
bedraggled robes were removed and the mud washed off her.
The attending nurse held the chunky gem to the light, and winter
gusted into her soul. She shivered and passed the crystal to an
aide, who sealed it in a plastic bag.

When the bagged prism was removed from the room by the
security officer, Lara began to fade at once. She lost iris reflexivity
and stiffened into an immediate and deathly rigor. The staff pronounced her dead. They wheeled her covered corpse into the
corridor, to await an attendant who would push it to the morgue.
By the time the attendant arrived, the wraith had faded to nothing but the imprint of where she had lain.

Later that night, the detective assigned to the missing corpse
examined the missing woman's jewelry. The craftsmanship of the
neck cord immediately held the detective's attention, with its
unique and baffling intricate design. The jewel itself appeared

simultaneously rough-cut and highly polished and shaped. He had never seen any gem like it, thick as a thumb and meshed with rainbows.

Peering into those crystal lights, the detective felt a peculiar chill, like a wind of cold atoms blowing brightly through him. He closed his fist over the stone and went to the examining bay where she had died and disappeared.

The swinging doors opened on an empty bay. Medical monitors stood inert. The exam table lay dark, already shrouded for the next trauma.

"G'day, sir."

The detective's long coat flapped like wings as he whirled about. "Where'd you come from?"

A swarthy woman in long, fluent black hair and wearing a priest's cassock stood beside the oxygen unit, where no one had been a moment before. "That's my crystal you have there."

"Who are you?" The detective reflexively reached for his badge.

"I have only a moment's clarity, sir," the woman spoke in a pleadful tone. "You must listen to me. You're in danger if you keep the crystal. Give it to me."

The detective showed his badge. "I'm a police detective. You know about this—crystal? What is it?"

The prism shone with a beautiful grace in his hand, like a small animal sitting vibrantly still. "It is dangerous."

"Why?"

The crystal's colors riffled in her dark eyes. "Those I stole it from will do anything to get it back."

"Yeah?" The detective's hand closed to a fist around the crystal prism. "And who are they?"

"They are dangerous."

"Okay." He slipped the crystal into the pocket of his coat and removed his handcuffs. "I'm taking you in for further questioning."

The woman offered no resistance. He cuffed her and turned to call for a nurse to pat her down. The clatter of handcuffs falling to the linoleum pulled him around. He stood alone in the empty exam bay, and at his feet the handcuffs gleamed, closed and locked.

INTERLUDE WITH AN ÆLF

BROYDO LED THE WAY OUT OF THE SEA CAVE WHERE HE HAD JUST slain a basilisk with the serpent sword. The hilt had annealed to his grasp, so tense had been his fright, and not until he stepped outside and daylight painted him in warmth did his cramped hand loosen. He rested the blooded sword tip in the sand and peeled his fingers from the hilt.

Before him, jigsaw horizons interlocked withered mountains and hill villages. Through a lens cube that she unfolded from her amulet-vest, Jyoti studied the villages. Hazings of distance peeled away, revealing salamandrines—glossily hairless people with newtlike features—busy at work. They had finished erecting the windmills and water flues they had packed away the afternoon before, and now they busily tended their cress paddies and wort fields. Children frolicked in school gardens in the midst of the village's blue-stone bungalows. And on the long highways that traversed the quilted fields, wagons cruised, powered by colorful solar vanes.

"Now that we've made it here, how will we ever find Ripcat?" Broydo asked. They had emerged onto a limestone escarpment among spiny, eroded mountains. Some maroon viperish thing thrashed in the oozing tidal pool below, beached until nightfall if it survived that long, and Broydo regarded it with fascination. He felt pity, convinced that the trapped sea viper was a vision of his own predicament, caught out of his element and surrounded by peril.

"We'll get help from the local authorities," Jyoti said matter-of-factly. She opened her aviso and transmitted a general distress signal. "We have to warn everyone about the dwarves and Duppy Hob."

"After what's happened in Saxar, news surely has preceded us." Broydo tore his attention away from the stranded sea viper and regarded the landscape. In the distance, he spied a trace that spiraled down the mountain and joined a path. That trail descended through a parkland of bulbous stromatolites and silky-frilled marine polyps to the farmed acres of the lowlands. "Let's follow that road down the mountain." He shadowed his eyes with his palm, gazing into watery horizons where the cultivated plains arrived at the sea. "Maybe we can find a meal along the way. I'm starved."

"Killing basilisks stokes an appetite." Jyoti winked encouragingly. She liked this earnest ælf. She had seen the fear in his face when he had peeked into the tidal pool at the sea viper exiled from its element as cruelly as they had been torn from their former lives—and yet, the next moment, his features brightened at the prospect of a meal. A voice squeaked from her aviso. She gave her name and title and described where they were, sweeping the wet land with her lens cube looking for something identifiable. On a nearby butte, she spotted a rocket pad and gave its location. "They'll meet us there."

"Who?" Broydo followed Jyoti along a slope of wild boulders to the trace he had spotted.

"Their foreign office is sending someone to meet us at that rocket pad." She passed the lens cube to the ælf and showed him where to look. "We'll warn them then about the dwarves. I didn't want to mention it on the aviso. If we're overheard, a panic could ensue."

Stromatolites stood like mossy stumps along the path of loose bricks and seashells. Tracks of small creatures—crabs, millipedes, waterspiders—wrinkled the scalloped drifts of sand that banked the brick path. "Life is so small . . ." Broydo mumbled.

"You sound like Dogbrick," Jyoti cajoled. "Are ælves philosophers?"

"Ælves are too practical for philosophy," Broydo replied quickly, "especially counselors, who must advise the leaders with pragmatic assesments, not ideals. But this quest has made me philosophical, margravine. To know that there is an author of worlds and that our lives are but dreams . . . does that not trouble you? Do we not seem so much smaller now?"

"I lost almost everyone I loved to the Dark Lord." Jyoti kicked at glittery shards of periwinkles and fish bones in the tide wrack. "Mine is a philosophy of survival. We *are* small lives and only together do we matter."

"We are united by a terrible threat," Broydo agreed, "but tell me, margravine, if I may ask, why have you given yourself to this quest? My grandmother, our clan leader, commanded me to see this through. But you—you've lost everyone, you said. Why do you care?"

"I lost nearly everyone, it's true, Broydo. But I did not lose heart." She placed both hands on her amulet-vest. "Charm saved me. Without my amulets, I'd have gone mad with grief. But the power in these hex-gems and conjure-wires has made my suffering bearable enough to still feel the pain of others. I don't want these worlds to end. And I don't want to lose the one good thing that came to me out of the terror of the Dark Lord."

"Reece Morgan—Ripcat—he is your consort." Broydo nodded with understanding. "I'm but seventeen summers old and have yet to know love. Even so I understand, margravine. I have been commanded by my clan—and you by your heart."

"They are the same, clan and heart, are they not?"

"You have been reduced to your lone heart—all that remains of your clan." The ælf's shoulders slumped sadly. "I am surprised that even the great power of Charm can heal such pain."

"Not all of my people are lost." Jyoti's jaw tightened as she remembered the others who depended on her to rebuild their dominion. "I have a brother yet alive and scores of survivors who managed, like myself, to elude the Dark Lord. Together, we will rebuild Arwar Odawl."

"It must be hard for you to be away from the ruins of the past you are striving to rebuild for the future." Broydo watched Jyoti's hands adjust the power wands in her vest, feeding herself more Charm to calm the disturbing thoughts the ælf roiled in her. "I'm sorry to distress you."

Jyoti offered a slim, reassuring smile. "We'll all be less distressed if we can stop Duppy Hob's invasion of dwarves and keep the dream of these worlds intact."

"If only we could find the others." Broydo led the way as they entered a vale of billowing scarves, the wind-ruffled tentacles of giant sea anemones. The ælf swatted them with his sword, and they retracted. "We must locate Old Ric and tell him what we know."

If the dwarves have not already found him, Jyoti feared. "The Shadow Eater—"

"Asofel," Broydo corrected her.

"Will Asofel be strong enough to stop all these dwarves?" She recalled the tall being of white-fire hair she had briefly chased in Saxar and doubted any one being could staunch the flow of maggot-warriors she had witnessed.

"The Radiant One is of another order of being," the ælf reported. "Old Ric believes Asofel has the strength to make the dream right again for the nameless lady."

"That strange nameless lady—" She lifted her chin curiously. "Who is she, Broydo?"

"Little is known of the Nameless Ones," the ælf replied. "They dwell beyond World's End, beyond the bright and burning Upper Air, inside the aura of the Abiding Star."

"They are creatures of light."

"Less substantial than we, and more powerful." His mind always felt as though it were rolling over when he thought of these entities for whom he was part of a dream. "In a way, I suppose, we are their shadows."

"Just as the dark worlds are the shadows of the bright."

Broydo accepted this with a nod. "Reece comes from a dark world, yet he seemed to me like a man of your own kind."

"Only his magic makes him different."

Broydo whistled. "But what a difference, margravine!"

"Often I wish it were otherwise." The steep trail they descended leveled among glistening brown fields of wort. "Though his magic has done so much to help rebuild Arwar Odawl, I would love him as dearly if he were only a man."

"I sense from your voice you would prefer that."

"I think so." She spoke to the ground, kicking at the pebbles in her way. "Magic troubles me. It is too remindful of the Dark Lord."

"A moment ago you spoke gratefully of Charm—and now you are troubled by magic." Broydo swung a querying look at her. "Are they not similar? They augment our natural strengths."

"Sometimes they distort us," she answered. "Charm has its dangers. My grandfather warned of that. He wanted his people to rely less on Charm and more on their self-sufficiency and ingenuity."

"He must have been a remarkable man."

Jyoti agreed with a small laugh. "Remarkable enough to be considered eccentric and ignored."

"Except by you."

"I loved my grandfather," she admitted with a shade of sorrow in her voice. "And I learned from him how to defend myself without Charm. But I cannot live as he lived, charmless, pretalismanic, independent of wizards and witches. I'm not as strong as he. I need Charm."

"We all do—except gnomes, of course." Broydo rattled his sword against the barnacle-crusted posts of a wooden fence. "They alone of the mortals carry Charm in their bones. Would we were all so blessed."

"It has always been the way among people to make themselves more than they are—with Charm, with machines." She flicked a look at him. "It must be the same for ælves."

"It is, of course." He plucked at his grass-woven shirt. "Look, unlike animals, we wear clothes! We must augment ourselves or we are not complete." He lifted the sword above his head. "Magic is the ultimate augmentation."

"And fraught with the ultimate perils—as the Dark Lord demonstrated."

"And so you would rather that your consort Reece be more like your grandfather, yes?"

Jyoti's gaze softened. "I'm swept off my feet just to know him at all. He's everything I've wanted in a mate—courage and compassion combined."

"I am terribly sorry, margravine," Broydo mumbled, head bowed, then added more loudly, "—sorry that I held the serpent sword and used it so poorly when Ripcat and Dogbrick were taken from us by the dwarves."

"I thought we had settled that, Broydo." She put a kind hand on his shoulder. "Don't blame yourself. The fact that you're still here and the sword is in your hand proves to me that you are an ælf of courage. Together, we'll get them back from the dwarves." *If they are yet alive*, she told herself, and then adjusted the flow of Charm from her power wands to quiet her anxiety. "Tell me about Lara."

"The ghost?"

"She was a witch from the Dark Shore, and she was trained by Reece. You traveled with her at World's End." Jyoti regarded the ælf closely. "What is she like? Is she beautiful?"

"Beautiful?" Broydo looked aghast. "She was frightful to behold. Her face was ripped to the skull—"

"You saw the wounds that killed her," she interrupted. "But deeper than that suffering, she must be a good woman for Reece to have followed her ghost here from the Dark Shore."

An impish smile lifted one corner of Broydo's mouth. "Are you jealous, margravine—of a ghost?"

"Jealous?" Jyoti shook her head sternly. "I'm simply curious."

"And I'm a counselor, who knows the emotions that move ælves—and people." His vivid blue eyes smiled. "We are not so different, people and ælves. Well, margravine, you must not worry about Reece's affection for Lara. She is a ghost—and you are a living woman."

A pulse of thunder lifted their attention to the skyport at the far end of the road. A silver-finned rocket reclined on its launchpad, surrounded by wheeling gulls scattering across the morning. Thunderheads cored with orange flames rose from the end of the road, and a star lifted into the blue day. The rocket swiftly arced out of sight, but its contrail etched the indigo zenith, pointing to where the ship had flown beyond the sky and into the Upper Air.

"Where is it going?" the ælf asked.

"Far worlds." Jyoti continued down the long road. Apricot clouds lingered over the launchpad. Farmworkers riding a giant sloth crossed their path, carrying harvest rakes to the cress paddies. They shouted and waved, and Broydo saluted them with his sword.

A white cumulus of rocket exhaust still floated above the sky-

port when Jyoti and Broydo arrived. Another ship was being
loaded for an afternoon launch, and salamandrine stevedores bustled between dray wagons stacked with bales of spices and herbs.
Forklifts conveyed the bales to the hold of the horizontal rocket.

The gatekeeper raised the spiked fence at their approach and
bowed, greeting Jyoti by her title. "Margravine!" He was a black
salamandrine with yellow blotches. "Welcome to Gabagalus!"

"We have urgent news!" Jyoti noted that the guard wore an
open aviso at the hip of his spun-gold raiment. "Dwarves are
invading from World's End under the command of Duppy Hob!"

"Margravine, you must still be in shock from your harrowing
journey here." Below his turban, the gatekeeper's shiny brow
creased with worry lines. "Dwarves? Please, pause for a moment."

Jyoti turned to Broydo for confirmation and saw that he had
wandered off into the skyport, drawn to a blazing outdoor grill
where salamandrines in kilts mingled, eating with their long, big-
pad fingers. Overhead, a flock of gliders in camouflage white and
blue slided across the sky on their way into the mountains from
where Jyoti and Broydo had descended.

"You are a head of state from a dominion of Irth," the guard
stated humorlessly. "I was posted here to await you as soon as
we received your distress call from the mountains. You must have
crashed at dawn, and the tide has swept away your balloon or
your boat."

Jyoti bent forward to speak directly into the gatekeeper's open
aviso. "We came to Gabagalus through a charmway from the
wilds of Zul."

"Charmways? Don't be silly." The yellow-marked salamandrine
took her arm and led her toward a solar wagon laden with crates.
He motioned to the cargo marked with ports of call she did not
recognize. "Margravine, Gabagalus is an interworld trade colony.
The prosperity of this entire continent depends upon the security
of these heavily underwritten agrarian enterprises. If there were
charmways, that security would be breached. Our trade partners
would be reluctant to invest in our harvests at the prices we now
command. You see? There can't possibly be charmways into
Gabagalus."

Validating that statement, heaven's drumroll rattled the tiles of
the arcade roof. A jet of green flame blazed skyward from the
crag where Jyoti and Broydo had entered Gabagalus.

"That's charmfire!" Jyoti thrust an arm toward the blackened stob that had been a weathered summit moments before. "By the Goddess! You've destroyed the charmway we came through! Why?"

"Please quiet down. This is a sophisticated audience—rocket mechanics, pilots—and they understand about charmways. But there are workers here who don't. If we give them cause, they'll spread panicky rumors of holes into other worlds. It's hard enough to get good farmers . . ."

"Listen to me." Jyoti took the guard by the shoulders. "Dwarves *are* coming through the charmways. Duppy Hob *is* directing an invasion. Sound the alarm!"

The gatekeeper's gold eyes slimmed. Slowly but firmly he removed Jyoti's hands. "You are in violation of our dangerous rumors law. Don't you see? There are no charmways in Gabagalus. I've already explained, that would destabilize our position as a reliable trading colony."

Jyoti's face clenched. "Your government is covering up these charmways. You don't want to admit you have a problem."

The guard's grip tightened. "I must ask you to come with me, margravine."

Jyoti lifted her face toward Broydo. But the soldiers had begun to wrestle with him for the sword and one had unsheathed her firecharm. The margravine chilled to witness this and froze motionless at what she saw beyond the sheet-stone walls of the rocket pad.

Rising out of the algal muck of the adjoining paddies, the pointed heads of dwarves whistled shrill war cries. They slogged ashore, unwearied by their descent from the mountains in stream currents and irrigation canals. Quickly, they hacked foot niches into the stone wall with their nimble hatchets and stormed onto the launch field.

Flares of green charmfire from the skyport guards cut into the first wave of muddy dwarves. The flames exploded the miniature warriors to shredded metal and papery embers of flesh. But another throng of dwarves soon spilled over the sheet-stone walls and more smashed through the spiked gate, shrieking their piercing berserker cries.

Jyoti tripped the gatekeeper and rolled his slim body under the wagon before he fully realized what was happening. "Do you have a weapon?" she shouted above the din of screaming dwarves and searing firecharms.

The gatekeeper shook his head and clawed at the ground, eyes spinning with fright.

"Then pray to your gods." Jyoti ducked around the side of the wagon, peering under the carriage, searching for Broydo. She sighted his bark boots scurrying toward her. Standing, she watched him running, knees kicking high, serpent sword stabbing the air in his jerking arm, and a dozen dwarves behind him.

"The sword!" she shouted, and a hatchet blurred over her head and struck her topknot, spilling her yellow hair over her face. When she brushed the tresses aside, she saw Broydo spin about and slash with the serpent sword.

Maggots flopped to the ground among the crashes of hatchets and armor. She ran to his side where he stood in a wide stance howling.

"Calm yourself!" She pulled him back toward the wagon, away from the slashing bolts of charmfire and whirling hatchets. "We have to find where they're coming from."

"Down the flues from the mountain charmway," the ælf guessed.

"There are too many. Look!" Jyoti's shrill stare pointed to soldiers falling back from the perimeter under a glare of blue-hot flames. The dwarves had seized a firecharm!

"Too many for the flues." The serpent sword trembled in his grasp. "What do we do?"

"There's a well out there—it's a charmway." Jyoti pushed him ahead of her. "Let's go find it."

Broydo dug in his heels. "Why do I have to go first?"

"You have the sword."

He curled around and held the shivering bone blade between them. "Take it."

She pushed the flat of the blade away with her open palm. "Smiddy Thea gave it to you."

"And I'm giving it to you." He closed her hand around the hilt. "There are too many. I will follow you."

"Stay close then!" The sword pulled her after it, its life in its balance, and she gave her body to it, let it lead her out from behind the wagon.

Star white streamers of energy arced overhead as some dwarf

struggled to fit a firecharm to its three-fingered hand. Jyoti let the serpent sword cut a path for her directly toward that star-welder's fire.

Maggots toppled on all sides, and Broydo hopped among the spasming gouts of white flesh. It took all his alertness to keep up with the suddenly slinky and swiftly agile Jyoti. So when a firecharm skidded under him and briefly tangled between his ankles, he jumped away from the green metal muzzle and wood stock. By the time he recognized it for what it was and twisted around to seize it, a dwarf had snatched it.

The scalded barrel pointed at the ælf's face. Doom would burn white from that black hole, and he did not blink.

A pale blur of bone blade thwacked the dwarf's helmet, and the armored dwarf convulsed to a maggot.

Broydo caught the firecharm before it hit the ground.

"The charmway is here!" Jyoti dashed among shards of the trampled gate, dwarves vanishing under her hacking sword. The swarming dwarves led her directly to the sewage duct, a concrete drainage pipe half-submerged in the algal pools behind the rocket pad.

"It stinks!" Broydo complained as they approached the scum-crusted duct. But he did not slacken his pace, for the drainage pipe glowed green within, packed with dwarves, and more of the manic minions spilled down the culvert in shrill pursuit, armor barely slowing them in the sludge. Threat surrounded them, and the ælf hurried to stay within range of the serpent sword, for he had no notion how to use the firecharm in his hands.

Gray water sloshed at his knees, and he hugged the weapon to his chest. Jyoti bowed first, bending to enter the cloacal tunnel, sword first. Maggots splashed in the fecal water, drowning. Broydo gritted his teeth and followed her into the tunnel, head lowered in humble obeisance within this shrine of final things and darkness.

BEASTMARKED IN MANHATTAN

DOGBRICK HEARD THE PAIN OF THE DWARVES. SOMETHING WAS KILL-
ing them in the charmways, and their death wails trilled at a
pitch his keen ears could read. The dying were far away. Yet he
could hear that they were dying swiftly, almost instantly, their
cries slicing to silence. No wounded shrieks followed. And many
died at once.

Soon he would be dead, as well. He had been shackled too
long without food in this cave, licking water from the dew-chilled
walls. Charmless without his amulets, he was starving. He felt
too weak to stand. All he could do was lie there among his
chains, staring through the open mouth of the cave with dull
eyes.

"Rest, Dog." Lara hovered like a mist, more felt than seen.
"Rest and share with me. Share."

A taste of moonlight colored the air, but Dogbrick lacked the
strength to raise his head. From under his salt-crusted mane,
honey brown eyes watched tenuous vapors weave Lara's phantom. She squatted before him naked, sensuous as smoke fumes
writhing, then dissolving in a gust of sea wind.

"I'm trying to hold on to you, Dogbrick," the phantom whispered almost silently, tickling the hairs of his long ears. "I need you. I don't want to fall into the Gulf."

He closed his eyes.

"Stay awake." The phantom suffused the space around Dogbrick, fraught with the odor of blue dusk. "Stay awake, or I'll slip away. The crystal prism has fallen to the Dark Shore. It's pulling me after it. Stay awake now."

Dogbrick heaved himself into a sitting position. Planetshine glossed the night sea. A moment ago, the ocean had been dull with daylight. The languid surf had lulled him asleep. He sniffed for the ghost.

The salt tang of spume carried a sour taint of guano from cliff rookeries. He swung his long head, reaching for odors and not finding the dry, cheesy stink of the dwarves. Yet he heard their dying. Louder and closer, their screams leaped like flames.

"You're awake!" Lara stood cat-eyed and transparent against the somber night sky. "I fell to the Dark Shore while you slept. Can you hear me?"

Through her naked outline, Dogbrick saw star fire shining out of seams among the clouds.

"I can only hold to Irth if you stay awake." She slid closer on the breeze. "I'm barely more than memory to you. But out there, on the cold world where the dwarves have cast me, I'm stupid. I can barely see straight. The fall has made me less. It took all my strength to warn the man who took the prism away from me. And he didn't listen. I know it. He has no idea what is going to happen."

The clouds healed their wounds, and Dogbrick sat in darkness. Surf laved dimly over distant reefs in the ebb tide. His heart pumped weakly, and a ponderous wave of weariness rose over him.

"Oh don't fall asleep again—" She clung to him for purchase against the nightward tug of death, the pull into the abyss.

A freshened wind spat cold rain, reviving him a little. He lifted his face to the wet night and found the strength to mumble, "Lara—stay close."

"I'm here." Her dusky body shone with feverlight in the black socket of the cave. "I'm close enough now to help you. I can dance for you and draw strength for you out of the ground. You won't have to starve for Charm. I'm a witch, you know. Reece trained me to do this."

She bent forward and kissed his cheek. At her touch, rainwater dripped down the weathered crevices of his face, and the apertures of his eyes flexed, seeing deeper into the dark, to the blind shapes of another world. He saw trees. Jungle birds fluted their cries from high galleries of looped vines. Lara danced naked among the pale boles, the leaf floor quaking under her whirling steps.

The witch drummed power out of the ground and up the sturdy trunks of the trees. Caval and Reece had taught her the steps and the chants, and the rhythms entranced her and gave her strength to dance cold halos onto the forest floor.

The light that Lara danced shifted dreamlike to the faceted colors of the crystal prism itself. Dogbrick's stare crisped. Lara's trancing dance had connected them to the soul-catcher. The crystal had held her ghost long enough that she could still see herself in it. Even from across the Gulf, the prism's lusters splurged around her.

Dogbrick's mind, loosened from his body by starvation and an absence of Charm, moved with the witch.

"Show us Reece Morgan," the witch commanded of the vessel that held her soul. And among its spectral shadows, they viewed Ripcat in rags standing stiffly on the rooftop of a gray brick building.

He sensed them, as well. Their abrupt presence jarred the hypnotic rigor that had held him in place on the parapet. His stance relaxed, which Duppy Hob did not appear to notice, so absorbed was he in using Ripcat's body as an antenna to broadcast instructions to Irth.

Duppy Hob stood between a ventilator hood and a water tower, an amber power wand gripped in both hands and held up to the sky. The wind sloughing off the Hudson brushed back his wild rye hair and pressed the black tunic against his stocky frame. Static broke apart what Duppy Hob saw of Lara and the beastmarked man in Zul, and he snapped alert in time to see Ripcat dive off the rooftop.

Duppy Hob ran to the edge and watched impassively as the blue-furred creature landed in a springing run atop a neighboring roof.

Ripcat darted among vapor pipes and air-conditioning sheds and, with another prodigious leap, crossed to an adjoining building.

He ran along a roof ledge until he found a fire escape below and dropped to it. In moments, he had clambered into an alley and sped through back lanes and warrens, not breaking his stride even at the fences but scrambling straight up them. He ran until his heart punched into his throat.

But the farther he fled from Duppy Hob, the thinner his memory of himself as Reece Morgan became. Crouched between trash bins behind a Chinese restaurant on Canal Street, he remembered nothing of his former life as a human being. He panted for breath and scanned the skyline for Duppy Hob. Gray sky rivered overhead, and no one moved upon the rooftops.

Mind racing, wild for escape, he reached inward, trying to see again his old partner Dogbrick. The image of that auburn face had jolted him awake and won his freedom from Duppy Hob— but now the vision had passed. In its place, he remembered what he saw when he was Duppy Hob's antenna: Lara's ghost in a hospital across the river. He could only surmise now that the crystal prism had been taken from her and was somewhere out there on its own—a piece of the cosmic child's soul.

Using the intuition he had honed as a thief in Saxar, Ripcat prowled the grim perimeters of Canal Street, sliding along the lee of old stone walls, slipping into doorways when anyone approached.

After a short while, he found a heavy cellar grating and forced it open with his inhuman strength, lifting aside the thick iron bars just enough to squirm through a cellar window into the back room of a garment thrift store.

Inside were crowded racks of clothing. Moving quickly, he donned a long winter coat, a slouch hat that obscured his face, and sturdy construction shoes to protect his numb feet from the icy pavement. Thus attired, he crawled out the way he had come in. An old ragpicker with whiskered chops watched with disinterest as Ripcat carefully replaced the heavy grating and strode away, his head bowed low beneath his hat.

In Duppy Hob's trance, where he had served as an antenna, Ripcat's mind had incandesced for a brief but critical moment with awareness of the crystal prism—the devil worshipper's prize.

He knew where it was. He could still feel it, thrumming distantly, beyond the river's gray slag.

Into a subway hole he descended, holding the long coat snug about him. He scrutinized a subway map set into the tile wall, the words speaking quietly to him, though he could not have read them aloud. After leaping the turnstile, he gazed down the track and heard rumbling vibrations before he saw the rails shining.

A metallic voice called, "Gate-jumper on the uptown platform."

The exit gate swung open before a uniformed transit officer, who approached smacking a nightstick against his palm. "Bad timing, buddy."

Ripcat waited until the officer nudged him with the stick before he turned and showed his beastmarks.

A silent shout stretched the officer's gaping mouth as he frantically backed away.

In one bound, Ripcat plunged into the dark tunnel, and when the cry of fear did finally come from the platform, more like a barking of shouted obscenities, he had already melded with the shadows. He continued on his way until train lights bobbed out of the darkness.

The engineer of the uptown express glimpsed a furred devil with long cold eyes and slender fangs bounding to the side of the track before the oncoming train. Even as the engineer whooped, the apparition was gone, if it had ever been there at all.

Ripcat leaped onto the silver, corrugated side of the rushing train, claws hooking the soft metal. His shoulders groaned, the speed of the roaring subway swinging his body horizontal. Passengers with their backs to the windows did not see him, but one straphanger did. Her mouth gagged open around a cry, and she stood momentarily paralyzed by the bestial visage from the pit gazing out of the shuttling dark.

When the other commuters saw her horror and looked over their shoulders, he grinned, trying to assuage their fright, and the sight of his fangs elicited terrified howls. Gracefully, Ripcat slunk away, climbing onto the roof of the hurtling train.

At Madison Square Garden, the express rolled to a stop, and he crawled out between the cars. Wrapped in his long coat, his smashed hat pulled low, he stepped onto the subway platform and moved with the disembarking crowd into the main concourse. He stopped under a departures monitor and the glyphs made sense to him, as they had at the subway map, their meaning remembered from some older dream of himself.

He identified the train that would carry him to New Jersey and the ramp where he could board. But just as he spotted the concourse exit that he wanted, a child eyed his beastmarks and bawled in terror.

Everyone stopped to look at him.

Jacket flapping, hat clutched in hand, Ripcat bounded over a long bench of cowering commuters. Screams and echoes of screams collided. Police whistles shrilled.

He dived through a tall portal onto the dim ramp way that led down to the trains. People threw themselves against the walls to get out of his way. With a single roar, he cleared the stairway to the train platform and leaped flights of stairs, sending conductors and commuters scurrying.

A cacophony of whistles, shouts, and terrified screams exploded down the rampway, and cringing citizens pointed the police to the chrome passenger cars with their doors open at the platform. An intercom voice urged calm as police charged onto the train, while under it Ripcat crept away.

He crawled unseen beneath flapping beams of flashlights, over cinders and soot-blacked ties. Minutes later, he rolled under a westbound train and latched himself by claws and wedged boots onto the rocking underframe. The clamor of the tracks shook his bones, but his beaststrength held him firm even through the deafening uproar of the tunnel.

In Weehawken, as the train slowed through a steeper grade past ancient tool-and-die shops, he climbed from under a passenger car and leaped from its side. He hit the ground with big, powerful strides, and his shoes dug deep gashes in the gritty soil of the abutment. Passengers smashed themselves against windows to watch him dashing between the iron stanchions, greatcoat filled with wind, blue fur streaked back from diabolic green eyes and razorous teeth.

He leaped a chain-link fence and slid on his heels down a gravel siding toward narrow and desolate factory buildings. Standing in a rainworn gutter on Hauxhurst Street, gasping for breath, he felt the crystal prism nearby. This thrumming sense led him past storefronts on Highwood to the stolid brownstone building that housed police headquarters.

The cold day helped him, for no one lingered in the salt-stained parking lot, and he came up from the back, among three squad cars and a riot wagon. He listened at a locked back door, then ripped the door open, the cold wood yielding to his brute tug with loud crackling.

He slipped into warm amber shadows in a storage room of drawn blinds. Metal shelves stood the length of the crepuscular storage room. The singing of Lara's soul led to a vault set in the building's cinder wall. His fingers listened to the tumblers, spun them quickly to their homes, and opened the thick door.

As soon as he tore the prism from its plastic bag, Lara stood beside him. Spun from tiny rainbows, her shape shifted with the light, more vague than she had appeared on Irth, where she had stood closer to the Abiding Star. She looked haggard, her eyes had sunk to sockets.

"Reece—" She touched him with fingers of cold wind. "Reece—is it you?"

"Come with me." He removed his hat and slipped the gold cord that held the crystal prism over his head. Out the splintered door he slid and jogged across the parking lot, to the slate pavements that led toward the river piers and the concrete karnak beneath the turnpike.

Dockside lanes flew by. He sprinted across a cemetery under the freeway viaduct and turned up JFK Boulevard, loping through tall gray grass. Startled drivers swerved, distracted by the sight of the blue-furred man. Several times, squealing tires drove him into the roadside thickets, until he was forced to move out of sight of the road entirely, clawing his way through a wicker field of bramble.

"Duppy Hob is using you." Lara tramped ahead through the nettles, garbed in mist, then fading from sight.

"I know he's using me. I'm his antenna." Ripcat slowed his run to a stroll and shoved icy branches out of his way. "He wants all the crystal prisms, because in them he has caught the soul of the nameless lady's child."

"He's using you even now." Lara pushed along beside him to where the verge of wild growth ended. North Hudson Park sprawled before them, a frieze of tree-lumped hummocks. Skaters

grainy with distance spun paltry motes of color on a glazed lake.
"Don't you see? Duppy Hob has sent you to retrieve the crystal
prism for him."

"No, I don't see." Ripcat strode onto the parkland sward under
the gray troweled sky. "I saw Dogbrick in my trance. He's shackled in a sea cave on the cliffs of Zul. The sight of him loosened
the trance enough for me to escape."

"Duppy Hob showed you Dogbrick. He used that image to
release you, so that you would rush to me and collect the crystal
for him." She disappeared in the gelid air, fading before him like
the smoke of his breath. Her voice continued invisibly, "He
showed you Dogbrick because he holds him prisoner. I am with
your partner now—even as I am here with you."

"The prism holds you." He lowered the brim of his hat when
he sauntered onto the asphalt path. Distant barking rippled
through the cold air.

"Yes, young master. I feel strong near you. The Charm that
radiates from your skin of light gives me strength." Glitters of
snowflakes twirled in the wind, shaping her phantom briefly: her
ashen flesh, smudged with bruises, one eye agog, healed under
his gaze to the sable-tressed woman of his dreams. "But I am also
held by the sea cavern where last my wraith lingered on Irth. I
am there, too."

Ripcat turned his back toward a bundled jogger, and whispered, "Then you can communicate with Dogbrick?"

The reply came from behind, "He's very weak. Dying."

Ripcat knew this was true. He had seen the Dog in chains
without his harness of amulets, his famished and bedraggled aspect listless. "Please—don't let him die! Not charmless. That is
too cruel a death. Dance power for him, Lara. Save him!"

"You can save him! You are the magus, Reece." Lara formed
on the path ahead, her hair sodden, her body robed in mud. A
bicyclist slashed through her. "Tell me, how do we leave the
Dark Shore? How do we climb back to Irth?"

"I—I don't know." He clutched the crystal prism at his throat,
hoping for remembrance of magic. His senses glowed brightly,
but his memory remained dark. "I know nothing. I am only a
thief—Ripcat."

"Stop it, Reece." The battered woman stared urgently at him
and screeched as though he had struck her. "Stop it!"

He moved toward her and opened his coat to expose the crysal prism, hoping its Charm would calm her. "Lara!"

Skateboards trundled by, and kids yelped with alarm. They stared hard at his claws and furred face, not moving at first, not trusting their frightened instincts, until his fiendish eyes set on them. Then, they burst away, scooping up their skateboards.

Startled to find himself revealed, Ripcat pulled his coat tighter and hurried across the sward. Voices shouted after him, and he ignored them, his gaze rummaging among the cold trees for the ghost.

"You are Reece Morgan, the man who gave me myself," Lara persisted, suddenly beside him again, so healed and whole in her loveliness, her eyes starblown and twinkling with emotion. "You are the man I love. Put aside these beastmarks."

He bowed his head before the woman of his dreams. "I can't."

"You can!" she insisted. Her hands swiped at him, bodiless. "You put them on yourself. Take them off. Be Reece again for me."

Shielded by an elm, he paused and opened his coat to look at the crystal prism. Molten rainbows quaked. He fixed his attention deep in these spectral turnings, but no visions coalesced. "If I strip away this skin of light and become Reece again—what then?"

Her transparency stained the bark of the elm. "Reece will know what to do."

The prismatic shine of the crystal sharpened her lineaments, and he saw the childlike conviction in her face, the certainty that Reece knew best. His heart sank before her nearly mindless obsession with her past, with the magus. She was not human enough to recognize him in his new shape. She was, after all, just a ghost, not really Lara, only her shade.

Pity for this echo of a life moved him to nod his head in agreement. "Reece does know what to do. He created these beastmarks with his magic." Her lonely features shone so vividly he had to remind himself before he continued that she was merely an arc of reflexes sparking in the ether that carried ghosts and demons. "These beastmarks serve Reece, and so they serve us. I won't change, Lara. Not yet."

Her grave stare held him. "Then how will we get away?"

"Hush." Sweet woe softened his voice. "There is no getting

away. You were right all along. Duppy Hob is using me. This moment, his dwarves are closing in."

He heard their shrill whistles in the hazy distance, where the dogs yapped. The high-pitched chanting seemed to come from the stony tunnels underfoot, layered in echoes of muffled earth, resounding through brachial sewage pipes and emerging from the gutter drains.

"Do not despair yet." He put his back to the elm and plunged his alertness into the parkland. "I have a plan. There's a charmway in the marshes that I saw in trance, when the crystal prism came through from Irth. It's not far from here. I'm taking us there."

The phantom approved and drifted across the lawn. "On Irth we can warn the wizards. And perhaps with their help we can find the old master—Caval. He will know how to thwart Duppy Hob. It was his voice called me out of the Abiding Star to find and warn you. Yet I've sensed nothing of him since then. Perhaps he was a dream, an intuition of your peril that my love shaped with the memory of his voice . . ."

"Lara—" He waited till she turned, and he could see the familiar dark edge of her stare, her face pooled in black hair. "You have been in my dreams every night on Irth. Why?"

She smiled slightly. "You know."

"Were we lovers?"

Her smile deepened. "Is that what your dreams reveal of us?"

"I loved you—and you died." His voice faded in his throat, unworthy of voicing what he did not remember, what he had seen only in dreams.

"Yes, you loved me." Her image sharpened against the soot-stained sky, and the park with its shelves of rock and bare trees embraced them as a couple.

Screams from the lake broke their gentle interlude, and the ghost blurred away. Ripcat noticed joggers and skaters fleeing before he saw what pursued them. Dwarves, white and clad in dull metal, wavered in and out of sight among the gray snowdrifts that banked the lake.

Full out, Ripcat bounded across the park. He flung his instincts ahead of him, feeling out the contours of paths, hedged hills, and copses. Hoping to deflect people away from the charging dwarves, he made no effort to disguise himself. His hat flew off and his jacket billowed open. Mothers wailed and huddled over their children. Dog walkers leaned back, holding taut leashes. Some dogs broke free and chased, but none could pace Ripcat.

He sped uphill off the paths, wanting to lead the dwarves away from innocents. Across a hogback bristling with beeches, he flung himself, before a hatchet tangled with his ankles and sent him sprawling over the rooty ground.

Dwarves hacked through shrubs and seized him with their big hands. Hissing violently, he twisted and thrashed and met the hard wooden helve of a hatchet between the eyes.

DUPPY HOB'S TRAP

DUPPY HOB HELD THE CRYSTAL PRISM BETWEEN TWO FINGERS AND lifted it to the overcast sky. The sleazy winter sun nested in the facets.

What is a soul? he pondered to himself.

He sat on the roof ledge above Reade Street and angled the prism so that it cast splinters of wan light across the tar paper behind him. One splinter touched Ripcat where he lay sprawled backward on the cowl of a ventilator fan, and he roused.

"What is a soul but a shape that is its own shaper?" Duppy Hob said aloud and tipped a smile over his shoulder at his prisoner.

Ripcat sat up, holding his aching head.

"In pain?" The young man lifted the prism higher and walked it between his fingers. "Aren't you lucky I eat pain?"

The throbbing of Ripcat's head abated. He stood, and his body felt light and airy. "Where is Lara?"

"Dead." Duppy Hob spoke distractedly as he held the crystal prism close to one eye. "She was murdered by settlers in the forests of the Snow Range on Papua New Guinea. You were there, Reece. You should recall."

Anger coiled tightly in the pit of Ripcat's stomach. "What have you done with her ghost?"

"Ghosts come and go." Thin rainbows painted Dubby Hob's blond face. "You know how it is with the dead. First you see them, then you don't."

With a harsh growl, Ripcat pounced, claws flashing, fangs bared.

Duppy Hob did not stir. He merely said, "Stop."

Pain exploded in Ripcat and cast him writhing onto the tar-papered roof. He convulsed like a candleflame in a wind, stuttering toward blackout. Then, the pain disappeared.

"It can go on," Duppy Hob said, still not disengaging his attention from the dazzled core of the prism. "On and on and on. You know that. On Gabagalus I revealed myself to you. That was not an hallucination. Do you remember? Or have you forgotten? I'm the demon that haunts this planet, and I've been haunting it for more than six thousand years. You're in my realm now, Reece Morgan. Forget anything else but don't forget that again or the pain will go on and on—and on."

"Kill me." Ripcat gnashed his teeth, tautening his whole body for a desperate lunge. He had to act, knowing that within claw strike squatted the rapacious demon of history ravening for the souls of other worlds. Tar paper ripped under him as he jumped forward and slashed with his claws.

The image of Duppy Hob sitting on the roof ledge scattered like smoke, and the leaping Ripcat dived through the illusion and over the edge. He plummeted without a cry, down the heights of Tribeca toward unyielding concrete. Blind windows blurred past. An oil-stained puddle reflected his expanding beastmarks, bleared with the rush of falling.

Impact smashed him to bright blood and grots of skull.

A painful jolt twisted him free of the falling dream, and he woke on the tar paper within claw strike of Dubby Hob's indifferent back.

"On and on," the demon warned.

Ripcat flexed his claws futilely and lifted himself to his knees. His fur lay matted on his round skull and beads of sweat trickled on his snout. "I won't serve you," he swore through gritted teeth. "You'll have to break me first."

"I've told you before, Reece, you already serve me." Duppy

Hob scrutinized the crystal prism with the avidity of a suspicious jeweler. "In fact, look here. I've found what I've been searching for, thanks to this hex-gem you've returned to me—not to mention yet again your usefulness as an antenna. Without you, we'd never be able to view the Bright Worlds so clearly. Here—see for yourself."

Duppy Hob pulled himself around from where he sat on the ledge of the roof and spun the crystal prism between forefinger and thumb. Spectra flashed, and needles of rainbow threaded through Ripcat's pupils and wove in the dark of his brain a vision of Irth.

The crystal prism connected Ripcat and Duppy Hob to its companions beyond the Gulf: the Necklace of Souls that Old Ric wore. The eldern gnome wandered within a charmway's vault of raw rock. Beside him, like a slender, tilted flue of milky white light reaching through the vault's dome, a Radiant One stood.

"Come along, Asofel—" Old Ric waved to the slim ray of light. "Broydo is just ahead. I can hear the screaming of the dwarves."

"We are watched." Asofel's voice descended softly from the narrow radiance.

Old Ric crouched lower and swung a look around for others in the caliginous chamber. Distantly, shrill cries knitted the silence with anguish. "I sense only dwarves dying."

"We are watched from afar." Asofel hung like a vertical fluorescent tube, shining dully off facets of hewn rock. "Regard the Necklace of Souls."

The eldern gnome looked down at the crystals that looped the arrow embedded in his chest. Goat eyes stared back. "What is this?"

"Duppy Hob." Asofel's voice had thinned almost inaudibly. "Watch—and you will see him watching us."

In the prisms, Old Ric discerned tiny figures inside the agate slant of goat eyes. Two men stood on a rooftop in a skyline of dismal brick buildings and glass towers and near-featureless geometry. Looking closer, the gnome saw that one of the men wore the beastmarks of a cat—the skin of light that the magus, Reece Morgan, had put upon himself. Ric had first glimpsed this aspect of the shadow thing in Lara's crystal on Nemora.

With a cold stab of fright, the gnome observed Lara's crystal prism in the hands of the second man, a youth in a black tunic with hay-nest hair and eyes black as boreholes.

"I see Reece Morgan in his beastmarks," Old Ric announced, his snub nose touching the Necklace. "And another—a young man with Lara's prism."

"That is Duppy Hob." Gazing at that devil, Asofel felt his light draining into a great night. "I have watched him from outside the dream. I have tried to see to his purpose, but I have failed."

"What?" Distracted by echoes of dwarf screams brightening in the tunnel ahead, Old Ric glared impatiently. "What are you trying to tell me, Asofel?"

"We are watched by the devil worshipper—and he has a secret."

The gnome stepped closer to the taut rope of light. "What secret?"

"That I don't know." Peering through the dream into Duppy Hob, Asofel's energy seeped through dark space and down into the black of the cold ground sleeping. "He is a master of darkness. He has a secret, a terrible secret that he keeps from me in a dark my light cannot penetrate."

"Then how do you know he has any secret at all?" The eldern gnome stood with arms akimbo, staring up at the long wand of light. "Asofel, since we left Nemora you have been—distant. You have not shown your face once. Don't blame me that this task has dragged on interminably. You're surly just because the shadow thing squats on the Dark Shore out of your reach."

"No. There is something more."

Old Ric's gray eyes sparked irately. "What now? Listen, if you want to leave the dream and return to our lady, go ahead. I understand. I can find Broydo from here."

"Hush, gnome." The Radiant One sounded as irascible as the gnome. "I am a being of light. I am bound to do what is just for the one who sent me. But how can I act justly when I cannot see into the darkest corners of this dream?"

"You just want an excuse to leave." Ric dropped his arms to his sides and turned from the light. "Then, go. Speak with the nameless lady and see if her child moves again."

The thin shaft of light dimmed as Asofel listened to the darkness. "The one who watches us holds the child's soul."

Old Ric spun about with a frightened gasp. "Can that be true?"

"I believe so." The luminous beam brightened. "I sense it now. But I don't know how he has done this. He is the true shadow thing. Reece Morgan was merely a foil."

The gnome absorbed this with a startled expression of sudden conviction. "Then we must go to the Dark Shore—for the child's sake."

"I've told you, I cannot."

The gnome glowered and wagged a bulb-jointed finger. "You dare not."

"What does it avail us to squander our light in that darkness? Better that we confront Duppy Hob here among the Bright Worlds."

Ric offered a disapproving frown. "And how will we do that?"

"That is what he watches to see."

Shrieks leaped like rats out of the dark. Green shadows glowed upon the tunnel walls, and a clattering of metal plates banged closer. Dwarves rushed from around a bend in the tunnel, armor clanging. Then Broydo leaped among them, his serpent sword swinging. Helmets and breastplates crashed, and maggots skidded into the cavern.

"Old Ric!" the ælf exulted, gasping, sparking with sweat. "How did you find us?"

From behind him, Jyoti came running, an exhausted firecharm in her hand, the muzzle and stock battered from use as a club.

"Asofel found you." Old Ric motioned to a dazzling cord that hung from the dark heights of the cavern.

The ælf bowed reverently to the supernal being. "Radiant One—you are stronger yet. That gladdens me, for it grieves our enemies."

Old Ric crossed his arms in front of him, palms up, and Broydo clasped the gnome's hands in the ælfen embrace. "I feared for you, Broydo, when we lost you in Saxar."

"And I feared for our quest—and all the worlds." The ælf squeezed the gnome's hands urgently. "The magus that we seek is a beastmarked man, named Ripcat. But he has been taken by the dwarves." He tossed a wrung and grateful expression toward Jyoti. "This is the margravine, Jyoti of Odawl. We've been chasing dwarves through the charmways, trying to find him. We've shared the serpent sword and slain many dwarves, but we have found only more dwarves."

Jyoti gazed with a perplexed mix of dread, loathing, and wonder at the tall staff of light. So this was the Shadow Eater, the monstrous entity who had devoured her security squad and other innocent people on the sky bund at Saxar. Its inhumanity revulsed her, and she wanted nothing to do with it. Yet, the stakes at venture now outweighed even her outrage at those deaths.

She let her eyes touch its brightness. Despite her antipathy, its presence filled her with a portentous sense, like faded instructions from a dream. She could not tell if this ray of astral fire promised good or further ill, and she kept the ælf between herself and it.

"Aye, we know about Ripcat—and more," Old Ric told the margravine and the ælf. "Asofel tells me that Duppy Hob himself is the shadow thing who holds the child's soul."

"The dwarves—" Jyoti spoke up. "When I first saw the dwarves in the grottoes under Saxar, they were chanting for Duppy Hob."

"The dwarves have stolen the soul of the nameless lady's child!" Broydo brandished the serpent sword. "But where have they hidden this soul?"

"We must go to Duppy Hob and make him tell us," Old Ric declared. "But the devil worshipper hides on the Dark Shore. The Radiant One will not go there for fear of—"

"Not fear." Asofel's voice rang like a bell in the cavern. "I am a being of light. My motive is never fear." The Radiant One thinned to a brilliant filament. "Any journey we make to the Dark Shore is futile and almost certainly fatal. My power is of no use there. I cannot eat the light that deep in the darkness, at the limits of the dream."

"That is why the devil worshipper hides there." Broydo vengefully poked his sword at the shadows, still wrought with Charmed strength from the serpent sword's killing frenzy. "He has taken the child's soul beyond our reach."

"Can you not appeal to the nameless lady?" Jyoti asked. "This is her dream. Tell her about Duppy Hob and ask her to change it."

Old Ric shook his head. "Duppy Hob has slowly accrued enough power in the dark of the dream—in the lady's unconscious—to influence the outcome of the dream. No, whatever can be done to save the lady's child must be done here, by us."

"There is another." The tall thread of light moved, tracking across the chamber to one of the many tunnels that intersected at this vault. "Now that the dwarves are silent, you can hear him."

Old Ric led the others to the tunnel touched by the line of white light. Without the guidance of Asofel, whose wider senses penetrated more deeply the dark corridors, they never would have found this one charmway among the dozens so quickly. Far away, a growly voice called, weak yet distinct.

"That's Dogbrick!" Jyoti pushed past Ric and entered the charmway that led toward his voice. She emerged in a damp cave overlooking the stormy coast of Zul. Sodden with sea mist and chained to the wall, Dogbrick lay folded upon himself. Deprived of Charm, he had shrunk, and his fur hung like brown smoke on his skeleton. At the sight of Jyoti, he stirred, yellow crust broke at the corners of his mouth, and he mewled.

He had spent his last strength calling to the familiar voices he heard at the audible limit where sound and dream furl together. At Jyoti's touch, the Charm from her amulet-vest saturated him. Strength began to return at once, and he lifted his head to see Broydo enter with an aged gnome pierced by a barbed arrow—the famous Old Ric, who had eluded capture at Saxar.

Charm flowed through him from a brace of power wands that Jyoti placed atop his back. Pain sloughed away. As soon as he could speak, he panted, "Lara—is on the Dark Shore. The dwarves—threw her prism—into the Gulf—"

"Rest, Dog—we know this." The eldern gnome knelt beside Dogbrick and read his beastmarks. The long mane and short crop of the ear as well as the massive jaws told Ric that this was an early breed of gnomish beastfolk, obviously a mongrel of many generations. He pitied the masterless creature and made soothing sounds as he examined the shackles.

"Lara—" Dogbrick rolled to a sitting position and tossed his head back and forth, searching for her ghost in the grainy air. But the Charm from the power wands had already restored enough stability that he could no longer veer his senses toward the invisible.

"I still have my sword, Dogbrick." Broydo stepped forward, displaying the weapon. "But I do regret I did not use it well enough to spare you this pain."

Before Dogbrick could reply, the ground shook, sand sizzled

in streams from the ceiling, and the cloudy horizon of the sea rocked. Bellowing echoes resounded so loudly that sound became tangible vibrations, shaking everything around them. Broydo caught Old Ric as he toppled off his feet, and the two tumbled into Dogbrick.

He howled and pushed away Ric and his sharp arrow.

Jyoti rolled into a corner and gravity pressed her to the cold wall. The din of rocks exploding and crashing diminished swiftly to an eerie silence. Through the cave mouth, peacock hues of sky flashed among torn clouds. The sea had vanished.

"What's happened?" the gnome called out from where he lay pinned under Broydo.

Dogbrick clutched the power wands to his chest, pulling strength into himself sufficient to stand on the canted floor of the sea cave. Over the lip of the cave mouth, he peered out at cobalt vapors of sky shredding to black and starry shrieks of eternal night.

"We're falling into the Gulf!" Broydo cried out, watching the last blue haze of sky evaporate into darkness strewn with stardust.

"How can that be?" Old Ric struggled upright in the tilted cave. "Asofel!"

A ray of white light penetrated the dark cavern. "We've been trapped!"

"Asofel, what is happening?" Old Ric staggered toward the light. "Why are we falling?"

"It appears that we are inside a cage of rock," came the dispassionate answer. The Radiant One peered across time to the dream's edge. "Ah, I see that this cavern was designed by dwarves to peel off these abyssal sea cliffs and plunge into the Gulf at Duppy Hob's command."

"By the blind gods!" Broydo clambered to the cave entrance and winced into the buffeting cold. Planet swarms glowed like smoldering rubble among comet smoke and star fumes. He slid back toward the others, his face blinking with fright. "We're falling!"

Dogbrick howled to realize he had been a lure.

"Please, Asofel!" Old Ric lifted his whiskery face to the light. "What can we do?"

"Nothing," Jyoti answered in despair for him. "We've fallen off the edge of the Irth. We'll fall forever."

DEATH ON THE DARK SHORE

RAUCOUS MUSIC BLARED FROM EMPIRE OF DARKNESS. BALD MUSI-
cians in studded leather thrashed frantic sounds from their Instruments on the caged platform above the dance floor. A maximum-
capacity crowd surged below, on the concrete dance floor among
laser rays and strobes.

The band kicked down shards of thunder and metallic shrieks
as the dancing throng convulsed rhythmically to a concussive,
tortured song of speed-metal pain and loss.

The party's ecstatic suffering carried its anger and hurt to
heaven, and the fierce music smothered out of hearing the chanting that rose from below, out of the city's pit. In the building's
cellar, before the anvil-shaped altar, thirteen naked, hollow-eyed
bodies knelt under their fervent and droning invocations.

Duppy Hob presided over the gathering, striding before the
altar, his ritual rant barely audible above the tech-thump vibrations from above.

In the dark alcove that doubled as a charmway to Gabagalus,
Duppy Hob's outpost on Irth, Ripcat squatted. Duppy Hob had
placed him there. At first, the captive thought he was being sent

back to Irth, but the charmway did not open. As he hunched and watched the skeletal acolytes chanting, he realized that he had been plugged into this alcove to serve again as an antenna.

The sole source of illumination in the cellar shone wanly from the altar's inset bowl of quicksilver. Ripcat's green eyes saw clearly even in this vague light, and he noticed that the spindle-shanked chanters were comprised of the city's destitute, living zombies, glassy-eyed, stringy-haired, skinny, and hungry, the world's human refuse. Seven women and six men knelt before the altar of darkness, obedient to the demon.

Disgust churned in Ripcat at the fate the demon had imposed on these luckless souls. As a magus, he had loathed that this power fed upon the lives of others for fuel, and he had never practiced these abominable rites. Under a filthy dawn, they would shuffle out to the streets to wander the city, begging for money and food until their master summoned them again.

Ripcat wished dawn were upon them now. He shifted restlessly in the fetid cellar until Duppy Hob spun the crystal prism. Flickers of rainbows flurried through the cellar, and the sickening malodors thinned away. The darkness brightened with a trance force that obscured the chanters and the walls of glossy rock and revealed a vision—

Dogbrick, Jyoti, the ælf Broydo, and a bald, wizened, pink-bearded gnome pressed against the back wall of a cave—and with them, a tall, luminous man with hair like sunlight . . .

Ripcat pulled himself free of the trance. The fetor of corpses hammered him, and he saw Duppy Hob, black robes snapping as he rushed among the kneeling zombies. The spinning gem floated before him, directing him among the supplicants, harvesting the power of their decaying humanity, their bodies slowly collapsing into mineral namelessness.

Rainbow light stabbed his eyes, and again he saw the aged gnome with the arrow through his breast and a gold cord of crystal prisms about his neck. *Old Ric!* With a gut cramp of dreadful anger, Ripcat recognized the eldern gnome. Duppy Hob had seized the Necklace of Souls!

Grasping that somehow the zombies' abhorrent ritual was drawing the Necklace of Souls across the Gulf to the Dark Shore, to Duppy Hob, Ripcat lurched against the dreamstrength of the trance. He snapped alert to the dark and putrid cellar and struggled to shove himself out of the alcove. He thought that if he swatted a few zombies, he could disrupt the demon's invocation and give his friends a chance of escape.

Stone-jawed with determination, he rose to his feet. Duppy Hob reared up before him, black eyes glittering with reflections from the spinning prism. Fans of chromatic light opened in Ripcat's eyes and converged in his brain to a sunburst of white light that dropped him back into the alcove, deeper into Duppy Hob's trance. . . .

A sharp ray of light glinted upon the shackles chaining Dogbrick to the cave wall, and the restraints clanked open and fell away. The next instant, the ray widened, cooling to the image of Asofel. He wore white raiment whose glare nearly washed out his lynx-slanted face with its devilish, donkey eyes.

"We must brace ourselves with what Charm we have," the Radiant One warned. "We're going to strike the Dark Shore soon. What we must do there, we must do quickly. As a being of light, I cannot long survive there."

"Can *we* survive impact?" Dogbrick sat against the wall, rubbing a power wand against his sore wrists. "I have no amulets."

"I will share my amulets with you, Dog." Jyoti began unlacing her vest.

Dogbrick waved away her offer. "Then we will both die. Keep your amulets to save yourself, margravine."

"You can protect us, Asofel," Old Ric stated confidently, placing himself squarely before the Radiant One. "You have the power of giants!"

"I cannot help." Asofel crossed his arms. "To protect any more of you than the one I've been sent to serve would exhaust me."

"Then exhaust yourself!" Old Ric commanded. "The blind gods have brought all five of us together to serve the nameless lady. We cannot sacrifice these lives when we have the strength to save them."

Asofel stepped away with a rueful shake of his head. If he wished, he could step out of this dream. As a being of light, he was compelled to do what was just—and what seemed just to him at this moment was to return to World's End and report to his mistress. She should be informed of the true nature of the shadow thing, the malevolent strength that Duppy Hob had ac-

crued deep in the darkness of her dream. Other sentinels could
be summoned to help overcome the devil worshipper. . . .

Yet, he did not leave. He knew that if he reported the true
evil festering in the dream, the nameless lady would be aghast
and almost certainly wake the father of the child. Then certainly
he would collapse the dream. Worlds bright and dark would
cease to be. Once, he thought ruefully to himself, this had
seemed an acceptable conclusion to him, when the dream had
been unfamiliar. But now that he had known weakness among
these worlds and had experienced the ardor of survival, he better
understood these figments of the dream, these precious small
ephemeral lives.

Evoked by something strangely new that he felt for these mer-
elings, something akin to compassion for these next-to-nothings,
these creatures of shadow that aspired to light—he sensed now
another, a higher order of justice. He walked to the brim of the
cave mouth and gazed out upon the tiny stars in the blackness
of the Gulf. The four mortals with him would almost certainly
perish on the Dark Shore, and their loss did pain him—especially
the gnome and the ælf with whom he had discovered the vivacity
of these dream-held beings. But letting them die would preserve
his strength and purchase him the chance to destroy Duppy Hob
and save all the worlds.

"Asofel is cold with purpose," the eldern gnome explained to
the others. "We must look to our own protection. The Necklace
of Souls contains enormous Charm. We will hold together, and
I will share it with you all."

"No." Asofel held out a luminous hand for the eldern gnome.
"Sentiment will not endanger our mission. Come, Old Ric. Our
quest for the shadow thing takes us below to the Dark Shore."

"I will not leave the others . . ." Old Ric was saying when
Asofel's fiery hand shot from his wrist, spraying sparks as it
snagged the gnome by the Necklace and whipped him away.
The next instant, the Radiant One and the gnome dropped out
of the cave, into darkness. Asofel's radiant strength was sufficient
to carry them safely through the atmosphere to the ground.

Broydo scrambled toward the edge, wanting to follow, but
gravity pulled him back.

"Let them go, ælf." Dogbrick grabbed Broydo's grass-woven

garment and held him in place. "One is already dead—the other is not of our worlds. We can't follow them into the abyss."

Meanwhile, Jyoti had disassembled her vest, dividing the amulets into three groups. She had striven to connect the pieces into crude bracelets—amber power wands bound with conjure-wire to theriacal opals, far-see onyx, ingots of witch-glass, and strings of rat-star gems. Quickly, she wrapped the clunky assemblage around the wrists of Dogbrick, Broydo, and herself.

The ælf placed the serpent sword point down between them, and they each grasped a portion of the hilt and attached their linked amulets to the haft.

"To the Dark Shore!" Dogbrick howled into the blazing silence.

Old Ric heard the animal cry from the cerulean space where he and Asofel stepped down the broad stairwell of the wind. He looked for the rock vault fallen from the cliffs of Zul and saw it far off across the sky, a blazing meteor. Its fiery trajectory arced over wintry woodlands, flashed briefly in the forest's secret veins, the frozen rivers and streams, the lacquered lakes and ponds, the crusty snowfields, the green glass of icicled pines, and finally exploded among scrub oak and conifers.

The blast shattered the amulet chain that bound Jyoti, Dogbrick, and Broydo and flung them through space. Charm streaked from them like comet smoke. Dogbrick flew over the spires of the forest, shaggy arms and legs churning as if sprinting across the sky. Sprung energy from the shattered amulets lofted him toward ancient hills. There, mammoth old trees awaited him, bent under their burdens of snow like ghouls of winter.

Jyoti arrowed low among the boughs. Branches snapped away before her Charmed flight—until she struck the thigh of a giant oak. A splash of green fire and splinters of woodmeat dropped her senseless to the ground, and she lay there in a rag-doll sprawl under clumps of snow fallen from the shaken tree.

Clutching the serpent sword to his chest, Broydo hurtled through the attic of the forest, spanked by tossing tree limbs, pelted with pine cones and snow clods, yodeling a terrified scream. He burst out of the woods and soared over the silver platter of a lake. Gunshots cracked the cold air, and smoke puffed from canebrakes along the shore where two hunters stalked the sky. A bullet struck the ælf's forehead, shearing away all his Charm and denting his skull.

Below, two bearded men in Day-Glo red vests and hunter's caps slogged over the frozen shore of the lake to retrieve the weird thing they had shot out of the sky. It had landed atop a snowy bank beneath the wall of the forest, and they could see the crumpled figure clearly as they approached, appalled at first that they had shot what appeared to be a husky man.

As they drew closer, however, the body's ælfen features convinced the hunters this was not an ordinary corpse. The purpled skin, lichenous hair, and tapered ears astonished them. Curiously, the bullet had pushed in the ælf's brow and not broken the skin. The frost blue eyes stared upward at the dent with cross-eyed and death-locked fixity.

One of the men picked up the serpent sword, from where its blade had pierced a snowdrift. It felt light as plastic, though its haft of coiled gold looked metallic. When they attempted to pick up the ælf, he, too, lifted as easily as papier-mâché. He was so light that they had to weigh him down with tire chains in the back of their pickup so the wind did not carry him off.

Across the blue sky, Old Ric looked for those who had fallen and saw nothing but winter sprawled across the hilly horizons. And the horizons themselves folded like the interlocked fingers of a giant. Then even that wide view curved away as Asofel carried him down the steps of the wind.

A bristly hillside of leafless trees swung aside, and Asofel strode over peaked rooftops and a grid of asphalt streets. At their approach, the mercury-vapor streetlights blinked on and off though it was midday under a lucent blue sky. They came down between two brown industrial barns into a lot of iron-black trees. Children in a playground across the street squealed at the sight of them and rushed in every direction.

A premonitory shiver chilled the Radiant One the moment he touched the Dark Shore. He felt as though something huge and cold from deep within the dim planet laid claim on him. A silent and implacable hostility pervaded this world. It was the darkness of death, of the dream's deepest unconscious limit, the darkness locked inside matter, starved for light.

The sentinel refused to allow his dread to own him or even show itself. Like a prophet returned magnificent from a desert

transfiguration, Asofel strode across the street. The brash wind
flashed through his massed curls like reflected sunlight and obscured his long features in a bright nimbus. Behind him, among
the flapping streamers of Asofel's iridescent raiment, Old Ric
hobbled. Gravity weighed the gnome down, and even with the
power from the Necklace of Souls, it took all his stamina to keep
up with his luminous companion.

The sight of the arrow-pierced gnome elicited more startled
cries from the intrepid faces waffled by the chain-link fence of
the playground. Old Ric ignored their hoots and tugged at Asofel's robes. "Where are we going?"

"To destroy the shadow thing once and for all." Asofel approached a parked car with windshield veined in ice. He put his
hand on the hood, and the vehicle barked, spewed a gust of
white smoke from its exhaust pipe, and churred to life. "Get in."

"You can command this wagon?" Old Ric asked, and opened
the back door.

"I have enough energy for now to command the dream," Asofel
replied, and pushed the gnome into the backseat. "But we must
hurry. This far from the Abiding Star, my strength is taxed to
its limit. I cannot endure long down here."

Old Ric crawled from the back into the front passenger seat
and watched in fascination as the parking brake disengaged on
its own even as Asofel was still getting in. The Radiant One
slammed the door, and the car jumped away like a startled horse.
The gnome's head snapped back against the upholstery. He felt
them moving at great speed, but he could not see through the
frosted windshield.

"Oh Asofel, what will you do when we find the shadow thing?"
Old Ric fretted anxiously. He regarded the Radiant One with
hopeless confusion; in all their adventures together, he realized,
he had never understood his strange, taciturn companion, had
never been able to foresee what Asofel would do, or how he
would act. "If you use your light to destroy him here on the
Dark Shore, your life is forfeit. You will not have energy to leave
the dream," he added imploringly.

The steering wheel turned free of Asofel's touch as the entire
car embodied his will and sped along streets that would carry
them by the shortest route to where he sensed the presence of

the devil worshipper. He behaved as if this feat required his full attention, and he did not answer the gnome.

In truth, he had accepted the fateful possibility that he might exhaust himself here in this dream and die. That had always been the risk, but now it was a chance that had become more coldly real. He knew that death on the Dark Shore meant that his light would be lost, parsed forever among the inert densities of matter and the void. He would never rise to radiance. He would simply die.

That thought left him cold inside. And for once in his life, he was truly afraid. The final endarkenment did not exist where he originated. But in this remote world, destiny was derelict. Anything could happen. In a moment, a thinking, sensitive being could be reduced to insensate elements, bits of dull matter hoarding the merest sparks of light. The idea dizzied him with fear, yet he had to go on. Not only the dream worlds were in jeopardy but also the world above, that had lost so much of itself to this nightmare.

"You're not answering me, Asofel." The gnome shifted uneasily in his seat. "This arrow through my heart doomed me. I'm a deadwalker, and I have no hopes for myself. Yet I cherished a hope for you and the nameless lady we serve."

Asofel's luminous face dimmed, blue as star ash. "You are not afraid to die?"

Laughter pealed from the gnome. "Life offers far greater hardships than death. What is to fear?"

"Losing the light—vision, consciousness, the magical will."

A flicker of anxiety stamped the Radiant One's long face. "To lose all this and become less, so much less . . ."

A siren lashed loudly from behind them.

"What demon is that?" Old Ric shouted, hands over his ears.

Asofel sighed. *Another distraction.* The more time he had to reflect on dying, the less will he had to stay in the dream. He wanted to move quickly to the shadow thing and be done with this frightful task. Yet, he sensed the authority of the woman in the screaming car.

Asofel slowed to a stop. From the sideview mirror, he watched the police cruiser pull up behind them.

"You're not going to eat her shadow, are you?" Old Ric asked fretfully, craning his neck to peer through the slushy back window.

The police officer got out and walked toward them, and though her ferret face was masked by dark glasses and a patrol hat, her erect posture carried her astonishment that this snow-blind car had found its way down the road at all—let alone at high speed.

"Promise me you won't eat her shadow," the gnome persisted.

With a disappointed glance at Old Ric, Asofel got out of the car. His radiance dazzled the officer, and he quickly stepped closer to her while she winced. He intended to speak nine words to her inmost self, "Go back to your vehicle, sleep, and forget us." But as he got close he felt her life, her place within the dream and the living distance of her destiny. She was Janice Archer, mother of twins, now nine, divorced, dating an accountant from the state tax office, but most recently tending her father, who was dying of cancer at home under hospice care.

He stepped back, startled again by the vivid intimacy of each life in the dream. Gray, forested hills rose in adoration on all sides of this empty country road, and he realized with a shudder that those inert hulks of matter were as real and as authentic as the fields of light where he belonged.

The policewoman's eyes adjusted, and she gasped at the sight of him: long-faced as a horse angel with fleecy silver mane and eyes canted with wickedness.

Asofel spoke the nine words, and Janice obeyed at once. He went back to his car and, with one swipe of his hand, cleared it of ice. Then he got in, and they continued their journey across the Dark Shore.

RECLAIMING THE DEAD

OLD RIC EXAMINED THE NECKLACE OF SOULS, SEARCHING THE PRIS-
matic depths of its crystals for whatever he could find. But the
gems revealed nothing more than frayed rainbows.

"Touch the Necklace with your power, Asofel," the eldern
gnome entreated. "I don't have enough Charm here on the Dark
Shore to see anything in these crystals."

Asofel budged his gaze from the side window of the car, where
he had been staring at the landscape trundling past: uphill fields
and their constellations of nibbling sheep huddled under the
frigid wind. He himself had been wondering what the sheep's
locked existences felt like, but he had restrained himself from
reaching out to them. "I must conserve my power."

"The Necklace needs only the smallest touch of your Charm,
and we need to see what has become of the others. Where is the
witch-ghost Lara without her crystal prism? What has become of
our companions on the Dark Shore—the margravine and Dogbrick?" Old Ric looked at him in despair. "And where is Duppy
Hob? This is his world. He brought us here. Surely, he is watching
us. Should we not at least have the power to see what is around us?"

The Radiant One reluctantly extended a pinky to the Necklace. A small green spark arced to one of the gems, and the rainbows tightened in all the crystal prisms. Immediately, images appeared among the facets.

Dogbrick hung like an auburn pelt among conifer boughs. He had been hurled high into the hills, onto a ridge of old-growth forest. A small wind ruffled his fur, and his nostrils dilated, breathing in the scentscape and quivering at the news of strange animals.

"I've found Dogbrick," Old Ric announced excitedly. "He appears dazed. Is he hurt?"

Asofel reached across the dream and touched the nearby presence. "He is not physically hurt. But the impact has dislodged his memory. The same fate that befell his partner when he arrived on Irth as Ripcat. He is amnesic."

"Then we must restore his mind." Old Ric extended the gems to the Radiant One. "Without Charm of his own, his memory may never return."

Asofel returned his attention to the winter sheep under the vast clarity of the sky. "Dogbrick can fend for himself for a while."

Old Ric peered again into the gems of the Necklace and watched Dogbrick gingerly climb down among the brittle fir boughs. The cold did not trouble him through his shag. He moved agilely but timorously over the cushioned pine-needle floor, exploring the rambling mansion of cedar halls fairy-dusted with snow.

"Now show me Broydo," the eldern gnome directed, and the Necklace gems clouded to an opal milkiness. "Broydo—the ælf-counselor from World's End. Show me Broydo."

"He's dead."

The gems clattered against his skewered chest. "He had Charm! The serpent sword . . ."

"It was not enough."

Old Ric closed his wrinkled eyes, his jaw loose, mouth open, stunned by grief. Then, his teeth clacked shut. "We can't accept that."

"We have no choice, gnome." Asofel, brushing from his face strands of hair lively and bright as voltage, shifted to face Old Ric. "Don't you understand yet? We cannot dissipate our energy or compassion for these souls. We need all our strength to face Duppy Hob. He knows we're coming for him. He'll be prepared."

The stubbled chin of the eldern gnome thrust toward a brown hillside hazed in a lavender of cold weather. "He's out there . . . his corpse. Let us stop and retrieve his body. We owe him that much."

"Forget the ælf." Sparks crawled up Asofel's face. "Think of the worlds."

Ric's eyebrows knitted to a reproving look. "That is why he died. To save the worlds. He knew what we are about. He is one of our own in this strange world." The gnome's voice slowed under the weight of his conviction. "We are not going to abandon him here, even as a corpse."

Asofel grimaced but did not protest. The nameless lady had set this gnome over him, and though Ric's command defied strategy, it appealed to the Radiant One's small, awakened interest in these dream-bound lives. He slowed down and, again without having to touch the wheel, spun the car around and drove back toward the county access road where he sensed the body.

"Show me Broydo's body." The eldern gnome scowled at the Necklace of Souls, and it disclosed the interior of a log tavern with the ælf's cross-eyed corpse hung by tire chains from the rafters. Revelers with frothy mugs of fermented brew gawked and laughed and passed around the serpent sword.

The car stopped beside a cobbled stream of old leaves paned in ice. Old Ric looked about confusedly at the stands of sleek, dark trees. "Why are we stopping here?"

Asofel got out and crossed the small creek.

"Wait." Old Ric flung open his door and followed the Radiant One into the gray wood. "Where are we going?" He mumbled grouchily when Asofel did not answer and the loomwork of frozen creepers, iced branches, and rotted logs slowed him down. He fell behind among trees beswirled with mist. He almost panicked when he could find no other tracks but his own among the leaf-strewn, snow-patched ground. Then, the Radiant One's sullen voice summoned him.

Asofel stood beside an oak cracked to its pale pith. At the foot of the split tree lay a crumpled body. Streaked blond hair splashed the snow.

"It's the margravine!" Old Ric swept the hair from her face and saw that she bore no marks of apparent injury. Yet she did not breathe. "The charm of her amulets protected her body—but her soul—It's been knocked out of her."

The Radiant One did not wait for the gnome to ask or order. With a sound like fire, he lifted an arm to the sky and his hand blurred from his wrist, reaching into the empyrean where Jyoti's comatose soul drifted languidly, dissolving into the void. He fit her back to her body.

Quite unexpectedly, at the moment of fusion, as coagulated blood incandesced and flowed fluidly again and the soul shivered awake, Asofel felt the core of her, where the dreaming was born. It was the same lucidity he knew at his own core, and its beauty amazed him. A sole star spun light at the center of every living being, he marveled to himself, amazed that the thought had never occurred to him before.

Jyoti sat up slowly, memory dribbling back into her groggy brain. Asofel's Charm filled her with a paradisial air and calmed her while she remembered. When she felt strong enough to stand, he stepped away and walked back through the trees to the car.

Old Ric helped Jyoti steady herself, but his attention was held by the sight of tracks, footsteps, left in the duff and snow by Asofel.

"We haven't much time left," the eldern gnome began to explain to Jyoti, coaxing her to step more lively through the cluttered forest. "Asofel has become heavier—less light . . ."

Words shriveled in Old Ric's throat when he glanced at the Necklace of Souls and saw short, stout, helmeted warriors scampering among the trees waving hatchets. "Dwarves!" He cast an apprehensive stare over his shoulder at the empty pine haunts, and hurried Jyoti faster. "There are dwarves nearby."

Reflexively, Jyoti reached for her niello eye charms before she recalled that all her amulets had been destroyed, smashed to charmdust, by the force of their impact. The heavenly mood she had brought back from the dead vanished. The cold penetrated her once again, and she hugged herself for warmth as they barged through the undergrowth.

She felt groggy, as if woken from a profound sleep. Memory stood apart and watched her like a separate self, and she wondered if she was dreaming. Then, the horrid thought occurred to her that Reece had died at the same moment she had crashed onto the Dark Shore. She felt half her self because he was dead. Lugubrious sorrow sloshed in her, until she reminded herself that she was charmless on the Dark Shore and knew nothing for sure about Reece.

Asofel leaned against the cowl of the car, watching cat's-paw clouds pad across the blue sky. Despite the imminent danger he sensed all around them, he was struck by the fidelity of light. Even here on the Dark Shore, this universal radiance cast the shadows of each life. Each individual possessed light, no differently than himself or the nameless lady or the greater beings who dreamed her. They were all equals in the fateful shine of their lives. Some simply shone brighter than others. But their fatefulness remained the same. Their awareness, their sensitivity, and their very lives held together with frayed hopes were no different—no different than his own.

"Jyoti is cold." The eldern gnome opened the back door and ushered her into the car. "Asofel—did you hear me? Let's start the car and get going. I've seen dwarves nearby."

"They've come to destroy the serpent sword," the Radiant One said. "We'll have to hurry."

A tropical warmth filled the car when Asofel got behind the wheel, and clarity fit itself more snugly inside Jyoti's head. "The serpent sword could be a useful weapon against Duppy Hob."

"It was made by Blue Tipoo," the gnome said, slamming the door behind him as the car sped away. He angled his body in the seat so that acceleration did not jar the arrow, "The sword may turn his own magic back on him."

As they sped along, Old Ric held the Necklace of Souls in both hands so that Jyoti could search with him for dwarves ajog in the woods, hacking bramble out of their way with their hatchets. They converged on a log tavern in a grove of giant firs. Hatchets pounded windshields in the parking lot, and the shattering glass summoned patrons from the tavern.

Asofel swung the car through a fast, tight turn, and the Necklace of Souls flopped against Old Ric's chest. When Jyoti grasped it again, they saw horrified faces in the windows of the tavern. A man with a shotgun strode out the door, and a hatchet struck him solidly in the thigh, evoking a bellow of pain. A blast of smoke and flame streaks from the twin barrels of the gun ripped a dozen dwarves into a hundred flying parts.

Before the man could reload, more dwarves banged over the hoods and roofs of cars, flinging their hatchets through the windows of the tavern. The gunman retreated, and the dwarf warriors charged after him, shrieking with battle frenzy.

The cries lifted Jyoti's and Ric's eyes from the Necklace in time to see the log tavern swing into view around a curve in the road. Dwarves by the score darted among the surrounding firs, and a side window burst to glass pebbles, struck by a hatchet.

Asofel pulled the speeding car off the road and barreled through a wave of dwarves, thwacking aside the agile and crushing the slower ones underwheel. The jolting car accelerated toward the dwarves that packed the front door. The collision ruptured timbers inward and shattered the windshield as the car heaved itself inside the tavern.

Old Ric could only sit stunned when the car rocked to a stop with Broydo's dented, cross-eyed face an arm's reach away, hanging in the space where the windshield had been.

Jyoti moved before the car actually stopped: Flinging open her door hard and bowling over three dwarves, she rolled out. The plank floor slammed her with bruising force, and she groaned for Charm, wishing she still had her amulet-vest. Yet even without Charm, she moved crisply, overturning a table before two barreling dwarves and smashing a chair against the helmet of a third.

Trained by her grandfather to fight without Charm, she advanced swiftly into the room, swinging a barstool like a weapon. Panicked customers clawed past her, rushing for the luminous daylight in the smashed doorway. To get out of their way, she jumped up on a table and watched more armored dwarves erupt through the swinging doors to the kitchen.

"Margravine!" Asofel's shining voice cut through the noise of screaming people and squawking dwarves. "Get the serpent sword!"

She looked where he pointed and spotted the weapon on a barstool. A knot of men had clustered there, unwittingly defending the dwarf-killing blade with pocketknives and smashed bottles, desperately fending off the fierce, little warriors. With the limb of a broken chair in one hand and a dwarvish hatchet in the other, she clubbed her way toward the sword.

The men at the bar jumped for cover at the approach of the berserk woman. She seized the serpent sword from the barstool and swung it in a tight circle. Helmets and plate armor crashed among the tables and chairs, and maggots thick as trout skittered across the floor.

Old Ric jumped from the car and climbed atop the hood to disentangle Broydo's body from the chains. He lowered his dead companion into the car through the vacant windshield. After Jyoti dived into the backseat, Asofel threw the car into reverse, and Ric clung to the dash, legs flapping behind as the machine yanked him out of the tavern in a squeal of tires.

Rooster tails of gravel flared behind when Asofel turned the car back toward the road, fleeing customers leaping out of his way. Dwarves jumped out of the tavern's debris, sprinting onto the road, chasing the battered car until it dwindled away.

The eldern gnome, fallen headfirst to the floor of the car, found himself staring at Broydo's pushed-in face. A stewed odor enclosed him, and a fly from the tavern mizzled in his green hair. But before Old Ric could shove away in disgust, the fly flitted out the window on a slipstream of jasmine vapors. With a melancholy bong, the dent in the ælf's forehead popped back into place.

"By the gods, Asofel! What are you doing?" Old Ric pulled himself upright into the passenger seat. The car swerved violently, and he whacked his head hard against the side window. "Drake's blood! You'll kill us all!"

Asofel's hands grappled with the steering wheel, and the car weaved wildly, grinding onto the shoulder. He lifted his foot from the accelerator and pulled the car back onto the road, jerking everyone out of their seats.

Broydo popped upright, frosted blue eyes bulging. "I dreamt I was dead!"

"By the gods!" the gnome cried. "By the very gods, Asofel! What have you done?"

Noticing the serpent sword in the back, Broydo clambered over Old Ric to reclaim his weapon. Jyoti returned the blade and told him what had happened.

"Then I *was* dead!" The ælf trembled as though a cold hand closed around him. "Radiant One—I owe you my life. But what of our mission? What of Duppy Hob?"

"Do you have the strength to confront Duppy Hob?" the gnome pressed.

Asofel made no reply. What he had done was just, and a tranquillity accompanied his fatigue. He smiled out at the road, the destinal path, that led him deeper into this new world. He was not afraid now. Like an antelope that lifts its head and watches hyenas chewing its slippery viscera, he succumbed to a voluptuous fatigue. It was enough to hold on to the wheel. The road would lead where he had to go.

"If you have the strength to step out of the dream, go," the eldern gnome counseled.

Asofel's barb of a smile answered the gnome. The Radiant One had lost his luminosity. He had become wholly corporeal. His pale hair hung lankly over shoulders that appeared strong but not shining.

"At least we have the serpent sword." Broydo poked the blade at Old Ric's headrest.

"And each other," Jyoti reminded. "We have to make the difference—do whatever it takes—"

"Where I come from," Asofel spoke up, "there is no death. Our births are a splitting apart of ourselves. So there it is easy to believe the story we tell ourselves that God is light, radiant everywhere—and there is no evil. All the shadow things in our lives are simply darkness in the pupils of God."

At that moment, many leagues south, on the island of Manhattan, Duppy Hob lifted from his altar a slender glass blade, clear as air, sharper than a razor. In the gloom of the cellar, it shone like molten metal. He held it up to the congregation of chanting dead. Their voices had dimmed to whispers over the droning hours, and at the sight of the glass knife, they fell to silence.

Ripcat sat stupefied in the dark alcove, his eyes star-webbed with reflections from the blade. Entranced by the power of the long ritual night, he did not move when Duppy Hob stood over him. Nor did he flinch when the tip of the ceremonial blade pricked the top of his skull. So strong was the demonic paralysis that he remained still as the fine edge sliced under his scalp and slid cleanly along the cope of his skull.

Pain tore through the trance, and Reece jumped upright while the blade continued cutting the length of his neck, across his shoulder, and down the breastbone. At the soft underbelly, Duppy Hob seized the flayed pelt in both hands and rent it.

Reece Morgan screamed. His human head, shoulders, and chest emerged from the peeled hide syrupy with the blood of Ripcat's stripped flesh. At the end of the curling cry, he collapsed, and Duppy Hob yanked the whole of Ripcat's skin from him, tugging the fur from legs and arms. Naked, glossed in blood and curds of mucus, Reece's body shimmered in the aqueous light. The small ritual scars, arcane tattoos, and magic cicatrix that marked his power points held the light longer and burned coolly in the dark, where he lay like the dead.

Duppy Hob wrapped the hide of Ripcat around himself, knotting the claws at his throat, the legs around his waist, and the fanged mask atop his head as a bestial cowl. Triumphant, he strode to the back of the cellar, mounted the bellied steps, and shoved open the hatchway. A smoldering beam of sunlight annihilated the cellar's darkness and basked the kneeling chanters in golden fire. Their scrawny figures bleached suddenly to silhouettes and shambled clumsily up the stairs and into the alley, dismissed by their master.

"Wake up, Reece Morgan!" Duppy Hob called into the crypt sternly as the cry to Lazarus. "Come out from that stinking hole. It's a new day!"

Reece staggered naked and squinting into the light. Slowly, he mounted the rock steps, sun rays steaming away the oils, clots, and frayed integuments of Ripcat's shorn skin. In the alley, he stood cleansed of all gore, breath smoking in the cold.

Duppy Hob opened the side entrance to Empire of Darkness and exposed the debris of last night's revelry—torn garments, stomped cups and cans, crumpled posters strewn across planks stained with human effluvia. At the center of the sunstruck room, Lara stood, naked, sheathed in her long, black hair, transparent as fire.

DARK SONG OF THE SOUL

FLIES, IRIDESCENT AND CRAWLING FRANKLY OVER THE WINDOWS IN-side Empire of Darkness, droned like an electric current. They sensed the abrupt tension, the surge of taut stillness that signaled the onset of something calamitous. Their green bodies whined against the sunny glass, frantic with their vicious need to escape.

Reece Morgan entered the littered room and advanced among spears of sunlight toward the apparition of Lara. Mindless of the eerie silence that had driven the flies mad, he crossed the dance hall as in a dream—naked, muscles heavy, cold outlining his breaths in the yellow air.

Lara and Reece faced each other with stupefied recognition. Both hung stunned and wordless, entranced by Duppy Hob. He had placed Lara in the building to draw Reece inside. With that accomplished, the ghost shivered like a cooked mirage and faded away.

Reece groped at the empty space where Lara had watched him. While he groggily mulled what had happened to her, Duppy Hob selected a black, ceremonial robe from a back closet.

He pulled it over Reece's head and helped him slip his arms into the wide sleeves.

"You've served me well, Reece Morgan." Duppy Hob smiled, his unsmiling eyes drillholes to a crater of hell. "Your usefulness to me is presently at an end. Now that the child's soul is almost in my hands, you're free to go. But we don't want you wandering around the world searching for your identity naked, do we?"

Reece gazed vapidly at the flayed pelt of Ripcat, his mind a cloud, a wing with nowhere to fly.

"Now you look the role." Duppy Hob adjusted the collar of Reece's black robes and slapped his shoulder with satisfaction. "A prophet of doom. You can roam the planet warning everyone about the end of the universe as we know it. You will herald my coming. Go." He pointed out the open door to the dingy alley, where the sounds of the city squeaked unnaturally small and far away. "Go wander the streets of Manhattan. Tell everyone of the doom that is coming when Duppy Hob becomes master of this dream!"

Laughter like crackling fire followed Reece into the alley. Barefoot, the dazed man limped to the street, and his deranged aspect sent pedestrians veering.

Behind him, the laughter continued, cascading after Duppy Hob slewed downstairs to his cellar and the charmway. The alcove shone with luminous blue daylight and sparkling motes of snow crystals. Before crossing the threshold to a distant room of the world, the demon withdrew all his power from the building. He would not need Empire of Darkness again.

Blisters boiled along the walls and rafters, blackening to scales of ash. Chancres of rust gnawed the metal loft, and its girders groaned and sagged, pulling down mossy veils of dissolved plaster from the ceiling. With a loud popping noise, windows cracked, and flies swarming across the panes drizzled to black dust. Moments later, the building was reduced to an empty shell, its interior hung in rotted draperies of sloughed paint and chewed wiring.

Duppy Hob closed the charmway behind him and sauntered onto a country road. The sky's blue dome enclosed snow-patched hills and pine forest. Out of the dark doorways of the forest, dwarves scuttled. The demon drew his creatures to himself, and the hosts descended in their thousands, the hillsides trembling with white and metallic shapes as though the snow itself rose up armored.

"Bring me the Necklace of Souls, children." His voice rose straight into the empty sky, big with power, and billowed to stately thunderheads, a purple wall of malevolent force crested silver with the sun's horizontal rays.

At the sight of the empurpled storm front stacking clouds out of a clear sky some leagues ahead, Old Ric sat up taller in the passenger seat. "Where is that coming from?"

"Duppy Hob." Asofel's curved eyes narrowed, and he pressed the accelerator to the floor, fishtailing into a curve. "He's come for the Necklace of Souls."

Straddling the center line, a young man in a black tunic and animal skin blocked the road like some errant god of myth. At his back, tempest clouds towered.

Asofel held the accelerator down and pulled the car into the center of the straightaway, aiming for the youth.

With a braying cough, the engine died, and the car rolled to a stop close enough for all to see the dimpled youth in Ripcat's skin. Fiery spirochetes crawled through space around him. The wind gusted, and he broke apart into a black glitter of nothingness.

"He wears Ripcat's hide!" Broydo groaned and clutched the headrest behind Old Ric. "Where did he go?"

"Duppy Hob was never there," Asofel answered and peeled his fingers from the steering wheel. "He won't get too close. He's afraid I'll eat him."

"He sent his dwarves instead!" Jyoti twisted in her seat to check the side and rear windows. "We're surrounded by them."

Asofel hung his head. He listened to the dwarvish marchers climbing down the dream through the thousand narrow charm-ways bored through space-time by the demon Hob in his six thousand years of exile. All converged on this site—the arena he had selected long ago. "There are too many. One sword cannot hold off these legions."

"Can you start the engine?" Jyoti asked, nose pressed to the side window, watching glittery ranks of dwarves spill down the hillsides.

Asofel banged a frustrated fist on the steering wheel. "He's trapped us."

Hoping to spare the others, Old Ric climbed out the open windshield, and Asofel pulled him back in. "Let me go, Asofel. Let me return the Necklace I stole."

"What good will that serve?" Asofel strapped the gnome into the passenger seat. "We must not submit. Not to this evil."

"The devil worshipper is too powerful here on the Dark Shore." Broydo peered from behind the bone blade. "Let's cut our way out of here—as we did on Gabagalus."

"Duppy Hob has called down upon us all his dwarves." Asofel directed their attention to the higher ridges, where sunlight glinted like a star field off the helmets of emerging hordes. "If we try to hack our way through them, we will be overcome."

"You should have gotten out when you could." Misery wrung Old Ric, because he knew from what he saw in the Necklace of Souls that there would be no escape: every facet showed packed multitudes of dwarf warriors bursting from caves and sinkholes, helmets masking all but the bloodglow of their red eyespots. "I'm sorry I brought you into this."

"I don't like when you talk that way, Ric." Asofel's complexion of blue star ash darkened, flushed with anger. "You sound like you've given up."

The others sat silently, their eyes held by the wave of dwarves sweeping down the brown fields.

"We must not give up." Asofel pulled around in his seat, large face clenched with determination. "No matter what happens, we must fight. That is why I gave you my light when I found you dead on the Dark Shore—to defy Duppy Hob."

"You're weaker because of us," Jyoti observed dismally. Without Charm to bolster her, she lacked all hope they could survive the dwarf assault, and she sunk lower in the backseat. "Now we have to die a second time."

"Margravine, listen to me." Asofel reached for the words that could replace the Charm she craved. "I don't have the power to defeat Duppy Hob by myself, because I gave some of my light to each of you. I was reluctant to do that at first. I thought Ric was foolish for suggesting it. But I'm glad now that I gave you my light, because we're stronger together. That's what I've learned from Ric—from all of you. Power is strongest when shared."

"What are we going to *do* now?" Broydo wanted to know,

watching the army of dwarves swarming across the roadside ditches.

"Light cannot be destroyed." Asofel spoke aloud but to himself, gathering strength for the mortal act that awaited him. "My power is still among us. We just have to work together and not despair. No matter how powerful Duppy Hob looks, we must not forget that he is the shadow—and we have the light to drive him out. The survival of the worlds depends on all of us. I can't do this alone anymore."

"But what *are* we going to do now?" Broydo swung his head, watching the dwarves leap with shrill cries onto the roadway. "What now?"

"What I can." Asofel opened his door. "And I expect each of you to do the same—no matter how painful that may be."

Ric grabbed the sentinel's arm as he moved to exit. "I don't like when you talk this way, Asofel."

The Radiant One smiled, and for an instant the car interior dazzled like water braiding sunlight. "Good-bye, gnome."

A hatchet skirred through the open windshield and gashed open the seat where Asofel had been sitting. Other thrown hatchets smashed the grille and headlights and thudded off the rooftop. The occupants of the car threw themselves on the floor and cringed under the shrieking attack.

Asofel stood in the road with his arms upraised, iridescent raiment shining hotter. He did not have the strength to attack Duppy Hob and win—but the dwarves were weaker creatures, augumented out of mere maggots. Their energy in the dream floated upon the void differently than the life flux of natural creatures. He drew on that energy. He pulled it into himself from the very fringes of the dream.

Cries edged with anguish cut through the war whistles and trills of the dwarves. Maggots collapsed onto the roadway with wet slaps and clattering of armor. Upon all the hillsides and in the depths of the pine woods, dwarves wrenched free of the magic that had transformed them. Far into all the riddling charm-ways, maggots writhed, and the evil that had shaped them flowed directly into Asofel.

The Radiant One hunched over, hair of moon air darkening to nightsmoke, black lips curling back from snarling incisors. He turned on the stalled car, wicked eyes gleeful with Duppy Hob's power. With one tug, he tore away the side door and stuck his scorched head in the car, the human fabric ripping from his cheekbones and brow, revealing blackened skull underneath.

"Use the sword!" Asofel gnashed. His dark face knotted, veins bulging. It took all his strength to restrain the ferocity of the dwarves compacted in him. "The serpent sword!"

Broydo rose up on his knees to pass the blade to Old Ric, and he faced Asofel's blood-fire stare. In the black depths of the Radiant One's pupils gleamed two red eyespots.

"I can't do it." Old Ric refused to take the sword and cowered against the glove compartment clutching the Necklace of Souls. From the facets of the crystals, thousands of red eyespots fixed him in their empty gaze.

"I can't—hold on—much longer—" Asofel's grimacing face throbbed. "The dwarves—will kill—you—"

Broydo shot a terrified look to Jyoti, wanting her to take the sword. But the driver's seat and headrest blocked her from delivering a clean blow to Asofel.

She glared at the ælf. "Use the sword!"

Broydo thrust, and the bone blade pierced Asofel's chest and caught on his ribs. A scalded cry shook the car, and Broydo flew away from the sword, punched nearly unconscious by the pain that jolted through the haft.

Teeth meshed in agony, Asofel swung the hilt of the lodged sword toward the gnome. "Ric—help me!"

Old Ric, who had pushed himself up on the dash and sat half out of the car, locked his frightened gaze on the disheveled and charred creature before him. Asofel's devilishly angelic lineaments had burned to a vague semblance of sooty hair on a ridged skull patched with singed rags of flesh. . . .

The eldern gnome took the sword's grip in both curled hands and drove the cutting blade deep into Asofel's body. Vibrant agony jarred Ric and threw him to the floor. Glimpsed briefly, Asofel's visage shone with feverish beauty again, then the devils' torment yanked him out of the car and cast him onto the road.

Asofel lay writhing on the steaming asphalt, his heart visibly throbbing through the amber casing of his rib cage. The serpent sword stood upright in his chest, vibrating as it destroyed the dwarvish magic he had pulled into his body. Its bone blade and gold-coiled haft incandesced briefly, then went still and dark.

The sentinel drifted on a sea of pain. Outside the dream, the pain would have been light, and he would have grown brighter for all this suffering. Trembling with cold, he felt himself growing darker. Yet he felt no fear. He had known it would be like this, and he had wanted it. The dwarves were finished. Duppy Hob was less. These thoughts gave meaning to the pain, just as the gnome had said.

The I at the center of his suffering shone with the last of his radiance, blazing with all that remained of his consciousness. In moments, weariness would deliver him from pain. Until then, he burned with his hurt body on the melted tarmac, glad for the pain, glad for the last of his life, all of him given away, for the love of a dream, all of his light given to darkness.

Lightning jumped down from the storm clouds at the far end of the road and staggered closer. Out of the thunder, Duppy Hob strode. His approach frosted the remaining windows of the car, and the glass collapsed in opaque granules, shaken by the blast. He jammed the heel of his sandal against Asofel's throat and wrenched the serpent sword from his torso.

"Stop!" Old Ric shouted, and struggled upright.

Jyoti shoved him back in his seat and averted her eyes from where Duppy Hob had raised the sword overhead with both hands, blade pointed down at the maroon, pulsating heart. A brilliant flash erased the gnome's face. When the glare faded and his features returned, pieces of the sun burned in his big eyes.

Broydo wailed with despair.

A ray of cold fire touched the ælf between the eyes, and he curled up asleep on the backseat. Jyoti shook him by his shoulders until his eyeballs clicked into place. Stunned out of his mind, Broydo groaned as from a nightmare, "Asofel is dead!"

Horror-struck, Jyoti kept her face turned away from the smoldering glow outside the car. In the rearview mirror, she saw the patch of road where Asofel had fallen, the asphalt melted to his outline, its edges licked with flame, and only ash where the body had been—a white bed of crushed diamonds—and a blackened stick for the sword.

In the mirror, a slippery demon pranced around the incinerated body, its cobra-hooded head a huge leer of needle-thin teeth. But when Jyoti dared a glimpse over her shoulder, she saw Duppy Hob as a jet-eyed youth dancing under Ripcat's hide.

"You see it, too," Old Ric whispered. "Duppy Hob is a demon."

"And Asofel is dead!" Broydo's teeth clacked with fright. "The serpent sword burned with him! We have no weapons against the demon!"

"Except the Necklace." Jyoti shared a wild look of hope between the gnome and ælf. "You said that the Necklace helped your clan, Broydo."

"It broke the demon Tivel's spell," Broydo recalled excitedly.

"But I'm not Tivel." Duppy Hob's voice shook the car, and the roof peeled away with a screech of violated steel. "I created the Necklace of Souls."

Old Ric stood up on the passenger seat, and a whirlwind whipped him into the sky. With the child's soul in his grasp, Duppy Hob had no further cause to hide his power. His human disguise shredded like snake molt, and in his place an ether devil blazed hotly on the Dark Shore.

The cold of the Gulf condensed the devil's ethereal form to a gargoyle with wings of red lightning, and he soared with Old Ric in his talons. Below, thunderclouds sheared to long scarves of fog and dissolved among frozen hills bunched together like dirty eggshells.

Desolate with grief, the eldern gnome moved to pull off the Necklace of Souls and end the perfidy of his existence now that Duppy Hob had triumphed. A webbed claw stopped him. With a voice like glass grinding to sand, the demon announced, "You are coming with me to the garden of the nameless lady. You will negotiate with her for me, while I hold secure the child's soul in the Necklace. She may try to snatch the soul back, but that will not avail so long as I hold even one of the crystal prisms. She is to give me her dream and make me a god. When that power is mine, when all the universe is mine to command, I will release the child's soul from the Necklace and the child will move again in her womb."

Old Ric clutched at the Necklace of Souls. "The child's soul is in *here?*" Shock pierced his shock at finding himself in a demon's claws high above the hazy blue curve of a cold world. "All this time—*all this time*—I held the child's soul! I paid for it when this cursed arrow pierced my body! The quest could have ended then."

"Quest?" The demon's lightning face flashed hotter. "Thievery! You stole my soul-catcher."

"Demon—speak not of thieving," Old Ric shouted into the viperous face. "*You* stole the child's soul!"

"Yes, I did," the demon agreed triumphantly. "Even as my dwarves were casting me into the Gulf during their rebellion, I used what power I had to drop the Necklace of Souls into the Labyrinth of the Undead. From there, I was able to focus it from afar, slowly, tediously, over thousands of Earth years, to lens the light of the Abiding Star and gradually absorb the soul of the child. Now it is mine!" Duppy Hob hooked a claw around the Necklace of Souls as they rose higher and starlight tapped in the indigo. "You are in my power—two million days of power come to bear on this one day, this one hour of victory! You will obey me—because you have no choice."

Lightning exploded overhead with an oceanic roar, and the demon smashed into a wall of stars so violently he dropped the gnome. Old Ric tumbled into free fall above the azure crescent of the atmosphere. From one corner of the sky, among a sprinkling of tiny stars, the moon hung like a pulpy, rotted thing.

Duppy Hob snatched the eldern gnome from his plunge and stood him upright in the violet shine above the sliding jet stream.

"You're trapped on the Dark Shore!" Old Ric laughed hysterically, mad with horror.

"No, no! Wait now . . . Let me think. We can't cross the Gulf with the Necklace of Souls in parts." The demon's sharp fingers upheld the lone prism that had housed Lara's soul. "I must rejoin the crystal prism to the others before we can leave the Dark Shore."

Old Ric folded his twisted hands over the Necklace. "You have not the power to rejoin the prisms," he challenged.

"Power!" The demon snarled. "I have more power than I can use. It will take more than power to rejoin the Necklace. If the witch had not slain my servant Blue Tipoo, I would summon him to accomplish this tedious task. As it is, I will have to do the work myself. Wait here."

As Duppy Hob dived through the wind, disappearing among frosty strata of clouds, Old Ric took the Necklace of Souls in both his bent hands and trembled to think of the child's soul he wore. That he had nearly removed from his shoulders the very prize he sought hollowed him with anguish. He looked about for a place to hide under the rumpled darkness of outer space.

With Jyoti dangling from one taloned fist and Broydo from the other, Duppy Hob returned. His slitherous tail lashed onto Old Ric's leg and pulled him down from his climb toward the moon.

"There's a lot of work to be done," the demon said, taking Broydo by the arm and leading him across the fluorescent glass roof of the sky toward the sun. "Ælf, you will work the bellows."

Auroral curtains of ionized gas hung in cathedral tiers, shrouding invisible lines of force from the planet's magnetic field. Wide as the horizon, the shining draperies buffeted in the solar wind. Duppy Hob shackled Broydo to the drapes with cuffs of pain. At the demon's command, the ælf ran along the world's rim, propelled by magic hundreds of leagues at a step. He flew across the planet, dragging immense sheets of plasma, then doubling back and fanning the sky fires to gusts of blue-and-violet flame.

"Now margravine, your task is to gather lightning bolts from the flames of the bellows and stack them for me." Duppy Hob set Jyoti in the electric wind blustering from the whipped curtains of plasma, and her brindled hair lifted from her head, stiff with static.

"And you—" Duppy Hob jabbed a fiery finger at Old Ric. "Stay still. Don't move or you'll be burned to a cinder, and I'll have to use the ælf for my negotiator."

The eldern gnome remained motionless against the black wall of space and watched the others toiling. Broydo already gleamed with sweat, his stocky frame running hard to pull the vast sails of light after him, back and forth across the slippery roof of the sky. When he fell, sparks flew along his skid path, and he jumped to his feet, grimacing with pain.

Jyoti, too, moved with alacrity, knowing that any delay meant violent suffering. She reached into the clouds of blue fire that Broydo pulled from the auroras and came out with fists full of eelish bolts. Sweat flew like sparks from her florid face as she stacked the blue-hot tangles of lightning, turning them so that their oppositely charged ends locked on to each other. By the time she had linked all the bolts into an incandescent chain, Broydo came huffing across the world, dragging another full sail of captured energy.

Duppy Hob wrapped the chain of electric bolts that Jyoti gathered around Old Ric's shoulder, connecting the sizzling edges to the facets of the crystal prisms. The labor required all his attention, and his horrid face grew eyestalks that pressed close to the sparking crystals, swiveling aside only to search for more bolts. "Hurry, ælf! Run! Run! I need more power to open the Necklace. And more later to close it. Hurry, margravine! Stack the bolts quickly. If the Necklace is open too long, the child's soul is forfeit—and so are all the worlds of the dream."

Broydo and Jyoti moved as swiftly as they could. The ælf threw himself skidding across the sky, spewing sparks and screams of pain yet scooping even more energy from the solar wind. Jyoti emerged with armfuls of spitting bolts, blisters disfiguring the sides of her neck and face where the asps of energy had bit her.

By their extreme effort, the demon garnered enough energy to open the gold, binding cord and reattach the lone crystal prism. The Necklace of Souls pressed more heavily on Old Ric's shoulders, and the greater charge of Charm quieted the loud horror that had been resounding in him since he learned that he had possessed the child's soul all along.

Distantly, the eldern gnome heard music—the dark song of Lara's soul. It eked out of the crysal she had worn and was amplified by the others.

Duppy Hob heard it, too—and more. Lara's ghost had joined with the dispossessed energies of all the souls that had been caught by these crystals over the ages. Powerless on the Dark Shore, Lara had sunk into the crystal. She had joined the drifting shades in the spherical corridors of the Necklace, had hovered mindless among them, just another lost soul—until she realized how her mind separated her from the other souls. She was a witch of the Dark Shore. She knew how to dance power.

Since Ripcat was taken from her by dwarves in the winter park, she had been dancing, pausing only when the demon turned the pressure of his awareness upon her. The dancing had pooled the tenuous energies of the lost souls, rekindling their rageful memories of capture and servitude. When Duppy Hob rejoined Lara's gem to the others in the Necklace, the wrath of all the souls in each of the gems resonated to a ferocious chorus.

The demon staggered back a pace before the blare of focused ire, eyestalks shrinking with hurt.

The sight of the demon's wide jaws agape with pain inspired a homicidal impulse in the gnome. He grabbed the arrow shaft that had pierced his breastbone and, threading an agony that not even Charm could mute, pulled it through. With a scream that ripped the air, he drove the barbed arrow into the underbelly of the demon.

Instantly, Duppy Hob bled fire. Flames spurted from under the webbed fingers that seized the impaled shaft. His eyestalks shot straight outward, fixing Old Ric with savage amazement. Then, the demon curled around himself trying to contain the flow of fiery ichor, dripping from his wound like clots of lava. Caught off guard by the witch's haunting, he had relaxed his psychic grip on the gnome, and the arrowhead had driven deep. If he pulled it free, his life force would drain away. Yet, if he left the barbed shaft in place, its toxins would eventually kill him.

The Necklace of Souls! his pain screamed in him, wild for a way to heal himself.

Old Ric's feet skipped on the glassy surface as he turned to flee. The demon unclasped from its agony and snagged the Necklace with its claws. But the claws had no strength. Even the gnome's withered hands were strong enough to restrain the demon.

Duppy Hob's blinding pain stymied him, and he groped at Old Ric like a withered crone. Every mote of his being burned with frustration. So close to the child's soul that would make him immortal when the lady was forced to turn the dream over to him—so close to immortality and yet too mortally weak to seize it—he embraced the eldern gnome in his snake-leather arms, and the two collapsed in a tangle of thrashing limbs.

Broydo's cuffs dissolved the moment Old Ric stabbed the demon, and he and Jyoti shambled to help, clumsy with exhaustion. But before they could reach the struggle, the demon and the eldern gnome rolled down the sky, spinning astral blood like a meteor. Lightning crackled along their shining trajectory.

Jyoti grabbed Broydo's arm and pulled him after her, down the sky, along the glittering curve that pierced the clouds. In the thunderheads, they flew blind. The fog darkened abruptly, and they crashed into a dewy cave wall. The roar of surf boomed, shaking the very air of the cavern.

At the mouth of the cave, crimson twilight streaked the sky above Gabagalus. Mountainous waves swelled out of the dark sea and smashed against the headlands, sending frothy walls of ocean crashing onto the sprawling plains of cress and wort. Duppy Hob and Old Ric wrestled on the rock ledge above this seething night sea, their frantic bodies silhouetted by phosphorescent explosions of spray. The cliff boulders boomed, and foam reared up behind them like a giant's face white with fury.

Jyoti and Broydo each seized one of Old Ric's arms and yanked him free of the grasping demon. With a kick, the gnome sent Duppy Hob toppling backward over the precipice and into the churning waves, the demon's piteous cry swallowed whole by the howling tempest of the sinking continent.

RETURN TO THE GARDEN

OLD RIC, BROYDO, AND JYOTI MOVED DEEPER INTO THE CHARM-way as waves sloshed through the cavern at Gabagalus. By the slim glow from the Necklace of Souls, they made their way through dense darkness to a rock ledge where the susurrant noise of the ocean did not reach. There, they examined the eldern gnome's wound and found it open but not bleeding.

"By the bones of drakes," Old Ric complained, "I feel no pain, no weakness! I could have removed that cursed arrow long ago!"

"Thank the gods you waited till you did." Broydo squeezed the gnome's shoulder affectionately. "And I think now we might more correctly say blessed arrow."

"It wasn't the arrow that stopped Duppy Hob from taking the Necklace of Souls." Old Ric turned to each of his friends, though he could see them only vaguely in the dark. "It was the witch Lara. She rallied the lost souls of the Necklace to assault the demon. They surprised and weakened him."

"Can you see Lara in the crystals?" Broydo asked.

"And Reece Morgan," Jyoti queried, almost too frightened to

ask. "The demon stripped him of his beastmarks, but we haven't seen his body. Is he yet alive?"

The eldern gnome lifted the shining gems close to their watchful faces. Lara gazed back at them from the jeweled facets, her languid black hair framing a whole body unmarked by wounds. Winter sunlight leaned through her transparent figure, and within the window of her body they saw a snowy sward of parkland, bunched gray trees, mummied joggers, brisk dog walkers, and a blond-haired man in black robes with cardboard wrapped around his feet trudging along a bike path.

"It's Reece!" Jyoti's voice wobbled to echoes through the blind charmways. "He's wandering through a city park on the Dark Shore."

Lara strolled beside him, her shimmering white raiment blowing in a ghostly breeze. Duppy Hob's spell had broken, and Reece startled awake to find himself clutching a crumpled dollar bill given him by a passerby during his tranced walk from Tribeca.

"Young master—"

Reece glimpsed Lara beside him, her dusky face smiling quietly. She blinked out of sight, then appeared farther along the cinder path, a shadow of sable tresses and swarthy skin clothed in veils of light. Again, she blurred to nothing and then glittered back into view at a distance, beckoning him from a mound of black, glacial boulders.

Into a narrow crevice among rocks overgrown with frozen grass, Lara slipped. He staggered after her, clutching himself against the brutal cold. Glancing about for dwarves or some other sign of Duppy Hob, he wedged his body into the gap between the boulders where the ghost had retreated. He turned his head sideways and had to exhale all his breath to squeeze through.

A cold blue day expanded across crystal peaks of ice mountains. He crouched with surprise before the wide vista and glanced back the way he had come. The parkland of gray trees, the joggers, the skyline of Manhattan had been replaced by a mountainside of frost-veined cliffs. And high overhead, adrift in the azure sky, the glassy disk of Nemora gleamed.

"There are charmways to the Dark Shore everywhere." Lara's ghost hung in the air beside him, pale as water. "Duppy Hob built them throughout his exile. Sometimes strangers wander into them and lose themselves on Irth."

"Lara—where is Duppy Hob?" Reece stared through her at the crevice in the scarp where he had emerged and worried that dwarves might appear at any moment. "The child's soul is in peril."

"The child is safe now." Lara's black hair blew across her face in an untidy wind he did not feel. "Duppy Hob's power is broken. The others will explain. They are coming. But I cannot stay. I've led you here to the Calendar of Eyes, to the tallest peak on Irth, so that we would be close to the Abiding Star, to the Charm I need to speak with you this last time."

Reece placed a hand in her emptiness and felt nothing, only his joy at seeing her whole and his sadness, watching her fade. "Don't go. Tell me what has happened."

"I have no time." She pointed into the sky at the silver-white glare of the Abiding Star. "I'm going there now that Duppy Hob's power is broken. We are free of him, and I am going to where I belong, back to the Beginning, back to the light of creation."

Reece opened his arms to her imploringly. "Stay with me."

"I've already stayed too long." She touched his unhappy face with her empty hand. "I am a ghost, young master. But I am a ghost who has lived again and made a difference among the living. My death is easy to bear now."

"And you are truly free, Lara?" The magus searched the young witch's eyes and found stars of joy in her stare. "Duppy Hob has no hold on you?"

"All that remains of our bondage to that devil worshipper is the pattern of sigils that tattoo your body." The ghost placed two fingers over the small, cicatrix pentagram that marked his flesh where his collarbones met. "This is the central emblem. Break this star, and your bond to Duppy Hob will end. And so will your magic in the Bright Worlds."

Reece did not hesitate. He scooped up a flat shard of flint and slashed its edge across the cicatrix star of flesh. Blood streamed down his chest, and the air chilled colder. Deprived of magic, his body began to shiver.

"Now you are free, too, young master." Lara's smile expanded even as her form slimmed away. "A new life begins for you—and something wider opens for me."

"Lara!" Reece cried into the emptiness where she had disappeared, and the cold shook him free of his vision. For a long moment, he leaned into her absence, his trembling hands holding daylight and the frail smoke of his breath. Then, the pieces of what she had told him fit together, and he lowered his arms and squinted up at the Abiding Star. Unfathomed happiness opened in him deeper than the chill from the frigid air or the hot pain of his cut flesh. Lara had smiled. Her suffering was truly over.

He hobbled toward the escarpment, seeking warmth in the charmway where he had crossed from the Dark Shore. His name resounded from the crevice with a joy muffled in echoes, and a moment later Jyoti pulled herself through. They embraced in the fusing cold, mute with excitement to find themselves in each other's arms again.

Old Ric and Broydo emerged from the charmway, hands shielding their eyes from the radiance of the Abiding Star. They tugged at the lovers and pulled them back into the cleft of the rock wall. And there, in the warm daylight, they shared their stories.

"Where is Dogbrick?" Reece asked when each had spoken.

"On the Dark Shore." Old Ric offered the Necklace of Souls to the daylight, and Charm composed the rainbows within to a view of Dogbrick. He sat in a splash of sunlight among giant cedars, and at his side several shaggy bipeds shared handfuls of nuts with him. "When we saw that he was safe, we chose to follow the Necklace of Souls to you, here on the Calendar of Eyes."

"Who are those creatures with him?" Reece tilted his head and watched Dogbrick munching nuts and signing satisfaction to the others.

"We thought you'd tell us," Broydo replied. "You're from the Dark Shore."

"I've heard of sasquatch . . ." With wonder, Reece observed the forest hominids slapping their brown pelts, imitating Dogbrick, who barked with laughter and nearly choked on a nut. "We have to go back for him."

"In time," Jyoti promised, "the dominions will conduct a thorough survey of Duppy Hob's pathways to the Dark Shore. We'll retrieve Dogbrick before he gets too friendly with the natives. But for now, Old Ric, you must return the child's soul to its mother. If you wait for us to equip ourselves with charmware, we'll escort you."

Old Ric demurred with a shake of his bald head. "The dwarves are gone. I'm sure the path ahead for me is clear."

"This is too important to leave to chance," Reece said. "Wait for us to get amulets and firecharms, and we'll make sure you reach the nameless lady with her child's soul."

"The blind god Chance has favored us this far," Broydo answered with merry eyes. "But I am not blind, nor is this eldern gnome, and we have seen the Forest of Wraiths in the gems. There are no dwarves in the woods where my clan dwells. We've seen none of those maggot-warriors anywhere. Asofel destroyed them all."

"There is a monastery on the ridge below this slope," the eldern gnome said, slanting a crystal prism to show the others the Charmed view of the mountain flank. "The Brotherhood of Wizards will welcome you, margravine. And by the time you tell them what has transpired, and they arrange for you to be equipped, I will have climbed beyond World's End and into the garden. Go, you two. Hurry while there is still some warmth to the day, before the Abiding Star sets and catches you charmless on the mountainside."

Jyoti thought to protest. But the afternoon had already darkened toward amber, and there was no question of them continuing with the gnome and the ælf without Charm. They huddled in farewell and shared the soft brightness of the Necklace of Souls. Charm laved them in peacefulness, and when they separated they each carried some of that serenity.

Fear returned only later. As they skidded down the mountainside and Charm waned for them without amulets, they worried for the Necklace of Souls and the child's life within it. "How will we know if the child is safely returned?" Reece fretted. "The dream of these worlds could end at any time. I have no magic anymore, no way to save us."

Jyoti paused on the rock trail overlooking the maroon domes of the monastery and took his hand. "We're just a man and a woman now, Reece. We'll have to live with uncertainty the way people have always done. But at least we can live this unknowing together."

"And with Charm," Reece chattered as cold numbed the blue

tips of his face and limbs. "The future always looks brighter through an amulet."

They laughed together despite their dread and the cold it fed upon and hurried down the stony trace, arms locked, hearts shining.

The eldern gnome and the ælf watched after them from the threshold of the charmway until they dipped from sight. Then, they returned to the cave and followed the images in the radiant gems—the emerald glints of the Forest of Wraiths that brightened as they progressed through the lightless tunnels. The sepulchral sounds of echoed footfalls and slow seepings relented to tolling birds and chattering monkeys, and soon they emerged among knolls of crimson pearl mushrooms and groves of eel-branched trees.

"My home!" Broydo shouted.

"Silence or you'll call squid monkeys down on us!" the eldern gnome berated him with a serious scowl, then burst into laughter. "We have come full circle, ælf."

Out of the hollow trees, green-haired ælves emerged, summoned by Broydo's shout. Soon an excited throng had gathered in the grove, milling about their clansman returned from his long travels and gawking openly at the Necklace of Souls that had once purged them of the demon Tivel's curse.

By the time Smiddy Thea arrived, a carnival atmosphere ensued. Gourd lanterns hung from the boughs, feast planks buckled on their trestles under the weight of burl-bowls brimming with honey berries, nut pastes, roasted tubers, monkey stew, and blue wine. Beneath her sea-green locks, her blue-black face grinned happily, netted in wrinkles yet unmarked by the pocking disease that had once gnawed the clan's flesh.

Old Ric did not linger to celebrate. He stayed among the ælves only long enough to extol the bravery of their clansman Broydo. Then he allowed the entire clan to accompany him through the jade avenues of the forest while he followed the images in the crystals of the Necklace. Scouts rushed ahead, searching for bull lizards and squid monkeys but finding none.

Old Ric knew there would be no obstacles now. The Necklace of Souls hummed on his shoulders with a magic greater than Charm, and he was not surprised when they arrived in a somber glade of towering ebony trees and found a ladder of plaited vines hanging from a dark zenith.

Broydo clutched his friend. A vagrant sorrow touched the ælf when he gazed up into the darkness where the ladder disappeared. "I will lead the way."

"No, Broydo." Old Ric crossed his arms, palms up. When the ælf took his hands in the ælven clasp, the gnome told him, "The circle is complete. I must go alone into the garden. That is what she wants."

The eldern gnome climbed the ladder without glancing back. As he ascended, the vines untangled beneath him, and by the time he mounted out of sight into the dark heights, only threads of aerial roots wavered where the ladder had been.

Old Ric crawled out of the ancient well near the garden. He clambered down the massive skewed stones and their iron braces forged in magical glyphs, and he moved quickly under the clustered lights of fireflies, through the garden's selvage hung with dewed webs and the onyx husks of beetles.

"The day is nearly done," said the Lady of the Garden. "For a while I thought I would have to wake the child's father." She awaited him in the stone pool beneath an aspiring helix of clematis and hanging roses white and yellow, afreight with golden bees intoxicated by attar. Their bumbling droned louder than the rapturous parings of distant music that filtered through the evening air.

"My lady, I have returned the soul of your child." The eldern gnome pulled himself onto the lip of the marble pool and lifted the crystal prisms in both hands. "A demon from the Upper Air has captured the child in these hex-gems."

"I saw what you endured in my dream." The young woman lay on her back in the garden's pool, rubbing sleep from her eyes as she bathed her swollen belly. "Drop the Necklace into the water."

Old Ric hesitated a moment, his last moment, before he remembered where he was. Nothing availed denying the Lady of this Garden. He removed the chain of hex-gems and waited for his mortal wound to claim him. No pain followed even when he released the Necklace and it slipped into the water with a small splash.

A smile lit her quiet face. "The child moves!"

Old Ric lifted to his toe tips, gaunt face grinning. "Then the worlds *are* saved!"

"They are my child's caul," the lady said through her smile. "My dream will teach this small one compassion and the greater aspirations of the heart. No, I will not conclude this dream yet."

"Oh thank you, great lady!" Old Ric bowed, suddenly almost weightless with relief. Only one sorrow remained to mar the joy of his adventure. He looked hopefully at the happy woman grasping her large belly. "I have a matter that gravely troubles me, my lady." The eldern gnome settled back on his heels. "Asofel—"

"Is dead—I know this." The young woman's magisterial gaze hooded sadly. "I feel his loss here in the palace. Even as my dream is stronger for the light he has sacrificed."

"That is just it, my lady." The gnome stepped forward beseechingly. "This is your dream. Can you not perhaps dream Asofel back to life?"

The lady peered up through her inky tresses from where she had been marveling at the child moving in her womb again. Sadness dulled her voice, "No, Old Ric. My magic is not strong enough to revive a Radiant One. Asofel is gone. He gave himself that my child would live, and he will be honored in our memory always."

Old Ric hung his bald head and backed away.

"Is there anything more, old one?" the woman's voice called after him.

"Nothing more, my lady." He knelt to climb down from the pool. "I am glad for your child. I am glad for you—and for the worlds."

"Then follow your gladness out of here, gnome, and return to the worlds." The young woman lay back in the pool, and her hair spread like blood in the water. "Asofel is no more, but his light cannot be destroyed. It is part of my dream now and has given me the strength to make some small adjustments. I hope these will please you."

Old Ric did not tarry to question the nameless lady. Her child lived. The worlds were saved. On airy legs, he ran over cobbles aswirl with golden leaves, one hand at his chest, feeling for the arrow wound and finding none.

Blooms and fronds dimmed under the slantwise shadows of enclosing night. Evening's purple bleared into violet overhead, fading toward the ultratones of the invisible, and within the utter black of the void no stars glimmered, no moon glided, only shoreless depths of emptiness ranged. Upon those alien reaches, another life dreamed, fugitive of all light, the child's father, who even in sleep informed the ill-shapen, deranged, and malevolent forms of darkness that circled closer out of the night. Duppy Hob had been this Nameless One's shadow in the young woman's dream. What had that shadow become in the dream now that the demon had been broken?

The eldern gnome scurried through the deranged darkness of bracken and flowers and arrived breathless at the ancient well. Not sliding glimpses to either side, he bolted up the skewed stones, amazed at his renewed vigor. He descended the ladder into frosty blue brightness.

The plaited vines dropped him onto the crescent face of a snowdune. He tumbled to an ice field and spun upon his reflection. In the wind-brushed panes of ice, he saw himself—his hair fleecy red and full, all wrinkles gone from his face save one vertical line of worry between his handsome gray eyes—stamped there by his sadness for Asofel and the fearful thoughts of darkness that had accompanied his descent from the night garden.

"Da!" a small voice piped from the morning mist. "I found you! I found you! Now it's my turn to hide!"

Old Ric whirled upright on his knees. He recognized that child's voice by its wet lisp. It was Amara, his youngest daughter—who had died many years ago . . .

A young girl with pallid face and slim shoulders draped in braided loops of russet hair slid across the ice and into his arms. "I found you!"

Young Ric grabbed the child and faced her from far back in his heart, astonished. He stared hard at her until he saw through his fears and his hopes to her actuality—and the fact that a new life had truly begun.

the dominions of *Irth*

Saxar

Zul

the Qaff

Andeje Crag

Keri

Malpais Highlands

the Falls of Mirdath

Lake Apocalypse

Spiderlands

Old Shard

Dorzen

Ux

Mount Szo

Moodrun

Elvre

Rainbow Forests of Bryse

Arwar Odawl

Drymarch

Sharna-Bambara

Floating Stone

Mere of Goblins

cloths of Heaven

Palace of Abominations

the Reef Isles of Nhat

JB 96